Steven Popkes

God's Country

Steven Popkes

God's Country

Walking Rocks /Book View Café

Also by Steven Popkes

Caliban Landing

Slow Lightning

Welcome to Witchlandia

Simple Things

Cover design by Wendy Zimmerman
Cover illustration © 2020 by Wendy Zimmerman
Published by Walking Rock Publications in association with
Book View Café Publishing Cooperative
www.bookviewcafe.com

ISBN: 978-1-61138-902-9

To Wendy and Ben,

And also David, who insisted this one be first

Table of Contents

Part 1: In Loco Parentis

"It is true, we shall be monsters, cut off from all the world; but on that account we shall be more attached to one another."

"Even that enemy of God and man had friends and associates in his desolation."

—*Frankenstein*, Mary Shelley

Chapter 1.1: May, 1997

"All parents are dysfunctional," said Cindy's friend, Portia. "It's the nature of evolution. They start as children and teenagers—normal and useful members of society. Something about becoming adults warps them." "I won't be like them," said Cindy Fiske grimly.

"We probably can't help it." Portia waved her hand in the air. "It's in the genes. When you get to be thirty and have a big strapping boy like my brother, you'll just naturally turn hateful. When I get to be forty and my little girl has left me, I'll probably dye my hair bronze like my mother and try to pick up the gardener."

They were walking around the fountain in Plaza Frontenac. The mall's faux Tudor buildings had been built thirty years before and were showing their age. It was a cloudless spring day. The heavy heat of the sun threatened to bludgeon them into a beatific stupor and fool them into thinking it was already summer. The sweat ran down Cindy's spine where her backpack rested. As they walked from light into shadow, the shock of cool air reminded them that it was still spring. Belief in summer was premature.

"You haven't left home yet," Cindy pointed out.

"My mother is acting out her part a little early." Portia admired clothing through the Neiman-Marcus window. "No doubt when she fully reveals herself, I'll be shocked and dismayed." Portia turned her body and ran her fingers over her torso, comparing her body to the display. "I would look good in this, don't you think?"

Cindy angled her body in conscious imitation of Portia, then gave up. Portia clearly had the same figure as the manikins. The dresses put into the windows would never fit Cindy. Both girls were fifteen but that was where their similarities ended. Portia lived in Creve Coeur, a wealthy suburb of Saint Louis. Her house was big enough that she, her brother, and her parents could successfully avoid each other indefinitely. She had that thin, tanned look that came from tennis and ballet lessons starting when she was four.

Cindy lived near Tower Grove in an ancient community of four squares that dated back to the late nineteenth century. Where Portia's house was newly built, with brass fittings and a chandelier in the foyer, Cindy's family had inherited their home from her grandfather. Grandpa Fitzie had given up on the renovation craze of the seventies. He'd gotten as far as stripping the house to the stylish bare brick walls and board floors, and stopped there. Similarly, Cindy did not have Portia's aristocratic features. She retained her child's round face even while other parts of her body became more adult. With her big chest and round hips, Cindy selected baggy clothes and envied Portia's long neck and thin shanks.

They had met at the City Museum as children and had been friends ever since.

Portia noticed Cindy looking in the window. "Not that dress. They cut that dress to fit someone like me. If you bought it, you'd look like either an aging housewife or a slut. You need something more like this." She drew Cindy along the window and inside the store. "You have a more 1940s figure. This one would be good for you."

The dress was red and dropped to just above the calf but with a slit in the side that came up nearly to her mid-thigh. Its bust was full. Cindy wasn't sure it wouldn't just make her look fat.

"Try it on," ordered Portia.

Cindy checked the price tag. It was over two hundred dollars. "Unless there's a knockoff at K-Mart, I'm never going to own this."

"I didn't say marry it." Portia pulled it off the rack. "Go try it on."

The dress seemed to fit, but there wasn't a mirror in the dressing room. She walked outside. Portia's eyes widened as she looked at her.

"What?"

"Look in the mirror."

For a brief moment, Cindy wondered who stared back at her. It was a flashy, no-nonsense sort of girl. The kind of girl that would go out on the town and find herself singing with the band, take home the lead guitarist, and break his heart the next morning. Take no prisoners. Damn the torpedoes. Full speed ahead.

"Am I good or what?" Portia said as she dropped her hand on Cindy's shoulder.

At that moment, Cindy knew she had to have the dress. Fish need water and the whole world needs oxygen. Cindy needed that dress.

"Loan me two hundred dollars," she asked Portia in a low voice.

"No can do. The cards are all maxed out. My, but you do look good."

Wordlessly, Cindy went back to the dressing room, knowing what she was going to do without ever really saying it to herself. She took off the dress and hung it up, put her jeans and blouse back on. Then, as casually as if she had been doing this all her life, she stuffed the dress in her backpack.

Outside, Portia waited for her.

"Let's go," Cindy said quietly.

As they left the store, a wail erupted from the speaker over the door. Cindy remembered she hadn't removed the tag.

Portia stared at Cindy, knowing instantly what must have happened.

It seemed that the plainclothes cop materialized out of the air in front of her. She couldn't raise her gaze to his face. She could only see his nameplate: Nametag Harvey.

"Excuse me, miss," he said. "Can I see your backpack?"

"Oh, damn," said Portia. "I forgot to buy that. Here, let me get that now."

The cop ignored Portia. "You'll have to come with me."

He took Cindy outside where his partner, Nametag Turner, was waiting. The three of them walked between the stores into a narrow alley, the arresting cop trailing, the partner leading. Their car was at the end.

Harvey stared at her for a minute as Turner moved behind her. "Do I have to cuff you?"

Cindy shook her head miserably.

"Okay," he said. "Do you have any ID?"

Cindy hesitated, then gave him her driver's permit.

Harvey looked at it for a minute. "Fiske. That name rings a bell."

Turner spoke up. "Jake Fiske?"

"Yeah. That's it. Fiske. City detective out of North Jefferson." Harvey stared at her. "Are you Jake Fiske's kid?"

Cindy didn't see how it could get any worse. Maybe her dad could help her. She nodded.

Harvey nodded. "Give Jake a call."

After a moment, Turner replied. "No answer."

Harvey pondered a moment. "Let's take her in. We can call again from the station."

They carefully and impersonally eased her into the car and closed the door. Harvey was driving. She saw a glimpse of Portia as they left Plaza Frontenac. A moment passed, then they were on the highway heading south. A turn onto Highway 40 and they stalled in traffic.

"Great," said Turner.

"Don't sweat it. Things will break out in a moment."

Sure enough, the traffic loosened and they ferried across the highway as they would a river. Cindy stared out the window. People glanced at her in the back of a squad car, then looked away. One man Cindy didn't recognize stared at her until the squad car pulled away. Stared at her and mouthed her name.

oOo

Jake tried hard not to be judgmental. There were a hundred thousand ways of living and none of them were right. Everybody was just trying to get by. Jake liked to get along.

As a tavern, Mississippi's was small, with barely enough floor room to hold perhaps five tables. The bar was barely seven feet long. The dartboard was placed next to the great, black ovens where Brendan ritually barbecued pork ribs and steaks every morning. One whole side of the room was a gilded front window, heavily curtained so only a strip of transparent glass showed.

Jake entered and looked around. Brendan was behind the bar, and a huge man sat on a stool.

He raised a finger to Brendan as he sat down. "First beer of the day, Brendan. Make it a good one."

Brendan nodded and uncapped a tall bottle. "Tripple bock. From Holland."

Jake nodded and sipped. A nice full, though light, flavor with a hint of sweetness.

"I'm Connie Samoan," said the big man.

"I know."

Jake had no idea if Connie was a Samoan or not, or even if Connie was his real name. Connie was big, with shoulders perhaps three feet across. He was heavy as a sumo and he sported Hawaiian shirts. The rumor was he had once actually been a sumo wrestler. Who was Jake to disagree?

"Sam Forestell said I should introduce myself to you," Connie said.

"I see."

"He said you were the person to see."

"How is Sam?"

Connie chuckled. "Still in East Saint Louis, so he's still in Hell."

Jake smiled. "I heard you want the Mexican's old turf."

"He doesn't need it anymore."

Tom Haberman, the Mexican, had disappeared a month before. The department had been taking bets when it would be confirmed that he was dead. Connie's approaching Jake counted as confirmation, but Jake couldn't talk about it. Pity.

"True. Did you kill him?"

Connie shook his head. "Wasn't me. I heard he got carved up by one of his girls and dumped in the river."

"Really?" Jake didn't believe it. But let it go.

Connie nodded. "I even know the girl. She's one of mine now."

Jake shrugged. No skin off his nose as long as it didn't make any waves. "Here's the deal. You can cover from the bridge out Chouteau and south to

River Des Peres and from the Arch to Laclede Station. That's where I have friends."

"How much?"

"Six grand a month, a month in advance—until I know for sure you won't get carved up by the same girl that got the Mexican." Jake's cell phone vibrated against his side, but he ignored it.

Connie nodded. "How much after?"

"An even ten a month."

"Christ, that's a lot."

"Not really. The Mexican didn't operate the street trade and you won't, either. The cheapest girls you have are two hundred a trick. Ten tricks a day, six days a week, is twelve thousand a week or forty-eight grand a month. So, I'm asking less than half the take of one girl a month. You have a lot more than one girl. Some of them get a lot more than two hundred a trick." Jake grinned at him.

"I have other expenses."

"And I'm sure you'll be able to overcome them. You look like an excellent businessman. Besides, I need some of that money to grease the skids for you. It's not all gravy."

Connie nodded. He looked around the room and out the front window, then leaned on the bar heavily to stand up off the stool. When he was fully vertical, there was an envelope next to Jake's beer. Brendan reached up and pulled it below and out of sight.

Connie drained his beer and put the glass down. "Nice talking to you," he said as he reached the door. A momentary flash of sunshine and he was gone.

"How much was it, Brendan?"

"Six thousand," Brendan said quietly.

"Bank it with the rest." He sipped his beer. "I wonder if he did hit the Mexican. If he didn't, who did?"

"You want another Tripple?"

"No," Jake said after a moment. "I'm off to home."

Jake's house was only two blocks away. He walked down the alley and stood behind it for a minute. Just the way his grandfather had done when the two of them walked home after a bender down the street. That was long ago, before he had quietly backed Brendan to start Mississippi's.

He looked critically at house's brickwork. It would probably need tuck pointing this year. Inside, the setting sun lent a red glow to the brick walls. The floor boomed when he walked, thick timbers butted against one another. Should seal them this year. Maybe put down a new floor. The bricks gave the house a burnt earth smell.

Jake's cell phone vibrated again. This time he answered it.

"Jake Fiske? This is Barry Hunter in Westwood. We have a Cindy Fiske here with an ID for your address. She says she's your daughter."

"What did she do?"

"Shoplifted a dress down at the Plaza Frontenac."

"Shit."

What to do? Go down for her? Try to keep it a secret? Call Anya and tell her now? Tell her later?

"I'll be right down."

oOo

Bill Wallace could see the Alton, Illinois, bridge as he banked gently south. The Alton Bridge was always his landmark to stay out of the Lambert Field airspace. Right on time, he passed over the Missouri River and followed it towards the small Creve Coeur airport where he was based. From the perspective of the cockpit of his Cessna, this cloudless day and still sky seemed made for flying.

He entered the pattern and in a few moments was settling down on the runway, gentle as a warm breeze in summer.

Bill tried very hard to avoid thinking about anything other than flying when he was in a plane—for safety as much as pleasure. But as he was taxiing over to his tie-down, he couldn't help feeling satisfied with the trip. Lifeworks, Bill's company, had very few investors, but any biotech effort took a fair amount of money and so those investors had to have deep pockets. Bill's largest investor was VCI out of Chicago. VCI was a euphemism for Fred Hibbert, a retired sugar farmer who lived in Chicago to be close to his grandchildren. Fred liked to see people in person, and Bill didn't think it a hardship to fly a couple of hours to say hello. Consequently, every few months Bill saddled up his 182 for dinner and a show down near the Loop. This time, however, it had been more than just a face-to-face update.

Bill liked to think of Lifeworks as Doctor Jekyll and Mister Hyde. Upstanding, staid Doctor Jekyll spent his day analyzing name brand products, and supplying formulations to grocery and pharmacy chains to make their own, generic, products. Doctor Jekyll helped these chains find vulnerable products, determine what they were made of, and figure out the most efficient method of producing them. Doctor Jekyll was self-funded.

Mister Hyde, on the other hand, delved into overlooked areas of research and determined new and patentable alternatives to those same brand products. Mister Hyde had so far been able to discover a new tranquilizer and two new muscle relaxants he had then licensed to Eli Lilly. Doctor Jekyll was well known and respected. Mister Hyde was a secret known only to a few pharmaceutical clients and to his own investors and employees.

Bill liked Mister Hyde. It satisfied him a great deal more than developing copies of famous brands of laundry soap and lip gloss.

This time he was going for the jackpot.

Six years ago, Bill had taken a chance on a brilliant but odd ("oddly brilliant", as he had told Fred) researcher named Anya Fiske. It was part of a larger plan to develop a suite of drugs to be brought all the way to market, following in the footsteps of firms such as Genzyme and Novartis. Fred's pockets were deep but not that deep, hence the secrecy until they had a product.

Now they did. Anapyridol had passed the first round of toxicity tests and was ready for human clinical trials. The initial patents were in place, with several refinements to be filed as soon as the press was informed. He couldn't wait to tell Anya. He thought about her for a long minute, her dark hair and eyes, high, almost Indian cheekbones. He knew he had a crush on her. It wasn't the first time he had been attracted to an employee. Bill had indulged only once, and he was still paying alimony so he was content to worship from afar. Still, he always found himself irritated when he thought of Jake. Jake didn't deserve her.

Bill finished tying down his plane and found the BMW in the parking lot. He caught the Mill Road and then Interstate 270 and stalled immediately in traffic. *Damn.* His own fault for not listening to the radio. He wished he were flying over this. The traffic edged forward, foot by foot.

He thought for a moment and then caught I-64 east. He'd get off on Lindbergh and work his way on the back roads. No reason to wait here. He was congratulating himself right until he stalled out *again* on Clayton. *Damn.*

A police car showed its lights and edged slowly across the lanes past him. Idly, he looked at it; he wasn't going anywhere. It took a moment for the girl in the back seat to register. Had he seen her before?

Last year. Company picnic in the state park. Anya's fifteen-year-old daughter.

He stared. The girl stared back defiantly. Then the squad car was across his lane and exiting the highway on the other side.

Hm.

Maybe he had two things to tell Anya.

oOo

Anya examined the MRI. The picture was a slice from the forehead to the nape of the neck, far finer in detail than that available to any axe murderer and with much less mess. Anya chuckled to herself. Bill thought she had an odd sense of humor already. A few times Anya and Jake had gone to a movie with Bill and whoever he was dating at the moment—always somebody beautiful, always somebody accomplished. The laughter between the couples never coincided. If she and Jake thought something was funny, Bill would only wonder why. It made Anya smile to think of it. Bill and his very smooth sense of humor. He didn't like edges.

It was one of the things she had always found attractive in Jake. Jake liked edgy. He liked sharpness, even if he was the one being skewered. One Saturday afternoon after they had begun dating, he had forgotten one right after the other: his socks, where he had left his pants, his gun and his shoes. When he finally found his shoes, he just sat on the bed and stared at them, exasperated.

"What the hell will I be like if I ever get Alzheimer's?" he growled to the room in general.

Anya, who had been watching this for half an hour, said: "How would I tell the difference?"

He stared at her for a good four seconds and Anya had time to think she'd messed up another relationship. Why can't you just be smoother? Nicer? She wasn't sure.

Then Jake exploded into laughter and lay back on the bed. "Good one," he said when he could speak.

Anya shook her head. It was a ploy of her mind when it was bored. Quick! Think of something more interesting and follow that! She had to check these MRI's.

The color of the MRI showed activity levels as measured by blood flow. In an ancillary radiograph, she could see uptake of Anapyridol tagged with radioactive oxygen in the brain of a chimp. The MRI image was of a human brain. The chimp radiograph showed the neural reaction of the posterior superior parietal lobe—that area of the brain that was involved in the orientation of the body in space. Secondary activity in the prefrontal cortex— the attention association area—was also strongly shown. This was the reaction she had predicted of Anapyridol in the brain. Instead of exposing subjects of the Anapyridol toxicity study to the radioisotope she had used in the chimp, she relied on the activity levels shown by the MRI. Glendel's group at Washington University had written a program they called an analogic imager.

Most physiological structures in vertebrates were closely matched either physically or developmentally. The reptile jaw had at least 4 bones. The mammalian jaw had one. The quadrate and the articular bones had migrated into the middle ear to form the hammer and anvil of the mammalian middle ear and left the dentary behind to become the mandible.

The analogic imager operated from developmental rules from several species, including chimps and man. The funding had come from the McGovern Institute for Brain Research at MIT. The brains of man and his closest relative, the chimp, had been given close attention. Using the analogic imager, Anna could morph a map of the chimp brain onto that of a human being if the chimp had followed human rules of development. In something like Anapyridol, this was especially important since it was intended to target some structures that were particularly well-developed in the human being. The raw pictures were informative but didn't show the level of detail she needed.

The images were closely matched.

Anya breathed a sigh of relief and sat back in her chair. She hadn't been too concerned by the toxicity studies—the animal studies had not shown any toxicity, even in the chimps. There was always a risk, but it was not terribly high.

But the target of Anapyridol was the unique human brain. There was really no telling what the drug would do until it was actually used in human beings. Now, at least, she had evidence the drug was targeting the right areas.

"Hey, there," Bill said as he came in the room.

Anya smiled at him. "Good news. Look at the MRIs."

"You tell me what they say."

"Brain activity we hoped for. Anapyridol might work."

"Wow." Bill sat down. "Any side effects?"

"Some reports of euphoria. Nothing unexpected."

"Look out, Prozac. Here we come." Bill frowned. "Hibbert is willing to front the money for the human trials when we go to the FDA. But he wants to meet you first."

Anya felt cold. "No, Bill. We agreed—"

"You can't stay in the background forever."

"Who says I can't?"

"I do, for one. Fred Hibbert, for another." Bill leaned across her desk from her and looked her in the eye. "You are my best-kept secret. Fred needs to be let in on it, too. He's paying for us to go on. Without him, we have to sell what we have and move on."

Anya shook her head. "I've spent over ten years—"

"I know. So does Fred. It's just dinner and drinks. We fly up to Chicago and back on the same day." He spread his hands. "You don't have to be shy about this. There aren't fifty people in the world that could do what you've done."

"I'm not shy."

"Good. What would you say to him?"

Maybe it would be all right. It had been nearly twenty years since she had left Moscow. Maybe it was time to quit worrying. "I guess I'd start with d'Aquili and Newberg's work—"

Bill shook his head. "Not yet. They're too much on the fringe."

"Fringe?" Anya laughed. "They're respected in the field—"

"Anya, they were studying religious experiences. It'll turn Fred off. You don't need to attribute anything to them. Just talk about your own thoughts."

Anya leaned her head back. "Okay. Based on their work—and I won't attribute it—it occurred to me that the relationship they had shown between the orientation association area and the attention association area could describe a mechanism by which human relationships are mediated. This behavior was shown in chimpanzee studies but such studies, since they involve an organ unique to humans—the human brain—could only be termed inconclusive. During the toxicity studies, surveys were administered before and after administration showed an increase in social responsiveness."

"Jeez. That sounds like a paper in *Cell*."

"Human relationships: big problem. Drug will fix better than club to head. You give us money." She snorted. "There. Is that better?"

"Much. Keep that in mind. We'll work on trimming it down tomorrow."

Bill looked down for a minute, and Anya had a moment of misgiving. "Bill," she asked. "Did something go wrong in Chicago?"

"No. When I got back—" he paused. "Anya, I saw Cindy in the back of a squad car on the way here from Creve Coeur."

"Why the hell didn't you say so, Bill? Jesus Christ." She pulled her cell phone out of her purse and dialed Jake. He picked up immediately.

"What happened to Cindy?" she asked immediately.

"Calm down, Anya. I've got it under control."

In the background, she could hear mutterings and office sounds. "You're still at the station."

"Out in the county. I was just talking to the Sergeant—"

"What did they say she did?"

Jake sighed. "She tried to lift a dress over at Frontenac."

"She shoplifted?"

"It's okay. I've got it taken care of—"

"I'll meet you at home." She hung up. "I'll see you later, Bill," she said as she ran past him out the door.

She could only see a vision of Cindy in jail until she reached her car. Sitting behind the steering wheel, she found herself weeping. *Did I come all the way over here for this? What kind of a mother could I be—didn't I tell her what it could be like? What kind of things she might have to do to survive—what I had to do to survive?*

Of course not, she said to herself coldly as she wiped her eyes. *You barely told her anything, didn't you?*

It's not my fault. She tried to convince herself. As she drove out of the parking lot towards Saint Louis, she found herself thinking of the house in Tower Grove. If only they lived somewhere else. Maybe it could be different. If only she didn't hate that damned house so much.

oOo

Like many of her friends, Cindy ornamented her room. Some girls she knew liked posters of boy bands or stuffed animals. Portia had carefully calculated her parental shock value and picked advertisements using models with various pierced anatomies to decorate her wall. Cindy was less interested in shock value than comfort. Her walls and shelves were decorated with samples of things she would like to have done and pictures she would like to have taken. Over the bed was a collection of snapshots she had bought from an antique dealer in Soulard: GIs from World War II and Korea in front of the Pacific Ocean. Postcards from France, London, Moscow. Over her desk was a big picture of a collie. Cindy had never had a dog. Anya didn't like them.

Cindy knew the shoplifting was a big deal. She was in real trouble. Jake took her aside when they got home and spoke about juvenile hall, jail, and prison.

"You're not a Creve Coeur bitch like Portia—" he started.

"Don't you call her that!"

Jake stopped and breathed for a minute. "No. You're right. She's not the one that got caught shoplifting. You are. But if she had, you can imagine her daddy would have had her out without a mark on her makeup."

Now was the time to butter him up a little bit. "So did you."

She could see him trying hard to be stern. "You're damned right I did," he said. "But what if those guys hadn't known me? That was just luck. You can't depend on just luck. You either have to have money or power, or you have to keep your nose clean."

Cindy looked at the ground, feeling sullen. "Okay. It was a stupid thing to do. I just wanted to…" For a long moment, she remembered what that dress had felt like against her skin, remembered looking in the mirror and seeing that grinning woman looking back. Damn the torpedoes. Full speed ahead. "I just wanted to look nice."

"Jail doesn't look nice on anybody."

"I know."

Home, she got out of the car and went up to her room. She looked in her mirror and saw herself twenty years in the future, living in a trailer south of Saint Louis, two, maybe three, kids and a dog, smoking a cigarette, staring back at herself, wondering what happened. Heck. She was alive, wasn't she? Shouldn't she want to live?

Anya came into the room.

Anya sat across from her silently for a long time. Cindy didn't look at her. She couldn't look at her mother without feeling guilty. Jake had grown up in this house. Grandpa Fitzie had worked for the gasworks, and Great-Grandpa had been one of the contractors when the Municipal Theatre had been built. Jake had been cozy in this house since Great-Grandpa had built it.

But Anya had been born in Siberia and had gotten to Moscow by doing things of which she still would not speak. It was one thing to fool Jake. Anya couldn't be fooled.

"Look at me," Anya said quietly.

Cindy glanced up and then down at the floor again.

"Look at me." Anya grabbed her neck.

Cindy yelped and closed her eyes. Then she swallowed and looked back at her mother.

Anya released her and sat back. "It is easy here. Back in Russia, the policemen might have broken your legs. Or raped you. Or ignored you until it occurred to someone that your parents might be called. And it wouldn't have been over a beautiful dress—you would never have been allowed to get near a beautiful dress. It would have been over a potato."

Usually she just let Anya's lectures wash over her but this time it was just too much. "Oh, come on, Mom. It's different here. If you had been a biochemist over there, we would have lived in a better place than *this*."

Anya's face grew pale. She reached forward, held up her hand as if she were going slap Cindy. Cindy stared straight at her, disbelieving.

Slowly, Anya lowered her hand. "Don't tell me what it would have been like. You know nothing."

The shock of the almost slap drove anything else from Cindy's mind. Cindy couldn't recall ever being slapped. Or spanked.

Anya stood. "Stay in your room. You may come down for meals and to go to school."

"How long?"

"We shall see." She closed the door quietly behind her.

Cindy found her eyes stinging with near tears. She could deal with being grounded. She could deal with not having a single dress or shirt or pair of pants that didn't make her look like an overfed Kansas geek. But she didn't deserve to be slapped. She knew better than that. The fact the slap hadn't happened didn't matter.

She was getting out of this house. One way or the other. When she hit eighteen, she was going to run as far and as fast as she could. Seventeen. Sixteen, maybe.

Why wait?

She'd have to get out of Tower Grove. She was surrounded on all sides by areas that weren't the best—a fifteen-year-old white girl late at night by herself was taking some pretty big chances. She could catch the bus down on South Grand. That might get her as far as the train station on 16th street. It was only a couple of miles away. She had some money. She could catch the late train to

Kansas City—they'd never think she'd taken the train. From there, she could take a bus anywhere.

Cindy packed up her clothes and waited for Jake and Anya to go to bed. Jake slept heavily, but Anya often tossed and turned for a while. Cindy dozed, and when she awoke it was nearly midnight and the house was quiet. She wondered if the bus was still running. Cindy decided to make her way to the street and see for herself. The bus stop was well lit. There was a convenience store. If the bus didn't come in an hour or so, she'd come back and wait until tomorrow night.

Out the window and down the fire escape to the alley, then pussyfooting down the cobblestones until she was out of sight and hearing of the house, followed by a dead run down to South Grand.

As she sat on the bench, the cars streamed past. It was cool and she was glad she was wearing her sweater. A couple of cars slowed down to look at her and then sped up. As *if* she looked like a hooker. Besides, there weren't any streetwalkers here. They were farther uptown.

Then a black Lincoln with tinted windows pulled into the store parking lot and next to her. The driver's side window came down.

"Need a lift, honey?" said a big man in the front seat.

Cindy stared at him. All her life she had been told not to take such chances. But his face seemed kind.

If you've got to live, it's better to live.

"Okay. I'm going to the train station on 16th Street." She got in the car on the other side and put her backpack on the floor. The seats were plush and the inside of the car was quiet. "I'm Cindy... Swales." She said at last.

"Pleased to meet you," said the man as he swung out into traffic. "My name's Connie Samoan."

oOo

After he left Lifeworks, Bill had a pleasant dinner with Kathleen Morris, as he did two or three times a month. Kathleen lived in Town and Country, a suburb a couple of steps above Creve Coeur on the evolutionary scale. She was a pleasant, talkative woman. Bill had gone to MIT at the same time Kathleen had attended Wellesley. Bill had married once and it was a disaster. Kathleen had tried twice with somewhat more success, since she had two grown children to show for it. Bill could barely mention his ex-wife's name without bile, but Kathleen was still quite friendly with her ex-husbands, something Bill envied. While she rarely talked about her exes, her children were often a topic of conversation: a boy named Raymond, who had dropped out of Washington University to guide for a rafting company in Sacramento, and a girl named Marsha, who was attending Tulane and living passionately with another girl whose name Bill could never quite remember. Bill often had fantasies about

Marsha and wished Kathleen would talk more about her. He felt somewhat embarrassed by this and hoped Kathleen never suspected his interest. Regardless, whatever Kathleen said about Marsha was not what Bill had in mind, anyway.

With both marriages out of the way and the children out of the house, Kathleen had directed her considerable energies into creating and maintaining her own venture capital firm. Kathleen had inherited deep pockets and was still cordial with her ex-husbands, who had deep pockets themselves. VenCap was not a big player, but it had bankrolled bigger companies than Lifeworks and done well in the nineties. Bill and Kathleen had been friends for close to thirty years and never once had either mentioned the possibility of Kathleen investing in Bill's company. But the possibility was always there, adding a certain spice to their relationship.

After dinner, they had drinks down in Soulard. As they listened to the live blues and watched the river, Bill watched Kathleen and thought about Anya. Comparing the two women was like comparing paper and epoxy; the two were so different as to make comparisons all but impossible. Still, he tried. Anya was dark, muscular as a small gymnast, with faint weathered wrinkles around her eyes and on her cheeks. Her skin was coarse from years in the cold and some mysterious privation. There was a faint scar that ran alongside her nose and crossed over the corner of her lips, its origin another mystery. Anya carried with her a sad wariness, as if she was waiting for the moment when everything would be taken away. Anya took nothing for granted. Over the years, Bill had quit making generalizations or even making broad statements, since he knew Anya would challenge them.

On the other hand, Kathleen expected things to turn out right for her. Tall, with long legs and delicate fingers, she spoke with her hands as much as her voice. Her hair was a darkening blonde and her eyes, blue. Intelligent, beautiful, and rich, things had always been easy for her. No pain had ever injured her for long. Bill loved having sex with her. She had no fear of being hurt and therefore no part of the act was closed to her, save by those things she liked and those things she didn't.

Sex with Anya, Bill surmised, would feel uncertain and strange, a hidden, dangerous, and attractive country populated with landmines.

Kathleen leaned over to him and kissed him gently behind his ear with lips and tongue. Her signal she was ready to leave. They ended up in Town and Country. Afterward, as they lay intertwined together, neither able to speak for breathing, he was filled with a warm affection for her and smiled against her hair.

Bill awoke around one and gently left the bed so Kathleen wouldn't awake. He took his clothes out into the hallway and dressed. He made his way downstairs and out into the night. The cool air felt good against his face, and he drove back to Lifeworks with the top down.

The building was empty when he let himself in. He spent the next hour checking proposals left for him by the salesmen: an equivalent of Zantac—Glaxo's patent would expire next year. A new repackaging method for selling ibuprofen. After he had disposed of them, he reviewed Anya's results. Things looked much better than she had said. MRIs of the subject groups were well within expected tolerances. He leaned back in his chair. Anya did not expect to see the same responses documented by d'Aquili and Newberg in any of the trials; the therapeutic dosage was much too small. But the dosage was far below toxicity. Bill wondered what it would be like.

It couldn't be any stronger than the LSD he had taken at MIT. Or the mescaline. Or the psilocybin. College had been a time of experimentation, after all.

He went upstairs and measured out two drops of purple liquid onto a scrap of filter paper, a triple dosage of Anapyridol but still a far below a toxic dosage. Anapyridol was similar to LSD in that respect. The active dosage was measured in micrograms. A hundred milligrams was a ten times any dosage they'd ever use in therapy.

Bill held the filter paper with a pair of tweezers and stared at it. It looked like the blotter acid he remembered from the seventies. He swallowed it—a taste of soap and cinnamon. He wondered what it would be like. The surveys said a certain euphoria and feeling of connectedness. He glanced over to the screen saver of the PC on his desk, vibrant colors melding into one another. If I'd had that when I was in college, I'd never have graduated. I'd have taken mescaline and stared until my eyes bled.

Nothing seemed to happen for perhaps an hour. He checked the time. Nearly three in the morning. Then, for a moment, his vision stretched like rubber. Colors blended in. He tried to speak—

—and was sitting in front of his machine, watching the colors.

It was like awakening from a long and exciting dream, only to have it evaporate when he tried to remember it. Something important. Something profound.

"Something," he said out loud. "To do with this computer." He chuckled, feeling good. He noticed the time on the wall clock. It was nearly seven in the morning and he didn't feel tired.

He could barely remember a thing. That was worrisome. He wondered if it was going to interfere with memory creation when they marketed it.

"Hell," he said. "What did I do for the last four hours?" Maybe he had stayed in the building. Once, on some orange barrel, he'd had a quintessential profound epiphany where he knew and understood all things, only to find out later it was the exact moment he had pissed himself. Hopefully, if he had done something like that here he'd had the good grace to use one of the potted plants. Better look around.

He stood up. At that point, he realized he was naked.

oOo

Go to work, Anya told herself. *Jake said so. You can't do anything moping around the house.*

What if she phones? What if she comes home, broken and bleeding, and I'm not here?

We'll take turns, he had said. *I'll stay here for half a day. Then you. How about that?*

That is nothing! she wanted to cry out to him. She's my baby! She's out in the streets. I drove her away. She's never coming back. Like everything else in my life, she left and she's never coming back.

But it was the house that decided her. The thought of staying in this dingy, dank, dusty hovel in the midst of American Corporate Wealth was intolerable. The other houses were painted and had been refurbished or, in a couple of cases, gutted and restored. Only this house still looked a hundred years old. Only this house still smelled of Jake's grandfather, as nasty and evil an old man as had ever lived.

Sure, the old man had said. *Move in. Be nice to have some new blood in the family. Hybrid vigor,* he had said, and lingered over every curve of her body, every day that he lived with them until he was just lying there in his bed on the floor above them, only the sharp smell of oxygen keeping him alive. Even then, his eyes followed her across the room, burning. Only the final feebleness of impending death had kept him from touching her or whispering things into her ear. His slyness kept him from being caught, and deep embarrassment had kept Anya from speaking of it.

After all, she had thought to herself. *Someday he'll be dead, and Jake and I will still have to live together.* One of the lessons she had learned in the Soviet Union was never to burn your bridges until you were fully certain they were too rotten to support you.

If she could, she would have razed this house to the ground.

So, she fled to Lifeworks, her eyes dull and red and her thoughts as sluggish as when she used to drink herself into a stupor back in Siberia.

Bill looked up from her desk when she came in. "You look like hell."

Anya nodded. She looked more closely at Bill. He looked as if he had slept in his clothes. "You don't look much better. Did you need something?" She gestured towards her chair.

Bill looked at the chair, confused for a moment. Then jumped up. "Oh, sorry. You had the report on your desk and I sat down here, reading it."

Anya put down her purse and sat heavily in her own chair. She ran her fingers over the desk. It was clean. The PC on the right corner, the report centered in the middle, a picture of Jake and Cindy to her left. Seeing Cindy in the picture made her want to cry again, but she wouldn't. This isn't how you got to Moscow, she scolded herself. This isn't how you got out of Russia.

"I was wondering if Anapyridol would interfere with memory formation."

Anya shook her head. "I don't see why. There is some hypothalamic involvement in its action but not within the therapeutic dosages. I suppose…" Her voice trailed off. Come on, she said to herself. Keep a grip.

"Anya," Bill said quietly. "What's wrong?"

"Cindy ran away list night. We haven't been able to find her."

Bill whistled. "Wow. You don't have to be here. You can go home, you know."

She smiled at him. As if going home would be any improvement. "I have the cell phone. Jake is home now. I'll go home in the afternoon."

Bill nodded and looked uncomfortable. Anya suddenly felt very affectionate towards him. She realized Bill was what Americans called a gentleman. This seemed to mean that Bill would earnestly attempt to do the right thing without ever really understanding the situation. The bumbling sincerity touched her like many things she had seen since she had come here. As clumsy and demanding as an idiot child.

Anya shook her head. To work. "So, does Mister Hibbert need more papers or reports to back up our dinner conversation?"

Bill started. "Probably not, but it would look good. Fred's a busy man. It will probably be a couple or more weeks before we get up there." He looked up at her. "But you can't go to Chicago while Cindy is missing, can you?"

What a soft, naïve country, she thought fondly. I whored my way out of VECTOR to Moscow. Stole the emigration papers of a crippled postal worker. Turned in my own brother as a dissident to delay the secret police long enough to make it to Israel. I stayed in Israel just long enough to make a new identity before I abandoned Tel Aviv for the United States. Do *this*? Oh, Bill. I can do anything.

"I'll manage," she said.

oOo

Jake knew the time to catch a runaway is in the first week. After that, it gets progressively harder to find them that at all, much less find them alive. Jake figured out what had happened the next day and put out the word to every station in and around Saint Louis. Nothing.

It didn't always happen that way. Jake had arrested more than one young prostitute with a missing person in her record. Sometimes, the record was over ten years old. It all depended on the first week. A girl gets picked up by somebody nasty and is found in an alley, missing various parts that make identification difficult. If she lasts a month, then she likely finds a depth where she can tread water. For a while.

Cindy was a smart girl. If she'd decided to really run—and Jake believed this was no plea for help but a desperate attempt to get away—she'd put as many miles between herself and Saint Louis as she could. That meant car, bus, or train. Jake didn't think she had the money for plane fare and it would be harder, since she was underage. If she had a ride lined up, then the best they could do was put out a picture out on the wire and wait. She'd had at least six hours before they found out she'd gone. Six hours at sixty-five miles an hour— and she'd probably go faster—was about four hundred miles along interstates that went to Kansas City, Chicago, Memphis, Columbus, or a hundred places in between. If she hitched, it would take her some time to get a ride—not much, but some. And if she didn't get picked up by some freak, she could still make some distance. And getting farther every minute.

A bus wouldn't go as fast, but it could go anywhere. Trains were the easiest and the first place Jake checked. Buses were the second. Planes, the third. Nothing. Nada. Zip.

Anya called him and asked if she could go to Chicago. Absolutely, he said.

It was good she was going to be gone for a bit. He had some people to see, and it would be easier if she wasn't around. Jake always felt he had to protect Anya from the dirty side of America. From what she'd told him of her life in Moscow, she'd been pretty well protected by her family. They were nothing like the hookers and junkies he dealt with every day.

He'd find Cindy before Anya got back.

oOo

In the early morning hours, Bill had wandered all over the Lifeworks facility to find his clothes and determine what he'd done. He found his pants around the loading dock and his jacket in the processing room. He found his shirt and tie carefully hung on a hook in manufacturing. Both his socks were looped over the top of the lyophilizer. His underwear was carefully arranged to adorn the knob of the clean room. Bill, more or less clothed, had sat at Anya's desk for nearly an hour until she had come in, trying to figure out where four hours of his life had gone.

Fred didn't want to wait two weeks. He didn't want to wait two days. Fred strongly suggested that Bill bring Anya up as quickly as possible. This was clearly impossible, since Cindy was missing. But when Bill asked, Anya gave him a look like a dark hole carved out of a snow bank, called on her cell phone, and spoke on it briefly.

"Sure," she said lifelessly.

"You want to go home and pack?"

Anya shook her head. "I always have an overnight bag in the car." She chuckled and looked at him.

The weather was dicey all the way to Chicago: line squalls and instrument minimums from Alton to Joliet. He landed at Meigs next to the aquarium— Fred had an apartment in the city. A taxi was waiting for them. First, they stopped at the hotel and dropped off their bags, then continued on to Victor's.

He didn't want Anya to feel intimidated by Fred. Bill tried to explain that Hibbert could be brisk at times. Anya waved him away.

"He couldn't be worse than Gorbachev."

"Gorbachev? Mikhail Gorbachev? Where did you meet him?"

But Anya only smiled wanly at him and didn't answer. She stared out the window until they got to Victor's.

Victor's maître d' seated them in an enclosed booth where Fred was waiting for them. Bill was surprised. This was more private treatment than he was used to. Fred stood up when they approached. He walked around the table and seated Anya. Anya smiled up at him, and Bill felt vaguely jealous.

"So, this is Anya Fiske," Fred said with a smile as they sat down. "Bill tells me good things about you. According to him, you are going to make us all rich."

Hibbert wore a jacket over a t-shirt and jeans. He was small and had the look of an older man trying to look young. He had no jewelry and an open countenance—as if he were an ascetic attempting to look stylish.

Anya smiled quietly. "You and Bill are already rich, Mister Hibbert."

Fred laughed. "Rich-*er*, then. Call me Fred."

She sipped her wine and dabbed at her mouth delicately. Bill thought she looked delicious.

Bill leaned back and watched them. He realized suddenly that this was the Fred and Anya show; Fred had only needed Bill to bring the two of them together.

Anya leaned forward on the table. "Anapyridol has a terrific potential. Not only as a Prozac-like drug. It can also—"

Fred waved his hand. "Spare me. Bill has brought everything down to my level. I'm very satisfied with your technical expertise."

Anya straightened in her chair. Her face retained her smile, but all other expressions disappeared. "I'm glad you're pleased, Mister Hibbert."

"Call me Fred," he said. "Bill? Could you do me a great favor? I'd like to speak with Anya alone for a bit."

"That's not appropriate, Fred," Bill said slowly. He looked at Anya and then back at Fred. "I'm the head of Lifeworks. It's my company. You need to talk to me, not one of my employees."

"I know." Fred spread his hands. "She's the golden goose, Bill. My money is in her hands every bit as much as it is in yours. Look, I've always liked talking to people one on one. Let me have this chance with your very own miracle worker."

Bill looked over to Anya. She shrugged and smiled. It's your call.

"Okay." He checked his watch. "I'll go have a drink and be back in fifteen minutes."

On his way to the bar, he thought of every possible response he could have made that would have kept him at the table.

Hindsight is always twenty-twenty.

oOo

Anya couldn't figure out what was going on. She almost declined, but some deep instinct kept her sitting there as Bill walked away.

Fred turned back to her. "I'm very impressed with your career. Ph.D. in biochemistry from the University of Moscow in 1979. Several papers in polypeptide synthesis. Institute of Human Research. Wonderful stuff."

"Thank you." What's this all about?

"The papers you published after you came to the states weren't like that at all. 'Neurochemistry of Synaptic Destruction.' 'Role of the Posterior Superior Parietal Lobe in Personality Disorders.' Very interesting stuff but very different. Where did that come from?"

Anya became very still. She didn't like where this was going. "I've always been interested in neurochemistry. As soon as I had the opportunity, I took it."

"Of course." Fred grinned. "You know, I was able to trace Anya Gamova from Tel Aviv to New York but I couldn't trace you from Moscow to Tel Aviv. What's up with that?"

"Why were you trying to trace me at all?"

He waved his hand. "A standard background check. The same sort of thing I did to Bill when we first started working together."

"Clearly the records must have been lost—the Soviet Union did fall and I am here, Mister Hibbert."

"Absolutely." Fred ran his finger over the tablecloth as if it were a map. "Call me Fred. Since I couldn't follow from Tel Aviv to Moscow, I looked around Moscow to see what I could find. That's how I found your papers— which was difficult in itself since all of your referenced publications had ceased operation when Gorbachev abdicated. So did the Institute of Human Research, for that matter."

"It was a hard time for everyone."

"I understand. Anyway, in my search, I did find some interesting papers by an A. Gamow. One was, I think, 'Autoimmune Induced Parietal Lobe Epilepsy and Personality Changes.' What do you think of that?"

The goose was cooked. The game was up. The sudden relief shook her. She almost laughed. "What do you want, Mister Hibbert?"

Fred stared back at her, his smile in place but empty. "Call me Fred."

"Is that all you want?"

"No," Fred said slowly, staring at her. "How long were you at VECTOR, Anya?"

Anya returned the look for a long moment then threw her head back and let the laugh escape. Fred Hibbert knew enough to send her to Hell.

She wiped her eyes. "The KGB kept up the Institute as a fiction of where we worked. It gave us credentials when we went to conferences. It was supposed to confuse the Americans."

"It worked for a while."

Anya carefully rearranged her napkin. "Alibekov recruited me just out of graduate school. He had me working with Sergei Popov. I was there for twelve years."

Fred nodded. "What were you doing there?"

Anya smiled wickedly. "First, I worked with Popov on his myelin experiments. It was a wonderful idea. Splice the gene sequence for myelin into a strain of bacteria and then infect the host. The host, of course, builds antibodies for the bacterial protein. But part of the bacterial protein is now myelin, so the antibodies are active against that as well. The bacteria are destroyed by antibiotics, but there's myelin everywhere—nerves are coated with it, brain cells are swathed in it. A couple of weeks after the infection clears, the victim's own antibodies start consuming his nervous system."

She chuckled and nodded. "Popov was a genius. We were much better at this sort of thing than you Americans. Your heart was never in it."

Fred leaned back in his chair. "They called you the Dark Lady."

"That came later."

"What happened?"

"Well." Anya sipped her wine. "Popov took the project as far as he could using different strains of bacteria. He ended up using *Legionella* to great effect. I had something different in mind. I went to General Kalenin—something I thought I would never do—and he set me up in my own lab. Sergei was happy for me." Anya leaned forward towards the table. "My idea was much more precise than Sergei's. I didn't want to kill somebody or make them sick. I wanted to change them. To make them more docile, say. To destroy their language skills or their ability to read. I used the same tools as Sergei did but not in bacteria. Bacteria are a blunt instrument for this sort of thing. I developed a strain of coronavirus with a gap I could plug with whatever DNA that interested me. First, I played with the genes coding synaptic receptor proteins—acetylcholinesterase, for example. In a little while, I could give you a common cold. You'd sniffle for a few days and then two weeks later. BAM!" She slammed the table. "It would be like injecting you with curare. More importantly, I had a scalpel I could use to peel away the layers of the human brain and see what they did."

Anya smiled at them both and drained her wine.

"What would happen if I reported you?" murmured Fred.

She ran her finger around the rim of the glass until it moaned. "Probably not much. I haven't done anything illegal since I've gotten here. They debriefed Alibekov and then gave him a job. Now he runs his own company. The same with Popov. Both of them are here now. I don't know what happened to Kalenin."

"Then why keep it a secret?" Fred scratched his chin.

Anya didn't answer immediately. "The human brain is unique—you know that. That's been the problem of our research all along. Once you get past a certain point, you have to have human subjects. Rats and mice and chimps just won't do. My work was... Let us say the 'Dark Lady' is on several lists. Prison is probably the least of my worries."

She rubbed her fingers together and looked back at him. "So, now you know all my secrets. What will you do with them?"

Fred stretched out his hand. "Nothing."

"Nothing?"

"Nothing at all. I expect we'll have a long and productive relationship."

"That's hardly reassuring."

"I like mysteries. You were one. It's as simple as that."

"You can blackmail me, I suppose."

His eyebrows lifted. "Why should I want to do that? I have enough money. You have no real power out of Russia—you've decided not to have any. Think of it as intense curiosity about the human condition and leave it at that."

"Mister Hibbert—"

"Call me Fred."

She laughed again. "Fred. That's not much of an answer."

"It will have to do for now."

He waved to a waiter in the distance who appeared astonishingly quickly. "Try the garlic shrimp."

oOo

Bill couldn't concentrate on dinner. Anya was quick on her feet and witty. She positively glittered as she spoke. Bill couldn't seem to catch up to the conversation. Mostly, he listened. He felt utterly captivated. Fred left them right after dessert.

The two of them took a cab to the hotel. Bill had come up here with a hazy idea of trying to make a pass at her but now that seemed silly. She was lovely and smart. But for God's sake, her child was missing. What sort of evil cad was he, anyway? He settled for walking her to her room.

She opened her door, turned to him, reached up, and pulled his lips to hers in a long, tingling kiss. Still licking his lips with her tongue, she drew him inside.

Afterward, he lay there in an amazed, half-conscious glow. Anya breathed softly, already asleep.

Sex as good as this came with a sense of profound significance, a link to a larger, deeper world. He felt connected to all things.

As Bill had felt the other night after he'd taken the Anapyridol. He had been sitting at his desk, watching his hands make trails in the air. He felt open and vulnerable but excited. There was a deep rumble to the world like a slow rumbling voice saying something important Bill couldn't quite understand. For a moment, he could see the world from the outside. Everything was connected. The distance between them, between the inside and the outside of the world, was mere illusion. The wall between him and the world was a soft, greasy barrier to be discarded as easily as a snake's skin, grow thinner and thinner until—*pop!*—it was gone. He stood up, done with barriers, and walked through his factory—as if anything could be defined to be his. Money didn't matter. Possessions didn't matter. He could feel all the people in the world touching him. Shirts didn't matter—he took his off. Pants didn't matter—he tossed it to one side—until he stood on the little balcony outside his office with the cool spring wind blowing deliciously over him.

He was an empty vessel joined to the great reservoir of life. All his life he'd never taken anything like God remotely seriously. But now, perhaps he'd have to rethink the matter. God is love, he remembered from his childhood, and was struck ringing like a bell with the love he felt for the people in the cars he saw driving, the planes he saw flying, the people moving inside the offices in the other buildings.

You can't keep this to yourself.

Back inside and clear in his mind as ever he had been, he pulled up the company web page. Next to them, he pulled up the papers Anya had sent him over the years: the molecular structure of Anapyridol, its manufacturing requirements, its mode of effect. One by one, he took the files and uploaded them to the website.

Sitting there, staring at the computer, he spoke aloud. "As soon as this wears off, I'll pull these papers from the site." His words seemed to roll away from him as if into a dark well. The answer rolled back as if he'd heard it said aloud. I'll just have to forget I did it.

Bill sat up in the hotel room, suddenly and completely awake. Anya rolled away.

The website!

Hastily, he grabbed his clothes and made his naked way down the hall to his room. He started up his laptop and connected to the internet. Sure enough, linked to an unlabeled button, he found all Anya's work posted for the world to see. Every patent they'd applied for, every secret they had kept, every deal he'd made with the FDA, was blown. He checked the number of hits—just a few.

He erased the files and button and flushed the server cache, glad for the first time he'd decided to host their server himself.

He had no idea if he'd done it in time.

oOo

By the next day, when Anya returned, Jake had to admit he'd struck out. He'd called in every favor to every street pimp he knew or heard of. Every cop he knew. Every john he'd let go and held on to the name for later. Nothing.

He filed the expected missing person report, his stomach jumpy and sour. Cindy was gone. He was surprised to find the house so different when he knew she wasn't there. Cindy's voice was higher than Anya's; he missed the counterpoint of their conversation. He missed the smell in the bathroom of that flowery shampoo she liked. He even missed the twisted tension in his stomach whenever he talked to her, that weird feeling of being manipulated and in control at the same time.

After a week, both he and Anya were wrecks. They sat across from one another at the big table in the kitchen. Anya was still going to work, but Jake had taken a leave of absence.

The week turned again and again nothing. At that point, the four walls seemed to close in on him and he left for Mississippi's. There he made a call. After an hour and two Irish Coffees, Connie Samoan came in the door.

He sat across from Jake. "What's wrong, man? You look like shit."

"My daughter ran away."

"That's pretty bad." Connie sipped his whiskey. "So, what's so urgent I had to come down to see you? You got your money, just as we agreed."

"I need help." Jake stirred his coffee. "You took over the Mexican's turf. But the Mexican had connections, too. I want you to ask around about Cindy."

"I don't even know what she looks like."

Jake pulled out a picture. Cindy in a green dress and a scowl. She didn't like that dress at all.

Connie examined the picture carefully.

Jake tapped the table. "You don't want *me* to go around asking. It would be bad for business. If you do this, I'll cut my take in half."

"In half," said Connie and looked at the picture. "Maybe cutting down to forty percent would incentivize me even more."

"Don't push it."

Connie stared at Jake for a long minute, then put the picture in his pocket. "All right. I'll see what I can do."

oOo

Cindy lay back in the big bed. The rooms at the Hyatt were huge, and they had the biggest bathtubs she'd ever seen. The place smelled of money.

She took a bath and carefully shaved herself as Connie had taught her. Cindy had seen for herself how a girl shaved in this particular manner excited her "clients" (Connie's words) but she didn't understand it. Then she bathed herself again and rubbed lotion where she had shaved so it would still be smooth and any cuts wouldn't be noticeable.

She slept for a little bit so she would be rested when Mister—she checked the card Connie gave her—Bonifacio came in. Then she brushed the sleep out of her hair and dressed for the occasion.

When Connie had suggested she come to work for him, she figured out right away what he had in mind but she didn't let on. She made him repeat what he wanted from her over and over, each time taking a little layer of glamour off it and coming closer to the truth. After about the third explanation, she saw the light dawn in Connie's eyes and he started laughing.

"You know exactly what I'm getting, don't you girl?"

She grinned.

"I won't be a street hooker," she said.

He looked at her, and for a moment she was scared—was this some line she crossed? Maybe she wasn't supposed to tell him what she'd do. Hell with that. If he got rough with her, she'd go back to daddy. This wasn't California they were talking about. It was Saint Louis, and she knew how things were.

"I don't do street work," he said shortly. "I work with good girls and rich men for a whole lot of money. You play your cards right, being as young as you are, you'll do well. You aren't a virgin, are you?"

"Not since I was fourteen."

"Good. Stick with me."

He'd taken her to his apartment near the river and they'd had sex—with a rubber, since she wasn't on the pill yet. He said he'd take care of that tomorrow. He was a lot more fun than her old boyfriend, Paul Steele. Or, as she'd thought of him, Paul Squeal.

Over the next week, she was with four men. Two here at the Hyatt, one at the Marriot, and one at the Executive. They were all older men but not so terribly ugly she had to pretend they were somebody else. Sex had been mostly just okay—though Mister Browning, at the Executive, had been terrific. But Connie had told her the client always needed to think it was fun. She didn't find it hard to convince them. Connie gave her more money than she had ever seen.

The first thing she wanted to do was call Portia, but Connie said that was the quickest way to have her daddy find her. Maybe she'd see Anya and Jake again someday, but not right now. Not when she was having this much fun.

Connie got her the dress she'd seen at Plaza Frontenac and she'd modeled it for him. He said he could do better and took her to Strapless in Clayton. The blue dress hanging next in the closet was one of those. It fit her well enough to make her look her age but strong enough to make her feel in control. "Worldly" was the word she used to herself.

"Always start off clothed," Connie had said. "People value what they have to work for."

When Mister Bonifacio came in the door, she was standing on the balcony watching the river, framed by the early evening light. As his eyes lit up, Cindy smiled back. This was too good. She was *never* going home.

Chapter 1.2: July, 1997

He had to get rid of her!

Connie gunned the motor even though he couldn't move two feet. The traffic on Lindberg did what it wanted to do; here, drivers were not bound by traffic laws. If someone wanted to stop—which apparently had happened—it was the solemn duty of each driver to slow down and stare carefully before going on.

Oh, she was sweet, Connie thought savagely. So quick and young. She was already making more than his best—that baby virgin flesh commanded a high price. Connie knew exactly how attractive it was. He'd tried it himself and then cut himself off. A good woman was no different from a drug: given half a chance, either one could own you.

Even so, he thought he had it under control. Just play her as long as she was able. Not too many at first, because what he was selling wasn't just the nice sex and the cute face; it was the softness. The vulnerability. Push her too quick and she'd get hard too fast. Then down comes the price.

Besides, he liked her.

Not that he would let that interfere with business. Business came first. As young as she was, she understood that.

So, play her a while. Make sure she got some change of her own—nothing compared to what he was actually getting for her. But not enough to let her get too greedy. Too much money spoiled a woman. If he played her just right, he could have another Traci Lords on his hands.

Then Fiske wanted to see him.

Jesus sweet fucking imperial *Christ!* Why the hell did she have to be Fiske's daughter?

Connie groaned as he turned onto Washington towards the bridge. The simplest way, of course, would be to kill her and dump her body way, way, *way* far away from here. But if he did that—and Fiske figured it out—Connie would be done for. It was slightly better for him if she were found alive. Even if she was found to be a whore. But not *much* better. Connie would still be done for, but he figured he could make the case it wasn't kidnapping.

Except maybe it was. She was fifteen. Maybe it was like kidnapping children. The willingness of the child meant nothing. Christ! Maybe he *should* kill her.

But not here. Not in Saint Louis. Not Connie—somebody else had to do it. But who? Where?

Connie didn't yet know who, but he had a good idea where. From Saint Louis everything drained downhill and across the river to East Saint Louis. He had to see Sam Forestell. But you didn't just see Sam. You made an appointment. Connie called on his cell as he crossed the Eads Bridge. Sam agreed to meet him for dinner.

Damn. He was going to have to get back by midnight to check on Cindy. Maybe he'd get lucky and Bonifacio would take care of the problem.

The Chicken Shack was patterned after the old fifties chrome restaurants, right down to the red booths and Formica tabletops. But it had seen better days. The plastic was patched with red tape and the waitresses looked like reformed prostitutes. Maybe they were. Connie didn't recognize any of them, but he was a Saint Louis boy.

Connie nursed a cup of coffee for nearly two hours until Sam showed up.

Sam Forestell was a thin, tiny man. He was white but Connie didn't care. Money was money. Power was power. Sam carried himself with authority. Connie never underestimated him. A knife didn't have to be big to be effective and Forestell always reminded Connie of a pale, narrow blade. Connie explained what had happened.

Sam did not change his expression. His dark eyes and narrow mouth didn't move. *Snake eyes*, thought Connie. *Stone eyes.*

"You want me to take this girl off your hands," Sam said precisely. "No."

"I can get the money. Forty, fifty easy. I can afford it. You know I can."

"I know that. You've got the Mexican's territory. I helped you set it up. I'm an investor. Now you're fucked." Sam shook his head. "You're not a good risk, Connie."

That blew a chill down Connie's back. "You said yourself that Tom Haberman was ready to be taken, and you were right. We have a good deal, here. I've just run into some unforeseen problems."

Sam shrugged. "She knows who you are. She knows where you work. We could take her and put her through the circuit and if she came out alive, she could still finger you."

Connie felt desperate. "Maybe we could put her out in the foreign markets. She's sweet, Sam. Really sweet. Maybe you could send her to China or Hong Kong."

Deep in Sam's eyes, Connie thought he saw a flicker of interest. "Here's her picture." Connie brought out the picture Fiske had given him.

Sam studied it. "Maybe. Wait here."

Sam left the booth and Connie took the chance to wipe his face with the napkin. Maybe coming clean with Sam wasn't such a bright idea. It was too late now.

Twenty minutes later, Sam returned. He pulled out a pen and wrote an address on the napkin. "Go get the girl. When you have her, take her to this address."

"They'll take her to Hong Kong?"

Sam shrugged again. "I don't know. I don't own a piece of you any more, Connie. I sold them you and your problem. That's the address of the new investor. They'll take care of everything."

Connie stared at the napkin. "But—" He looked up. Sam Forestell was gone.

oOo

"Tell you what, Sam," said Norman casually over the phone. "One girl isn't enough. I'll make a trade, though. I'll take Connie's territory if you take over a piece of the Alton crib."

Sam couldn't breathe for a long minute. His cell felt cold and alien in his hand. For a moment, looking into the kitchen, he caught the eye of one of the cute Puerto Rican cooks. *Barely a boy*, he thought. *With a soft mouth and big eyes.*

The cook realized Sam was watching him and dropped his eyes.

"Sam?"

"Excuse me?" he squeaked. He was standing in a tiny alcove made by the propped open door of the kitchen and the wall next to the coat rack. Two of the walls were covered with dirty red carpet and the third gave him a window through which he could watch Connie.

"Maybe you're not interested—"

"I'm interested." Breathe, Sammy. Breathe. "How much of the Alton crib?"

"Say, the south side."

"Does that include Joe Cori?"

"Sure," laughed Norman. "I don't much care for Brother Joseph. I'm not partial to white folks. You might get along with him better." Norman coughed. "Present company excepted, of course."

"Of course." Sam kept his response neutral. Norman wasn't somebody he wanted to get angry. Sam was higher than Connie in the food chain, but Norman was the bigger shark.

"You tell Connie to bring that Fiske girl around here. We'll straighten things out. Then hustle your ass over to Alton and introduce yourself to Cori.

I'll fax you what you need to know and call ahead." Norman hung up without saying good-bye.

Sam clicked off his cell. The little alcove seemed like the only safe place in the world.

Norman must know what he was giving Sam. Alton. It was five or six times what Connie had and Sammy was on the ground floor. *Connie must be sitting on something big,* he thought.

Sam felt cold. Something big enough to blow little Sammy away like a snowflake in the wind. Maybe this was even better than he'd thought. Maybe he was better out of Saint Louis. Could Norman be getting ready to try to make a big push into the city? Sam didn't see how. Norman had a lot of firepower, but he didn't match up to Big Boy or Leonardo.

Whatever it was, the possibility of Alton was more than big enough for him. *Mom,* he thought. *Your little Sammy is entering the big time.*

Sam gave Norman's address to Connie and said good-bye. *Poor Connie,* he thought as he drove north to Alton. It was like being a tadpole between a hammer and an anvil.

The fax came was coming out of the machine as he came in through his door. He read it quickly. Brother Joseph's schedule was filled. He was a man of prodigious appetites. Sam wasn't surprised. He listened to Brother Joseph's radio station regularly. While Sam wasn't exactly a believer, he enjoyed a good Hellfire and Damnation sermon. An occasional fall on his knees for other than carnal purposes was good for his soul.

Getting ready to go, Sam chose his suit carefully. Hard but not mobbish. Sam settled on a lovely double-breasted blue. He smiled. It was rare he got to dress this way.

The Alton Bridge gently lit the darkness against the sky. Seeing it, thinking about his new found position, Sam felt suddenly heavier. Weightier. He was a businessman.

oOo

Norman carefully hung up the phone. He was happy enough with the trade. Sam would make good on the Alton crib and Joe Cori was out of his hair. Though it was just business, Norman had an antipathy towards preachers. Perhaps it had come from his upbringing back in Charleston. Every Sunday, his mother had dragged her husband, Frank, her son, Norman, and his sister, Irene, to an eternal round of Hell and Damnation preaching that began with sunrise services on Sunday and didn't end until the entire family collapsed, exhausted, into their beds that night. Norman's father had escaped first, disappearing on a trip out for a pack of cigarettes. Norman had hated him for his easy ability to escape.

Norman had been forced to wait four more years before he was able to get a job and enough money to buy a gun. Then he was set. A quick hold up of a liquor store down the street and a hotwired Chevy got him to Atlanta, where he sold the car to a chop shop. For a few years, he muled heroin and marijuana from Miami to Memphis until things got a little too hot for his taste. He took his savings and, after much soul searching, bought a sweet little Cadillac DeVille and drove in style all the way to East Saint Louis.

Sam reminded Norman of himself, twenty years ago. All hot get up and go. The tremendous urge to make something of himself. To imprint himself into the very sidewalks and the walls of buildings.

"Who was that?" came LeRoy's voice from the back of the house.

You get responsibilities when you get family, he thought. *Duties. You get a legacy. Even if he isn't your own child. Even if he might not even reach twenty.*

"Sam Forestell," Norman called back as he walked back to LeRoy's room.

LeRoy liked the lights out. His dark young face shone in the glow of the monitors. In the dark, mused Norman, you couldn't see the bones in his face. His wrists didn't look so skeletal.

LeRoy looked up at him. "Well?"

"Connie was desperate to dump the girl. Does that make him a good source?"

"Sure." LeRoy shrugged. "I still don't trust him."

"No reason why you should." Norman rested his hand on the boy's shoulder, testing it thoughtfully. Maybe a little more meat on him. Maybe the new drugs the boy prescribed for himself were working.

"Anyway," said the boy. "We need her. Look at this." He drew up a set of web pages. "This is the Lifeworks site today. See? Nothing." A few clicks on the keyboard. "But last week, you can see it all: drug chemistry, toxicity studies, references, stoichiometry—though they didn't get that exactly right."

He fiddled with a second computer and brought an image like a collection of multicolored beach balls connected by soda straws. "This is what they think it looks like. And they're right in the native form. But they don't take into account the interaction with the receptors. They're not expecting it to kink. Here is what it looks like when it's at the sites."

The new image looked to Norman exactly the same. He chuckled. "I can see the obvious differences."

"Yeah, right." LeRoy laughed. "You don't see nothing."

"How old are you again?"

LeRoy grinned up at him, pure boy. "Fifteen."

At a moment like this, he looked just like his dead sister. Norman felt a surge of sudden, bitter longing to see her again. "You can figure all that out, eh?"

LeRoy turned back to the screens. "Some fifteen-year-olds can throw a ninety mile an hour fast ball. But me?" he said with satisfaction. "I understand carbon."

Norman heard a beep from one of the computers. LeRoy looked over and read the message. He bent down and opened the small refrigerator under the table. LeRoy pulled out a juice box and a pill organizer. "We can't match the production run they have," he said as he carefully arranged his pills. "We want to use this girl to get into white suburbia. Lots and lots of teenage kids with burnable money. For that, we need pills. Needles just won't do. So, for that we need to get Lifeworks to do the work for us."

"You think this will go over?"

"Maybe. It plugs into all the right sites." LeRoy grinned at him.

Norman couldn't have been prouder of him if he'd been his own son. "Not bad, LeRoy. Not bad at all."

LeRoy nodded. He scooped the final pile of pills off the table into his hands, poured them into his mouth, and chugged down the grape juice. It took him several tries to get them all down.

"Yuk. The protease inhibitor is really bitter." He shook his head. "Uncle Norman?"

"Yes."

"Don't ever let anyone convince you different. AIDS sucks."

oOo

The secretary's name was Maybelle. She led him down a maze of corridors and stopped at a closed door. Sam could hear voices on the other side. Maybelle knocked and put her head inside.

Sam could see a tall, bony young man, perhaps thirty, standing and staring back at him, a morose expression on his face. His face was wide with sharp, jutting cheekbones and narrow eyes.

Maybelle opened the door a little further, and Sam could see Brother Joseph Cori, sitting at his desk.

Joe Cori was a big man, maybe fifty, with a big belly and a heavy neck. His hands were broad and muscular, with scars across the fists betraying a violent past. Sam felt as if he were in the presence of royalty.

"Thanks, Maybelle. Come on in, Mister Forestell. This is my son, Ethan." He stood and gestured towards the young man. "He was just leaving."

Ethan turned and stared at Joe for a moment. "Yeah. I suppose. There's not much more I can say here." He brushed past Sam. He and Maybelle walked loose-limbed down the corridor.

Joe motioned for him to sit down.

Sam sat down across from him.

Joe didn't seem to notice him. "I wanted to meet you. And all," he said absently. He lay his hands flat on the desk as if he were about to declare it *healed!* as he did on his daily television show. He drummed his fingers for a moment.

Suddenly, he looked at Sam. "Have any children?"

"No."

Joe nodded. "'Sharper than a serpent's tooth' and all that. It's true, you know. They are ungrateful. They take your whole life…" His voice faded off for a moment. "My son—my *son*—said everything I did here was built on lies." Joe's voice boomed into the room. "As if anything built on the glorious birth, death, and resurrection of Jesus could be a lie. As if my whole life as a minister has been a lie. As if Jesus himself is a lie. That's what they're teaching him in graduate school."

He shook his head. "My son is smart. He's smarter than his daddy. He's studying astrophysics down to Washington University and considers things that are more than my feeble mind can comprehend. But can he comprehend the mind of God? Can he understand that Jesus died for his sins?"

Joe slammed his hand on the desk. "No, sir!" he thundered. "That he cannot."

Joe took a deep breath and seemed to look around. His hands came back to rest on the top of the desk, wiggling like so many fish in a school. Silence grew in the office.

"My daddy was a preacher," Joe said in a calm voice.

Sam wouldn't have changed this conversation for anything. "Really?"

"He worked the Revivalist circuit all across the South. 'Brother Jimbo Harrison. If he couldn't save you, the Devil would surely have your soul.'" Joe chuckled. "He changed his name because Cori was Italian and people might think he was Catholic. He needn't. The Coris were Protestant three hundred years ago—even Italy had to have a few, I suppose. He started in the twenties with Amy Semple MacPherson and split off from her in the thirties to go on his own way. He was over fifty when I was born."

"You were close to him?"

"Oh, no. I hated the son-of-a-bitch." He drummed his fingers for a minute. "He wanted me to come into the business, as it were. It was just another way to separate gullible, scared people from their money. I changed my name back to Cori as soon as I could and left town. He didn't hold it against me. It was probably a relief to him. He was near seventy when I left. He didn't hate me, then."

Joe leaned forward on his desk and worried a broken bit of skin on his palm with the other hand. "No. What frosted him was that I got saved. Billy Graham saved, too. In Indianapolis, Indiana. On September the eighteenth. In the Year of Our Lord, nineteen hundred and seventy-two. I figured I had to make peace with the old man. I went home and tried to save his soul. Made him so mad he dropped dead in the living room right in the middle of my sermon on how he had to change his ways." Joe made a sound in the back of his throat that could have been a cough or a chuckle. Sam couldn't tell.

"Here, look at this," Joe opened a drawer and pulled out an envelope. "Daddy used this trick. Bob Tilton used it again. See here? That's two cents. Next to it you can see it says: 'Do you need money?' The idea is the receiver takes the two cents, prays over it, and sends it back. With a check. Daddy took the check and threw out the prayer request."

"So, you wouldn't use such things?"

"This was the first thing I sent out when I started my ministry." Joe leaned forward. "But here is the difference: I take the prayer request and offer it to God."

Sam was confused. "What difference does that make?"

"It makes all the difference in the world. A person makes a prayer, writes a check, and sends it to me. I take that money, pass on the prayer, and use the money in the furtherance of our holy mission. By passing on the prayer I have completed the transaction. It has become sanctified."

"I don't understand."

Joe sighed. "Ethan didn't, either. Here, let's take a different one." Joe pulled out another envelope containing a plastic glove and a flyer. "In this one, the petitioner has some affliction. He takes the glove and rubs the afflicted part and then mails the glove—and a check—back to me. I take the money, pray over the glove, and use the money to run the station. This has made the signing of the check an act of faith—a prayer, if you will. I accept that prayer in the spirit it was offered and add my own prayers. Now, ask me what Ethan asked me."

Sam tried to think like a graduate student in physics. "Why is the check necessary?"

Joe smiled widely. "Exactly. In your position, you already know the answer."

It was like the dawning of a blinding light. "Money is the token of worth," Sam stammered. "By associating it with the prayer you've elevated the worth of the prayer in the mind of the petitioner." And everything else of worth in the world.

Joe beamed. "I couldn't have put it better myself. I can see we're going to get along well."

oOo

Cindy made Connie open the sunroof. Connie wouldn't let her stand up and let the wind blow over her—too many cops around, he said. She gave him her sexiest pout and held her hands out, feeling the summer wind run over them. She wanted to shout, she was so happy.

Mister Bonifacio—she'd kept calling him that even though he'd told her to call him Dominic since she could tell it turned him on—had been just a flat-out good time. He had taken her downstairs and danced with her in the hotel bar. It had been a terrific place with lights moving back and forth like an old disco. She had obeyed his instructions and acted all daughterly (or grand-daughterly, in this case) but she was having so much fun she couldn't help touching him every now and then when the shadows came across them. After a while, it was clear he was having trouble keeping down his grandfatherly appearance so they came back upstairs.

He'd even been fun in bed. He wasn't too fat so she didn't have to make up anybody for him to be, and he'd really liked the way she'd smoothed herself out. Dominic had insisted on doing it three times, which got a little tiresome— she was ready to call it a night after the first one—but he was the customer and it wasn't like it wasn't fun. She was just a little tired.

Midnight rolled around, and she slipped out of bed and took a quick shower, gathered up her things, and slipped out the door. Dominic had the sweetest little smile on his face. She wished she could be there when he woke up—give him something nice in the morning—but Connie said Mister Bonifacio didn't like to have anybody there when he woke up. She'd have to ask Connie about that. It seemed to her that he might like it if she were there for him in the morning.

Still, she sighed to herself. *I suppose it's better I get a good night's sleep, too.*

But when she got into Connie's car, she was just too excited to sleep. Connie said they had an errand to run over in East Saint Louis. She said fine.

It was an early summer night. The moon was big and yellow and reflected a buttery streak down the river. The waterfront was lit up like Christmas and she could hear a saxophone wail and echo over the causeway. The Eads Bridge looked utterly black. It broke up the moon as they drove under the girders. The air had that warm, close feeling, like nestling together after making love. *Sex*, she thought to herself. Connie said she should never call it making love. It was unprofessional.

They pulled up in front of an old brick house among other similar houses. Cindy was familiar with the style: two completely vertical floors terminated by a broad asphalt roof. The porch pushed out of the front with a poured concrete base and columns and covered by a shingled awning. It was like hundreds of houses she'd seen in Webster Groves or University City. In the hot summers, the brick gradually absorbed the heat, and by July the interior was a baking kiln. The only thing good about this sort of architecture was that it beat the Tower Grove house where she had grown up.

It was a far cry from the Hyatt.

"What are we doing here?" She stared at the two dark men lounging on the porch. They looked bored but watchful.

"You have an appointment."

Yuk! she thought. Cindy had figured she'd been getting the plum jobs because she was so young. Eventually, she'd have to pay some dues. She just didn't expect to pay them so soon.

Connie led her up the steps. "Connie Samoa," he said to one of the two men.

"Yeah. He's expecting you. Go on in."

The door opened into a brightly lit hallway. Cindy blinked and looked around. The walls were white and the floor was the color of honey. Framed pictures were carefully hung in the rooms she could see with track lighting above them. Cindy had been in the Saint Louis museums on field trips and these paintings had a similar feel to them.

Connie looked around nervously while Cindy admired one painting in particular. It was fairly large, perhaps two feet square. A man sat in a red chair with only his back visible, his business mysterious and inscrutable. A woman dressed in a yellow blouse and white dress sat to his left, playing something that might have been a piano. A woman stood to his right, dressed in a grayish blue dress. She could have been singing.

What struck Cindy was the light that fell on them. It made the yellow blouse and white dress positively glow. The red-backed chair was the color of sunset. The blue dress was a cloud. In fact, the more Cindy looked at the painting, it seemed that the people playing music or singing or whatever were incidental. The real subject of the painting was the light. The people, checkered floor, and draperies were there to tell the story of the light. As people could be used to tell the story of money or Christ be used to tell the story of God.

"Hey, there!"

Cindy started. *Wow,* she thought. *If I had written that on the report for the MFA field trip I'd have gotten an A for sure.*

It was a skeletally thin black boy roughly her own age. He had come downstairs. "What are you doing out here?"

"Connie Samoa," Connie said stiffly.

"You were supposed to come in the back way," the boy said accusingly. He saw Cindy and his eyes widened slightly. Cindy knew that look. She smiled at him and he almost smiled. He clearly was sick in some way. Cindy wondered what was wrong with him.

"The guy outside just sent us in," said Connie, oblivious.

Connie whispered to her. "The kid is LeRoy Parkin. Norman's his uncle."

"Norman?" whispered Cindy back.

"My boss." Connie shook his head in irritation.

Cindy found herself liking the boy.

"Okay," the boy said. "You and the bitch follow me."

Cindy felt as if she'd been struck.

So much for first impressions.

oOo

Orphira sat outside Lieutenant Charles Holmes office. She leaned her head back against the cool concrete wall and closed her eyes. Her hair was short and tightly curled against her black skin, so the coolness of the wall soothed her. The Saint Louis Police Department didn't use a partner model—officers were assigned as needed—but they did pair up people for training. This had been mentioned multiple times at the Academy. She couldn't hear what was happening inside but she knew, anyway. She could script it as if it were a play:

> HOLMES is an old cop who has seen better days. He fiddles
> with a pencil as he talks to FISKE.
>
> HOLMES
>
> This isn't up to you, Jake. It's a departmental rule. You knew
> it was coming down to this. She's new to the department. You
> have to be her mentor.
>
> FISKE
>
> I can't do vice detail with a woman. What am I going to do?
> Stake her out and wait for someone to proposition her?
>
> HOLMES
>
> Like you haven't done that before.
>
> FISKE
>
> Not with somebody I'm training.
>
> HOLMES
>
> Doesn't matter. It's policy. Every officer gets trained when
> they come into the department.
>
> FISKE
>
> How can I do good cop/bad cop with her? What pimp is going
> to take her seriously? If I have to shake down some dealer,
> who's he going to go for? Okay. I have to show somebody the
> ropes. But if I got to do that, I want a mean son-of-a-bitch
> who can help out in a fight.

That is, unless it wasn't about her being a woman but instead was about her being black. She could script that, too.

Well, Officer Fiske, I'll be better in a fight than you will ever be. My old sparring partner and ex-husband is Homicide Detective Joe Brobeck, National Karate Championship, 1998. I've probably been in twenty times more fights than you. None of that hold your punch crap, either. Joe studied in Okinawa and over there you wear armor until you get your brown belt. After that, they take the armor off, and if you get hit it's your own fault. So, don't worry about that. I'm a better shot than you, too. I've seen your scores. I'm smarter than you are. I left the force and spent four years in Silicon Valley, writing software for the web, and I'd be wealthy now and not being transferred over for you to argue about, if I hadn't made the mistake of holding onto the options and not cashing out before the bubble burst. I came back to Saint Louis and back into uniform just in time for you to be yelling about something that was out of style twenty years ago.

Lucky me.

The corridor smelled of cleaner and bleach—the Gravois station handled a lot of prostitution and drugs, and the cops here had a horror of AIDS contamination. She had liked her little house in San Jose. Right now, she wondered why she left.

The door opened with a slam. Jake came out first and Charlie stood in the doorway.

"Officer Doyle? Let me introduce Jake Fiske. You'll work with him until you find your feet."

"Charmed," said Jake distractedly. He looked terrible, as if he had been carrying a load of bricks for days.

"Likewise," Orphira said.

"Okay. Come on, let me show you your desk," Jake said, leading her along. "It's right next to my desk."

Orphira felt a little disoriented. She felt no hostility from him at all.

"Is that where your last trainee worked?"

"I've never had a trainee." Jake looked back at her and shrugged.

"How did you manage that?"

"My grandfather was on the force for a long time. He brought up most of the officers in charge. He handpicked Duck to replace him."

"Duck?"

"Did I say that? I meant Holmes. Duck is what Granddad called him. It's not what people call him anymore. Anyway, I worked that connection as long as I could to avoid getting a trainee. I didn't want the extra work." He shrugged. "Which is why Donald Holmes kept it a secret until it was a done deal. He probably didn't want me to try to mess it up. It's probably getting to be some kind of black eye for him. I knew it couldn't last forever. You play the hand you're dealt, right?"

They came to an open area office filled with desks. Jake led her to a pair facing each other. "This particular desk belonged to Jerry Mack. He retired three months ago. Now it's yours. That one is mine." He smiled distantly again at her.

Orphira had never found it easy to like people. Especially white people. Especially white men. But Jake didn't seem to change his behavior even a little bit when he left Holmes, white, and started talking to her, black. That counted with her. The little hitch in people's voices, the sudden shift of the eyes and quirk of the mouth made her helplessly angry. But this little Irishman—Fiske was an Irish name, wasn't it?—didn't seem to notice or care. Maybe she had scripted things wrong.

"What did Lieutenant Holmes tell you about me?"

"Not much. He knows me pretty well. I like to figure things out on my own." He rummaged around in his desk and pulled out a folder full of paper. He started rummaging through it.

"Ah. What have you figured out?"

"I figure you're Papa Doyle's daughter from University City. I heard you'd given up the force and moved to California. I didn't know you came back." He looked up from the papers. "Does he still play over at Blueberry Hill? I used to go listen to him." His voice trailed off and his eyes stared into the distance. Then he shook his head. "Good times," he said in a grim voice and continued reading the papers in the folder.

Probably some case he doesn't want to share. "Is my father in that folder, Mister Fiske?"

"No," he said distractedly. "My daughter ran away a few weeks ago and I'm trying to find her. I asked if I could take a leave of absence to go find her, but Duck doesn't think it will do much good. That's what we were talking about in there." He looked up at her. "What do you think, Orphira? Do you think I ought to quit and go look for her? Do you think I can do any good?"

Orphira realized that what she had taken for distraction was instead a deep and abiding pain.

"I don't know, Jake," she said carefully. "Do you think she was abducted?"

"I'm not sure." Jake leaned back in his chair. "She went upstairs and snuck out the fire escape. The kid down at the laundromat saw her walking down South Grand. He looked away, and when he looked back, she was gone. She could have been caught right then." Jake shook his head. "Or she could have just got a ride."

"Let me see what you've got. Maybe I can see something you didn't." She held out her hand.

He looked confused for a moment. Then, like the sun coming up, she saw it dawn on him that she was offering to help. This was the sort of things people did for one another.

A slow, shy smile came out over his face and she realized she liked him.

"Better call your wife, Jake," she said quietly, glancing over the papers. "We're going to be here a while."

oOo

Cindy wrinkled her nose. The back of the house smelled of cigarette smoke and beer. A door next to the kitchen led them to a dark building that looked as if it had been bolted to the house as an afterthought. There were perhaps half a dozen men lounging in the outer room, sitting on old threadbare sofas outside a single door.

"In here," said LeRoy. "Just the bitch. You stay outside."

The room was shadowy but not so dark she couldn't see a middle-aged black man sitting at a desk as she entered. He gestured towards a chair.

Cindy sat down. She tried to look provocative but it didn't come off. She just felt stupid.

"Do you know who I am?" His voice was deep and clear. It was loud in the room and made him seem bigger, scarier.

"You're Connie's boss, right?" Her own voice seemed painfully thin. She squirmed, suddenly embarrassed at the short skirt. Cindy had a horrible, little-girl feeling that she was doing something wrong, but she didn't know quite what it was.

He nodded. "My name is Norman Parkin. You were brought to me as a problem to be solved. Do you know why?"

Cindy shook her head.

"Your father is Jake Fiske, Saint Louis Police Department. It's a bad idea to use the children of police officers in this business."

At the mention of her father, Cindy sat up. They couldn't do anything to her. The relief made her chuckle.

Norman stopped. He stood up and came around and leaned against the desk, staring at her. She grinned at him.

He spoke quietly. "You may be thinking that because your father is a policeman that nothing can happen to you."

Quicker than she could see, he slapped her across the face.

Cindy yelped. Her mouth filled with the metallic taste of blood. Her ears rang.

"All that means," Norman continued as he sat back down, "is that we must not get caught." He tossed her a box of tissues. "Don't spit on the floor. I don't want a mess."

Cindy sat back down, trembling. She held a wad of tissues to her mouth. When they filled with blood, she tossed them in the wastebasket and wadded up another. She never took her eyes off Norman.

"As I was saying, this cannot continue. One way to solve this was to bury you in the Mississippi. Or I could send you to work as a pretty white girl overseas in, say, Sudan or Indonesia. You're young and strong. You could last a year or more."

"Please, sir," she said. Her voice came out shakily.

"Or I could send you home."

Cindy's face lit up. At that moment, the money, the clothes were forgotten. "Let's do that."

Norman chuckled. "You would owe me. You would work for me."

"Name it."

"Later," he said in that mild, lethal voice. "I will." He stood up. "LeRoy will get you some ice to put on it. Connie will take you home." Norman stood up. "Good-bye."

She stood up and stared at him. She wanted to ask him if he really would have killed her. If the soft, lethal voice and the slap were just being tough on her. But something in his eyes stopped her, and she decided she didn't want to know.

oOo

Norman left his office and came into the house by the kitchen. He nodded to Damulin and Talbot. They nodded back, relaxing as they sat back to their coffee.

He walked to the front of the house and stood in front of *The Concert*, feeling as always refreshed as he looked at it. He would have to re-read Edward Snow.

It had upset him to know that Connie and the Fiske girl had even seen the painting, much less that they had been admitted to the front door. He had considered getting rid of Connie and the girl, both. Unlike Connie, he was much less concerned with killing a cop's child. If Norman were ever caught, that would be the least of his worries.

Once he had calmed himself down, he realized LeRoy was right when he said that having the front door be the forbidden entrance was just going to create problems. But Norman had been raised in this house and he didn't want to change too much of it. Maybe it was time to rethink his position. Besides, it was clear that neither the girl nor Connie had any idea what they were seeing.

Norman noticed that LeRoy was watching him from the hallway.

"It went well, don't you think?"

LeRoy nodded. He looked away.

Norman sighed. "What now?"

"You didn't have to hit her."

"Hit her?"

"I saw her face when she left. It had your fingers all over it."

"Did you give her ice?"

"Yes."

Norman shrugged and turned back to *The Concert*. "She wasn't taking us seriously. She was thinking herself safe because Fiske is her father. That had to change. You know that."

"I know."

"You called her a bitch."

LeRoy nodded. "Part of the job."

Norman suddenly looked at LeRoy speculatively. "You like her, don't you son?"

"Don't call me son," said LeRoy with a shy grin. "Being compared to my father is insulting to you."

"You do. I can see it in your face." Norman walked over and grabbed him around the shoulders. The two of them walked back to the kitchen. "I thought you didn't like white girls."

"Norman!" LeRoy's face took on a deep color.

"Okay, okay." Norman let him go. "I wash my hands of it. Who you date is your own business. But not employees. If you're going after this girl, wait until we're done with her. And for the record, I didn't slap her that hard. Just enough to get her attention. How about some ice cream?"

"Christ, Norman." LeRoy pulled a tub of mint chocolate chip from the freezer. "I bet you even used the Darth Vader voice on her. I'll be lucky if she ever wants to see me again."

oOo

Why was she always so sad?

Tess Durbin stared out the car window. She sipped from a half pint of vodka that Sam had given her and stared out again. Sam sure had a nice car. She had to give him that. A long, dark green Buick. One of the sporty jobs. It only looked like a third cousin to one of those huge floating sedans. But she still didn't like him. Norman, she liked. Norman with his deep voice and his big hands—she used to be Norman's favorite a long time ago. He used to tell her she was a sweet as cherry pie. He even sounded as if he meant it—which counted a lot for her, since it was well known that Norman didn't much care for white women. But maybe it was the contrast that had attracted him, she being so pale and all. With her black hair and milky skin, maybe he had liked the look of them together.

It didn't last. *Nothing lasts*, she told herself. Was she always so sad? When did it start? Her friend, Lola, had been killed when Big Boy tried to take out the competition. Leonardo wasn't even scratched, but Lola and three of Leonardo's boys were shot to pieces. Was she sad before that? Was she sad before Gary split? Before he found out she was hooking again, and came and took her little Monica? Was she sad before the judge said that not only couldn't she get Monica back but that she couldn't see Monica anymore? Was that when it started? Or did it start when she found out she was just another Norman Parkin asset? Was she sad before that? When did it start?

She let the air conditioning blow on her face. The cool air felt good, like a light breath of winter across her eyes.

No. She supposed she had reasons to be sad, but it seemed to her she'd been sad years ago, in high school. Back in Milan, Missouri—as rough a small town as there ever had been. Even then, she'd had this hard knot of melancholy in her chest. Something neither love nor sex nor motherhood could ever loosen. Maybe that's how she got here in the first place.

Tess watched through the window as the Buick negotiated the short square turns between blocks. She glanced over at Sam nervously turning the wheel. There was no relief coming from him. Besides, he was too small and skinny to be of any use to her. She liked big men. Not that she was all that choosy. Some women were actors. Or nurses. Or wives. All of them were working girls. She was a working girl, too.

"Listen," said Sam tensely. "You're not one of his regulars."

"I know that."

"But I think he'll like you. Besides, none of his regulars are available tonight."

She knew that. Vanessa had been to confession and the priest told her she had to give Joe up. Vanessa was a good Catholic girl, and neither slaps nor bruises nor the broken arm Sam had given her had changed her mind. The other two girls had gone to ground, and Sam hadn't been able to find them. Tess knew Norman wasn't going to like the way things were going.

"You told me all that three times, driving up here. Lighten up, Sam." She smiled at him, a big, dazzling smile that should have told him everything was all right. He didn't notice, so she turned it off. Not that she minded gay guys, but Sam ought to go get laid or something.

"Are you going to be okay? You feel good? Here. Take something." He reached into his jacket pocket and pulled out a leather wallet. It opened on the seat. In different pouches, as organized as an old lady's sewing bag, were little plastic bags of pills. White pills. Red pills. Orange caplets. Silver capsules.

"I didn't know they still made Quaaludes," she said idly.

"Take what you need."

She picked two downers and washed them down with a little vodka. After a few minutes, it seemed that knot of sadness in her chest didn't pull quite so hard.

Sam pulled into a little Best Western near the highway and told her what room he was in.

Just because she couldn't feel it didn't make anything less sad, she thought as she walked up the stairs.

Joe Cori was sitting at the table next to the balcony door, reading loosely stacked papers. He was still wearing his suit. He looked up at her over his reading glasses when she opened the door, nodded, and went back to his reading. She felt suddenly confused and sad again, standing in the doorway not sure of what to do.

"Come on in, darlin'," Joe said without looking up. "Sit down for a minute and I'll be right with you."

Tess sat on the edge of the bed, her purse in her lap. She wished she had another downer but even if she had, she wouldn't have taken it in front of a customer. There was no surer way of getting in trouble with Sam. Sam had made it clear: Tess didn't want to get in trouble with him.

After a moment, Joe took off his reading glasses and tucked them absently into his suit pocket, and started loosening his tie. "The work's never done, is it?" he said and glanced at her.

She forced a smile. "I guess not."

He looked at her a moment, then away as he took off his tie and jacket.

The Best Western room had two double beds. Tess was sitting at the foot of the one nearest the door. Joe sat on the other, his back against the headboard.

"What's your name?" he asked.

Something in the way he said it made her turn to him. Joe was watching her. *Oh, God*, she thought. *I'm messing this up already. Sam is going to be so mad.*

"You have a name, don't you?" he asked gently.

"Tess."

"What's the matter, Tess?"

That was wrong. They were supposed to talk to *her*, not the other way around. That's the way things worked.

"Nothing," she said and gave him the same bright smile she had given Sam. Sam missed being dazzled by his orientation but there was nothing protecting Joe.

His eyes widened a little. "When you do that you are so pretty," he said. "It lights up the room." He leaned forward and in a loud whisper he said, "But you don't mean it."

Tess felt wary. Just what did Joe want?

Joe moved to the edge of the bed opposite Tess and leaned forward with his elbows on his knees. This close, Tess realized how big he was. Most fat men moved like they were held down to the earth with steel ropes. But Joe moved gracefully, as if he were so strong or so light the earth barely held him at all.

"This is why people like me have regulars," Joe said confidentially. "Everybody knows what to expect from one another. I don't want you to come here and beat me with a whip or tie me up or handcuff me to the bed. I don't want you to dress like Eva Braun or dance like Lisa Minelli. What I want is a girlfriend for the night. At the end of the night, you'll go back to your life and I'll go back to mine. Sometimes I like to sit up late and get drunk while we watch an old Elvis Presley movie. Other nights, I might want to have as much sex as this old body can possibly take. On occasion, I'll get drunk and bawl about my dead mother."

Tess stared at him. When he spoke to her, it was like there was no one else in the world.

He took her hands so she had to turn around and face him. His eyes were open and wide, warm and brown as the earth. "Tonight, I'm in the mood to do nothing but listen to you. So, darlin', what's making you so sad?"

It was as if his face filled the world and she told him all of it, from the beginnings when she was a child. Lola dying. Gary leaving. Losing Monica. She might have talked for ten minutes; she might have talked for two hours. She had no idea. It was enough that he listened.

It was so natural and easy, that when he pulled her towards him, she opened as easily and as naturally as the grass opens to the sun, as trusting and forgiving as when she was a little girl.

oOo

Orphira knew Jake was coming down the hall long before he came in the room. There was a booming, happy voice as Jake said Hello there, helped carry Clara's folders, clapped Duck on the back—she smiled to herself. Ever since her first conversation with Jake, she could only think of Captain Holmes as Duck. She returned to the report on a gambling bust down on Leland. You'd think people had better things to do with their money. *Although*, she thought, *you get better odds on a crap game than the lottery.*

She didn't look up when Jake sat at the desk across from hers. "You're happy this morning."

"Guess why?"

Orphira looked up and knew instantly. It was written across his face. "Cindy came home last night."

"Yes!" The word exploded from him as he leaned across the desk. "I was getting set, too, to start checking the hookers across the river but she came home." He laughed and leaned back in his chair. "I didn't find her under some barge down near Cairo."

"Better make an appointment for her." Orphira didn't look up. She didn't want to see his face.

"Appointment?"

"Your wife will probably do it."

"What appointment?"

"Jake." She looked up. "I know she's your little girl. But she's been gone a month as a runaway. You know she's been up to something. Get her tested."

Jake thought for a minute. "I don't care what she's done. She's come back."

Orphira sighed. "This isn't something to be forgiven. It's an issue of public health. If you don't want to put it on her record, take her down to the clinic in Soulard. They know what to look for."

Jake stared at her.

Orphira stared back. "You've been on vice longer than me. You know how things are."

Jake looked away. "Boy, you sure do know how to blow a good mood."

She chuckled and returned to her report. "That's what my ex-husband used to say."

He left the room and returned a few moments later. He tapped his finger in front of her until she looked up. "You're right," he said. "I'll pick her up and take her this afternoon. Do you know the doctors over there? One that won't make it too humiliating for her?"

Orphira looked up at him. She let him look her in the face for a long half minute to give him time to think about what he said. "Why would I know the doctors over there? Why would you *think* I know the doctors over there? Do you think every black woman knows all the doctors in all the public health centers are so she can find out if she got herself knocked up the night before when she was out with her man?"

"I'm sorry. You mentioned the clinic in Soulard. I thought—"

"I know what you thought."

Jake's face turned red and he stood up and started to leave the room.

Orphira spoke suddenly. "Hiller."

Jake stopped. "Beg pardon."

"Ask for Doctor Hiller. If he's still there. He was good enough for me." She grinned at him.

Jake looked as if he didn't know what to do. He turned and left without a word.

Still grinning, she returned back to her report. *Hell. This might be fun after all.*

oOo

The boat wasn't large as houseboats go, but the woodwork was new and the trim was freshly painted. The deck was clean, and there wasn't any trash lying around. Sitting in lawn chairs on the aft deck, Cindy and Connie could see distant lights travel across the highway bridge. The night was damp, motionless, and black. A light fog or mist—Cindy couldn't quite tell—lay over the trees, the farmland, and the feeder streams and pools, wrinkling like a blanket.

"This is great," said Connie with a relaxed sigh.

This is what's great about men, thought Cindy, grinning. *They can think a mosquito-covered, half-sunken boat in the middle of a stinking river is great.*

Connie got up and lit a subdued lantern inside the boat. A small apartment with kitchen, bedroom, and sofa all in easy reach. Like a small trailer or mobile home on the water. Inside, the houseboat was just as neat and clean as the outside.

"You want a beer?" asked Connie eagerly.

Cindy stared at him for a moment. Then she realized she was actually on a date. A real date. Like in the movies. Connie had asked her out. It didn't matter—right then, anyway—that they had been given a job to do. He had asked her out, anyway.

"Sure," she said. "I guess."

Cindy felt older, somehow. She was uncertain what to do next. If Connie had been a client, she would have known exactly how to proceed. But since this was a date, the terrain was a little murkier. Cindy liked it. "Is this where you live?"

Connie came back with two Coronas. "I wish. I have a little place down near the stadium. Maybe in a couple of years." They clinked bottles and Connie took a drink. "But I own it. Bought it last year." He spread his arms around. "Three hundred acres of prime bottom land. I can farm it for a while. Or build a casino. There's an old warehouse away from the river I could use as a construction base. But it would take backers. Money. Payoffs. Farming is a lot easier. I haven't decided."

"You could leave it alone. Let it just grow back to birch and creeper."

"That, too. But that's not the best."

Cindy thought for a moment. "How did you buy it? I mean there are three casinos on the west side of the river already and the highway is covered with strip malls. How could you afford it?"

Connie was silent a moment. "Well, I didn't exactly buy it. I sort of inherited it."

"From who?"

Connie examined the bottle for a moment. "It's not important. How did you get out? You didn't climb out the back door again, did you?" Connie sipped his Corona.

"No," she said. "I told them I had a date."

"It's a little late for a date."

"I did have a date. With Portia. She dropped me off just before you picked me up."

Connie nodded. "They're letting you go out on a date?"

"What are they going to do? Lock me in my room? You know how well *that* worked."

Connie shrugged. "My dad would have beaten me black and blue for running off."

"And look how well you turned out."

Connie started and looked at her but she grinned at him. After a minute he smiled back and watched the road. "Are you going to be all right with this?"

"It's a little late to be asking that." Cindy sighed. She felt safe at home— something she'd never thought about before. But she missed the fun. All of her friends seemed distant now. Interested in different things than what she was interested in. Even her best friend, Portia, was hard to talk to. Cindy hadn't spoken to anyone of where she had been or what she had been doing—she wasn't sure how it would be received. Even by someone as open-minded as Portia. It made things hard. She missed the money, too. She was getting as much as $200 a time. Now, to get that kind of money she'd have to steal it from Mom.

Until now. Cindy sipped the beer. "Two hundred bucks is two hundred bucks. I've been in Mom's lab lots of times. I know where everything is. It took me a week, but I have all the access codes—it's not like she's trying to hide them. If somebody comes, call me on the cell." She reached in her pocket, pulled out the little phone, and held it up.

"Put it on vibrate," Connie said dryly. "I don't want this to be like some bad movie."

She reset the phone. "Now you can call me and I'll enjoy it."

Connie glanced at her and turned back to the road. "It's just as well Norman made you quit. You're too smart for that business."

Cindy didn't answer. She watched the lights on the highway. People were trying to get home after a long day of work, of visiting strip malls, after buying a pizza or a loaf of bread.

"A normal fucking life," Cindy said softly. That's all she wanted while she was sitting in that chair across from Norman, the burn of his hand hot on her face. All she had prayed for. Let me get home. Let me leave all this. Just give me a normal life.

If Connie heard, he made no sign.

"You want another beer?" he asked quietly after a few moments. "I've got Dos Equis. Tres Equis. I've even got Tecate and some lime to go with it. The refrigerator's packed."

"No." Cindy looked at her beer. She hadn't even finished a third of it. She used to drink it right down when she had the chance. Now she was being offered as much as she wanted. "I don't want to get sloppy."

"Okay, then." Connie checked his watch. "About ready to go?"

Cindy stood up and threw the bottle as far as she could. The bottle sailed out of the light, and she waited for the splash. She heard nothing and then gave up. "Yeah. I'm ready."

oOo

When Joe had asked for Tess a second time, she was pleased but didn't think that much of it. She honestly liked Joe. He had made her feel better than anything or anyone had for a long time. He listened when he had no earthly reason to and when she had sat across his thighs—the only practical position given the size of his belly—he had made a decent effort to make sure she had fun, too. In Tess's experience, this was pretty unusual. But Tess told herself, her experience had never ascended more than a level or two up from a streetwalker. She imagined, or more accurately, hoped, the higher-priced girls had a better class of client.

On the way to the hotel she was struck by a horrible suspicion. What if he was going to try to convert her or study her or, worse, what if he was one of those guys that really liked for her to talk about her life or something? She shuddered. The idea of talking about what she had been through to some sinister leech was more than she could stand. Maybe she could lie to him or something. She was unhopeful. On matters of the body, Tess could lie like a trooper: scream like she was experiencing orgasms from Christ himself or that she really, really, liked the taste of semen or that size didn't matter and sure, it happened to lots of guys. But in matters of the mind, what she thought about things or where she had grown up, she had trouble keeping a straight face. The line may have seemed odd to some, even to Tess herself, but she could tell when the giggling started that some part of her, at least, kept precise and careful track of what was going on.

But Joe had treated her courteously. Just like before, he was working when she got there. She waited for him to finish and—that was when she understood what she liked about him—at the moment the papers were stacked and put away, Tess became the center of his attention.

Then Joe asked for her *again*, and she realized she had found a regular that she liked. Not a guy that just liked her. For reasons she did not understand, this made her even sadder, and a couple of times she begged Sam to let her off. It was her period. She wasn't feeling well. She had explosive diarrhea. Anything. Because Joe deserved better than a sad prostitute. Instead, out of loyalty she listened dutifully to his radio station, even though she'd been raised as good Catholic girl from Town and Country and found his sermons distasteful. Still, she sent away for the plastic prayer rug and the blessed medallion and the rest of it. It was amazing to her how much of it there was.

oOo

It was late now, nearly eleven. Connie pulled the Lincoln off the highway. A few minutes later he drove behind the lab. The parking lot was empty.

"You better wear these," he said. He gave her a pair of latex gloves.

Cindy nodded grimly. She checked the phone again and then pulled the gloves on.

As she left the car, Connie grabbed her shoulder.

"Good luck," he said.

She smiled at him. "Piece of cake. I rip off my mother every day."

Getting past the back door was easy—the access code for the building was the same for all doors. She stood in the darkened lobby and looked around. Cindy couldn't remember the cleaners' schedule, but she heard no sound.

Cindy took the stairs; she had no idea if the use of the elevator was tracked. She'd read on the internet that some places logged such things. Of course, maybe they logged the opening and closing of doors. Probably, they logged the use of an access code. So, if the theft was discovered it would be tracked back to Anya. Anya would figure out it was Cindy pretty quickly after that.

She shrugged. She'd cross that bridge later. If the theft was discovered, she'd likely have more to worry about than Anya's disapproval.

Anya's lab was on the third floor. It took a different access code. She keyed in the one she'd found in Anya's purse and sure enough, she got in. It was like a video game: each level took a different key.

She knew where Anya's desk was and that was where her certainty of things ended. From here on, she was working on guesswork and intuition.

Anya's desk was in the alcove just outside the lab. From what Cindy knew, the lab was where the animal test work was done. Anya wouldn't be using it now, since Anapyridol was past development and into trial production. Still, Cindy came here first to see what she could find. With any luck, Anya had left some of the pills here to analyze or something.

She rummaged through the desk. Nothing. No codes. No pills.

Okay, she thought. They had finished their first production run—Anya had been clear about that. So, where would they keep the pills?

Cindy knew that Lifeworks didn't manufacture much of its own material—in the years Anya had worked here, there wasn't much Cindy hadn't heard at one time or another. Real production was farmed out to various contract manufacturers. What little Lifeworks had in the way of such facilities was limited to experimental runs and research. The question was: had they received the material and, if so, where had they put it?

She looked through the paperwork on the desk and found a copy of the receiving receipt, a lot of ten thousand units of Anapyridol.

"Wow," Cindy breathed. That sure seemed like a lot to her.

It was likely the lot had been received. How many bottles would that be? Ten bottles of a thousand? A hundred bottles of a hundred? How would it be packaged? Where did they put it?

"Damn it," she said and stood up. She left Anya's desk and went back to the corridor. "Let's be logical about this. Where wouldn't it be?"

It wouldn't be in Bill's office or anywhere else in administration. It wouldn't be in the lab. That wasn't controlled enough. Cindy had heard a lot of bitter dinner conversation in the last year, while Anapyridol was going through the preliminary human studies about the level of detail required by the FDA. It wouldn't be in the actual production facilities or animal experimentation for the same reason. But there might be a controlled holding area in production. Wasn't there also a drug room near here? Cindy vaguely remembered Anya bitching about signing controlled substances in and out because of FDA rules. Once the human trials started, they didn't have the same freedom that they'd had with the animal work.

Work methodically, she thought. Work logically. She walked the corridor, looking for anything that looked like a drug room. Sure enough, there was one around the corridor. Locked with a keypad. She ran through all the access codes she had memorized. The fourth one worked, and the door swung open heavily.

It was like being in a pharmacy. A row of Prozac jars next to a collection of packages reading Zoloft, Wellbutrin, Ritalin. But nothing interesting and no Anapyridol. In the back of the room was a large locked cabinet such as would hold guns or, she hoped, stronger drugs. A sign-out pad hung on a hook attached to the front. Cindy ran her finger along the list: morphine, OxyContin, cocaine—she could make some good money here if she wanted. Finally, near the end of the list, Anapyridol. *Yes!*

But there was no keypad. Only a hole for a circular key like something for a bicycle lock or—*damn!*—a gun cabinet. She looked through Anya's key chain. Her heart sank. All of the keys were straight. Not a round one in the bunch. She looked through Anya's keychain again to make sure. Nothing.

"Okay," she said softly. It had to be around here, then. In her mother's desk? In Bill's desk? She'd look in Anya's desk first.

Cindy turned and Bill was standing in the doorway.

He was leaning against the door frame as if he were tired. There was something odd about his eyes, and every moment or so he looked around as if he were watching something she couldn't see. And he was naked.

She gasped and looked down.

He looked down at himself, too, then looked up. "What?"

"You're naked."

He shrugged. "She told me someone would come."

"Who? Mom?"

Bill shook his head. "I knew I would try to hide it as soon as I found out I had exposed it. So, I forgot I had done it. Fortunately, I didn't succeed."

Huh? "Uh, Mister Wallace. I've got to go."

"It's not in there."

"What's not in there?"

He stepped over and stood very close to her. His penis brushed her jeans. "What you're looking for." His eyes were dilated and his breath had a curious, sweetish odor.

She looked down at him, then up at him and raised her eyebrows meaningfully.

Bill glanced down and stepped back. "Sorry."

"What am I looking for?" Cindy asked. This was getting more and more interesting. She wondered what Bill was on.

"Anya's dream. My project. Anapyridol. I knew someone would come to get it. We mustn't keep it to ourselves." He backed out of the room and beckoned for her to follow.

He padded silently on his bare feet as they walked back to his office. He held the door for her and closed it after she entered. Then he went to his desk and pulled out the lower right drawer.

"Here they are," he said. One by one he pulled out brown jars, each labeled "Anapyridol, 100 µg." When he was finished, there were ten jars on his desk. He beamed like the father of a newborn son. "Aren't they beautiful?"

Cindy sat down across from him.

He put on his reading glasses and looked them over carefully, picked one. "Here. This is the one for you."

She took it from him. "This one? How come?"

Bill shrugged. "The therapeutic dosage is 200 micrograms—two pills. But nothing really happens until you take 800 micrograms—eight pills. We started seeing some heart arrhythmias in the chimps at five grams you're safe. We've found twenty pills is optimal." He smiled beatifically.

Cindy hefted the jar. It was heavy and slick in her hand. "Where's your car?"

"Next lot over. I didn't want to scare you away."

"How did you know I was coming?"

Bill shrugged. "I didn't know when. I've been here every night for two weeks."

"Did you know it would be me?"

Bill shrugged. "You never know who's coming for you."

"What does this stuff do?"

Bill seemed to ponder that. "It's a blessing," he said finally.

A few moments later Cindy was looking out the window as the Lincoln sped away, the jar in her lap.

"How did it go?" Connie said as they turned onto Highway 40.

She held up the jar wordlessly.

"Good. I was worried there might be trouble." He pulled out a thick envelope and passed it to her.

"Trouble," Cindy repeated as she counted the money. She leaned back in the seat and closed her eyes. "Connie, how much did you charge for me?"

Connie didn't answer immediately. "About two grand. Sometimes a little more. Sometimes a little less."

Ten percent, she thought. *Two hundred bucks is two hundred bucks.*

Cindy sighed. "I'm underpaid."

oOo

She was too sad, Sam thought savagely to himself. She was too sad? He'd show her what fucking sad was. He'd slice her open and sell her kidneys!

Except he wouldn't. Tess had become Joe's favorite. When scheduling prevented Tess from getting together with him, Joe got testy. He refused other girls. He made disparaging comments about Sam's orientation. He mentioned Sam's mother.

From anyone else, this would have become a matter of honor—even Sam had honor of a sort, though he would have been the first to admit that honor took a swift back seat to expedience. But Joe was different. Joe had a higher calling. When Joe spoke, Sam wanted to listen. And damn his mother—or his pride—if Joe spoke against them.

Sam's customary methods were useless, then. Okay. He was a creative sort. Drugs might work. He tried Tess on various kinds: Benzedrine—Sam's personal favorite—didn't work any better than Seconal. Seconal didn't work as well as OxyContin. And OxyContin didn't work at all. Sam tried Prozac and Zoloft, but they took too damned long. A week later and she was still sad. Joe always wanted her, and he always wanted Sam to help her get better.

"You're a goddamned pharmacy," Joe had thundered at him.

Sam had quailed and decided to pursue the last resort. He would ask Norman's advice.

Sam had been to Norman's many times and knew not to go in the front door. When he had heard Connie had inadvertently been shown in the front, he was appalled at Connie's luck. Not only had he lived, he had also gotten to see Norman's paintings. Sam had hinted he'd wanted to see them for years. Norman had ignored him.

When Sam pulled up in front of Norman's house, he was half-tempted to just walk in the front way. Half tempted. That was how the Mexican had gotten on Norman's bad side. Not that it was the only reason that Norman had backed Sam and Connie in the takeover, but Sam was convinced that was the final feather on the balance.

Sam, then, faithfully stepped past the two men standing outside and entered in the back door to wait his turn. Tonight, he was alone. Only LeRoy was sitting at the desk outside Norman's office, with perhaps fifty plastic bags of pink pills.

"What are these?" Sam asked, always interested in pharmaceuticals.

"Shut up," said the boy, and went into Norman's office.

Sam amused himself, wondering how he would deal with LeRoy if the occasion ever presented itself. Then he heard LeRoy and Norman arguing.

"Ten's not enough," LeRoy said. "You heard what she said. It takes four to get off. You know people are going to want more than two and a half trips in this first lot. Less than four, and you just get euphoria and shit. We got to do better then give them depression relief."

"I don't want to risk more than five hundred in the first lot."

"You better. We need to make a bang in the first try and then jack up the price."

"You give some little white boy from Clayton twenty of them and he blows out his heart, we're not going to make squat on the deal."

"Tough. That's how many I put in the bags."

"Out of the question! That's ten percent of our stash!"

LeRoy started to speak and then looked outside at Sam. He closed the door, and Sam could hear shouting through the wall.

Without thinking, Sam counted out two pills from ten bags and put them in his pocket. Then, he sat down and tried to look innocent.

After a few minutes, LeRoy came out, clearly angry, and grabbed up all the bags. From a drawer in the desk, he pulled a box, put the bags in the box, and headed into the house.

Norman came out, his face like thunder. "What do you want?"

"I wanted to talk to you about one of the girls. Tess. Do you remember her?"

Norman shrugged. "What the hell do I care about her? She's your problem now."

"I need your advice."

"Yeah?" Norman laughed. "This is a first. What's the problem?"

"She sometimes claims to be too…sad to work." Sam felt ridiculous—not a safe feeling in his life. He waited for Norman to give him grief.

Instead, Norman looked at him quizzically. "Wait a minute. This Tess. She's a pale white girl with dark hair? Thin little thing?"

"That's her."

"Sad Girl. Oh, I remember her. She'd cry if a mouse got caught in a trap. Hell, I never knew what to do with her. I kind of liked her, though, so I sent her up to Alton. I never figured she'd last this long."

"She has."

"So, ice her. Nobody's going to be looking for her."

"I…can't. She's become the favorite of an important client."

"No client is that important—wait. You're not saying she's the favorite of Joe Cori?"

Sam looked at the floor. "Yes."

Norman laughed again. "That is a pickle. Have him buy her out. Let her be his problem."

Sam felt stricken. He would never have an excuse to speak with Joe again. He'd be limited to just watching him on television. "That's an interesting idea."

"You don't like it. I can tell. Joe brings in a lot of money." Norman considered a moment. "You tried all the drugs?"

"Everything. Downers, uppers, Prozac."

Norman whistled. "You might just have to wait on the Prozac. It takes a while."

Sam felt miserable. "Okay."

"I'll ask LeRoy if he can think of something." Norman clapped him on the back. "All the other girls are doing fine, eh?"

Sam nodded.

"Then you're okay. You'll think of something. Just don't slap her around. It makes her sadder." Norman smiled at him. "I know."

Sam found himself standing on the back porch. He made his way mechanically to his car and drove a few blocks to a McDonald's. He bought a Happy Meal and threw everything out but the French fry bag. He put his twenty pills in the bag and folded it shut. Maybe this would work

oOo

Sam had said no more than two as he gave Tess the bag. Two had made her feel pretty good, but she was still sad. Tess wanted to do better by Joe.

No more than four, she told herself. There was always a buffer in these things. After all, it wasn't as if this was smack ordered from some shaking junkie in North Saint Louis. This was a real pill with a real pedigree—you could tell from its shape and the printing embossed on the side.

So, she took two more before Sam picked her up, and pretty soon the world took on a slick sheen and she saw rainbows around the lights. Every reflection had glittering points surrounding it and the colors changed character: purple became smooth and mysterious, red became thick and muscular. Yellow looked shy and blue wasn't telling anybody anything. She felt something in the back of her mind, coiling and uncoiling. Sam didn't notice. He just muttered to himself continuously like he always did.

Then it was like an eye opening inside her. An eye looking around with a searchlight gaze at everything she had ever done, every person she had ever seen, every word she had ever spoken. A loving eye. A womanly eye. For a long, timeless moment, the only reason she existed at all was to be observed.

Her heart pounded and she coughed violently. She opened her eyes— when had she closed them?—and looked around at the world. The eye belonged to somebody, but Tess had no idea who. Only that looking at the world for this somebody was a wonderful task. Look at Sam. Look at how slight and ridiculous he is. How sad he is. She wanted to reach over and rub his cramped shoulders. How is he so different from me? Aren't we all the same?

She looked through Tess, and Tess heard *her* thoughts.

Sam dropped her off, and everything seemed distant and close at the same time. As if the world curled around itself so that everything was touching.

Inside, Joe was waiting for her, but this time the papers were in a neat pile in front of him on the table and he was staring at the wall. The depth of his sorrow was palpable.

"Honey," she said sitting across from him. "What's the matter?"

"Nothing," Joe said, looking up at her. "Don't worry about it."

It was like another voice speaking through her. "Come on, now. You've listened to me. Now I'll listen to you. What's going on?"

"Just my son," he said. "Nothing new. Just my only son, who won't talk to me anymore. I called him today and I knew it could be the last time." Joe spread his hands. "Am I such a horrible person that my own son won't speak to me?"

Tess felt as if she could see deep into him. He would have wept if he could, but he didn't really know how. This must have been what he looked like when his wife had died.

She shook out four pills, looked at size of him and shook out two more. "Here," she said. "Take these."

"I don't do drugs," Joe said, and mechanically pushed them away.

"Look, honey," she said and stopped his hand. "There is nothing in this world that wasn't put here for a purpose—you've said that yourself. There's a time and place for everything, whether it is good loving or a pill to take the sadness away. This is the time for the pill."

Joe stared at them for a moment. "Is six too much?"

She put them in his hand and brought him a glass of water.

After a moment or so, Joe threw back his head and swallowed the pills and drained the water. Tess felt instantly better doing something kind for someone who had been kind to her.

They lay next to one another in the bed. Joe rested his head on her shoulder and draped one arm across her chest. For a little while, Tess thought he might go to sleep, and she found herself disappointed. Surprised, she realized she had other ideas.

Then Joe gently cupped her breast, and Tess smiled and turned to him, ready, eager. Joe's eyes burned.

Afterward, it took her a good twenty minutes to catch her breath. Joe had been amazing—hell, *she* had been amazing. It had been like a wonderful dance where each partner knew exactly what the other partner wanted. She slipped into a sort of dream state, floating as if in water. She only opened her eyes when her drying sweat made her cold in the hotel air conditioning. Joe had left the bed.

He was standing in front of the window, watching the interstate. In the distance, the Alton bridged loomed a graceful ghost over the city. He was naked, his belly swollen below his chest like a square sack. His shoulders, back, and legs were strong and muscular from the effort of holding up that great weight. "What did you give me?"

"I don't know. Sammy gave it to me and I took it. I gave it to you."

"Did you feel the touch of Him? His Breath blowing through you?"

She got up from the bed and came over and leaned against him. "It felt like a woman to me."

Joe seemed to think for a minute. "I felt it a long time ago. When Billy Graham brought us down to the stage and we stood before him while he called to us, called us to accept Him, to open ourselves to His love. I stood there, surrounded on all sides by people, soft women, hard men, jostling among ourselves, rubbing against one another. And for a moment, it was like He was breathing for all of us. His breath gave us life in the beginning and it was still keeping us alive. 'Amen!' I cried. Amen."

He turned and took her by the shoulders. "But tonight, I felt Him speaking to me. Looking through me. Moving through me—through us as we were there on the bed. There was no sin in this. No evil. For He was with us. This is a calling. This is a ministry." Joe shook his head. "But how can I trust a drug? How can I trust a pill?"

"You don't," Tess said and it was again like a voice speaking through her. "You trust Her or Him. The pill isn't anything."

Joe let her go and looked down. "How many do you have?"

Wordlessly, she pulled out the bag Sammy had given her.

Joe hefted it in his hand and she could see him working it out. She was excited and scared and calm all at once. Tess felt as if she was standing at the very edge of an adventure.

"Okay," Joe said and let his breath out slowly. "We're going to need a lot more of these."

Chapter 1.3: August, 1997

Joe brought them together in the Mark Twain Conference Room of the same Best Western where he had been spending every third night with Tess. Barely a handful, but Joe's Savior had done more with less. Joe saw Tess in the back of the room, smiling at him. Joe smiled back. He hadn't felt this certain, this light in his heart, since Edna had died. Not all of it was due to finding this clear channel to God. A good portion was due to Tess. Blessed in love and sealed together with the Holy Spirit, Joe was ready to marry her right now, but Tess wouldn't hear of it.

"It's too early, love," she had sighed, lying next to him. "We have a mission. We're going to need everything we have. You would lose the station and everything else if you publicly married a call girl."

"Mary Magdalene was a prostitute," Joe said earnestly.

"I don't plan on losing you to the cross," she said, laughing. "We can wait."

Joe waved to her again, and from the back of the room she blew him a kiss.

Not everyone was here yet, but Joe decided it was time to start.

The room was mostly filled with women and only a few men. All of them personally introduced to the pills by either him or Tess. The best working women and working men of Alton—he smiled to himself. The term had never been more apt.

"Folks," Joe began, using the let's-be-comfortable voice he had perfected on *Hour with Jesus*. That was right for this morning. Thunder and lightning were unnecessary. "I thought it was time we all met. We have all experienced the joy of communion and now we must plan our campaign." He warmed to his subject. *Ethan was wrong,* he thought. *I had always believed from the day Billy Graham had laid his proxy hands upon my upturned face.*

"We are going to break up into groups. Most of you know Tess and she'll organize you by location. Then we're going to plan our attack block by block, neighborhood by neighborhood. First, we will take Saint Louis for the Lord. From there, the nation."

His voice dropped. "For this is a war against Satan and we who have so directly experienced God's love must be ready to use all of our strength and power to win it. It is God's Plan we will be fulfilling and God's Holy Purpose we will bring to pass. There is no sin in His service and no act done within His will that He cannot redeem. This is why we have been brought here together and this is why we will be victorious." He smiled at them and they beamed back at him. *This is what I was put here for,* he thought. *This is what I was meant to do.*

"Now, Tess, if you will help organize everybody, we'll get to work."

Tess smiled at him and for a long moment all he could see was her face.

oOo

Not for the first time, Sam wondered if Connie had set him up. Now Sam was stealing. But not just from anybody. From Norman Parkin! What the hell was he thinking?

It was Connie's fault.

But how the fuck could he have set Sam up? It was Norman's idea to trade Connie for Alton. Unless Connie was in on it. Sam could see Connie's huge, sweaty face in his mind, the fear in his eyes like broken ice in the river. No. It couldn't have been Connie.

Lord knows it couldn't have been Joe.

Sam rattled around his mother's old house like a bullet in a shoe. It was filled with her things: the little glass horses he had bought her in Florida. Her collection of miniature Japanese teapots—he picked up a Satsuma that had been her favorite. Admired the brown top and orange body. Admired its tiny perfection. God, he missed her.

Ever since he had resigned himself to losing Tess to Joe, he had taken to watching Joe's *Hour with Jesus* every morning. It was contact with Joe, even if from a distance. Tess was Sad Girl no longer, what with the pills he was slipping her and her newfound love. (Call it that, he said to himself. Why should women have all the luck?) Tess positively glowed. If Sam hadn't known better, he would have thought she was pregnant.

Maybe he should just come clean with Norman. Hadn't Sam asked his advice a few weeks ago? (The night he first stole from him. How was he going to explain that?)

It was Tess's fault. She'd manipulated him. He'd break her neck if she didn't belong to Joe.

Joe had asked him—*personally!*—for more pills. That was when he should have gone to Norman. That was when he could have made it look like initiative. That was when he would have looked like an entrepreneur.

But that was two weeks ago. Two weeks and over a two hundred pills. And now Joe wanted even more. Norman was going to discover this any day. Sam had to come up with a plan, escape or otherwise.

Calm yourself, Sam, came a firm and gentle voice in his mind. *Yeah, Mom,* he thought. *Yeah.*

When did he become so afraid?

Your whole fucking life! screamed a part of him.

Not so, Sam, came the same gentle voice. *You weren't afraid back when you were running your own little gang. Before you were tapped by Norman. You were working for yourself. Back then, you felt safe as long as you had Tiny Tim with you.*

Sam reached in his pocket and pulled out his knife. He flipped his wrist and with an oiled snap, more felt in the hand then heard, it opened. He admired the glint of the light of the honed edge, the oriental flavor of the mother of pearl handle, the heft of it in his hand. As knives went, Tiny Tim wasn't large. The blade was actually legal. Sam turned his hand in the air and smiled. Like the old song, it's not the meat, it's the motion.

Mom never steered him wrong. The answer to his problem—the answer to his prayers—was to be as he once was.

The starlight was barely visible in the glare from the city as he drove along the river on the East side. Never the St. Louis side. If it happens on the east side of the river, nobody cares. Things only matter when you cross the river or go North into his own home town of Granite City or South towards Cairo. Here in the evening shadow St. Louis cast over into Illinois, the only things he need fear were people with knives and guns. Norman was here, but what was Norman but a man with a gun? Sam had never feared such things before.

He stopped in front of one of the local dives south of the bridge. Its sign was partially broken and only a buzzing picture of a partial cocktail showed that it was there at all. That was okay. Sam didn't need to know its name. He got out of his car and stood outside, watching. From the number of cars, there weren't many patrons. Sam was a well-dressed white guy; he looked like an easy mark.

Sam went in and looked around. Two guys drinking separately at the bar, a big guy in a shiny Cardinals jacket and a smaller one in a flannel shirt. The rest of the place was empty. Perfect.

He went to the bar himself and ordered a Manhattan. The black bartender stared at him. With his best swish forward, he changed his order to a Tequila Sunrise. Again the stare. Finally, he settled on a Whiskey Sour. He sipped it a moment, looked around nervously, paid, and went outside. He stood leaning against his car, waiting.

A moment later, Big Guy came out. He saw Sam leaning against his car.

"You want some action?" Big Guy said with a leer.

"In the worst way," Sam said smiling.

"You got money?"

"You'll have to take it away." Sam pulled out his knife and held it loosely at his side.

Big Guy stopped for a moment, weighing the new situation.

Sam needed to sweeten the pot. "I have five thousand dollars in my wallet and I'm looking for a fight."

"You found one." Big Guy slipped out of his jacket and wrapped it around his left forearm. Then he pulled out his own knife, a beautiful, black ten-inch switchblade.

Sam stepped away from the car. *Darkness, violence, and death,* he thought. Who needs Saint Louis? *This* is night life.

Big Guy feinted a couple of times and stepped forward. Sam didn't respond except by moving back, step for step. He'd had enough of a wait to look over the ground. He knew how many steps brought him out of the parking lot and into the road. Two cars to his left and his own to his right. Behind Big Guy was the club. Plenty of room.

Big Guy leaned forward and slashed across at Sam's eyes. Sam stepped back again, and the slash cut air. As quick and supple as mercury, Sam stepped inside Big Guy's reach as the knife swung away and lightly cut across Big Guy's chest. It was only over his ribs—nothing to get upset about. Nothing like what Sam had been through before he ever had a knife.

Sam stepped back, and the return stroke again sliced through the night air. Big Guy moved back, bellowing. Sam followed, step for step.

Sam remembered the first time he'd ever understood what a knife could do. It was a little brawl in an alley near Lafayette Square. The kid with the knife wasn't more than twenty, and his knife had a blade less than two inches long. The other guy was older and huge, built like a brick wall and bent on tearing the kid apart. But the kid stayed calm and proceeded to carve that guy up like a Christmas ham.

Something like what Sam was planning right here, right now.

Big Guy tried to shield himself with his jacket-covered arm and strike with the knife. Sam came up from underneath and cut him across the back of his hand. Big Guy howled. This time, Sam stepped forward, and as Big Guy hurried back, his knife arm swung out. Sam stopped the arm with his left hand and cut down across the inside elbow, then stepped back, smiling.

With the tendons cut, Big Guy's arm flopped uselessly, his knife still held as if it could do any damage. Big Guy stared at him, his other hand held out to grab him if he came close again. Sam circled, leaving a space where Big Guy could run back to the diner. Big Guy took the bait, turned, and Sam came in behind and slashed the back and side of Big Guy's knee. Big Guy went down, rolling, and came against Sam's car.

Big Guy threw a handful of gravel, and one rock hit Sam in the face. For a moment, Sam stumbled and fell backwards, surprise. Big Guy jumped, using his good leg. Sam rolled out of the way, and Big Guy landed heavily where he had been. He grabbed Sam's jacket and dragged him back.

Sam was furious now. He rolled back on top of Big Guy and kneed him in the groin, took the man's cut elbow and twisted. Big Guy screamed and let him go.

Sam jumped up and stared at him, breathing hard.

Big Guy was holding his elbow, glaring at him.

Sam could hear commotion inside the bar. Time to bring it home.

He flicked the knife at Big Guy's eyes, and the man flinched away. Sam dropped the angle of the slash and came back across Big Guy's throat. Blood spurted, and Big Guy tried to cry out something but gurgled and fell back, twitching.

Sam jumped back to avoid the blood. He watched for a few seconds to make sure of the wound. Satisfied, he ran to his car, started the car, and gunned the engine out of there.

Driving up the river road at eighty, he grinned. *Mom, you were right.* For a moment, he remembered her as she had been at the end, eaten up inside by cancer, living from pain pill to pain pill, pleading with him when she was awake enough to recognize he was there. A lump rose in his throat as he crossed the river. He was sorry he'd had to kill her. Even now, years later, he still missed her.

Put that away, she commanded.

Dutifully, he obeyed and pushed away the grief. He was at last what he had once been. Mom was right. Mom was always right.

oOo

Every time Tess called Sam she wanted to hang up. Not because she was scared of him anymore. She wasn't. With Joe, and God, on her side, Sam need never scare her ever again. He was a little man with little ideas and he was, she saw at last, deeply afraid of what she and Joe were doing.

But it didn't matter.

Every time Sam came in, it was like dragging around an anchor to the past.

Tess picked up the phone and put it down. She picked up the bottle of pills—Divinidine, Joe had called it with a laugh. A pharmaceutical connection to God. Better faith through chemistry. She shook the bottle. There wasn't much left. She picked up the phone to call Sam and put it down again.

Tess looked out to the parking lot. There had to be another way.

The pills had to come from somewhere and Sam was too small-time to manage it by himself. He was probably getting his pills from Norman.

She picked up the phone. This time, she dialed Joe. He should be in his office now. Tess knew his show schedule by heart. Gloria put her through instantly.

"Hello, honey," Joe answered warmly. "Did you see the morning show?"

She smiled into the receiver. He never failed to make her smile. "I did for a minute. I was busy talking to some new recruits."

"Good. What's up?"

"We're getting low. Sam's not coming through."

In her mind's eye, she could see him nodding. It was as if they were connected.

"Well, we knew this day would come. Just tell Sam to either get us Divinidine in the amounts we need or push us up to his supplier."

"You know that has to be Norman."

"You know Norman has to be fronting this for someone else. These aren't back-alley pills. This stuff is drugstore quality."

Tess sighed. Dealing with Norman was a whole new level up from Sam. Norman didn't run scared. "You should call him. I don't think he'll listen to me."

"I suppose." Joe fell silent a moment. "Do you think Norman knows who Sam's supplying?"

Tess felt cold suddenly. "Joe, I don't think Norman knows about us at all."

"You think Sam's stealing from Norman? No wonder he's scared all the time." Joe was silent a moment. "I don't want to get Sam killed."

She waited for Joe to work it out. Tess had little love for Sam.

"I'll call Norman," Joe said finally. "Maybe I can make Norman see that Sam is doing us both a favor."

"Whatever works." Tess didn't believe it. She figured Norman would whack Sam on pure principle.

They spoke softly on the phone for a moment before the two of the hung up. She lingered over the call, one hand resting on the receiver.

Charity begins with me, she thought. *Maybe Norman will surprise me. After all, no one is beyond redemption.*

oOo

This was inevitable, thought Cindy, staring out at the window into the hot August rain. The third floor of the house was her terrain. There she was queen.

Of course, her room wasn't all that big and it was down the hall from the mausoleum that Grandpa Fitzie's room had become. Now, *that* was a nice room. All it would take was a complete gut job, add a bathroom, and build new closets. Cindy had considered staking out the room in a sort of geographical *coup d'état* for a long time. But so far, she hadn't done anything about it. Her own room was reasonable enough in size. She had her own phone. In the winter, the furnace sometimes didn't quite reach and it grew cold. Often, she spent time studying wrapped in a blanket.

But her parents didn't come up here. And when she looked out the window, she could see north up Grand towards the city. The night Cindy had returned, Jake and Anya had held on to her like she was a life raft and they were drowning. This room had seemed a grotto of safety. A place where no one, not Norman or Connie or even her own parents, could come.

That had lasted about a week.

After that, Anya had to go back to work and Jake had cases to figure out. When they left, Cindy could see the fear in their eyes. Would she be there when they got back? It didn't exactly make her feel good, but somehow this interest excited her. But days passed and she was there when they came through the door and, little by little, they relaxed. Even the night she had a "date" (with Connie, no less—though, of course, *they* didn't know that) made less of a ripple than she had expected.

Now it was the end of August. They were at work. School would be starting soon. She lay on Grandpa Fitzie's old bed, staring out through his big picture window, watching the rain fall.

Cindy left Grandpa Fitzie's room and returned to her own. She idly fingered through the clothes in her closet. All browns and grays of her high school uniforms to the clothes Mom liked her to wear. The jeans in her drawer and a few shirts added a pale splash of color. A far cry from what she had been wearing in June.

Her phone rang and she picked it up, thinking for perhaps the thousandth time she should have her own cell phone.

"Cindy!" cried Portia on the other end. "You're home! I've been trying to call you for a month."

Note to self: *Don't forget that Portia is your alibi for the date with Connie.* Somehow, she had to clue Portia in. "Yeah. Things have been pretty hairy here since I ran off."

"I imagine." Portia paused. "You can tell me about that, you know. I won't freak or anything."

"Oh, I know." *Yeah,* thought Cindy. *As if you would be able to handle it.* Or, she thought, *maybe I'm wrong. Maybe Portia could handle it.*

"Were you beaten and starved or something?"

Or maybe not.

Cindy skipped answering. "So, what's happening?" Cindy sat back on her bed, staring at the drab clothes in her closet. She deserved so much better.

Portia didn't press it. "I'm having a party."

Cindy sat up. "Get out of town. What did you do? Lobotomize your parents?"

"Almost," Portia said smugly. "They're going away this weekend to—let's see. How did she say it? 'Patch things up.' Down in Grand Cayman, where they spent their honeymoon."

"That's good, isn't it? I mean it's not like they get along."

"Come on, Cindy. 'Patch things up?' More likely this will just rip the scabs off of the way things are. The first three days on the island will go really well while they're giddy with sex and booze. Then, I predict on Wednesday, they'll wake up and look at each other and share exactly the same thought: Why am I here with *you?* The vacation will go downhill from there."

"Wow."

"The best I'm going to get out of this is released on my own recognizance for five days. Which I plan to use well. Think of it as good-bye to sixteen. I'll be seventeen in a few weeks. End of the summer. Step one is a huge party that with any luck will last three days and get at least four girls pregnant." Portia fell silent and Cindy could hear her considering. "Pregnant and in jail. Are you in?"

Cindy laughed. "Absolutely. I'll tell Jake and Anya it's a sleepover."

"If I invite the right people there won't be much sleeping. Do you need a ride?"

Cindy smiled into the phone. "No. I'll bring a date."

oOo

Joe slowed the Lexus down and eased it to the curb. He turned off the lights and sat looking down the hill to the house where Norman lived. It took no great thought or detective work to find out about it. Joe had been coming to East St. Louis since long before Norman got here. Norman had killed François Michaels to get a piece of the action. Joe had known François and liked him—a young black man whose French forebears had not the foresight to move to the west side of the river. When Cold Norman had taken François out, Joe had never found it in his heart to warm up to him. It was always just business. That had been a long time ago.

Though Joe had never been here before, he knew about the place: how the front lights had been taken out and the windows blackened to eliminate targets. How Norman insisted that business be done in the back of the house and the front never used, and how he posted two guards on the front porch to enforce it. This had never made sense to Joe. Why do your illicit business in the back of the house? If you lived in the front of the house, you were more exposed, regardless of how black the windows were. Maybe if you reinforced the front of the house—which made no sense, either. After all, if you were going to go through the trouble and expense to rebuild the front of the house, why have illicit activities in the back?

Joe knew secrets when he saw them. He could smell one here.

He rubbed his hands together. Clenched and unclenched his fists. He was never this worried when he was younger. Back before he was saved, he used to like coming over to the East side; the rougher the better. Joe looked at the back of his hands. The scars covered the knuckles like a road map and like a map; each one told where he had been. One scar crossed the back of his fingers from a knife fight in the parking lot of that little bar on the river road. Another showed where a tooth had split the skin over his knuckle. He wasn't sure where that had happened. Or when.

Joe took a deep breath. He was here to negotiate. Violence shouldn't be necessary.

"God's work," he said to himself. "Just remember you're doing God's work."

He started the car. After it caught, he turned on the lights and let out the clutch. The car pulled away from the curb and eased down the street. He was here to negotiate, but first he had to get Norman's attention.

Joe stopped the car and got out and started walking up to the porch. He could feel the guns pointed at him. His eyes adjusted as he walked to the porch. Two men stood up.

"What do you want?"

Joe smiled and brought out his most friendly voice. "Hello, gentlemen. I'm Joe Cori. I'm here to see Norman."

The two men looked at one another. The nearest guard held the gun on Joe. The second man held his pointing at the ground, ready.

"I don't want any trouble—" began Joe.

"Shut up," said the nearest guard and shook the gun in Joe's face.

Joe reached over and took the gun away, backhanding the man to the floor. The other guard brought up his gun but Joe stepped outside of his arm and slammed his left fist into the guard's face. The man hit the porch at nearly the same time as his gun.

When Joe turned back the remaining conscious guard was just getting to his feet and pulling a knife out of his pocket. Joe grabbed the arm holding the knife, pinning it. With his other hand he picked him up by the shirt and slammed him into the wall. The man fell to the ground, the knife forgotten as he tried to just inhale. Joe waited a moment until he was sure the man could breathe. Then he carefully struck the man in the back of the head with the heel of his fist. The man went down, shook a moment, trying to get back up, and then relaxed.

Joe picked up the guns and the knife, and checked each man for further weapons. Nothing. He put what he found in his pocket and checked each man again to make sure they were merely unconscious and not hurt any worse.

Then he stood up and grinned. "Gentlemen. I still got it, don't I?"

The door had been nailed shut, but nothing a determined shove couldn't break.

Joe wasn't sure what he was expecting: a huge chemical drug factory? Sexual slavery? An army readying their weapons? Instead, the room was well-lit, with only two chairs and a short bench. On the walls, framed and presented under track lighting, were some of the most beautiful paintings Joe had ever seen. A soft Mozart was playing.

Joe closed the door quietly behind him and turned back to the paintings. He didn't recognize any of them, though they had that Dutch feeling he saw when he'd visited the museum in Forest Park. One in particular of three musicians, two women and a man, was lit inside as if painted on a window. That one seemed familiar.

None of the paintings were labeled. *Of course*, Joe thought. This was Norman's treasure. Norman knew each one of these paintings as well as his own name.

Norman came down the hall, looking down and lost in thought. He stopped when he saw Joe. His startled expression went blank. Joe knew Norman was going to kill him if he didn't get a reason not to.

"I think these may be the most beautiful paintings I've ever seen," he said in a low voice, meaning every word. As a preacher, Joe understood the value of sincerity, especially when it was true. He sat down on the bench. "That one, especially."

Pride and caution worked Norman's face. The result was a sort of cautious pride. "That's the prize of the collection. It's—"

Joe held up his hand. "Don't tell me what it is. If you tell me what it is, I'll start thinking about how you must have gotten it. I just want to enjoy it for a moment."

The silence in the room deepened. Norman took one of the chairs next to Joe and the two of them gazed at the painting. Eventually, the moment passed.

"Are they alive?" Norman jerked his head towards the front of the house.

"'Thou shalt not kill'" quoted Joe. "They'll feel pretty sick when they wake up. I wouldn't fault you for getting a doctor to look at them. I'm rusty and might have hurt them more than I intended."

Norman nodded. "What do you want?"

"About ten thousand of these." Joe pulled out a plastic bag from his jacket and handed it to Norman.

Norman's expression didn't change, but the long silence he took as he studied the pills told Joe he'd guessed right. Sam had never told Norman he had been giving the pills to Joe.

"Sam isn't allowed to sell very many of these. They're a new product and we don't have that many of them."

"Ah," said Joe, taking back the bag back from him. "So, ten thousand of them is out of the question?"

"I didn't say that. What are you proposing?"

Joe folded the plastic bag carefully and put it in his pocket. He wasn't sure how much he should tell Norman. How much did Norman know about the drug? "We've found Divinidine to be useful in the church."

"'Divinidine'?"

"My pet name for it—Sam never told us what to call it." Joe sighed and leaned back against the bench. "As I said, we're finding it useful."

Norman frowned. "I don't like distributing through a church—too many people know each other's business."

"We're not going through the church." Joe glanced at the painting again. *Such light.* "Do you remember Tess Durbin?"

"Yes. She used to work for me. Now she works for Sam."

"No, now she is my fiancée."

Norman's eyebrows went up. "You're losing it, Joe. Your church is never going to hold still when their pastor marries a prostitute."

"That's my business," Joe said shortly.

"Suit yourself. I meant well."

Joe didn't speak for a moment. "We're converting through the call girls. Tess's friends."

Something in Norman's face seemed to open to an expression Joe didn't know how to read. Some connection had been made. Some mechanism had been triggered.

"Does Divinidine enhance sex?" Norman said slowly.

Joe could feel a broad grin come across his face. "You better believe it."

Norman leaned forward. "I can meet ten thousand. Not a problem. But I have an idea. Tess's friends are limited. Even if you go through Sam, all you'll get is Alton. I have a line into a call girl network that covers Saint Louis—about forty times what you'll get out of Alton."

In spite of himself, Joe was excited. "That's a huge step."

"And I can supply infrastructure: shipping, packaging, manufacturing. You name it."

Joe stared at him. "Norman, why do you need me?"

Norman returned the look. "We haven't been able to sell it. You have a sales organization. Are you going to use your shows?"

"Not yet. We're going to stay undercover for a while."

Norman nodded. "Good idea. So, Brother Cori. Do we work together?" He stuck out his hand.

Joe clasped it. "We work together."

oOo

"It's not my fault," said LeRoy, glaring at Norman.

Norman, for his part, glared back. It was inconceivable to him that he had these thousands of pills and couldn't sell them. Who wouldn't want them? Wasn't every American searching for God? Last time he looked at the paper it seemed that the Post-Dispatch was falling all over itself saying how religious the whole damned country was, *especially* St. Louis. You couldn't drive to Kansas City without being peppered with evangelist billboards. Well, here Norman was not only selling God at a very reasonable price, he had packaged it in a safe, easy, and convenient pill. And he couldn't unload a hundred of them!

But don't take it out on the kid.

He waved his hand between them and looked away. "Yeah, I know. It's not your fault."

Mollified, LeRoy turned back to his PC. "Maybe we're going about this wrong. Look, we're on the street trying to compete with cocaine, heroin, and ecstasy. We're an unknown quantity making inflated claims. Also, the speculation we read about Anapyridol suggested that it was intended as a socializing drug with anti-depressive and anti-psychotic effects. Kind of like oxytocin with a kick. You're not going to get any interesting recreational effects until you get beyond the therapeutic dosages—something we've been avoiding until we get our feet under us."

"Yeah? So?"

"So, maybe we need a new venue. A place where the competition isn't so fierce. And maybe we should be less cautious."

Norman shook his head. "Right now, this drug is undiscovered. We get a bunch of overdoses and the DEA is going to get interested. I want to stay in the honeymoon as long as we can."

LeRoy threw up his hands. "Make a choice, Norman. Either we keep trying to nickel and dime our way to market penetration or we find a new market."

"Let me think about it." Norman turned away from LeRoy, towards the front room. He did his best thinking there, drinking in the collection.

The trouble was, the kid was right. Norman knew they needed a new approach. Drugs were like any other pyramid scheme; you needed willing converts to carry the message and do your selling for you. Until you created a small cadre of dedicated users to carry the word, you didn't have anything.

Norman almost walked into Joe before he saw him. Norman stopped and stared at him. Joe? Here? In the collections room? He must have come through the front door—Norman and LeRoy had been in the back and had never seen him. Didn't he have guards for this?

If Norman had been carrying a gun, he would have killed Joe completely out of reflex. As it happened, unarmed as he was and as big as Joe was,

Norman had to consider what to do next. He was about to call out to LeRoy to get the guys in the back.

"I think these may be the most beautiful paintings I've ever seen," Joe said in a low voice.

Norman stopped. He almost smiled. He stopped that, too. Then, he stopped himself from saying, "Really?" Norman decided that maybe Joe wasn't so bad after all and that he could let him live until he understood what Joe wanted.

Sitting across from Joe and only half listening, he thought about the guards out front. It was vanity that kept that door open. He should have bricked up the whole wall years ago. But no, he had to have his secret pride. "Outside people drive by and never realize I have these."

Then he heard Joe speaking and it burst into his mind like a gunshot. He'd been looking for his cadre of believers and Joe had come and given them to him like a Christmas gift. Hookers! High priced hookers!

Norman knew Connie's operation backwards and forwards. Connie catered to two distinct populations: transient businessmen and affluent kids from the county. Businessmen he could ignore; they were dangerous since they could be caught at the airport and even if they weren't, they had no staying power.

But the rich county boys were another thing altogether. Once a kid got sweet on a hooker, they kept coming back. Hookers were safe: you could sleep with them and they disappeared. You didn't pay for a hooker to stay; you paid them to leave.

"Does… Divinidine enhance sex?" It wouldn't do to bet on hookers and then turn the men into melted candles. But Joe's sincere grin was more informative than anything he could have said.

After they finalized things and Joe left, Norman sat back down in the collections room. He sighed. A wave of fatigue washed over him. Why couldn't people get it right? Was there something intrinsically wrong with them? Didn't Sam realize he would eventually be caught? Now Norman was going to have to do something. What was it Caligula said? Something about it being okay to not be liked as long as you were feared? Words to live by.

But now Sam had gotten away with something. He had put something over on Norman. He had made Norman look foolish. Things like this broke the fear, and then you had to go and whack people until they were afraid again. It took time, and it took money. Norman tapped his lips with his finger, thinking.

Even though such rules were clear to any three-year-old, people had a way of conveniently forgetting him. Norman was going to have to whack Sam. Probably in some horrible, vengeful way as a lesson to other people.

On the other hand, he thought, the same grapevine Norman relied on to keep people in line meant that inevitably Joe would find out about such a lesson. It was pretty early in the game to put the fear of Jesus—the phrase made Norman smile—into your clients. That should happen later, when both partners were thoroughly dependent on one another and it was time to show who was boss.

He walked back to the office where LeRoy was sitting at his PC, staring into the monitor as if trying to bring forth sales of the drug by sheer force of will.

"Good news," Norman said.

"What?"

"We have a new partner for Cindy's drug: Joe Cori."

"How did you figure on that?"

"I'll tell you about it on the way."

oOo

"Hello," Cindy said, hoping it was him.

"Hey there, girl," came Connie's deep voice.

"Oh, thank God. Where have you been? I've been trying to get a hold of you for days. The party is day after tomorrow. I don't have a date and, what's worse, I don't have any clothes."

There was dead silence for a moment. "You better start at the beginning."

"First, I want my clothes. All of the ones you bought me. I want them this afternoon."

"Cindy, I have a business to run. I can't come over at a moment's notice."

"Second, I'm going to a party this Friday and I need a date."

"Friday's a big night."

Cindy grinned into the phone. She could tell he was going to say yes. They may not be lovers, but they were more than friends. Colleagues, maybe. "You're a big man. I'm going to a wild party full of nubile and willing teenage girls and desperately inexperienced teenage boys. Imagine how that will be for business."

"You have a point," he said reluctantly. "But I have a new business venture. Something Norman's put me on to. Friday is going to be difficult."

"Oh." Cindy put all of the disappointment she could into that one world. She could feel him melt right through the phone.

"I guess I can manage something."

"That's really terrific. Can you bring my clothes over? Please?"

"I suppose."

Then all it took was clearing it with her parents. That was the easy part. They were happy as clams she was friends with Portia. An upper-class girl living in Town and Country could only be a *good thing*.

Connie would only pick her up before Jake and Anya got home. Not that she blamed him, since she was pretty sure that Jake knew who Connie was. Cindy being seen in the same *neighborhood* as Connie would probably get somebody hurt.

As they drove down the street and turned onto Grand, Cindy slipped out of her jeans and put on her dress. She had thought for a long time what to wear. A lot of the things Connie had bought for her gave too much of the wrong impression. The idea was to suggest, not to proclaim. Finally, she had come back to the red dress she had shoplifted back in May—a lifetime ago.

"Damn, Cindy," Connie said laughing as she changed. "Give a man a warning next time. I might have driven into a ditch or something."

"Think of it as a reward for being such a nice guy."

"I'll keep that in mind."

She straightened out the dress and brushed her hair. She hadn't felt this happy in a long time.

She had a horrible thought. "Connie, could any of these county boys know you?"

Connie shook his head. "I doubt it. Some of them might have been clients, but I don't manage underage connections myself. I have another kid do it—gives me somebody to blame. Otherwise I get a child abuse rap. It's not worth it." He smiled at her. "And they do all my recruitment for me, too."

"What about me?"

Connie shook his head. "Except for you. You were worth it. I thought you would go far. Out of this business into porno movies, maybe. That could have been a gateway to something else. Real movies. Recordings. And me there all the way to manage you." Connie shrugged.

Cindy stared at him. "You're kidding."

"Nope." He looked at her. "Don't feel bad. It was a long shot, anyway. We're both still alive. Norman's got me in some new things that should turn out all right. You're part of that."

"The pills my mom developed."

Connie nodded. "Which brings me to my next item of business. You and LeRoy are going to talk to Mister Bill Wallace about a stable and continuing supply."

"What?"

"Can't have a business without a supply. I'll be there to back you up, but hopefully I won't be necessary."

Cindy considered this and watched the traffic. She didn't feel so happy now. "When?"

"Tonight. After the party." Connie glanced over to her as he drove. "I told you Friday would be difficult."

"But the party is going to last all night. I wanted to finally have some *fun*."

"You'll have fun. Don't worry. About midnight, we'll leave to go get some booze. LeRoy will meet us there. You'll have your talk with Mister Bill. LeRoy will go back across the river, and I'll take you back to your party." Connie handed her his cell. "Make the call."

Cindy held the cell for a moment, then flipped it open and dialed Lifeworks.

oOo

Sam was feeling pretty good as he took the exit for Corondelet. The house was dark, but Sam took the steps two at a time. He didn't even fumble for his keys—it was as if his fingers knew them even in the dark. Nothing like a good fight to get the glands percolating. Suddenly he remembered the cook in the Chicken Shack he'd seen a few weeks ago. Maybe it was time to wander over there and see what might develop. Sam was whistling when he stepped inside the foyer and turned to close the door.

Someone grabbed Sam's shoulders and threw him against the wall. He hit the wall as he was pulling the knife out of his pocket. Whoever it was expected that and slammed Sam's hand against the banister. Something cracked with a pain that seemed to light up the room. He couldn't even scream; it took too much breath. Then he was thrown across the room and landed kidney-first across Mother's wooden chair. Sam cried out. Who the hell was it? He could see two figures but not their face in the light from the street.

"Shut up," Norman said.

Jesus Fucking Christ!

Why the hell hadn't he thought to keep a gun in the living room? There were knives in the kitchen, a forty-five in the den under the sofa, a thirty-eight in the bathroom, two nine millimeters upstairs, and a shotgun in the closet— the shotgun was the closest. He could shoot left-handed if he had to. Or he could get to the bathroom.

"I'm gonna' puke," Sam made retching noises.

"Shut up. Get in the chair."

"Man, I don't wanna' throw up on the chair."

Norman pulled out his own pistol and pulled back the hammer. He brought the barrel to Sam's eye. "Get in the chair, Sam," he said quietly.

The round black hole mesmerized Sam and he found himself scrabbling into Mother's chair.

"Turn on the light," Norman said.

Sam pulled the switch on the lamp, and the room suddenly sprang into sight. He blinked a few times.

Norman sat across from him on the sofa, his pistol easy in his lap, and the hammer back in place. LeRoy stood leaning against the wall at the corner of the sofa, silent and watching.

"What's the matter, Norman?" began Sam. "What's the problem? We can work it out—"

"I spoke with Joe Cori this evening."

Balls it out to the last, he told himself. What have you got to lose? "Yeah? So what?"

Norman smiled at him coldly. "Cold Norman" was right. Sam could see him weighing what he was going to do like a butcher measures out a cut of steak.

Norman pointed the gun at Sam's feet and pulled the trigger. The room roared. Sam jerked back in the chair, absolutely certain Norman had blown off his foot.

He looked down, and there was a bloody hole in his shoe just at the edge of his toe. Blood leaked out on the floor.

"Jesus Christ, Norman!"

"You listen to me, Sam. You aren't worth much more than a gnat's ass to me one way or the other. Give up the attitude. I know about the pills."

Sam grabbed a wad of tissues from a box on the table and tried to stop the blood.

"It's just a toe, Sam," Norman said tiredly. "If I wanted to blow off your leg, I would have."

"It's my toe."

"You've been stealing from me. I should kill you now but you're marginally worth more to me alive than dead. I like the way you manage your girls." Norman held up the pistol. "So, I'm going to cut you some slack. I'll deal with Joe Cori from now on. You run your girls in Alton. If I even think you're fucking with me, I'll rip your eyes out."

Norman motioned to LeRoy, and the two of them left the house.

Sam pulled off his shoe and hobbled to the bathroom. He held toilet paper to his foot and waited for the bleeding to stop.

"Son-of-a-bitch," he said to his reflection with a grin. "I'm going to live."

oOo

Portia's house was big. Every time Cindy saw it, she was reminded how rich Portia was. This place was huge. Three floors, and each floor seemed to be a block long. A lawn so flat and green it looked like you could swim in it. But there was no need: the pool was right there out the back porch.

She and Connie arrived in the late, tawny evening. The sunlight had become golden and a flat, animal heat welled up from the earth. When Cindy stepped out of the car, the heat threaded its way under her dress until she felt as if she had been oiled. Things clicked into place. Connie, huge and dominant, taking her arm delicately. Walking up the walk, feeling the dress shift across her breasts and stomach, feeling the eyes in the windows turn her way. She gave them a little smile—a smile she had learned in the weeks she had been away. Cindy knew she no longer looked fifteen. She looked eighteen, twenty. As timeless and as sexy as Cleopatra or Helen of Troy.

Portia came out the front door and took her hands. She whistled. "Don't you look positively *decadent!* I love it." She turned to Connie. "You must be the cause. Come on in." Portia pulled Cindy away from Connie as they entered the house. "He's huge. Honey, I've got to tell you. You don't look like a virgin anymore."

Cindy grinned at her. She felt ready to sin.

The party was loud, and there were plenty to drink. She started to take one but Connie caught her eye and shook his head. They had work to do later.

Reluctantly, she just drank a diet Coke. So many opportunities. So little time.

By the time the sun set, she was dancing in the main room with a tall, handsome senior who would never have asked her name last spring. Now he looked at her as if he were starving.

In a long slow dance, she held him close but not too close. Not like she held Mister Bonifacio, for instance. The way to stay in control here was to skirt the line but not cross it. Then after the next dance, she sent him to get her a drink and disappeared over by the pool. He'd find her or he wouldn't.

She sat down on a chair in the shadows.

"Now, that was cruel," came a voice beside her.

Cindy started and turned. It was Donnie, Portia's brother. "I thought you were in college."

Donnie nodded. "Taking a summer break from Ivy League Hell. Hanging out and enjoying myself. Why do you think Portia was allowed to stay here by herself?" Donnie pointed to himself. "Good old responsible Harvard Man will make sure young Portia Does Not Stray."

Cindy giggled. "You're not doing a very good job."

Donnie shook his head solemnly. "I'm doing a terrific job. Ask Portia. Ask Mom and Dad when they get home—no, never mind. Don't ask them. They won't be in a talking mood." He sipped his drink and lifted it towards her. "I'd offer to get you one but I'm afraid you'll disappear."

"I wouldn't disappear," she said in a low voice. "But I don't want a drink."

Donnie stared at her. "Are you really fifteen?"

"Yes." She sat back in her chair and relaxed. *Okay,* she thought. *I'll act normal for a bit. That ought to be fun, too.*

Donnie sighed. "It's not alcohol, anyway. Just soda. I don't like drinking."

"Fair enough." She watched him for a moment. He had this intense interest in the people around the pool. At first, she thought it was the girls. Most of them had bikinis on but one or two had conveniently lost their tops. But it wasn't that. He gave them no more attention than anybody else there. Cindy wondered if he were gay. But he didn't seem gay.

"So close together," Donnie murmured, sipping his soda. "So far away. Ever wonder how far away people are from one another?"

"Not often."

"I'm not surprised. Most people think of it as a natural condition. But it's not. The boundaries between us are artificial. They can be erased by a wave of the hand." He waved his hand.

Donnie turned to her and regarded her with the same unflagging interest he'd given to the people by the pool. "You think you're so far away. But distance can be obliterated in an instant."

Before she could do anything, Donnie touched the tip of her nose.

"See? Distance eliminated. The bubble around you is broken." He turned back to the pool. "But it doesn't stay broken. And it shouldn't. You can't bring people together by breaking anything. You have to draw them together. They have to want to come together from within."

Cindy laughed. "What are you on?"

"These," said Donnie simply and handed her a pill bottle. "Four. Drugs in general scare me but not this one. I might try another couple more of them in a little while." He leaned towards her and she leaned away. "It narrows the wall between us from this great brick monster down to something as fine and delicate as a soap bubble."

He held up his hand and pointed a finger to one side. "You know, if you wet your own hand with soap, you can gently poke your finger through a soap bubble." He slowly penetrated the imaginary soap bubble in front of Cindy. It was the single most erotic thing she had ever seen.

Donnie lifted his eyes to her. "And it won't even pop. It's like you and the soap bubble are one."

They stared at one another for a long moment. Cindy came to herself and shook her head. She looked down at the pills.

Donnie sat back and turned back to the pool. "Take them. I have more."

She stood up and backed away, stumbled against the door, and turned away from him.

Connie was waiting for her. "It's time to go."

Connie had already explained to Portia it was a booze run, so getting out of the party was no big deal.

After a moment, she changed back to her jeans. At that particular moment, she didn't want to feel sexy at all. Connie chuckled, but she ignored him.

The pill bottle dropped to the floor, and she picked them up and looked at them, holding them away from Connie so he couldn't see. She opened it and shook them out into her hand. They nestled pinkly in her palm.

She recognized them immediately.

oOo

Bill liked living a double life.

It was as if he had come to resemble his own company. He was the Jekyll and Hyde now. Anapyridol had released a spirit in him, and he was born again.

By day he ran Lifeworks, both in the normal operations of testing shampoo and reconstituting hairspray, and in the designing of the protocols for the human testing of Anapyridol. But at night, his own personal Mister Hyde came out. Always unknown. Always unpredictable. Some nights he wore himself out making love with Anya on the sofa in his office, breaking whatever illusion of stamina he had against the rock of her desire. Her touch kindled him, burned him alive, and he lay afterward merely inert and joyful ashes.

Other nights held other surprises.

He had given ten thousand doses to Cindy without a thought. The spirit fire within him had promised this. Bill had not questioned it. But now he waited. Cindy—or whoever was chosen to come—would return for more.

He kept secrets—many secrets, he chortled to himself—from Anya. From Hibbert. From everyone but his own personal spirit. To her he brought what he was and from her came the rewards.

To everyone else he wore a mask to cover his laughter. To Hibbert, it was the dutiful businessman talking to his investor angel. Such and such a profit was to be made. Such and such a plan was required by the FDA. Of course, we would only need ten thousand units, but wouldn't a hundred thousand additional units for research be more prudent? It would be bad to run short. To Anya it was the mask of the conciliatory lover, grateful to be given small snatches of her time. Go home to your husband. What we are doing is wrong, but I must see you again. Always laughing. Always enjoying the dance. To the rest of his staff, including Anya, he was still Mister Wallace, giving out orders and making decisions. Sometimes he would joke about it.

"Anya, I wonder if Anapyridol could compete with Viagra or Levitra?" Bill asked, laughing inside. *Damned right it could! Look what it's done for me!*

Anya, thinking that his performance was due solely to her and the spice of their illicit liaison, would smile kindly. "No," she would say. "I think, in fact, that there may be some sexual dysfunction we'll have to tackle. The weakening of the boundary function in the psychology of the patients might contribute to that."

It was all he could do to keep from howling.

But he could not hide from the spirit in his mind, the eye that watched him and watched through him. While she shared in his jokes and smiled at his laughter, there was no dissembling to her. She saw him from behind, through both him and the mask. When her eye opened within him, it was like being loved inside out.

Bill liked giving things names. With the spirit he was no different. He tried Mary. Georgette. She Who Must Be Obeyed. None of them worked right, though she never complained when he tried them on her. He was an actor on her stage and he was performing for the Queen. Queenie? Oh, give it a rest, Bill.

Eventually his waiting was simply ended. He sat back in his chair, feeling mellow and heavy from an hour with Anya on the office sofa. Funny, he mused. He and Anya had settled into a routine of sorts. Anya always worked late. But a couple of days a week, she came storming into his office about twenty minutes after the staff had gone home, took off her clothes, and had him right there on the sofa or the carpet or the desk. Once they were done, she stood up, went into the private bathroom he had next to his office, and took a quick shower. Then she kissed him good-bye and left. Sometimes they talked about Anapyridol or the production facility or new projects. Just as often, she left without saying two words, and the only sign she had been there was the smell of her perfume in the air.

And so on this particular day, he was sitting back in his chair, fully sober and straight but comfortable, considering whether or not to take some Anapyridol. This was a game he played with himself every evening. He always gave in, but it was exciting to tantalize himself. The phone rang.

"Bill?" Cindy said as soon as she recognized his voice. "This is Cindy."

"Cindy!" he said heartily, still playing Doctor Jekyll. "Good to hear from you. Do you want to talk to your mother? She's around here somewhere."

"Cut the crap, Bill," she said pleasantly. "We have business to discuss."

"Okay," he said seriously. "When?"

"Tonight. I'm bringing a friend." She hung up.

He replaced the phone in its cradle. Curled and quiet in the back of his mind, he could feel that she was pleased with the way he was handling the Queen's business.

Working on the Queen's business was an image he liked. Thinking of her as God scared him.

oOo

"Why the hell do I have to go?" LeRoy sat in his darkened room, his face shiny from the glow of his PCs. He fumbled at the keyboard, knowing what Norman was going to say. *He'll sigh first,* thought LeRoy. *Remember to be patient.*

Norman sighed.

LeRoy smiled to himself. It wouldn't do to smile right then. His uncle was a proud man, and disrespect was easy to discover. Not that Norman had ever hurt him. From the day he had arrived, Norman had unfailingly been his loving uncle. But you didn't hang around somebody feared by cops and thugs alike without learning a little caution. While Norman was a good uncle to LeRoy, LeRoy knew he wasn't called Cold Norman for nothing.

"I haven't got any sons," began Norman slowly. "You're the closest thing I have. I'm going to give you the business one of these days, and you have to learn how it works. I know you haven't got the heart for it right now. But you're young yet. And you've been protected. It's time for you to show yourself. Nobody's going to respect you if you just appear suddenly out of the ground."

LeRoy looked up. "I could fuck it up pretty fast. I don't know anything about this stuff."

Norman shook his head. "It's okay. I'm going to give you a cell phone. I'll call you, and you keep it open with the earphone in. I can hear everything in the room. If you get in trouble, I'll tell you what to say. If the connection breaks, you can interrupt what's going on and call me back."

"You..." LeRoy grinned. "Want me to wear a wire?"

Norman laughed. "It's a funny world."

"What do I say, then?"

"Tell Bill about how we're gearing up. We need him to keep the FDA satisfied and still order us ten thousand a month."

"That's a lot of pills."

Norman shrugged. "That's what Cori says he can move. Remember, this stuff is cheap. No middleman, and we're dealing with pharmaceutical production. No cops yet, either. It's honeymoon time, and we'd be stupid to squander it."

"I guess."

"What the hell's the problem? You were the one all excited about this stuff?"

LeRoy turned away and stared at one of his screens. It was time for his medication. Automatically, he opened the small refrigerator and pulled out the pill box. He carefully placed each pill on the table and pulled out some seltzer. "That was before I found out I was going to get my hands dirty. I just like my quiet little computers." *Sigh now, Norman*, he thought, as he swallowed the pills.

Norman sighed.

"This is as easy as it gets, LeRoy. Bill is one crazy white guy, all by himself. He's got no guns to speak of. You're not going to find a better place to learn the ropes."

"Okay. Okay." LeRoy waved him away. "I'll go."

"And it's a chance to meet that white girl you like."

"Get out of here!"

LeRoy seethed all the way across the bridge, up route 40, and into the Lifeworks parking lot. Norman sat next to him in the back of the Caddie the whole time and ignored him. Occasionally he sighed.

They pulled next to Connie's Lincoln. Cindy got out and waited for them. LeRoy didn't want to leave just yet.

"You got the cell phone set up?"

LeRoy nodded and patted the pocket of his jacket.

Norman nodded. "You'll do fine. Get on out there."

LeRoy stepped out of the car. He saw Cindy's eyes widen a moment and regretted the crack he'd made when she had been brought over to Norman's house.

She surprised him. "Come on," she said and turned away towards the back door of the building. LeRoy followed, enjoying a moment to watch her rear swaying back and forth.

Inside the building and up the stairs: Cindy knew her way around. LeRoy followed just behind her. She turned a corner to an office and opened the door.

A tall white man was sitting behind the desk. "Cindy!" He smiled at them.

Cindy walked over to him. "Bill, this is LeRoy Parkin. LeRoy? This is Bill. He owns this whole set up."

"Hardly," said Bill. He held his hand out to LeRoy.

LeRoy listened for Norman, but there was nothing forthcoming. Of course, Norman couldn't see what was going on. He could only hear it. Hastily, LeRoy put out his hand and shook with Bill. He didn't like it. It made him feel somehow fooled.

"I'll hang out in the lobby or something," started Cindy.

"No," LeRoy said firmly. "Stay."

No one could fool him. Not about carbon. LeRoy felt the nervousness fall away from him like a shed coat. Stage fright. Nothing but stage fright.

Bill said, "What can I do for you?"

He could hear Norman's voice. "Just like we said."

LeRoy thought for a minute. "I thought you'd be naked."

Norman muttered angrily in his ear. "You're fucking it up."

Bill looked faintly taken aback. "Not tonight, son."

"You're not on the stuff right now." LeRoy spoke pleasantly, as if it were not important.

Cindy looked at Bill. "You're taking those pills?"

Norman yelled into his ear. "LeRoy—"

LeRoy said quietly: "Trust me, Uncle." And turned off the cell.

"Well, yes," said Bill.

"Jesus." Cindy stared at the ceiling. "I knew you were on something. But not this stuff. Next, I expect you'll start going on about how we are all one person. One people. The only border between us is our skin."

LeRoy nodded. "That's the feeling. Right, Bill?"

Bill stared at them both, one then another, like a midnight deer caught in the oncoming headlights. "Yes," he said finally. "Yes, it is."

"Okay, Bill," began LeRoy amiably. "I caught your website a while back. Before you changed it back again. I was the one that went through it and figured out what you had."

Cindy leaned against the wall. "Too many surprises."

"What's fun about Anapyridol," continued LeRoy, "was the cute way you figured out how to get it across the cell. Using signal transduction was a stroke of genius. At first, I didn't think you realized what you had done. I saw how where the kink in the acetyl group was going to happen as soon as it encountered a dehydrogenase in the blood stream. Then I realized you were using that kink to get it across the blood-brain barrier into the posterior superior parietal lobe. Once there, the normal synaptic enzymes would break it off, exposing the purines—which also broke the signal carrier so it would be digested like a normal protein. Anapyridol, now exposed as neopyridol—my name for it—started doing its thing. I was impressed." LeRoy smiled at him.

Bill stared at him with his mouth open. Cindy was shaking her head. LeRoy drank it in. *Think I'm just some halfwit black kid that lives on the street, will you? You ain't seen nothing yet.*

"Wow," said Bill. "You should talk to Anya."

"I'd like to. Then I went and looked at Newberg and d'Aquili's actual work and realized that Anapyridol is going to dissolve the sense of boundary in human interactions." LeRoy leaned forward. "It's going to be one hell of an aphrodisiac."

Bill started to grin and wiped it off his face so fast LeRoy saw it but Cindy didn't. "You really should talk to Anya. She knows far more about Anapyridol than anybody."

LeRoy nodded. And there was something going on between them. Cindy clearly didn't know about it. "No doubt. My point in telling you this is I really understand what you're doing. I understand the drug. I can move—right now—at least ten thousand units a month. I've projected at least fifty thousand units a month by Thanksgiving. All without the FDA being any wiser."

Bill frowned. "You're not what I expected."

"I can't tell you how often I've heard that." LeRoy rubbed his hands. "That's how much I *think* I can move. We have a honeymoon right now, Bill. No one knows Anapyridol exists. The longer you can keep it in clinical trials, the more we will both profit from it."

Cindy sat down suddenly. "I do not believe this." Then she looked distracted and sniffed the air around the sofa. "Reminds me—" and stopped. She stared at Bill for a moment.

LeRoy didn't know what she was thinking, but it looked ominous. "The big problem is production. Can you keep up with that sort of demand and still keep it secret?"

Bill seemed lost in thought for a moment.

Yes! He saw it happen. Bill had quit looking at him as a scrawny black kid. Now he was looking at him as a partner. That's what had to happen for this to go anywhere. It was all well and good for Cold Norman to terrorize his suppliers. But LeRoy just couldn't pull it off. He had to go all colleague on Bill's ass.

"For a while," Bill said slowly. "Say six months. By Christmas it would be too hard to hide."

LeRoy gave him his best grin. "Fifty million dollars by Christmas. More, even. Half of it yours."

Bill smiled in return. "Sounds good." He stood up.

LeRoy came over to the desk and shook his hand.

Outside the office, LeRoy felt the nervousness and shyness come over him again.

Cindy stopped "Why was I in there?" She turned and asked him.

"Uh—"

"You wanted to impress me, didn't you?" She smiled at him.

LeRoy could feel his cheeks burn. He stared at the ground. "I guess."

"That was sweet." She kissed him on the cheek. "Can I borrow your cell?"

"Cell?"

She pointed to his pocket. "I saw you switch it off."

Dumbly, he handed it to her. She smiled at him again.

"I have to call home." She stepped away, dialed a number, and spoke into it. What she said was almost in a whisper so he couldn't tell what it was. Then she handed him back the phone, still warm from her touch. He glanced down and looked at the number. He didn't recognize it.

"Come on," Cindy said. She took his arm, and they walked out to the cars.

All the way there, LeRoy couldn't get past the feeling of her arm in his.

She kissed me, he thought. *She kissed me.*

oOo

Cindy's mind kept ringing around and around. LeRoy talked to Bill like he was a biochemist himself. Bill clearly believed him. Bill was on the stuff. It was an aphrodisiac, for God's sake. All she could think of was Donnie, talking to her at the party, about how all people were all connected. Nothing was separate. There were no boundaries. The whole thing scared her.

Especially this freak kid. This brain. This weird fucking little genius. Why should he be so special?

This was getting way, way too deep.

It was sitting on the sofa that clued her into it. When she smelled the perfume, LeRoy's aphrodisiac comment still echoing in the room and Bill smiling. He knew it worked like an aphrodisiac. Probably with that rich lady he sometimes had as a date.

For all Cindy knew, they had done it right here in this room and the smell of the perfume was hers.

Then she knew this was why Connie was involved. They were going to sell it through the other call girls. Hell, she would have been involved if Norman hadn't yanked her out of it. Maybe Jake being a cop did help her.

Somehow, she had to tell Jake. Jake would know what to do. But how? And without telling him she was part of it?

And when they were walking out, LeRoy looking at her with cow eyes, she figured out how to do it. She'd call from LeRoy's phone. Call and whisper and hope like hell she got Jake's machine instead of him.

Tell him what? She thought. The hotel. It had to connect with the hotel — the management there never seemed to even notice her. And the night she and Mister Bonifacio had gone dancing there, nobody had said a word, even when he was practically groping her on the floor.

Someone else answered and she panicked, tried to recover, failed. "There are drug deals going down at the Hyatt, Room 609. Big drug deals." It sounded tinny and inadequate, even to her. "Really big drug deals." She wanted to mention Connie or LeRoy or Norman. But that would lead them straight to her. She said whatever came into her mind in a hiss and hung up. She stared at the phone despondently. No one would believe that.

She turned back to LeRoy and smiled at him. He smiled shyly back. He wasn't ugly or anything, was he? And he was smart. Godawful smart. Cindy hoped he didn't figure out what she had done.

Cindy took his arm, and it was like a little spark of electricity fading into a comforting warmth.

I wonder what he's really like, she thought.

oOo

Bill stood at the window and watched them leave. Fifty million. He chuckled as he counted out six pills and swallowed them. Orange juice made them go down easier.

Cindy and LeRoy looked back at one another when they stepped into their cars. Good kids. Maybe they'd go to a movie or something sometime.

The two cars left the lot and he was alone.

Absently, when he felt the first tinglings and stirrings in the back of his mind, he started unbuttoning his shirt.

"Fifty million," he said out loud and laughed. Chump change. The projected revenues of Anapyridol for its antidepressive effects alone were three hundred million. As an adjunct to psychotherapy, that was maybe six hundred million more. Nearly a billion dollars just for its expected use. But no drug ever stayed being used for one thing. Researchers were always figuring out new uses for old drugs. That's what kept the merry-go-round going.

He sat down and waited for his Queen to come to him.

It sure was a good thing he wasn't in this for the money.

Chapter 1.4: October, 1997

After Orphira had completed her training period, Lieutenant Holmes had left her at the desk opposite Jake's. This meant he expected them to be working together. It also meant that when either of them was at the desk doing paperwork, reading forensic results, or talking on the phone—they invariably found themselves looking at one another. Jake found this funny and his chuckles were contagious. More than once, they had looked up at the same time and laughed. It was a friendly feeling, and Orphira found it comfortable.

That evening, when the tip came in, Orphira picked up the phone and answered it before she remembered the phone was on Jake's desk. Jake had taken off early to run some errands.

The voice was a hoarse whisper. Orphira thought it might be a woman's voice but it was hard to tell. A whisper is hard to attribute under the best of circumstances but this woman—if it was a woman—was talking over a cell phone and that muddied the waters even further.

"Jake Fiske, please."

"He's not here at the moment. I'm Detective Doyle. Can I help?"

There was a moment of silence on the other end of the line. "There's a drug deal going down. Room 609 at the Union Station Hyatt. Tomorrow at 11: 30 in the morning. It's big."

Without thinking, Orphira wrote it down. "What kind of drug deal, ma'am?"

Another moment of silence. "Heroin. Cocaine. Everything. You go there and you won't be sorry." A click and a buzz.

Orphira filled out a form on the call and left it on Jake's desk. Probably some prank.

She thought about it on the way back home to University City. The voice was a small continuous buzz in her ear as she walked up the long, unairconditioned stairway. July in Saint Louis is hot but it's nothing compared to the hellfire of August. Dog days, they call it. Damned right. It'll kill a dog in a couple of days if you let it.

In July, the heat baked all of the good smells out of the concrete and the asphalt. By August, what was left had come to a nice simmer: the rotten food in the dumpster behind Riddles Restaurant, the sour beer smell from the liquor store trashcans, and the vine covered chain link fence in the alleyway—a favorite watering place for Saturday night drunks. A good, rich stink that stewed in the air and seemed to settle in the stairway of Orphira's apartment building. It was a choice of what you could bear: the heat of the hallway or the stink coming in from outside.

The stink lessened as the stairway went higher. On the third floor, Orphira could barely smell it. Inside her apartment, smacked in the face by the wet towel of her air conditioning, she couldn't smell it at all.

Cooking was out of the question. She made herself a cheese sandwich and took a plate and a bottle of wine in the living room. The voice rang in her head. She thought she would recognize it if she ever heard it again.

Orphira looked around the room. What a dump. Brown paint splashed indifferently on the wall. Rattling old window air conditioner. Just a living room, a kitchen, and a bedroom. She should have stayed in California.

What? she said to herself. And miss the glamour of police work?

Orphira was already at her desk when Jake entered the office at eight thirty.

Jake smiled at her.

She smiled back. "Got something for you."

"What?" Jake shook his head and picked his mail out of his slot.

"Check your voice mail. I saved the recording."

Confused, Jake dialed the number. After a moment, he looked at her. "Any idea who it is?"

Orphira shook her head.

Jake shrugged. "Probably a crank call."

"You're probably right."

Jake stared at her for a moment. "And?"

"Let's check it out," she said amiably. "You can show me how it's done." She handed him a scrawled note. "I even wrote it down."

"I bet you did," Jake said sourly. "It can't be worth anything."

"Think of it as a training trip."

"You're past that." Jake shook his head and looked at the note.

"It's a pretty day." Orphira said quietly. "I'll buy you a hamburger."

"All right." Jake sighed. "You drive."

Jake stared out the window while they drove. It bothered Orphira. She wondered if something had happened at home. "Cindy all right?"

"Eh?" Jake looked startled.

"Cindy. Daughter. Ran away a while back."

Jake nodded. "She's okay." He fell silent again.

Okay, she thought. *Just drive.*

The Saint Louis Hyatt rose out of Union Station. When Union Station was built, over a hundred years ago, it had been the largest, busiest train station in the world. Hard times for the railroad had turned it into a gutted hulk. Like much of Saint Louis, it had been reborn. Now, where once trains had taken immigrants to the west, there lay an indoor pond full of paddleboats. There were shops where you could buy gourmet ice cream, a complete facsimile edition of every map Lewis and Clark ever made, or a walking stick made from an elephant's pizzle, all beneath the most beautiful hotel Orphira had ever seen.

The vaulted ceilings, the marble floors, and restored gilt furnishings resulted in the sense of being in the heyday of the British Empire, when all of these artifacts were bright-edged and new. The Hyatt built on that. The effect was somewhat spoiled by a preponderance of overweight tourists in Bermuda shorts but was still powerful.

"This is where we tell the concierge why we're here?" Orphira said softly as they walked across the marble floors.

"No. This is where we go directly to Room 609 and knock on the door. We're investigating."

"I don't get it."

They entered the elevator. "If we bring up the concierge it means we mean business. If somebody's there, we have to arrest them. We don't want to do that."

"We don't?"

Jake was silent a moment. "What happens if we bust somebody for possession and it sticks? The guy's assets get sold and some Missouri schoolchild gets new textbooks or something. We get zip. Now, if we investigate and see what's going on, we might be able to play the guy into something bigger. Then we call in the DEA and bust them on federal charges. His assets get sold and we get a much larger percent." He looked at Orphira hastily. "We, meaning the department, I mean. Not you or I."

"I understand."

Part way down the corridor towards Room 609, Jake spoke up again. "Besides, if we do talk to the concierge, and it's a false call, we're bothering him for no good reason. If it's a good call and we see something, we have cause. It's not like we're here to bust down the door."

"You're the senior."

"Is there a problem?"

Orphira stared at him as if he were joking, then away. She was still brand new here. Maybe this was the way things were done. "No problem. Should I bring out my weapon?"

Jake gave her a pained look. "No. Just watch what I do and act accordingly."

He looked up and down the hall. No one was in sight. She heard nothing through the door, but that was unsurprising. This was one of the most expensive hotels in the city. Sound-proofing was probably the first thing they did.

Jake sighed and knocked on the door.

After a moment, the door cracked open and a young girl peeked out. Orphira could tell just from seeing her shoulders and the way she held the door that she was naked. Great. They busted in on some businessman's Morning Delight.

The girl looked them both over. "You're not room service." Her eyes were so dilated they looked as big as teacups. "We ordered a pizza for breakfast."

Beyond her, on the table next to the sink, Orphira could see pills. She looked over at Jake. He saw them, too.

Tiredly, Jake nodded to Orphira. He pulled out his badge and showed it to her. "Open the door, please."

The girl hesitated a second. Orphira expected her to slam it in his face. She wondered what Jake would do then. Open it with a kick or something—she wondered how strong the doors were in the Hyatt. Jake was wrong. They should have brought up the concierge. Something bad was going to happen. Orphira felt suddenly sick inside. *Jesus, what if somebody gets killed?*

Instead, the girl nodded and held up her hand. "Just a sec." She called over her shoulder. "Donnie? Toss me your jacket."

"How come, Trish?" came from Donnie out of sight. A young voice.

Trish didn't answer. Orphira heard the sound of thrown cloth. Trish's eyes never left Jake's face as she put on the jacket behind the door.

Orphira looked at Jake. Jake just stared back patiently.

Orphira had heard of cops staring down criminals with sheer force of personality—who hadn't?—but it was always third-hand or fourth-hand. She had always considered it a myth. Something born out of the movies. Certainly, not from Jake Fiske. But here was a young prostitute, with obvious drugs and paraphernalia in plain sight, rolling over for him.

Trish opened the door. Donnie was a kid, maybe eighteen if he was lucky. Trish wasn't much older. Neither of them seemed particularly scared. Only a little subdued.

"Donnie, he's a policeman. A detective." Trish turned to Orphira. "Are you a detective, too?"

Orphira nodded and stepped back, keeping an eye on both of them. If something went ugly, she wanted to be ready.

Jake asked for and took their IDs. He ignored the pills on the table. Orphira figured he had some kind of plan. Orphira glanced over and read the address. Trish lived north of the Cathedral. Not much of a surprise there. Things changed pretty drastically north of Olive. But Donnie came from Town and Country—yeah, he could afford this. Probably put the room on his own platinum card. Jake nodded to Orphira, and she backed away to give him room.

Watch and learn, she thought. *Watch and learn.*

"What's this all about, officer?" asked Trish.

Donnie nodded, following her lead.

Jake leaned against the table and picked up one of the bottles of pills. "We got a tip about some illicit activity here and decided to check it out." He picked up the bottle and shook out a couple of pills on his palm. They were pink, professional-looking things. The bottle had no label. He held up one of the pills. "What are these?"

Orphira admired his casualness. She could tell from the way they looked at each other the pills were illegal. She wondered what Jake was going to do next.

"I have asthma, sir," Donnie ventured.

Jake nodded. "Detective Doyle will get your names. Do you mind if I take this? Just to show my boss it was a bad tip."

Donnie looked stricken, then gradually some color came into his face and Orphira suddenly felt she could read the kid's mind. There was going to be trouble. She felt herself tense and the focus of the room narrowed to the kid, Jake and Trish. A tingle came into her fingers. Hell, she wouldn't even need the gun to take this kid on.

"That will be fine, Detective," interrupted Trish hastily.

Orphira looked at Trish in surprise. She relaxed. Maybe this would turn out all right. She took their names while Jake stood and watched them. Her hand shook as she wrote in her notebook.

"Okay," Jake said when Orphira was done. "That's enough for now. We'll contact you if we need you further."

"Trish," Jake said as they started to leave the room. "It would be a good idea to keep this between us. You shouldn't have to tell anybody."

Afterward, in the car, Orphira had to ask him, "You want to tell me why we didn't arrest them both? Or do you think he's an innocent asthmatic and she's giving him mouth-to-mouth."

Jake chuckled. "She's a working girl and he's a kid with the means. And this is illegal narcotics of some sort—we'll let the guys at the lab figure out what."

"And we didn't arrest them because…"

"If we arrest her, we have to arrest him. Arresting Trish won't get us anything. She's not afraid of us." Jake shook his head. "But Donnie is a higher sort of boy. Arrest for him is a big deal. He won't be able to get into college back east or if he's already in, he could get kicked out. Let's see what we have and then, if it's anything interesting, we push him a little."

Orphira nodded.

Jake stared out the window. "Besides, we don't want to drag a good county boy all the way to the office for asthma medication."

Orphira smiled. "You're the senior."

oOo

I am like water, Sam thought. *I am like sand. Try to stop me and I will flow around you.*

He sat outside the hotel in his car, watching for Joe. Though it was fall, there was enough residual heat from the summer Sam had turned on the air conditioning.

Norman had made it clear he was not to talk to Joe anymore.

"Come on, Norman," Sam had pleaded. "Cut me in on this deal. Let me work with Joe. I need this."

Norman watched him speculatively. "Like you need to eat, Sam? Like you need to take your next breath?"

They were sitting outside on the porch of Norman's house. Norman had nailed a sheet of plywood over the door. The guards were now sitting in a car in the driveway. Sam didn't need to look in the windows to see they held guns. Something had happened to make Norman nervous. Sam wondered what it was but wasn't curious enough to risk asking.

"Take the rest of the girls in Alton," Sam pleaded. "I'll do whatever Joe needs. I'll run the pills for him. I'll be his right-hand man. I'll rub his big-ass belly if he wants me to. Just let me in on this."

Norman didn't say anything but his eyes took on that cold look Sam had come to recognize. Trying to be as unobtrusive as he could, Sam rested his hand on his pants pocket. It was unlikely he could get the knife out before Norman's goons shot him, if it came to that, but its slim precision comforted him.

"What's it to you, Sam?" Norman said quietly. "Have you got a thing for him? He doesn't swing that way. You know that. Besides, he's got Tess." He grinned. "She's prettier than you."

Sam faked a grin in return, shrugged and looked down. "It's complicated."

"Did he convert you? Did he bring the light of Baby Jesus into your heart?" Norman laughed. Then he stopped as he watched Sam's face. "Jesus. Is that it?"

Sam turned away and stared at the goons in the driveway, his face burning. "Not exactly."

"If you're going to start doing charity work, you're not much good to me."

Sam snapped around to Norman. "You don't have to worry about that. This is personal."

Norman sighed and leaned back against the post. "Well, I hate to get between a man and his religion. But the fact of the matter is that Joe and I are partners. Neither of us trusts the other enough to let there be any middleman between us."

Norman spread his hands. "That's the way it is, Sam. You stay away from Joe. He's got nothing to do with your business anymore. You just stick with the girls in Alton. Be a good boy and maybe I'll throw in Granite City sometime down the way. Harry's been hinting for years he wants to move back to Chicago, anyway."

Sam nodded and left him.

I am like water, he thought. *I cannot be denied.*

Sam opened up a tiny battery TV. He tuned it to Joe's station. Purchasing it had been an eye-opening joy. The stores sounded like retail litanies: Best Buy! Circuit City! Wal-Mart! The world of consumer electronics put Joe Cori within his grasp.

Joe was starting his sermon. Though the initial invocation was always the same on *Hour with Jesus*, Sam could tell from the cadence it was one he'd seen before. He turned down the sound and watched Joe move across the sound stage, first coming into the audience, stroking them and getting them ready, asking people how they were, and gently eliciting spontaneous testimonials.

Sam knew they were really spontaneous since he'd managed to get admitted to the audience three days before. Not that they didn't do their homework. The audience had to fill out long questionnaires, and several of them were brought into private interviews. But Sam was looking for plants and he didn't find them. Sam didn't know show business or the evangelism trade, but he could smell a lie from six blocks away. He was sure Joe had picked out who he was going to talk to long before the cameras were rolling. He was equally sure that the testimonials were genuine—he'd seen Joe's talents that day in Joe's office. After a few minutes, Sam had been perfectly willing to tell the story of any part of his life. If Joe had asked it, Sam would have been saved right there, genital warts and all.

Sam watched the miniature Joe start his sermon. Joe leaned forward to make his point, then pulled back to let the audience think about it, leaned forward to drive that point a little farther home, pulled back, and make a joke about it. Sam didn't need to hear him to know what was happening.

He turned on the radio and tuned it to Joe's station. This sermon was a new one that Joe had been pushing lately. It had to do with the authenticity of being saved.

"...how do you know you've been saved by the healing power of Jesus Christ and not fooled by the devil? For it's not enough to just say the words— words are never enough. Saying you won't drink isn't what keeps you from drinking. Saying you will refrain from evil thought and deed isn't what keeps you from doing it. Satan is infinitely creative in how he tries to pull you from the path, even to the point of masquerading as our Dear Lord. As it says in the gospel, 'many are called, but few are chosen.' Well, friends, first you have to look deep in your heart and see the glory there. That's how you know who you've given your heart to. But that's not enough. If you're saved in a phone booth, the first person in line outside is Satan, ready to tempt you."

At that moment, Joe walked down the stairs of the Best Western, looking for all the world as if he were a businessman starting his commute.

Joe preaching silently on the tiny television. Joe extolling virtue over the radio. Joe in person, getting in his car and going to work.

Sam smiled to himself. Joe Cori and air conditioning. Life was good.

oOo

Joe lingered on her kiss as he stood by the door. When Tess pulled away, he stood up. She straightened his tie.

"It's just like being married," she said.

Joe snorted. "No. Marriage will be much better."

She smiled at him. "That's hard for me to imagine."

Joe nodded. "I know. When I was married to Martha, we had Ethan. I was just starting out. It was pretty good."

Tess kissed him again, on the cheek this time. "You're starting out again. We don't have children and it's still pretty good."

Joe chuckled. "Yes, it is."

"I'll get things ready here for a bit and meet you in the lobby at two. Don't be late."

Joe nodded, then smiled. "Hey, maybe you're right. Maybe it is like being married. I'm whipped already."

"Go on and get out of here. I'll see you this afternoon. Remember, we're going to be in the Lewis and Clark Room."

Outside of the hotel door, Joe stopped as the early October sunlight struck him with unexpected heat. At least it wasn't August, when the steam boiled off the river and made soup of the air, a thick bouillabaisse coating the armpits and groin. Normally, Joe didn't think about his size. But in the heat, he felt pockets of sweat collecting where flesh rolled over flesh; it was hard not to notice. He sighed. By October the weather had finally turned.

God loves me, he thought. *God and Tess.*

He walked down the stairs to his car, a sharp new Lexus he'd bought earlier in the year. Joe had never liked it, new car smell and all. It was too soft, too easy. When he drove the Lexus, he had the illusion that he was in a stationary room and the road and other drivers moved past. He didn't like the feeling.

As he pulled out of the parking lot, he noticed Sam's Buick across the street. He turned north towards the station, and the Buick pulled out behind him. Joe frowned. That was going to have to be dealt with. He had enough problems. Being stalked by a homicidal pimp didn't make his life any easier.

He spent the morning taping another *Hour with Jesus.* His sermon was titled, "The name of the road doesn't matter as long as it gets you to Jesus." More on the same theme. Groundwork. It was all groundwork.

Joe had always liked mixing the sermon with working the audience. It made the message easier to swallow. A real sermon, where everything stops and the audience shuts up and listens to some geezer shouting at them from the pulpit, just didn't connect the right way. You had to reach out and grab them. That's the way his father had always preached. Joe had qualms about old Jimbo's goals, but he had no hesitation about his methods. They worked.

Besides, it was fun.

Joe pulled one woman from the audience to testify. He guided her in the right direction and when she was ready, he let her speak. What she actually said didn't matter. It just had to have the right flavor to it: the wayward path, the sudden light of salvation, the glory of following the Will of the Lord. It had to have the right shape. Set it up right and the testifier would do your job for you. And come willingly back to the office for private instruction if you played things right. But Joe didn't like to do that even before he met Tess. It complicated things in his mind. He wanted to lead his flock, not diddle them.

Joe always kept his director in the corner of his eye as he worked. Phil could tell when he was getting off track and caught up in the moment. Joe counted on him to signal it was time to get back on message. Phil wasn't signaling today, which meant Joe was on target, but he looked unhappy. Joe would have to talk to him after the session.

The woman sat down and Joe returned to the sermon. In a few minutes, the tears streaming freely down his face as he spoke of the wisdom, the glory, and the almighty love that flowed down only from Jesus Christ upon the faithful here on Earth. He was in the game. He was on the money. He was in the groove.

When the session was over, Joe went back to his office and took a shower. Then he returned to the studio and found Phil.

"What's going on, Phil? You looked like you were sucking on a lemon during the taping."

Phil looked around and pulled him onto a vacant sound stage.

Phil was a short, balding Jew from Brooklyn that Joe had saved in a Queens revival, back before Joe had decided it was time to stop the traveling and settle someplace. Phil and Joe had studied the market for a year and decided that Alton was the best place to be. Not so far South there would be too much competition but just Southern enough to have a fertile ground to cultivate. The big Catholic presence was enough of a challenge to spice the deal. Phil rarely had anything good to say. Every Sunday, Phil came down to the altar and was saved. And every Sunday, it was like watching a man rend himself. Joe thought Phil might have been better suited to Catholicism with its regular confession, but he kept his opinion to himself. He didn't want to ever lose Phil. A better director couldn't be found.

"Your presentation is really good. I saw tears on the face of a couple of men in the audience. You're on a good roll these last few weeks. The post show surveys suggest you're really being effective." admitted Phil. "But effective for what? You're broadening the message."

"What does that mean?"

"If there are many roads to God, then why should anyone pick *you*?"

"I know," Joe said smoothly. "But we need to broaden our message to increase the market share. You've seen the numbers. We've saturated our base."

Phil nodded. "But the solution to that is to go national. Get a slot on one of the networks—pay them off if we have to. If you dilute the message, we make increasing market share harder, not easier."

"I don't think so." Joe leaned towards them. "We have to make sure people feel they can come to us, saved or not. They can't be made to feel they're beyond saving. If we stoke up the fires of Hell too much, they'll be a wall between us and our audience. We've got the converted. The audience surveys tell us that. Now we have to extend that appeal beyond them."

Phil shook his head and looked dubious. "I don't know, Joe. If we make things too broad, the converted won't feel special enough. Brother Tilton is coming back on line pretty soon—looks like he beat the Florida charges. If our base is disaffected, they might vote with their feet."

Joe smiled. "We'll keep them. We'll keep them and get more. Balance is the answer. We've just got to strike the right balance."

Phil shrugged. "Let's see how it goes. I'll change the surveys to track the base and see if they're wavering."

Joe rubbed the back of his neck, thinking. "Be careful on that. Sometimes, the fact of asking the question is enough to perturb the mind of the faithful."

Phil chuckled. "Heisenbergian religion?"

"What?"

"Something Ethan mentioned. Heisenberg said the observer couldn't help but interact with the thing he was observing."

Joe stared at Phil. "You've been talking to Ethan?"

For a moment, Phil looked as if he'd said too much. Then he relaxed. "Sure. I've known Ethan since he was born. Shouldn't I talk to him?"

Joe put his hand on Phil's shoulder. "Of course. We haven't been getting along so well lately. I guess I'm a little jealous."

Phil smiled at him gently. "Fathers and sons always have a rough time. Don't worry. You'll get through it."

For a long moment, Joe couldn't speak. He felt a sudden pride. For all their differences, Joe could see how smart his son was. Maybe he doesn't have to believe just yet. Maybe it will come in time.

But always when these thoughts came ran the dark river under them: but if he dies before he's saved, he has nothing.

"I'll do that," Joe said at last.

Lunch was with a group of Christian investors. Joe told a few jokes and referred most of the tax questions to his financial people. Then it was one o'clock and he was back in his car on the way to the Best Western. In his rear view mirror, he saw Sam's Buick. He was going to have to do something about that.

oOo

It took Jake more than the twenty-minute drive home to calm down. Going through the motions at the Hyatt and then holding it together for the rest of the day was like keeping a poker face for a solid seven hours. He saw his face in the rearview mirror. He would never worry about playing cards again.

To hell with it.

Jake pulled off the highway and took Broadway towards to the river. He pulled off at the Gateway Arch, got out, and walked around the green. The evening summer sun gave everything a golden character. There were people milling through the park, watching the descending sun.

What was he going to do?

When Orphira had rolled out that message, the room filled suddenly with the stench of doom. Jake knew the hotel, and he knew the time. It was the same morning slot he'd set up with the Mexican a long time ago.

He kept turning the situation over in his mind all the way to the Hyatt. How the hell was he going to get out of this? Delay was the answer. Delay. Delay. Delay. Figure out later what was going on.

Best case: it was late morning. This late anybody who had been together the night before was out of there. Afternoon delight didn't usually start until around one.

Middle ground would be they would interrupt some poor businessman's last gasp of fun before checkout. Damage control. He would have to give Connie a break.

Worst case: action and drugs they could bust on. A bad combination. How was he going to contain it? He'd have to be the one to question the concierge, not Orphira, so when the regular reservation came up he could squash it.

When that girl Trish answered the door, he just about gave up right there and then. Thank God, none of Connie's girls knew who Jake was. He didn't know Trish, and Trish didn't know him. But she played it straight. Yes, Detective. No, Detective. If Orphira hadn't been there, the girl might have tried to close the deal with a blow job.

Now it was over. He had the pills in an evidence bag in his pocket, and Orphira thought he was able to pull this off out of his wisdom and experience on the force rather than plain, dumb luck.

So, what was going on?

Somebody was ratting on their game. Ratting on Connie or ratting on him? Why would they call him? Was he being set up? Or did they mean to get Orphira—was it intentional they called when he was out with Connie?

Okay, he told himself. *Hold on. Connections to you are unlikely. The Mexican is dead. As soon as you realized it, you cleaned out the Mexican's place. Even that little houseboat of his that Connie likes. The Mexican is gone. There's nothing left of him but a few cases of Corona. You're clean and safe. Connie's different, though. He's exposed. Who would rat him out? Connie's working for Norman now. Sam's over in Alton. Would Sam do it? Is Norman setting Sam up? Try as he might, Jake couldn't turn this one around to any angle that held up. Okay. Forget about Norman and Sam. What about one of Connie's girls?*

No connection there unless *Connie* was setting *him* up. But why? What percentage was there in getting rid of him? Connie had to know Jake had protected himself. If Connie was too stupid to figure it out, Norman sure as hell knew. Norman wouldn't piss on Jake to put him out if he were burning alive, but he still wouldn't let Connie rat Jake out. The fire would rain down on all of them.

A little calmer, Jake walked back to his car. There was a parking ticket on his windshield. He looked around for the meter maid and saw her. He whistled at her and when she looked up, he flashed his badge. She nodded, and he tore up the ticket and got back in the car.

Off route 30 to Arsenal, then down Alfred Street to the house. He unlocked the door and stepped inside. The house smelled of brick and mortar. He stood in the kitchen for a moment and enjoyed it. The same smell he remembered when he was a kid. Back in the olden days when he and the Mexican were going to McKinley's. Good times.

"Honey, I'm home," he called, not expecting an answer. Anya was no doubt still at work. Cindy was probably out with some friend.

He heard Cindy call down to him. The sound of her voice made him grin. A sudden urge to cook sent him rummaging in the cupboard. Maybe it was thinking about the Mexican and high school—long after Mom and Dad had driven off the Discovery Bridge and Gramps had taken him in. In high school, Jake had wanted to be a chef. He'd gone to culinary school, too. But Gramps hadn't taken to the idea and sent him to the Academy to be a cop.

Absently, Jake broke a half dozen eggs, separating the whites and yolks as he did so, a quick, unhurried motion, graceful and unconscious. It wasn't so bad being a cop now. He had money in the bank. Gramps's house was his. He had the bar and, after training from Jake, Brendan was making the best barbecued pork in Saint Louis—it had been written up in the Post-Dispatch and everything. True, nobody knew Mississippi's was Jake's. And, true, nobody knew how much time it had taken to get the barbecue just right and how long it had taken to train Brendan. But a secret victory is a victory none the less.

A *soufflé*, he thought. It had been a while since he had made one.

Cindy was standing in the doorway.

"Hey, honey," he said as he pulled the cheese out of the refrigerator. "How was school?"

"Okay, I guess." She paused a moment. "Jesus, Dad. Are you going to shoot the eggs into submission?"

Jake stood holding the cheese and staring at her. Then he laughed. "Oh, yeah."

He put the cheese down and emptied his pockets onto the table. He unstrapped the Glock, and opened the small safe in the cupboard and put it away.

Cindy sat at the table and fingered some of the things that had come out of his pockets. She picked up the medicine bottle and looked at it. "What are these?"

Jake buttered the bowl and sprinkled it with Parmesan. "Something we pulled in today." Something I should lose.

He made the béchamel sauce and put it aside to cool, and joined her at the table. Jake picked up the bottle and dropped the pills in the wastebasket.

"Should you really do that, Dad? Isn't that an evidence bag?"

Jake nodded. "I took it off a kid just to scare him. It's probably some prescription he got from his parents to make him feel good."

"But Dad, what if it's something important?"

Jake looked at Cindy. "Like what, honey?"

Cindy looked uncomfortable. "I don't know. Maybe it's cocaine or something."

Jake watched her for a moment. "Is there something going on at school you want to tell me?" he asked softly.

"No," she said shortly. "I just figured if it was evidence of a crime you wouldn't just throw it away. It seems... wasteful."

Jake continued to watch her squirm. Abruptly, he decided to let it go. "Don't worry about it."

He returned to the table and added the egg yolks and the remaining cheese and seasoning, folded the stiffly beaten egg whites in carefully, and poured it into the baking pan. He placed it in the oven. "Eat in forty minutes."

oOo

Cindy couldn't believe that after all the anguish she'd had over calling Jake—forget anguish. This was downright panic!—he was just going to throw those pills *away*. She wanted to reach across the table and slap him. Hard. The way Norman had slapped her.

As soon as Jake pulled the soufflé out of the oven, they started to eat. As always, it was incredible what her dad could do in the kitchen. The soufflé was light and airy, with a hint of spices that escaped identification.

Anya called to say she was working late, so the two of them watched TV for a while. Then Jake went to bed.

Cindy went back to the kitchen, pulled the pills out of the wastebasket, and put them on the table.

There was more than one way to commit a felony.

oOo

Anya sat in her car staring at the back door. She couldn't face going into the house right then. She could hear the car cooling in the dark. She leaned back in the seat. Bill's face suddenly swam up behind her closed eyes and she caught her breath at the physical memory of him touching her. Her legs were still shaking.

Anya opened her eyes. The urge to fall asleep was almost overpowering, and it just wouldn't do to wake up here in her car at first light. Not that she would last until then. Tower Grove was pretty safe compared to some parts of Saint Louis, but sleeping in a car in an alley was asking for trouble.

Anya shook her head. She hadn't been entirely sure of her motives when she'd first slept with Bill. Some of it was in response to the disturbing conversation with Hibbert. Part of it was because Cindy was lost and she felt bereft. There was a little—maybe more than a little—self-protection involved there.

Now everything was muddled. The sex was nothing short of amazing. Addictively good. Not that she couldn't drop the affair instantly if she felt it was necessary. Anya was an expert in jettisoning baggage when survival was at stake.

But it mixed things up.

She got out of the car and stretched. It wasn't that late—perhaps eleven. But in the mercuric glare of the street light, the windows in the house were dark, empty sockets. Only a pale light shone through the kitchen window.

Thirsty. Once inside, she turned on the light and rummaged in the refrigerator for something to drink. Nothing but beer. She settled for a glass of ice water and sat at the table.

The icy glass felt good against her forehead. Her life was too complicated. Job, husband, daughter, lover, house. She should just get a damned dog and be complete.

She drank a long gulp and started to put the glass down. But Jake had left an evidence bag on the table. Wearily she brushed it aside and set the glass on the table. What sordid crime did this bag represent? If it was important enough to bag, what was it doing on her kitchen table? Idly, she picked it up. A brown, non-descript, generic medicine bottle. The pills spilled out of the bottle. For a long moment, nothing registered. Pink pills. Brown bottle. Evidence bag. Pink pills.

Anya opened the bag and shook out the rest of the pills. She suddenly found herself wide-awake. These could be anything, she told herself. She scratched the pink coating off until a fine white dust coated the tip of her fingernail. It looked like a crystalline snow.

This is going to be really stupid if I'm wrong, she thought as she licked the dust.

It was that same strange bitter, soapy taste they had worked so hard to cover in the toxicity trials. It had confounded the double-blind tests enough that they'd had to hide it. Anya remembered trying endless juices until she had found a diabetic orange test drink that covered the taste.

In an evidence bag. Jake must have been tired. It had been years since he had accidentally brought home evidence. Anya wondered if Jake could hide it so Duck wouldn't find out.

That meant that Jake, or somebody Jake was working with, had found Anapyridol at a crime scene. Maybe it would be something comfortable and easy, like a homicide of one of the workers at Lifeworks who happened to have some pills in their pocket. Anya shook her head. She felt hollow inside. Jake worked vice and unless you were rounding up prostitutes or busting a cheap crap game, vice meant drugs. Jake must have found this in a drug bust. She dropped it in the trash. Either he'd look for it or he'd forget it.

Anapyridol was on the street.

Now what was she going to do?

oOo

The afternoon meeting filled the Lewis and Clark. This time, there weren't twenty or thirty reformed prostitutes. The room held three hundred people, and there were folks standing in the back and crowding in the doors to get a glimpse of him. A cheer erupted from the room as Joe entered. He waved to them. Tess was waiting for him at the front of the room. He had to shake hands and talk to people just to make his way to her. He glanced at her and she blew him a kiss.

He was suddenly filled with confidence. This was going to happen.

When he had finally made it to the podium, he had to stop and wait for the applause to die down. It gave him a chance to give Tess a quick hug and to catch his breath. He could smell the electricity in the air charging him up, filling him with the power to do God's Holy Work.

He stepped forward and grabbed the microphone. The room quieted.

Joe looked around the room and grinned. "Pretty good for only a few months' work, isn't it?"

The crowd roared back at him that it was.

"Back in June," he said as they stilled. "We started with sixteen women. Sixteen faithful. Sixteen good servants of the Lord. Stand up!"

Tess's sixteen friends stood up and blushed as the rest of the room applauded.

"But we're not going to stop there, are we?"

NO! came the response.

"No, we're not." Joe looked back at Tess beaming at him. "Our good friend, Miss Theresa, has given you all assignments. You all know where you're going next. With any luck, by spring we'll be going public with God's Holy Word all across this great nation. So, keep still yet. Keep doing what you are doing. Like a seed, God's work must begin in the secret places and then break through into the full light of day. Have faith, my brothers and sisters. We will come into the light!"

The room shook with the shouts of "Amen!" They stomped their feet. They clapped their hands. Finally, Joe waved them quiet. He thought of Trish. She had taken herself out of circulation once she'd been caught by the police. An excess of zeal. The young man was a regrettable casualty. Someone who would be brought into the fold later.

"But we must be careful," he said. "Do only your assignments—no more. No less. We are in the margins here between legality and morality. We must not trip over one, pursuing the other."

They cheered him and he beamed over them.

"You all know what Miss Theresa means to me. Let's make it official." Joe waved Tess to him. He pulled out a box and got down on one knee. "Theresa

Durbin, will you marry me? Tell me quick. My knees aren't what they used to."

She leaned forward and whispered in his ear. "You old fool! It's too soon."

"Marry me, anyway," he whispered back.

Tess held his face with her hands and smiled. "You're still a fool," she mouthed at him. "But you are my fool."

"Of course, I will," she said loudly, and nothing more could be heard over the crowd.

After the meeting was finished, the two of them sat at one of the tables, tired. They held hands in companionable silence.

They kissed, and Joe left. Tess had wedding arrangements to make.

He was whistling in the early evening crispness as he walked down the stairs to his Lexus. He saw Sam's Buick. The good feelings blew away, and only weariness remained. He walked over to Sam's car and rapped on the window. It opened, and Sam looked up at him.

"Sam," said Joe levelly. "What are you doing here?"

Sam looked away and back again. "Looking for a room?"

Joe chuckled. "What am I going to do with you? You can't keep following me."

"You can ignore me," Sam said hopefully.

Joe leaned on the window. "I can't do that. I can't have you around all the time. You know that."

Sam gripped the steering wheel. "Don't send me away."

"Sam—"

"Don't send me away." Sam composed himself. "I'm not hurting you. I'm not calling you. I'm just being nearby." He looked up at Joe. "In case you need me, you understand."

Joe looked back at the hotel. "You're scaring Tess."

"She doesn't have to be scared of me," Sam said in a rush. "I never touched her. Not once. And I never will, now that she's with you. You tell her that."

"Oh, Sam."

"I won't go," Sam said sullenly. "You can't make me. I'm not doing anything wrong."

For a moment, Sam reminded Joe of Ethan when he was a little boy, obstinately clinging to some idea or toy, refusing to give up. *Oh, Lord.*

Joe shook his head. He slapped the roof of the Buick and stood up without a word. Back in his car, the sun descended over the river. He pulled out of the parking lot and headed for home. He saw Sam's Buick pull in behind him.

Oh, Lord, take this cup from me.

But there was nothing to do but drink.

Joe pulled his cell out of its holder on the dash and rang a number.

When the voice spoke on the other end, Joe began without preamble: "Norman? We have a problem."

oOo

After the party at Portia's, Cindy's social life closed down to a deep, dark hole. It surprised her to find she preferred it this way. It was so much easier and more comfortable than trying to figure out where Norman's drugs were going or who was screwing who in Connie's stable.

Connie called her up a couple of times. Cindy snuck out, and he took her out to dinner or down to the houseboat. One night, when the river was still and she had finished drinking six or seven of Connie's Coronas, she found herself shouting obscenities at the cars crossing the Veterans Memorial Bridge. She asked Connie if he'd give her a rifle. She figured the wind was in her favor; she could hit maybe one a two of them. Connie gave her a cup of coffee.

It came to her through the aching hangover the next day that there ought to be a better way for a fifteen-year-old girl to spend her time.

Even so, she didn't try to do anything more. Now she was back in Rosati-Kain High School. Jake had smoothed the way with some excuse or explanation. Cindy didn't know how he had done it. She knew there was some story she should remember, but she ignored it. Cindy had wondered what she would say to her friends.

What did *you* do over your summer vacation?

Well, after I ran away, I was a call girl for a couple of months. Then I got involved with a psychopathic drug dealer and his strange, yet not unattractive, nephew. I helped them steal pills from my mother's company a few times. Actually, I didn't really steal them. The naked, crazy president just gave them away.

That wouldn't go far in a Catholic high school.

Cindy had decided to just ignore the question. Otherwise, she'd have to come up with a plausible lie. Something that fit in okay with her running away. She was sure that everyone would know about that. Something beyond the story Jake would have her tell.

The question had resolved itself. Except for Portia, Cindy found she was no longer interested in her friends. They, it seemed, weren't interested in her, either. Maybe running away had its benefits. Or maybe they thought she'd contracted something while she was gone. They were right, as far as that went. She'd contracted a terminal case of not giving a shit.

The phone rang. Without thinking, she picked it up and answered. "Hello?"

"I'd like to speak with Cindy Fiske, please."

The voice was naggingly familiar. "I'm Cindy Fiske," she said.

"I'm Mariah Rendquist. Portia's mother?"

Now she remembered. No doubt, she wanted to warn Cindy off. Cindy, who had run away, shouldn't associate with a high-class girl like Portia.

"What can I do for you?" Cindy said sweetly. What was that saying? Don't let the bastards get you down? Only in Latin.

"Do you know where she is?"

Cindy shook her head. "No. I haven't seen Portia since—" Oops. She almost mentioned the party. "Oh, for at least a couple of weeks. Why?"

Mrs. Rendquist's voice cracked, then settled down. "Portia didn't come home last night. Actually, she might have been gone since night before last. Jerry—Portia's father—didn't see her this morning, and I left early so we thought she was just sleeping late. And last night, we figured she had a date. But this morning she wasn't in her room."

"I'm sure she's all right, Mrs. Rendquist."

"I suppose. But Donnie's been saying the strangest things. And now he says he's dropping out. He's hasn't been home all week, but at least he's been calling in from his friend in town—"

"Donnie's gone, too?"

Cindy could hear Mrs. Rendquist pull herself together over the phone. "I'm sure they're both going to be all right. But if you see Portia, you will be sure and call me, right?"

"Absolutely, Mrs. Rendquist."

Mrs. Rendquist was silent a moment. "Cindy, if you know anything and you're just trying to protect her from us getting mad, I understand. But I'm really worried. If you know anything, please tell me."

"Mrs. Rendquist, I have no idea where Portia is. But if I find out, I'll call you."

Cindy sat on the edge of her bed, staring out the window for a full minute, thinking about Portia. Donnie going off the deep end was bad enough. What if he'd given Portia some of that stuff? She'd left the tip for dad and the next evening, he'd had some of those pills in the evidence bag. Nothing important, my ass.

Cindy tried calling Connie but got nothing. Either his cell was switched off or he wasn't taking calls. She wasn't sure leaving a message was safe, so she didn't.

Pills in 609, the Morning Delight Room.

It took two bus changes to reach Union Station. Cindy had plenty of time to talk herself out of this. She was arguing with herself all the way up the elevator to the door of the room. This was stupid. Portia probably isn't here. If Donnie got those pills from somewhere, they didn't have to involve Connie, and they didn't have to involve Connie's stable. They certainly didn't have to involve her. A couple of times on the way over, she considered if Portia was a good enough friend to stick her neck out this way. If she wasn't there, and it was just a girl and a guy, she'd just go on her way and pretend it was the wrong room. Unless she knew them. What if Mister Bonifacio was there? Would that make Connie mad? Norman?

Cindy rubbed her temples. She didn't know. She didn't know anything.

Then she was in front of Room 609. All she had to do was knock.

Instead, Portia opened up the door.

"I knew it was you," she said. She gathered Cindy in her arms and hugged her. "It's so good to see you."

Inside, Portia was by herself. "Archie's already left." She wrinkled her nose as if she smelled something. "Can you imagine anyone ever naming their baby Archibald? I mean, here's this gross little wailing thing comes out from between your legs and the best name you can come up with, the word you're going to call him all his life, that's going to shape his world, the name that can make his whole life good and terrific, and the best you can come up with is Archibald? Calling him Archie is the best thing you can do for him."

"Who's Archie?" Cindy sat down at the table. There was a small plastic bag of pink pills.

"Guy I met at the party. One of Donnie's friends. We hooked up. He bought the room."

"He did?" That didn't make any sense. The Morning Delight Room was always reserved.

Portia nodded. "Yeah. You didn't know him? He knew your date."

"Ah." So much for Connie's anonymity.

"Archie turned me on to the pink pills. You have got to try these."

"That's okay."

"No, really." Portia came over and sat across from her. "This stuff is so great. I mean, you can connect with the whole damned *world!* It's like there's nothing between you and anybody. I mean nothing. And when you really get high on it, it's like something wakes up inside of you. Something big. Something huge. Like the rest of the world is watching through your eyes."

Portia put her hand on Cindy's arm. It made Cindy uncomfortable. There was something about the touch she didn't like.

"The best part though. *The best part.*" Portia leaned forward and dropped her voice. "The sex is completely incredible. I mean it's like beyond anything you can ever experience. You're having sex with every part of your body and your mind. And when you come? It goes on and on and just vibrates inside you."

Portia laughed and rubbed her hand on Cindy's arm. "Sometimes you can get off just by touching someone else. Anywhere. With any part of your body."

Cindy pulled her arm away. "Sounds… pretty good."

"You have no idea. Want some?"

"Not right now."

Portia shrugged but was clearly disappointed. "Suit yourself."

"Portia, your mom called."

Portia stiffened, then forced herself to relax. "I expect she did. How did you find me? Did Donnie tell her I was here? I've only been here since last night, and I'm going somewhere else after this."

"She's just worried."

"I bet. Let's see." Portia counted off on her fingers. "I ran off with Archie on Monday. So, I wasn't home Monday night. Then Tuesday rolls around and they haven't noticed I'm gone, yet. Now, it's Wednesday. I bet they called this morning. Right?"

Cindy nodded.

"It's good to be predictable." Portia picked up one of the pills and turned it against the light.

Cindy leaned forward. "Portia, you shouldn't be taking these. They make you crazy. That happened to Bill. My mom's boss. Donnie, too."

Portia studied the light reflecting off the edge of the pill. "When I take a few of these, someone wakes up inside me. Someone who likes me. Someone who listens. Someone real." She giggled. "Someone who likes great sex. Isn't that worth a little craziness?"

Someone knocked on the door.

Portia didn't move. "Now, who could that be? You brought my mother along, didn't you?"

Cindy shook her head wordlessly.

"Then let's see who it is."

Portia grinned wickedly as she walked over to the door. Cindy couldn't see who it was, but she could see Portia's face suddenly fill with confusion.

"Cindy?" Portia said in a small voice. "It's your dad."

oOo

Jake thought he was in the clear. He'd dumped the pills. The Donnie kid was gone. Trish had been bailed out and was in the wind. As long as there were no more tips, he could think home free.

Orphira got a call.

Jake watched her out of the corner of his eye. Watched how she spoke in the phone. "Yes." "No." "Are you sure?" Then she hung up.

She was watching him.

Jake looked up. "What?"

"Cindy Fiske has been seen in the Hyatt. The manager thinks she went to Room 609."

Jake stared at her. "How do you know this?"

"When Cindy was missing, I circulated her picture around. This is the first hit."

"Really?"

"New manager, too." She pursed her lips. "I'm as surprised as you are."

Cindy? Jake shook his head slowly. *In the Morning Delight Room?*

He stood up. "Let's go."

oOo

The next few hours were like a tour of the Dungeons of Saint Louis. First, the station house, District 4. Then it was a couple of hours first talking with Orphira, then Jake. Then Orphira again when Jake started yelling. Then Jake, when he'd calm down enough to listen to her. No, she wasn't there doing drugs. Did she look like Portia? Did she look like she was high?

Then the two of them questioning her, asking again and again about the pink pills, about Portia, about the room. It was all she could do to stick to her story: Mrs. Rendquist had called her. She'd heard about the room from Donnie. (A lie, but there was no way she was bringing Norman and Connie into this. It would be a tossup whether Norman, Connie, or Jake would kill her first.) She thought she might be able to find Portia and persuade her to come home. If she hadn't learned to act for her clients in the beginning of the summer, she never would have pulled it off. Yes, Mrs. Rendquist had picked up Portia. No, they had no idea what she or her mother had said. Yes, Portia was in serious trouble. No, they weren't going to tell her what was going to happen to her.

Now, in Jake's car driving home, in the rain. Jake stared out the window, a miserable expression on his face. "Figures," he said.

Cindy watched the fall thunderstorm darken the sky. The streetlights came on. The water had started to come up to the curbs.

"How did you know about that room?" Jake asked hoarsely.

"I told you—"

"That was bullshit. Tell me the truth."

No, she thought to herself. "Portia told me about it. She'd been there before. I didn't know about the pills."

Jake nodded to himself. "It's a prostitute room."

"It is?" Cindy tried to get just the right surprise in her voice.

"Yeah." His hands tightened on the steering wheel. "Nobody much cares about prostitution, as long as it's not visible. As long as there aren't any minors involved."

"You knew about this?"

Jake looked at her defensively. "A little. Yeah. It's not something the department considers important. Drugs are important. People get killed over *them.* The Feds get involved. Smuggling. Things like that. But unless somebody calls up about a bunch of streetwalkers, we pretty much ignore it. Somebody could get away with it for a long time, if they weren't too greedy.

But now it involves drugs. Now it involves minors." Jake nodded in her direction. "Now it involves my daughter."

Cindy completed the thought. "Now it's important."

Jake nodded.

"Do you know who's involved?"

Jake squinted through the rain. "I have some ideas. I know some people. But I haven't been able to make any contact. We got a tip the other day."

Cindy kept her face studiously attentive.

"Somebody who didn't like the principals involved, I expect." Jake tapped the steering wheel.

"What do you mean?"

"Well, it couldn't have been just anybody because the call came through a redirect service."

Cindy held up her hands. "A redirect service?"

Jake sounded tired. "Every call into the department—into any district in the city—is recorded, along with the originating phone number. But if you want to cover that up, you set up an account with a redirecting service. Then you call an 800 number, type in your account number and the number you're calling. The service makes the call and doesn't keep track. The only record left behind is the original call to the 800 number. Since that's just one number, there are too many callers to sift out. Some cell phones are programmed to do it automatically."

Jake laughed humorlessly. "Not that Orphira didn't try. She managed to get all of the numbers that made calls to the 800 number at that particular moment. All 620 of them. Not one of them from a Saint Louis number."

"Not one of them?"

Jake shrugged. "Not surprising. Anyone who would use a service would want to cover their tracks. If it were me, I'd get a cell phone from Oregon or some place. Use that locally through the service. Maybe even use two redirects. I'm not sure how it would be traced. These services may be required to keep records, but you'd need a court order to crack it."

"But you would have been able to figure out any local phone?"

"Sure."

Thank God she'd used LeRoy's phone.

"Shit," said Jake. "Now I'm going to actually have to investigate this." He sighed. "Things were going so well."

oOo

LeRoy was tallying that day's sales of Divinidine when Norman burst into the room. He slouched in the chair across from Leroy and glared at the wall. "Tell me some good news," he demanded.

LeRoy sat still for a moment. As much as he loved his uncle, as much as he respected him and owed him for giving him a home when there was no other place for him to go, of late Norman had been making him nervous. Norman was showing a part of himself to LeRoy he'd kept hidden. Or, LeRoy thought as he watched the narrow angles of his uncle's face, LeRoy was only now admitting to himself who his uncle was. Maybe he had been seeing only one facet of the diamond and could now see the whole blood-covered gem.

"We're making a profit," LeRoy said slowly. "Divinidine was slow to start, but Cori's starting to bring in the money. And he's paying off the lots, just like he said he was."

"You know what I don't like about him?" Norman stood and half-turned back towards LeRoy. LeRoy couldn't see his face.

Norman shook his head. "He figured this out. He could tell which way I was going to jump from the day he came in here. Even that day, when I should have cut his heart out, he knew I wouldn't." Norman held his hands out in front of him. "He flattened two of my men and came in the front door as if he owned my house. As if my private front parlor was a public art museum. He discussed my collection and made me a business proposition while Damulin and Talbot were drooling outside."

Norman threw up his hands. "As if he had a right to tell me what to do. As if he owned me."

Norman shrugged. "And I took him up on it. Put plywood across my front door. Let him live—though to my credit, I had to think about it for a few minutes. It was a good deal he was offering me—one he's made good on. But even so, when he was standing there in my front room, admiring my paintings, I almost blew him away."

LeRoy didn't move. He didn't think Norman had been drinking. His uncle was angry, but he wasn't staggering. LeRoy couldn't smell any alcohol. As far as he knew, Norman had never done any drugs.

"Now he's given me the call I've been expecting. The call I didn't want to get." Norman sat back down in the chair. "Sam—stupid moron that he is— Sam has been *stalking* Joe. Now that Joe's plans are being threatened, it comes to me—to *me*—to solve Joe's little problem." Norman snorted. "What makes my balls burn is I'm going to do it. Not because I particularly want to—I like Sam. Sure, he's a cruel, psychopathic bastard, but if you get past that—" Norman started laughing. "Never mind. You can't get past that. It's not even a drawback. Except now he's gone stupid on me, and stupidity is a major sin in this business."

Norman waggled his finger at LeRoy. "Remember that. Never let stupidity get in the way of making a good buck." Norman fell silent.

LeRoy hadn't said a word during the entire speech. But the silence deepened, and Norman still didn't say a word.

"Uncle Norman?" he said cautiously. "Do you want me to get Damulin and Talbot for you?"

"Damulin and Talbot? Why would I want those two clowns for this?"

"I thought—"

"No. This has to be kept quiet. Sam has to just—*poof!*—disappear like the Mexican. You keep that sort of thing in the family."

LeRoy didn't like where this was going. "Family?"

Norman came around and drew him to his feet. He put an arm around LeRoy's narrow shoulders. "Everybody has to have a little blood on his hands in a Mom and Pop operation like ours. Now it's your turn."

LeRoy didn't quite understand how his feet started walking but the next thing he knew, they were entering the garage.

"You have your driver's permit, don't you?"

"Yes," stammered LeRoy.

"Good." Norman handed him the keys. "Wouldn't want to break any unnecessary laws. You drive."

oOo

Sam had the big television tuned to Joe's *Hour with Jesus*. He had cooked up a big bowl of popcorn. He could tell Joe was working to some kind of big finish. Maybe it wouldn't be tonight—the rhythm felt wrong. But the beat of Joe's shows kept pounding forward. Something was going to happen. Just in case, Sam recorded every show.

Joe was okay with it, he was sure. After the conversation he'd had in the parking lot, he could see it in his eyes. Joe approved.

Sam's role in Joe's life was still somewhat obscure—after all, this was early days. Joe himself wasn't so sure what was coming next. But Sam was sure to have a part in it.

Sam had begun to think of himself as the mysterious chronicler of Joe's ascent—and ascent it was sure to be. Joe's biographer, maybe.

Mom, he thought. *I'm going places.*

Tonight was a live show. Joe was in rare form. He was practically dancing across the stage as he first brought the audience to the brink of heaven, then showed them the cracks in the earth where burned the fires of Hell. Sam laughed delightedly as he chewed the popcorn.

In one pan shot of the audience, he saw Tess.

Sam nearly choked. *Tess? On the show?*

Joe was talking about the blessed state between a man and a woman when he stopped dead in front of her. He reached down and took her hand and brought her to his feet.

"This is what I'm talking about, friends. This woman—like any woman—and me—like any man—should be ready to be joined together."

Sam whispered to himself, "Oh, my God, he's going to marry her."

And it all lay in front of Sam at that moment, all of the set-up and now the payoff. To come to this. Joe was going to marry her. But that wasn't all. Phrases Joe had said in his sermons over the last months rattled through his mind: "It doesn't matter where the inspiration can come from—driving a car, listening to the voice of a child—as long as the inspiration leads you to Jesus." "Forgiveness wasn't just meant for the easy things, friends. Jesus forgave those who drove the nails through his hands. If He can forgive them, surely we can forgive each other."

It all came back to what Joe had told Sam that first day they met, how the act of the commitment of the money was what blessed and sanctified the transaction. It wasn't hanging out in a hotel room that took down Jim Baker. No one cared. For all have sinned and fallen short of the Glory of God. It was the violation of the sanctity of the transaction—the embezzling of the money— that took Jim Baker down. Joe knew that in his heart. He'd been taught that since he was a child—that was what he had been saying to Sam months ago. Joe had been laying the groundwork to take all of it—Tess, Divinidine, the religion—public.

My God, Sam thought, awed. *It's beautiful.*

The house went dark. The television blanked out to a mindless, fading dot.

Sam froze. He looked out the window and saw reassuring lights outside. He lunged off the couch towards the hall closet where he kept the guns. Why didn't he have a gun on him? No reason at all—he'd left it on the kitchen table when he'd been making the popcorn. *Foolish! Foolish! Mistakes like that will kill you. The shotgun in the closet was closer.*

He made it to the closet and stopped, listening. He heard nothing. He waited some more. The instant he turned the knob, it would be obvious where he was. Jesus, the house was so dark.

As gently as he could, he turned the knob, wondering when the last time he'd oiled the mechanism—had he ever, in fact, oiled it? It creaked. Shit! Hell with it. Sam yanked open the door and reached where he knew, exactly, where the shotgun was.

He felt a slashing pain across the back of his legs and he fell. From the shape and form of the pain, he knew it was a baton. Then another slash across his face and from the fire that exploded in his eyes, he thought he was blind for sure. Someone hit him stomach with the end, and he couldn't breathe.

"You just have to remember the right way to do things," Norman said conversationally in his ear.

In spite of the bursting purple bubbles in his vision, Sam scrabbled for the knife in his pocket. Even if he never breathed again, he could still take Norman with him.

He felt Norman's hand there ahead of him, and the weight of the knife was gone. Norman grabbed his hands and taped them behind his back, taped his feet together, taped across his mouth.

Gently, Sam told himself. *Don't panic. Close your eyes and relax. Start crying, and you'll drown in your own mucous.*

"You see, LeRoy. It's just not that hard."

Sam felt Norman—or was it the kid?—take his feet and drag him down the hall to the back door. Sam heard the car back up to the door and the trunk open. Norman opened the back door, and before Sam could do anything, Norman yanked him across the porch, and he bounced down two stairs and fell on his stomach on the edge of the trunk. The blow knocked the wind out of him.

Don't puke! You'll choke on it!

By the time he was able to breathe again, the trunk was closed and they were driving somewhere.

Maybe he'd be lucky. Maybe when Norman opened the trunk, he could get a kick at him. Knock him down or something.

Now the pain in his shoulders began, like lines starting in his shoulders and drawn down to his elbows with a soldering iron. Only the certain knowledge that if he started to cry he would be dead before the car stopped kept his eyes dry. He knew. After all, he'd done this sort of thing himself.

After a while, he couldn't feel his hands or his feet. His shoulders were useless, and from what he could tell, the fall against the trunk had broken something inside of him. At least, he felt something hurt inside when he turned and tried to get comfortable.

The car stopped, but he could still hear cars driving by. Good Christ, was Norman going to just dump him on the highway? Or was he just going to dump the car?

The trunk opened, and Norman struck him hard in the stomach. He hoisted Sam over his shoulder—*don't puke!*—and started carrying him up a set of stairs. Through a door and a few steps down, Norman let him fall to the ground.

A burst of white pain that subsided until Sam could look around. They were in a small dark room. From what he could see in the dim light of LeRoy's flashlight, one wall was brick. The other was part brick with a long door of iron above it. He worked at swallowing. The wall had been in the sun all afternoon. Sam could feel heat radiating from it. The heat and the injuries made him nauseous.

"You see, LeRoy, it's better to have someone completely disappear than to have any sort of body. Pinochet and Peron showed us that a long time ago. Bodies tell tales: how they were killed. When it happened. Who might have done it. All a disappearance leaves is a mystery."

Sam could see the boy watching uncertainly. He stared at the boy, pleading with his eyes, but the boy couldn't see him. LeRoy's eyes were all on Norman.

Norman took a tiny sledge from his pocket and tapped around the iron door. "The caisson workers built a little hidey hole here. Here's where they hid when they smoked opium or drank too much or needed to straighten crooked folk. It's not even in the plans of the bridge—I know that for a fact. No one but me has been here for years."

Something slid noisily, and the side of iron swung slowly open. Sam saw Norman shine a light in there.

"It's not empty, Uncle Norman. Looks like a body."

"I can see that."

"Whose is it?"

"How would I know? I didn't do it. Besides, it's all covered in mold." Norman shook his head. "This place should be empty."

"So, where do you want to take him?"

"This is still the spot for him."

The boy bent down over him, and Sam bent his body suddenly, using his own head to strike at the boy's. Their foreheads connected, and LeRoy staggered back.

While Norman steadied LeRoy, Sam thrashed about, looking for something, anything to be a weapon, a tool, something to cut the tape.

"It's all right, LeRoy," Norman crooned. "Just a bump on the head. You'll be fine. Think of it as a learning experience. You keep them conscious as long as you can because it keeps the witnesses afraid. Even tonight, there are witnesses: you and me. But when the actual deed is done, it's better done when they're unconscious. You sit this one out."

Norman helped LeRoy sit down on the steps. Sam had managed to thrash his way over to the other side of the room next to the door. Norman jerked him back to the center of the room and then jumped back, the way a fisherman jumps back from a shark he's just brought on deck.

"All right, Sam. It's time," Norman said. He stepped forward with the sledge. "Just a tap."

When Sam woke up, he was lying on his stomach. It was completely pitch dark, dead silent, and damp. For a long moment, Sam didn't know where he was. Then he remembered; he was buried alive. He started to cry, stopped himself. Then he thought, *So what?* Tears rolled off his nose.

"Sweet Jesus Christ," came a voice next to him. "What a baby."

Sam froze. He knew that voice.

It was the Tom Haberman, the Mexican.

oOo

Anya stared at the new mouse toxicity data. It looked as if Anapyridol was safe up to the toxic level. After that, the LD50 increased dramatically. Essentially, as long as the Anapyridol serum level remained in the safe zone, there were few side effects—progressive lethargy in the animal models. After a point, the animals stopped moving until the Anapyridol was metabolized. But once it had been excreted by the kidneys, they seemed to have no leftover issues.

But as soon as the level entered the toxic zone, side effects escalated rapidly. It wasn't a huge problem for the FDA since the difference between the therapeutic dosage and the toxic dosage was so great. Still, once the patent ran completely out, the obvious path would be to sell the drug over the counter. There might be problems then.

Of course, no one considered therapeutic doses on the street.

She pushed the report away and leaned back in her chair. For the life of her she couldn't figure out who was stealing Anapyridol and selling it on the street. For that matter, she couldn't understand out why anybody would buy it. *Dime bag antidepressants! Get your social awareness in a pill right here!* No. She couldn't see it. Anapyridol was pretty powerful stuff, but it wasn't something a junkie would be interested in. They'd get a better rush off cough syrup.

It was the how of it that stuck in her mind. The formulation of the pills was farmed out to the same manufacturing contractors they'd always used. If the contractors were safe for morphine derivatives, they ought to be safe for something as benign as Anapyridol. The lots came straight to Lifeworks and went in the safe. Only she and Bill were supposed to know the combination of the safe. They were the only ones registered with the FDA. She certainly hadn't sold Anapyridol on the street. She couldn't imagine Bill doing it. What would be the gain? Money? Anya was only a small stockholder but Anapyridol would make her far more money legally than she could ever hope to see as a recreational drug.

Anya walked down the corridor to the pharmaceuticals room and opened the safe. Just to check, she told herself. It was empty of Anapyridol. Only the morphine, cocaine and the marijuana derivatives were there.

Stunned, she stared at the safe. Her first thought was that somebody really did steal them. Her second was, Why the hell did they leave the cocaine?

Okay. First thing is to tell Bill.

Bill looked up from his desk and smiled at her. He really did have a cozy smile. She shook her head as she closed the door behind her.

"I was looking in the safe for the Anapyridol—"

"—and found it missing," Bill finished. He reached down and opened his left bottom drawer. "Here it is."

Anya looked past the edge of his desk. Sure enough: five jars, one thousand tablets apiece. She sighed. "That's a relief. Why did you bring them here?"

Bill closed and locked the drawer. "Well, it didn't really have to be in the controlled substances vault, did it? We just put it there to keep it safe, and it's just as safe in here. Besides, if we were ever really robbed, they'd just clean the safe out and throw the Anapyridol in a dumpster somewhere. I figured the pills would be safer here."

"You should have told me."

Bill nodded. He looked up at her, and his smile deepened. "I should have." He caught hold of her hands and drew her to him. "I've had other things on my mind."

One thing led to another, and now she was driving home, a pleasant weariness suffused throughout her body and her mind angry that somehow she'd lost control of the situation.

Jake was sitting at the kitchen, drinking a beer and looking miserable. Right then, Anya had to pull together enough energy to care. Maybe it would be easier to just leave. She reminded herself that for all of the great sex, she didn't really love Bill. And she did love, as much as it was possible for her to love, Jake and Cindy. Maybe that was what made things easier with Bill.

Anya sat down across from him. "Can I have a sip?"

Jake nodded and gave her the glass. It was just Budweiser, but at that moment it tasted fine.

She gave him back the glass. "Long day?" she asked helpfully.

"You could say that. Checked out a tip downtown and found Cindy and her friend Portia in a hotel room with a bunch of pills. Had to take them both to the station." He sipped the beer. "Cindy swears she was just trying to find Portia. Portia's mother was worried. Cindy knows more than she's telling, but I'm not sure what. Portia's mother admitted that she'd called Cindy, but I couldn't get out of Cindy how she knew where to find Portia. It was enough for Herrenwold to release Cindy to me. Portia was released to her mother. We'll see what the DA says."

Anya was silent for a long time, trying to fit this into anything sensible. "Cindy and Portia were in a hotel room together?"

Jake started. "You think they were there... together?" He clearly hadn't thought of that.

Anya shook her head. "Probably not."

"I hope not," said Jake. "Great. Gay daughter. Brings home her girlfriend for me to meet. 'Here are the grandchildren, Daddy. Made by me and Portia with our own little turkey baster.'"

Anya chuckled. "Maybe that's a shade premature."

"You think so?" Jake pulled at the beer.

"I'll go up and talk to her."

"Yeah." Jake drained the beer. "Tell her the facts of life."

The facts of life. The phrase rang in her mind as Anya walked up the stairs. She knocked on Cindy's door and heard a mumbled response from inside. Assuming it was some sort of "come in," Anya opened the door.

Cindy was sitting on the bed, leaning against the headboard, her knees drawn up to her chin.

For a moment Anya just looked at her. She seemed so young. The unconscious contortion of her body, the brooding expression on her face—it was like a painting titled, *Adolescent Female at Rest*. Anya tried to remember what she had been like at fifteen. Studying in a concrete block apartment building in Moscow. Worried that her father might get picked up on charges of contamination for just being a Professor of Western Literature. Mother had moved to the Ukraine by then, taken up with a minor bureaucrat Anya had never met. Maybe he hadn't been so minor. He had had a dacha up there somewhere. Briefly, Anya wondered what had happened to her mother. Her father had died of lung cancer before she'd finished her Ph.D., the consequence of those villainous French cigarettes he liked to smoke. Yet another reason to suspect him of contamination.

She sighed. There was almost no common ground between Anya and her daughter.

"What do you want?" Cindy said sullenly.

No. No common ground at all.

Anya closed the door and sat stiffly on the edge of the bed.

"Your father wanted me to talk to you about the facts of life."

"Oh. Good God." Cindy covered her face with her hands. "Didn't we talk about that when I was twelve? The time I had my first period."

"No," Anya said reasonably. "We talked about sex."

Cindy looked at her over her hands. "And the difference is…?"

What are the facts of life? Anya thought. *Just the facts. She was unsure of herself. How far would the truth actually take her?*

"No doubt you've had sex by now," Anya said calmly. "Many girls your age have. I'm sure you used some kind of birth control. You're not pregnant."

"I could be sterile."

Anya glanced towards her. "Please. That would hardly be likely." She continued. "Hopefully, you used some kind of protection. You have a significant chance of getting a sexually transmitted disease if you don't. Protection lessens, but does not remove, the chances. You can get the actual statistics from the net. I'll send you the sites. Then you should make a reasoned choice about whether or not you should have sex."

"A reasoned choice?"

Anya nodded. "Reasoned. No doubt if you've had sex, it's been most likely with a boy. I've seen you look at boys and haven't seen any indication you're a lesbian." She thought for a moment. Perhaps this was Bill's intent. To cloud her reason. What would be his purpose? His motivation?

"Mom!"

"The 'facts' of life are facts, Cindy. I'm just talking about things you already know." Anya considered for a moment. "Regardless of which sex you choose to sleep with, you should be aware, if you're not already, that any commitment made in passion cannot be considered reliable. This is true for all sorts of promises from 'I'll love you forever,' to 'I'll take you as far as Omsk in return for oral sex.'"

"Mom?" Cindy dropped her hands. The expression on her face was one of horror. *Good*, thought Anya.

"It sounds better in Russian." Anya smiled briefly. "Those are the basic facts from which you can draw your own conclusions. But they have little to do with life. Sex, like many things, is a tool for what actually counts in life: survival and power."

"Survival and power?" Cindy just stared at Anya.

"Of course." Anya nodded. "One must survive to do anything. Power over one's life is measured by the ability to choose options. The more power you have, the more choices you have. This is a fact I know: power over other people's life limits the choices one has over one's own life. A dictator can directly affect the lives of millions but can't go down to the corner to get a pack of cigarettes without danger to his own life. Therefore, consider your commitments to others carefully, since you must give up some of your own autonomy to fulfill them."

"Aren't you going to talk about sex? Love? Babies?" Cindy held her hand out to Anya. "You know, normal parent stuff? Like why you married Dad because you loved him and then had me."

"Your father is a romantic," Anya said. She smiled affectionately at the thought. "I'm fond of your father. Once I was out of Russia, I could afford to give up some autonomy for a person I cared for. As for you—" Anya laughed at the memory, "—that was a moment of unplanned and unreasoned passion and your father's Catholicism. Which I do not regret in any way. You are the daughter I would have hoped to have, had I been considering having a daughter. You are strong and have your own mind. You will do well in the world when you decide what you want to do in it."

Anya sobered. "But none of this changes the facts of life. And the facts are that if you do not control your own life, someone else will. If you do not invest in your own survival, you will not survive." The disbelief on Cindy's face told Anya that she still did not understand.

"You are young." Anya patted her leg. "You do not realize your own capabilities. When your survival is at stake, you can do wonderful things.

Things that in other circumstances would be degrading or disgusting but, since they save your life, are marvelous.

"This is all about what's going to happen to me if I run away again, isn't it? That's why you're saying all this." Cindy sighed. "Why did you ever leave Russia? I bet you were happy there."

"I was happy in Russia." Anya nodded to herself, remembering the good times at VECTOR. "But all good things come to an end. I could no longer do the work I wanted." What she could do even now with the techniques she had developed here and the freedom she'd had there. Nothing can be perfect, she told herself. Content yourself with that you can do.

"I had to come to America to do that." she looked fondly at her daughter. "Someday, no doubt, you will understand."

"Understand what?"

"The facts of life."

Anya stood up and stopped at the door. She turned back to Cindy thoughtfully. "I'm glad we had this talk."

And closed the door behind her.

oOo

"Will you shut up?" said Tom. "And keep still. This is tricky enough."

Sam froze. It's not easy to lie still with a dead guy next to you. Especially a talkative dead guy.

He felt a cold, wet strip leading from his mouth down his cheek and along the back of his neck. He had no idea what it was, but every horror movie he'd ever seen tried to get airtime in his mind.

Something cold and wet started working its way under the tape. Sam started to shake his head.

"I said, Keep still."

The Mexican's voice had a dry, rasping quality, as if he were speaking from the end of a garden hose. But it still held the same dangerous certainty he'd had in life.

The gag started to peel loose as it got wet. When it got to the edge of Sam's mouth, it felt slimy. That was enough, and Sam rolled on to his side and threw up. The gag fell off.

"Nice," said Tom. "You really know how to spruce the place up."

When Sam could breathe again, he rolled onto his back. He could still feel the slimy coldness at the edge of his mouth. He tried to spit it away, but it clung.

"I'm sorry you're dead, Tom," he said.

"Blow it out your ass."

The slimy strip seemed thicker now. It clung to his skin. It was wet and dripping slowly into his mouth. Water, by the taste of it, but musty. He tried to spit it out.

"That's all the water you're going to get," said Tom. "So, you'd better swallow it. It'll take a couple of days to get out of here."

"We can get out of here?"

"Just stay still and be patient." Tom laughed. "You've got time."

"Get the tape off my hands."

"Shut up and wait. I'm on a schedule."

"What?" But Tom didn't answer. Sam settled back. What else was he going to do?

Sam found himself sucking at the cool strip on the side of his mouth. The water actually tasted pretty good. It seemed to settle his stomach, too.

"You know," Tom said conversationally. "The only reason Norman let you and Connie whack me was he figured the two of you were too stupid to be much of a threat."

"I had nothing to do with that."

"Fuck you. I'm dead. I know things. I know, for example, that you paid Connie to put a bullet in my head after Norman offered you my territory." The Mexican chuckled. "For less money, too. That's the funny part. Norman's share of my take was a lot less than yours was."

"So, how come you're helping me?"

"I got my reasons. But you didn't know I was here, did you? Any more than Norman did? Connie knew."

Sam shook his head. "What are you getting at?"

"Mysteries are what the dead give the living, shit stain," laughed Tom. "Live with it."

"To hell with you," muttered Sam. He felt suddenly very sleepy.

"That's the idea."

Sam awoke feeling considerably better. The tape around his wrists had loosened a little, and he had feeling in his hands and feet.

"About time you're awake. You've been out for a while."

It was absolute dark. Only the desperate phosphenes of his vision punctuated the darkness.

It was cooler now. At least, Sam no longer felt he was in an oven. He sniffed the air. It had a tang of sulfur in it. Not strong, but definitely there.

"The air smells funny," he said.

"You don't miss a trick, do you? You're under the Eads Bridge—in it, actually. There are bound to be a few smells around here. It could be worse." The Mexican chuckled. "A lot worse."

The slimy strip had grown into a something that felt like a tube taped to his cheek, and it delivered a steady drip of water. The flavor had changed and was meatier. Heartier. Like a broth. What would a dead man feed me? Sam tried not to think about it.

"I used to love coming to the Eads Bridge at night," said Tom quietly in the darkness. "When it was so late even the cops were asleep in their cars, I'd come out and stand in the middle, looking up at the full moon hanging up there like a shiny penny. You forget things when you see them too often."

"You get me out of here, and I'll take you with me."

Rasping cough. "Right. Everybody makes promises to the dead guy."

"Everybody?"

But Tom wouldn't speak anymore.

In the dark, Sam slipped in and out of sleep. He could tell when he was dreaming because he was happy or he felt comfortable or he could see.

So, when the light seemed to come out of the walls and he found himself in a courtyard, he knew he was dreaming. This was just fine with him. Being awake was the nightmare.

The courtyard was below the ground; the walls went up fifteen feet or more. Trees and bushes bordered the place, and their roots or vines hung over the edge. It was an old place. The grass spread rampantly over the marble flagstones, and the roots of the trees grew through cracks in the smooth walls.

In the center of the courtyard was a broad, round fountain. The water shot up from the water, atomized high in the air, and fell back as rain. Beyond the fountain rose a stairway out of the courtyard. The steps were small, each riser no more than an inch or two. Above them, there was a blush of light against the trees as if the sun were beginning to rise. The glow in the sky was full of promise and speculation. Sam stared at it.

"Don't get comfortable." The Mexican sat on the edge of the fountain, watching Sam.

"What?" Sam said, startled.

"I'm here to give you a message."

"So, give it to me." Sam started to walk towards the stairs.

Tom grabbed him by the throat. "Look at me."

Reluctantly, Sam turned away from the stairs. The Mexican was standing now, towering over him. Sam had forgotten how tall he was.

"Okay." Tom pulled Sam around until he was between Sam and the stairs. "Two things. Whatever is up there is the same thing Joe is seeing."

"What is it?"

"I don't know. I'm told I can't know—not that I'm prevented from seeing it. Just that in my current state of death, I'm incapable of seeing it. This is as far as I can go."

Sam stared at him. Not being able to see the coming light seemed something horrible. "That's terrible."

Tom nodded at him grimly. "No problem. It was my choice. Just remember. First, it's whatever Joe is seeing."

That made sense. Sam had seen Joe was lit up inside. Now he knew where it came from. "What's the second thing?"

The Mexican grinned at him. "This is the best part. Joe's the one that set you up."

Sam stepped back, shaking his head. "What are you talking about?"

"Norman tried to kill you—left you to die, in point of fact." Tom chucked. "Joe put him up to it."

"But why?"

"He's going public. Your attention was, let's say, inconvenient."

For a moment all Sam could see was Joe, standing outside his car, looking down at him. That's why he had looked so sad. "You're lying—"

But Tom was gone. There was nothing between him and the stairs. Even the fountain had stilled.

Sam walked across the water and up the stairs. Each step brought him closer to the light. When he rose high enough to see it, he could feel her light shining through him, lighting up every dark corner and cranny inside him.

"Mom," he breathed. "I've come home."

He was awake when the iron, in a swirl of sulfur, broke loose and fell to the ground. The tape binding his arms and legs parted and he half rolled, half fell down onto the brick. It was day outside, and a dim light reached into the tiny room. After a few minutes, he leaned against the still-smoking iron door and shakily stood. To his eyes, adapted to no light at all for the last three days, the room appeared fully lit. He looked inside the alcove where he had been lying.

The body of Tom Haberman, the Mexican, was engulfed in cottony fungus. Streamers led away from him, some as fine as hair, some thick as cable across the floor and up the walls, draped from the ceiling.

"Thanks," Sam said.

There was a movement from the body—a sort of exhalation—that might have been a whispered, "Good luck." Then what remained of the body collapsed into a sluggish puddle.

Sam nodded and crawled up the stairs out of the room. He could hear the sound of pigeons. High above him was an opening. Stairs now led downward into the dark. He followed them, feeling his way around the turns until they stopped at a door, limned in light and smelling of sulfur.

Gently, he pushed at the door.

The iron joints stretched and parted like cheese. The door fell outward into the sun with a crash, and Sam was blinded.

He staggered out into the afternoon autumn sunlight. The heat reflected back from the concrete felt good to him. In a few minutes, he could see where he was, standing at the base of the Eads Bridge support on the Saint Louis side.

Cars rolled by next to the river. Pigeons wheeled and danced in the air. He could smell people thick all through the city. He could hear the deep hum of their conversations.

Sam tried to yell, but all he could manage was a cough. It didn't matter. He was alive. He was free. He was born again.

Chapter 1.5: December, 1997

LeRoy took a last look in the mirror.

Jacket. Slacks. Flowers. Tie. Everything a young black criminal should wear on a date.

"You sure this is such a good idea?" said Uncle Norman in the doorway.

"Never you mind," snapped LeRoy.

Norman chuckled. "Ah, to be fifteen again. Going out to dinner and a movie with a young hooker."

"Call girl," said LeRoy. "You told me she was a call girl."

Norman nodded. "True enough. But she still works for me. It's probably a bad idea to get involved with the help."

"I'll take my chances."

"It's not you I'm worried about." He turned LeRoy around. "Be careful. She knows a fair amount right now. She's still her father's daughter. She doesn't need to know any more than she has to."

LeRoy nodded. "I can still go?"

Norman stared at him then laughed. "Sure. Just be careful. I like Cindy. I'd hate for us to have to take care of her like we did Sam. Tell Damulin to drive you. Take the Chrysler."

LeRoy left the house. All six foot five and three hundred and seventy pounds of Damulin silently materialized out of the corner shadows to follow him to the garage. LeRoy pointed to the smooth, black Chrysler Le Baron. Not a car he would have chosen for himself, but he would take what he could. Until he had a license. Until he had a place to call his own.

Cindy was waiting for him at the corner of Kingshighway and Arsenal. She joined him in the back seat without a word.

LeRoy didn't know what to say. Instead, he nodded to Damulin in the mirror and the car started off in silence.

"This is such a bad idea," Cindy said suddenly. She looked at him. "You're dressed up. You're wearing a tie." She cocked her head to one side. "You look all right."

LeRoy managed a smile. It came to him that there was a problem with going out on a date with a prostitute, even a former prostitute. Could he believe anything she said? If she said he looked nice, was it true or something she was saying to make him feel better? Was it an act?

Cindy shook her head. "This is so not a date."

"Beg pardon?" He wondered if she had hooker-inspired intuition. LeRoy didn't know much about girls. Maybe they could read minds.

"You're dressed up like this was a date," she said patiently. "Jacket. Tie. Flowers. All of that says date. Look at me. I'm still dressed in the school uniform. I'm sitting up here and talking to you like this. Does anything about this remotely say date to you?"

LeRoy looked at her. The uniform was a plaid skirt with sweater-vest over a white shirt. The ensemble was clearly designed to fit over young girls who had not yet been struck by hormones. In fact, LeRoy thought, it was quite probable the designers never thought these girls so clothed would ever be infected by something as common as puberty. And if they were, it was their own fault. The sweater-vest limned the round curves of Cindy's chest and the skirt flared where it shouldn't. LeRoy wondered if Cindy had noticed this or if she saw something else in the mirror. Perhaps something fictional. The truth of the matter was that Cindy was pornographically hot in that outfit and LeRoy could never, ever tell her.

"Does it say," he said, his voice suddenly squeaky in his ears. "Dinner and a movie? No date need be involved?"

Cindy smiled and giggled at this, and LeRoy was dazzled, as if all the light of the waning December sun had been suddenly drawn to her face. When Cindy smiled, he forgot to notice her bosom. It gently suggested itself just below the line of his vision.

"I guess," she said and looked out the window. "What did you have in mind?"

oOo

The area around the Cathedral had been renovated some years before. It was now a haven of restaurants, galleries, and idiosyncratic shops. If a shop didn't sell something interesting, it disappeared quickly, since novelty was the main attraction. The neighborhood was edgy and tightly wound from its proximity to the war zone six blocks to the northward.

Ethan liked the walk here from his apartment near Washington University. He'd never been mugged. But then, Ethan had been shuttled around a lot of places before Joe and Edna had settled down in Alton, many of them a good deal worse than Saint Louis. It was also possible that the predators sensed he was as poor as the proverbial church mouse and had nothing steal.

Tonight, he had finished his preliminary exams and had decided it was time to celebrate a little.

In this tiny room, he pulled his secret stash of pocket money and a single credit card out of its locked drawer.

The card was a gift from his father, and Ethan loathed using it. He hated to owe anything to Joe. He'd managed a scholarship to SIU and then a research assistantship to Washington University. The stipend paid barely enough to keep for the room in a shared house and a more or less continuous diet of crackers and tomato soup.

Taking Joe's money made him queasy. He couldn't help thinking of some ancient retiree kneeling painfully on that damned plastic prayer rug and sending their life savings to Joe Cori's *Hour with Jesus*.

But eventually, the temptation of a cheap steak or fish would prove irresistible and by the end of the month out came the card. Every time Ethan put the card back in the drawer, he swore he'd never use it again.

This time, though, he picked it up without shame. He'd done something important. Henry Mathauser, his advisor, had even complimented him on his results. The preliminary exams were the first concrete step of accomplishment towards the degree. True, he was liberated only to slave in Mathauser's lab, under his direction, needing his permission and support for any actual equipment or project. And it was also true, there would be no increase in salary and that he would now have to work even harder and that most of the papers would have Ethan's name somewhere in the anonymous middle of the list of authors instead of the prestigious first, second, or last.

But it was a step, he told himself. His father had a right to be proud and probably would be, too, if Ethan were speaking with him right at that moment. Which Ethan was more than willing to do at some future date when he wasn't quite so angry at Joe for marrying again. Theresa. He'd never met her. Joe had mentioned the two of them had been on one of his shows, but Ethan would have actually had to watch one to see her. Instead, he'd gotten a call from Joe one evening to tell him about it and to read the announcement in the paper the next day. Joe had seen the picture of the two them. She was much younger than Joe—perhaps thirty-five or forty—and made up as if she were Tammy Faye Bakker.

A good night on the town might go a little ways to helping on that score. Put that nameless retiree's money to good use for a change.

Ethan put on his best slacks and a nice shirt. For a moment, he had a blank moment when he looked in the bathroom mirror. Were these the slacks he'd gone off to college in? Didn't he wear this shirt in high school? The shirt was tight across his chest and arms, but the pants were loose on him.

"Hooray for the tomato soup diet," he said to himself. "If I wrote a book on it, I could put Atkins out of business."

The air outside was sweet. It had rained the day before, and the December sun had come out. The day would be short, but the moment was precious. The bare trees were a glossy gold in the sunset light, and the earth smelled as if it had been washed in the blood of the lamb. The crisp evening lent a brisk cadence to people walking to and from their cars, finding places to eat, looking at dresses, jewelry, and knick-knacks in the window. It was too cold for fall, but still too warm for winter. No one was quite ready to give up the heat or embrace the cold. People stood in front of the windows only as long as the residual warmth of walking remained, and then moved on quickly.

Olivia's had a sidewalk section they kept stubbornly open against the weather. Ethan couldn't face going inside. He kept his jacket on, took a table, and watched the street lamps ignite over a trout immersed in a light cream sauce. He was surrounded by the murmur of people.

Now, *this* was living. Ethan figured if he could do this, oh, maybe two or three times a year, he might be able to manage the rest of graduate school.

His waitress took the card and he eased back in his chair. Maybe food was better than sex, he mused. You could enjoy it anytime. Of course, it had been a long time since he'd dated anyone. He could just have forgotten.

"Excuse me, sir?"

He looked up. The waitress had a funny expression on her face. She looked around and leaned over him conspiratorially. "I'm sorry sir," she said. "Your card has been declined."

Ethan felt the embarrassment flood his face. "Excuse me?" he squeaked, not really believing, not able to believe, what she was saying.

Her sympathy evaporated. Her voice rose. "I'm sorry, sir. Your card has been declined. We've been instructed to retain it."

"Oh," Ethan said just to keep her from saying it again.

She slid the check back to him. "We can take another card or cash."

"Ah." Ethan pulled out his wallet mechanically. He counted out his remaining cash. Just enough to pay the check but not enough for a tip. He gave her all of it and fled before she had a chance to return.

A block away, he sat on a bus bench to collect his thoughts. Had Joe finally cut him off? Did even the little money he'd used up over the years become too much? Had there been one too many arguments over the cosmology of creation? Had he realized Ethan hadn't intended to connect with him again?

Ethan rubbed his face. It had to be *her*. It had to be *Theresa*. His father wouldn't cut him off, would he?

Truth be told, Ethan told himself, he didn't really know. While his mother had always supported Joe pursuing God's Word, unless his father was actually around, she was indifferent to it. When Ethan had gravitated into science instead of theology, Martha had defended him. She'd listened to him explain the vagaries of distant star systems and the peculiarities of quantum physics with the same patience she'd given Joe when he expounded on the hidden secrets of Jesus and God's plan for humanity.

Looking up to the clear and starless sky in the December night, Ethan realized that she'd never been interested in either. Whatever his mother believed, she'd told neither Joe nor Ethan. What she had done, what was important to her, was to protect them from each other until the day she died.

The result was that Ethan didn't really understand how a man as intelligent and insightful as he knew his father to be could embrace a stumbling archaic mythology like Christianity. Fundamentalist Christianity. Revivalist Fundamentalist Christianity. It made no sense to him.

As he thought about Joe, it came to him that it must take an awesome amount of energy to continually have to keep fitting the narrow definitions of the Bible to the real world. It didn't take much to blow away the Bible—the instant you brought in the concept of time, any facts supporting the mythology evaporated. It took years for the light of even nearby suns to reach Earth. Determining the distance between stars that were five thousand light years away—to pick a period dear to his father's heart—was a fairly simple application of straightforward geometry. So, without reaching into biology or fossils or anything complex—just depending on geometry and *time*—the age allowed by fundamentalist creation was falsifiable.

Ethan breathed out slowly. No wonder he had such fights with his father. Ethan wondered if there had been one hour—no, one *minute*—that could have passed during the simplest of conversations where Ethan didn't unconsciously challenge the very binding energy of Joe's faith.

The will of it, Ethan thought with sudden respect. *The very effort of it.* To have to spend that much energy to believe something so patently unbelievable. To use such tools, like radio and television—whose fundamental operation was seamlessly derived from the same physics that challenged Joe's faith—seemed to Ethan to be nothing short of blind, stupid, and ignorant. Yet, his father was none of these things and still believed. Reason itself—the essential tool of human beings in a hostile world—had to be abandoned.

For a moment, Ethan saw his father reflected in thousands of people believing similarly over the years. No wonder Galileo was persecuted. No wonder Copernicus had been so careful. Faith was so inherently fragile, so incredibly effervescent, the slightest breath of reason could shatter it. No wonder it was defended so vigorously.

Then consider, Ethan told himself, Joe as a fifty-year-old man, lonely and bereft of his wife, estranged from his son, clinging with his failing strength to his belief. He meets a young woman who bolsters that belief, who looks up at him with stars in her eyes. What man could resist her?

It had been a long time since Ethan had dated, much less loved, anyone. but he could still remember how another person could suddenly and naturally become the center of the world. A pre-Copernican system about which everything revolved.

Perhaps Theresa is sincere, he thought reluctantly. Dad's sincere. He's been dodging con artists for a long time—the field was full of them. If she was sincere, then maybe she and Dad came to the idea it was time to cut him loose together.

Maybe it *was* time. Ethan could see them thinking that. It was ineptly done—they should have told him. But it was hard for Joe and Ethan to talk at all, much less to talk about Theresa.

Maybe it really was time, Ethan thought with a start. Maybe they were right.

Jesus Christ, he thought, appalled.

I'm going to have to get a job.

oOo

Connie eased himself down carefully on the lawn chair. The thin aluminum tubing creaked but didn't collapse. The strapping popped a couple of strands, but other than that, made no protest. Connie figured he'd have to buy a new one the next time he was in town. He relaxed, popped the top off his Corona, and settled back.

It had turned warm since the cold snap of a few days ago. A few mosquitoes had decided they weren't ready to settle down for the winter just yet and buzzed around him incessantly. Connie imagined they viewed him as so much real estate ready for colonization.

Normally, Connie didn't like boats much. Even on the Mexican's houseboat, Connie had to be careful not to move too quickly lest it start a queasy rocking.

Houseboats are like most things in life, he thought. *They are not built for scale.*

Even so, with the full moon peeking up over the forest and shining down on the river, a Corona in his hand and a six pack in easy reaching distance, he could see the attraction.

"Enjoying yourself?" came a voice in the darkness.

Connie sat up too quickly, and the aluminum tubing collapsed, pinning him for a moment. He stood up and ripped the tubing away. He saw his gun ready for him, just inside the doorway out of reach, but the light over the deck blinded him and he couldn't see into the shadows.

The voice laughed. "Worth the price of admission."

Connie licked his lips and looked longingly at the gun. Too far. "Who's there?"

"Connie? Don't you recognize my voice?" Sam came into the light. "Have I been gone that long?"

Connie watched the edge of Sam's knife glitter. "So," he said slowly. "Norman lied to me."

Sam smiled at him. "Not exactly. He certainly thinks I'm dead. By the way, I bring word from the Mexican." He feinted with the knife and Connie stumbled back.

"Relax," chuckled Sam. He slipped inside and came back out with Connie's gun before Connie could regain his balance.

"What do you want?" There was something different about Sam. He moved like a snake or a cat—Connie wondered if he was on something. He tried to see Sam's eyes, but they were hidden in the dimness.

Sam feinted again and this time, Connie stepped back, ready for him. Unfortunately, that meant one foot went off the back deck and Connie fell into the river.

He came up spitting and choking and *cold*. December didn't show in the air, but it had definitely come to the water. Sam grabbed the boat hook and held it out to him. Connie grabbed it and held on, keeping his head above water. Connie Samoan had never learned to swim.

"Easy, big guy," crooned Sam. He shook the boat hook, and it almost slipped from Connie's fingers. "I wouldn't want you to drown."

"What do you want?" His teeth chattered. It was hard to talk. The current kept trying to pull him under. The current tried to roll over his head.

Sam carefully kept him out far enough that Connie couldn't reach the edge of the houseboat. "You know where Norman is getting that special drug—you know the one I mean. You're going to skim some off for me."

"He'll kill me!" Connie sputtered and choked, suddenly underwater. He was jerked back to the surface.

Sam waited until he could breathe again. "Die now or die later, sweetie. I'd take die later if it was me."

"Okay!" Connie shouted.

Sam brought him to the edge of the houseboat and let him take hold. He stepped back on the deck and waited.

Connie slowly climbed up, trying to think, his body shaking

Sam was sitting in the other chair, sipping Connie's Corona and holding Connie's gun easily in his hand.

Connie shook water from his hands. "To hell with it," he muttered and stripped off his clothes. He immediately felt warmer. Naked, he balled them up and threw them in the river.

He stalked into the houseboat, dried himself off, and got a pair of sweatpants and a hoodie from the drawer, and a beer from the refrigerator. He was acutely aware that Sam was able to see anywhere in the small space and could shoot him before he could pull out any hardware. Not that he had any in his drawers or the refrigerator, he thought ruefully. He had always thought the Mexican was paranoid, the way he kept guns everywhere. Right up to the day he and Sam had shot him and dumped the body under the bridge. Then he thought maybe there was something to it. Of course, that didn't mean Connie ought to be paranoid. After all, it could never happen to *him*. Right?

Right, he thought with disgust.

Clothed and warm, he came back out to the deck, pulled another folding chair off the rack, and sat down. "So, now that you're back from the dead we're partners again?"

"Honey," purred Sam. "We were never partners before. You worked for me, remember? Until I released you to Norman. But things change, sweetie. We're partners *now*."

"Yeah," said Connie.

"Norman's about to cut you out of the deal, anyway," said Sam. "You're the middleman. He's tough on middlemen." Sam chuckled. "Believe me. I know."

"If he cuts me out, how am I going to skim any for you?"

"For us, dear. You'll do very well for yourself." Sam leaned forward. "First, you do know where he's getting the stuff, right?"

"Pretty much." Connie hedged. "But I don't have any leverage there."

"Your little girlfriend is all the leverage we need."

"Great." Connie stared out at the river, a lit piece of brown water in an immense darkness. "That's just fucking great."

oOo

Joe and Tess sat across the big double desk from each other. Joe was working over the general ledger report. Tess was going over Divinidine delivery figures.

Once, Tess's mother had said, "You never know what you can do until you have to." For years, when Tess had considered it, she had thought about it in terms of being a call girl. You didn't know what you could do until the client required it. But now, poring over pills purchased, pills allocated, pills dispensed, she had started to wonder if this was more what her mother had in mind. And how much everything cost! She had already come up with a round figure of one thousand converts by the end of the year. It took six pills to have the appropriate effect. Tess dimpled into a smile as she remembered how they had experimented with different dosages. After a certain point, ripping each other's clothes off just became inevitable.

Six pills twice a week was what they came down to. Twelve pills a week: 1 hit per week. 48 pills per hit month. 576 pills per hit year. A thousand converts would consume over half a million pills per year. Currently, Norman was charging a dollar a pill. Budget, then, for when he raises the price—a million a year. They only had a few thousand pills on tap. That had to change.

She leaned back in her chair. Don't worry about the money. Joe would figure something out. Worry about the supply. Say they had fifty thousand pills on tap. That's about over one thousand person-weeks. Currently, they had ninety-two people on the books. Tess pulled out her calculator. 11 weeks. 22, if they rationed Divinidine to once per week—think of it like Sunday communion. They would run out in January or March. If they had the money. If they had no more converts.

Tess sighed. This had been a shoestring operation long enough. It was time to bring it up to the next level.

Joe looked up. "Did you get Ethan a new card?"

Tess looked over to him, suddenly derailed from her line of thought. She nodded. "I had Maybelle get him a new card on Bank St. Pierre. Soon as he calls in, we'll deliver it."

Joe nodded and went back to the ledger. A companionable silence fell between them.

Tess glanced up at him over the desk and then went back to work. It was only since their marriage went public that she'd started working with Joe in his office. Joe had insisted a double desk be moved in so they could work opposite each other. He said it helped him remember their holy mission when he could see her. She was amenable. Being near him just smelled right.

Joe sat back in his chair and threw down the pencil.

"We need a miracle," Joe said morosely as he looked at the report.

Tess pulled down the lid of her laptop so she wouldn't be distracted. Tess didn't like to be distracted when she talked with Joe. She wanted to be able to give him her complete attention. Tess rubbed her finger as she waited for him to speak up. Her wedding ring itched.

"It looks like our television audience doesn't appreciate you the same way I do," he said. He looked depressed.

"Yes," said Tess simply. It was enough to agree. She didn't need to say she told him this would happen. That helped no one. Besides, she liked being married to Joe—something that had surprised her. It was as if a nervous, jittery, long-flying bird long inside her had finally been allowed to rest. She wasn't quite ready to say she was actually happy just yet. But Tess could see the country without a telescope.

"Contributions are down?" she asked.

"Down doesn't begin to describe it. The four-hand letter didn't bring enough to pay for postage. The guaranteed prayer medallion didn't get more than a few hundred phone calls. Even the prayer rug only broke even." Joe looked thoughtful. "We need a miracle."

"Surely it's not as bad as that."

"Oh, we're still in the black. But the writing's on the wall." Joe stood up and went to the window. Below his office, his ministry worked, busy as proverbial bees, in a complex of offices and production studios separated by tiny green grass squares.

"Any ideas?" he said to her.

"What?" Tess looked up, startled. *Damn*, she said to herself. I still haven't got this marriage thing figured out.

"A miracle," Joe said patiently. "Do you have any ideas?"

"Beg pardon?"

"I've been thinking about this. We have been touched by the living hand of Jesus. He's given us our mission. Maybe a miracle isn't too much to ask."

"I have no idea what you're talking about."

Joe shrugged. "I'm not too sure, either. But it seems to me with all of the faithful and all of our prayers, something might happen if we give it the opportunity."

Tess watched him speculatively. She had been thinking of what had happened to her in purely personal terms. "Isn't what we have inside—what we can give people—enough?"

Joe shook his head. "Not at all. That was the first thing I learned, way back when I got saved. If you don't have something to show, you don't have a flock. Do you think people get saved because of the Holy Love of the Lord? That's the goal, but that by itself doesn't get people to come down to the communion rail. You have to have something tangible. You can scare people there with the Fires of Hell. You can draw them there by showing them miraculous healing. But if you wait for them to figure it out for themselves, all you get are Methodists."

He tapped the window. "No. We need a miracle. Maybe we should make one."

Tess stared at him. "Falsify a miracle?"

"No. That never works. You get found out and you go down the tubes. That's what my daddy liked to do. Set up a miracle, milk it, and run like hell. There was no end of little two-week shrines he set up all across Texas and Alabama. And two weeks later, there was no end of little two-bit towns with a pot of tar and a bag of feathers, waiting for him to come back. We have the real thing here, Tess. Somehow, we have to make use of it. For the Lord."

Joe stared outside.

Tess could tell it was cold and wet outside, a true Missouri December. The clouds overhead darkened. She stood up and took Joe's hand.

"We need a bigger supply, too." Tess explained her figures.

"As if we didn't have enough problems." Joe shook his head.

"We'll figure something out."

Joe nodded and squeezed her hand.

Tess looked up into his troubled face. She went to the door and locked it. Then she started unbuttoning her blouse.

Joe's face lit up, and she smiled at him. There was more than one use for a double desk.

Outside, the rain turned to mist as it struck the pavement.

oOo

Cindy felt better the next day. Going out on a date with LeRoy seemed so incredibly normal. Sure, he was the nephew of a criminal gang boss. And they were chauffeured around by a bodyguard carrying a gun. But it was so much better than meetings at midnight with naked Bill and finding Portia in a drug-ridden haze. During the movie she actually felt okay. She even held LeRoy's hand—something she probably shouldn't have done. After all, she didn't like him that way. Cindy caught herself. It felt good to think like that instead of trying to figure out how she was going to make sure her client had a good time.

Normal—even a broken, silly normal—felt good.

She resolved that the next step should be to get Portia to talk to her.

It wasn't easy. After the hotel, Portia kept avoiding her. In Mrs. Jamieson's art class, Portia sat by herself in the front of the room. Cindy sat in the back. Mrs. Jamieson liked fixed seating, so Cindy was outfoxed.

Fortunately, in the spring she and Portia had made up their schedules to have as many classes in common as possible. So, Cindy waited for Mister Richard's calculus class—something Cindy had loved but Portia had loathed and done purely for the sake of friendship. But Mister Richards had the temerity to hit the ground running in September and kept it going until now, near Christmas. It was all Cindy could do to take notes, glance furtively at Portia to get her eye, and watch Portia coolly turn away.

Lunch time rolled around, and Cindy was ready to leap across the intervening seats and claw Portia's eyes out, screaming, "Listen to me! I only want to help you!"

Probably not the best of plans.

Portia took her plate, after carefully putting enough people between her and Cindy to make cutting in line a lethal offense, loaded up with macaroni, and sat by herself in the farthest corner of the cafeteria.

This alone told Cindy how bad things had gotten. Portia was never alone at lunch. While Cindy might be (or had been) her best friend, Portia was very popular. Her cynicism mixed with humor, wealth, and fashion sense, practically guaranteed followers. Portia had never taken them seriously, but she also never drove them away. As she had said to Cindy once, people who will do anything for your attention have their uses.

But like rats on sinking ships and birds during earthquakes, her followers had fled at the first taint of religious fanaticism. And, Cindy admitted to herself, Portia was exuding more than just a taint.

Cindy took her own plate of macaroni and walked over to her table. She set down her tray across from Portia and sat down.

Portia looked at her. "I thought I had made myself perfectly clear."

"Portia, we've been friends for years. Did you think I would really stay away?"

"I never thought you would turn me in to your dad, so I can't say what you would do."

Cindy stared at her for a moment. "I didn't do that."

"I ran off. The next thing I know is you show up at the hotel door." She shook her head. "I'm just gushing about Divinidine—"

"Divinidine?"

"The pink pills, all right? And right after you get there and I tell you everything, in comes your dad. You're a... what Littleton said about Shakespeare last year. You're a stalking horse."

"A what?"

"A stalking horse. 'He uses his folly like a stalking horse, and under the presentation of that he shoots his wit.' You're the horse the hunter sends in to distract the game so you can shoot them. I remembered because when Littleton read the quotation it so perfectly described how I used Donnie with my parents. That's what you are."

Cindy stared at her. *This is the drug. This has to be the drug,* she thought.

"I don't know why my dad showed up there," Cindy said slowly. "I didn't turn you in—I got in trouble, too! Look—" She suddenly felt overwhelmed by all of this. She buried her face in her hands. Her mother. Her father. Connie. LeRoy. Norman. Now Portia. *Sweet Jesus Christ.* Did everything have to turn to shit, or was it just her?

She rubbed her eyes and blotted any tell-tale moisture with a napkin. "Look," she said evenly. "Do you remember Sister Evangeline in fourth-grade summer camp?"

Portia looked cautious. "Yes."

"She struck you with a ruler when you insisted that it was every girl's right to pee whenever she had to. Remember that?"

"Yes."

"And you said you were going to get her, so you boiled about a bushel of poison ivy leaves and took the broth and soaked her underwear in it, and then carefully dried it and put it back in her drawer."

"I remember."

"And remember how confused we were when Father Gerard started itching?"

Portia giggled. "Yeah. I remember."

"Who got the leaves with you and made sure you were wearing your swim goggles when we were cooking the underwear? Who got treated with calamine right alongside you at the nurse's station with both of our hands as big as footballs? Who backed you up when you said we had been picking flowers and liked the ones with the red berries?"

Portia sobered. "You did."

"That's right." Cindy took a deep breath. "I didn't rat you out then. I didn't rat you out at the Hilton. I don't know why Dad came to that room, but it wasn't because of me." A tiny lie. "You either believe me or you don't. You decide."

Portia watched her for a long time. "Is the dress you wore at the party the one you tried to shop lift?"

Cindy nodded, not understanding.

"That is so cool. Did your big man get it for you? When you ran off, what was it like?"

Cindy relaxed. There was a manic glint in Portia's eye. She was clearly off her nut and drug-ridden, but Cindy could cope with that later. Now she just wanted to enjoy being forgiven.

oOo

The Grand Hall at Union Station looked as if it were lit by emeralds.

Donnie watched it, sitting on a bench. He imagined it as it must have been when filled with people entering with great fanfare, leaving in terror of getting caught, and standing there, not knowing where they should go. People sitting amidst their luggage, people having the ticket in their hand and that ticket being the only thing in the world they owned, people feeling like they owned the place, people in love. The place must have smelled of coal smoke, horse manure, and human sweat.

In his pocket, Donnie fingered a bag full of pills. Thirty pills—that's how many he'd snagged from Trish. Trish, who wouldn't speak to him now—getting busted put a dent in Divinidine sex. He felt betrayed. Abandoned. Wasn't he chosen along with her? Just a little hint of the police, and he'd been left behind. Christ had associated with thieves and lepers. Why not Trish?

He had a soda in his hand. Impulsively, he took the baggie and emptied it into his hand. A moment of thick pain in his throat as he swallowed the lot and then washed it down—*forced* it down, really—with his soda.

The Grand Hall was like a dome stretched long. The acoustics were amazing. He could hear everything.

After a few moments, the light grew brighter—it was no longer emerald the color, but emerald the *quality*. The *nature* of emerald-ness. A jewel of perfect light that seemed to grow brighter every minute. Was the light God? Was it even necessary for the light to have a name? Something recognizable? No. It was only necessary that it shine through him.

What need had he of Trish? This was enough. He put his soda in the trash. The urge to eliminate all impediments from his life—everything between him and the light—grew irresistible. Shoes? Unnecessary. Clothes? Remove them. The light was the only thing of importance. Fear? Discard it. Sight? Hearing? Gone, until there was only Donnie left and that was superfluous, too.

For a long time, Donnie just wasn't there. There was only the light. Golden and viscous, there was only the feeling of being bathed in warmth. There was no Donnie. There was only the sensation experienced by someone who would have been Donnie, had there been a Donnie present.

He realized he was there as he thought about that.

God was not here, he realized. Or, rather, he was no more or less here than any other place. Everything was formless and void.

Donnie remembered God's presence. At Portia's party. He remembered His humming undercurrent beneath the conversation surrounding him. He had even tried to give God's gift to Portia's friend, but it had been spurned. This didn't surprise him. Until that first day with Trish, being spurned was the natural order of things.

Trish had given him first the gift of her body, as if it were Christ's, then the gift of her witness, and then the gift of God himself.

God had revealed his solemn nature to him. This was the fruit of the other Tree in the Garden, manifested and ingested so that God could be revealed to Donnie without destroying him.

None of this explained where he was.

Fully aware now, he had no sensation of his body save the gross sense of warmth and comfort. Before he was aware, it was enough. But now he wanted to know where he was. He wanted his hands, fingers, and penis back. For a moment, he panicked.

He heard a voice.

"I need someone to pull a heavy load. To take my gifts to the heathen and bring them to me."

Donnie felt his voice in his throat. "Here I am, Lord," he said, suddenly filled with light again. "Here I am. Send me."

"Then wake up."

Donnie opened his eyes and looked around. He was on a hospital bed surrounded by a curtain. Beyond, he could hear medical activity. There was a small man sitting next to the bed.

"What happened?" Donnie shook his head. "Where is everybody? Where is Trish?"

The little man giggled. He seemed to glow with confidence and danger. Donnie immediately felt that he could trust him. Donnie knew that it was no accident to awake right now and right here to face him.

"You will see Trish again when it's right," the man said. "But now playtime is over."

"Who are you?"

"My name is Sam," said the little man. "It's time for us to go. We have work to do."

oOo

"Look," Jake said, trying to sound reasonable. "It's been a couple of months since we pulled in the county girl."

"And your daughter." Orphira watched him across the desk impassively.

Jake groaned. This was not going to be easy. "And Cindy. I remember. Have a heart."

"So, it's been a couple of months." Orphira crossed her arms.

"That room's been staked out ever since. Nobody's been there except tourists, and pretty boring tourists at that." Jake leaned back. "I think this is a blind alley."

"And the lab report?"

"They don't know what that stuff is. There's a lot of 'looks like' and 'resembles' in there but nothing concrete. It's either a brand-new drug, unlike anything that's been on the scene before, or that kid was right: it's his asthma medicine."

"Did you see a resemblance to any asthma medication in the lab report? I must have missed it."

Jake shrugged. Diverting a bloodhound was no easy task. "The kid said it came from Europe."

"But you decided we shouldn't send it to the national lab because 'it probably isn't worth the trouble.'"

And because I know the people at the Saint Louis labs. Jake made himself smile. "Don't you think our guys are any good?"

"I don't think they have access to European databases. But it turns out that I do. I sent a sample to a friend of mine in Saint Louis University." Orphira smiled sweetly at him. "She says that whatever those pink pills are, they're not a recognized formulation in any of the databases."

"Ah," said Jake shortly, trying to regroup. "Could it be experimental?"

"That's what Lucy thought. It's clearly a professionally made pill."

"All right, then. Could the kid be right?" Lead her. Don't push her. Jake was beginning to understand how Orphira worked. He saw suddenly how much alike she and Anya were. They shared the same drive to get things done. Dangle a problem in front of them, and they snatched at it and wouldn't let go.

Orphira frowned. "I guess. We should talk to Donnie again."

"And get the county on our back?"

"You said yourself Donnie was scared of getting busted. How about I just talk to him person to person—not as a cop but just as Orphira Newton?"

Shit, Jake thought. "If you think you can do it. It's a good way to get in trouble."

Orphira nodded and looked up Donnie's phone number.

Jake leaned back, exasperated. He watched her as she dialed, and it took him back to when he met Anya. For a moment the office was gone, and he saw the classroom where the course in immigrant law was being held. In those days, he'd thought he might want to become a lawyer. Night courses at UMSL to get ready to take the LCATs. Anya had been so small and perfect, with her exotic skin and fine hands, that it just took his breath away. But there had been a lot of pretty girls at UMSL. What had really interested him was the intensity she brought to the class. So, he'd had asked her to get some coffee with him. Six times, he'd asked, and each time she'd given him the same brusque "No" until it had become something they laughed about. She didn't like coffee, he'd found out. She liked silent films, light opera, art that made her laugh, and tea so strong it left chemical burns in his throat. And when they had finally slept together, he found out she was nearly as strong as he was.

Jake shook his head, and the room cleared. That was a long time ago. Jake felt old. No law school for him. Now he was just trying to protect himself.

"Yes, Mrs. Rendquist. I'm Orphira Newton. Can I speak with Donnie, please?"

Jake watched her. When Orphira relaxed she had a truly striking face: high cheekbones rounding down to a well formed chin, wide brown eyes. Her skin seemed to glow. She wasn't small, but she looked strong. For a moment, Jake wondered what it would be like to touch the curve of her hip, the swelling of her breast.

"I see. Can you hold on a moment?" Orphira put the phone on hold. "Jake? Wake up."

Jake started. Orphira snapped into focus in front of him.

"We've got a problem," Orphira said. "Kid OD'd on something and ended up unresponsive in the ER at Barnes. Then he up and left before they figured out who he was. Donnie Rendquist is gone."

oOo

Anya left Lifeworks early. She took the back stairs and walked clear around the building to avoid running into Bill. She didn't want to see him. She didn't want to see Jake or Cindy. She wanted to find some small hole in the wall and drink something foul and strong, and think things through. It felt as if everyone in the world had a piece of her, enclosing her in a web of obligations and secrets until she could no longer breathe.

She drove downtown below the brewery. The air was thick with malt and yeast. Anya liked the smell of beer, the smell of growth and ferment. The finished products such as vodka or ale were so often a disappointment after the promise of that scent.

The building that housed the Pale Horse was wedged into the street at an angle. The entrance was narrow, and the bar spread open in a broad triangle. Anya looked around as she entered—one obvious entrance. In case of fire, break the front glass window and jump into in the street. No building inspector or fire marshal had ever cleared this place.

Anya ordered a vodka martini and took it to a booth. She sipped it slowly. *No one could like the taste of a martini,* she thought.

Gin and vodka with an onion. The result was a taste not found in nature that burned away any illusion left by sweet fruit punch drinks. Here's the raw alcohol toxicity of the vodka. Here's the bitter kerosene of the gin. You want something sweet? Here's an onion.

She savored it.

All roads lead to Rome, and if all scenarios were impossible but one, that scenario was the road to follow. All pills ordered were accounted for. 10,000 pills of Anapyridol were custom-manufactured for them at MRD Labs. 10,000 were made there. 10,000 were shipped to Lifeworks and 10,000, minus those used for trials, analysis, and submission to the FDA, were accounted for. Nine large bottles of a thousand pills each, ten bottles of one hundred pills each. She didn't think anyone was close to her in the research—Anapyridol came out of her Russian work. Besides, though it was remotely possible there was another lab that had discovered or had even stolen the formula for Anapyridol, but they would never have the exact formulation she'd tasted.

Either she was mistaken about the pills Jake had found or someone was manufacturing Anapyridol somewhere else. Anya was sure of the pills. That meant the entire formulation, manufacturing, and design of Anapyridol had been stolen. Lifeworks was a small company; only she and Bill knew all of the pieces. Only the two of them knew what to steal. She hadn't done it.

That left Bill.

Anya sipped her martini again. Could he have been lying to her all this time? It was hard to believe someone could fool her that much and for so long. Especially since she'd been sleeping with him.

Anya shook her head. *Let's be honest.* In this affair, Bill was the one in control. She might have started things, but when the sex started to become incredible the balance of power had shifted. After all, what did he have to lose? He owned his business. He had no wife or children. He owned her research in return for stock. She, on the other depended on him for facilities. Lifeworks owned her research. Anya had a husband and child. She cursed herself for an idiot. She'd put herself in this position out of reckless abandonment.

Her cell phone rang. She looked at the number. It was one she didn't recognize, and she started to put it away. Then she thought it could be Cindy and answered it.

"Hello?" She sipped her martini.

A deep voice spoke to her in Russian: "Doctor Gamova. How have you been?"

She stopped breathing. She knew that voice instantly, and for a moment, fifteen years melted away.

It was Colonel Kalenin.

A nail-biting hour after she had told him where she was, he was sitting across from her.

Kalenin held up his beer stein. "I have developed a taste for Budweiser since I came here."

They spoke in Russian. It was comforting to speak in her native tongue.

Kalenin looked good. He wore a svelte dark suit and diamond cuff links. He had always seemed small to Anya, though still very dangerous. A snake can be small. Or a lynx. But he had always seemed a little lost in his baggy Soviet uniform. Now, as far as his clothes were concerned, he had traded up. His face still seemed searching, the brown eyes slitted behind his glasses.

"How did you find me, colonel?" she said in a low voice. Anya had thought her little life in Saint Louis obscure enough to hide her. Kalenin had disproved that idea.

Kalenin smiled. "Call me Sasha."

Of course, he wouldn't answer, she thought. He had never answered anything of the sort. Why should he start now?

Anya nodded. "How long have you been in the States? Tell me that, at least."

Kalenin nodded. "I came here two years after you did. Mostly, I keep to the West Coast. But, occasionally, I come out to Saint Louis to check up on you."

"Check up on me?"

"How have you been? You have the smell of trouble about you." He leaned forward in a way Anya remembered she had disliked. "Have you been naughty?"

"Hush," she said. Is this what Kalenin had become? A lecherous old man using his contacts to pursue (or blackmail?) Russian expatriates?

"Ah," he said in a sad voice. "So, we must move to another topic. Tell me, Doctor Anya Gamova, about Anapyridol."

Anya froze for a brief moment. "What are you talking about?"

Kalenin laughed. "Masterfully done but not quite quick enough. It has been your pet project for some time. I looked at the specifications—"

"How did you get them?"

Kalenin shrugged. "What the FDA knows, I know if I want to. Anapyridol resembles Product 22 in the old lab, doesn't it?"

Anya nodded. "I've made extensive modifications—"

"—as I saw from the specifications," Kalenin said comfortably. He beamed at her. "This is how globalization should work. Good, solid products on one side of the world are put to use on the other."

Anya stared at him. "What do you want?"

Kalenin's eyes turned hard. "I know you need help. I'm prepared to offer it. Product 22 has appeared on the street—oh, sorry! Anapyridol. Is that your doing? Making a little on the side?"

"No!"

"I'm not surprised. It's not your style. Come, Gamova. Tell me about Anapyridol. Tell me what you didn't put in the reports."

"Okay." Anya drank the remains of her vodka martini down in one gulp. She grinned at Kalenin. "Remember the personality boundary experiments I did."

"Yes," Kalenin said immediately. "We were investigating Geschwind syndrome. Product 22 reduced the personality boundary between individuals. It was a potentially powerful hypnotic."

"No. We must be precise here. What Product 22 created was *submission*. It was not a hypnotic at all, as it did not induce suggestibility."

"What's the difference?"

"If I *suggest* to you the building is on fire, you will actually feel your skin shriveling and burning. You will see flames erupt from the walls. Psychosomatic behavior will result. Product 22 could not induce that. Once Product 22 has been administered, if I say to you flee this building because it is on fire, your reaction would be to submit to my superior wisdom and flee the building. You would not need to see any fire at all."

"I understand." Kalenin leaned back and sipped his beer. "Anapyridol doesn't work the same way?"

Anya shook her head. "What I learned from Product 22 was how to access the cingulate gyrus with a drug. Submission did not interest me. I hoped Product 22 was inhibiting subsystems that resulted in a submission effect. I realized when I looked at the MRIs of the test candidates, I had stumbled into something far more interesting than submission—reptiles show submission. Birds show submission. Fish show submission. This was something much more uniquely mammalian. I had found personality boundary suppression."

"I'm lost."

"Think about primitive mammals—back in the age of thecodonts, when reptiles and mammals parted ways. Mammals developed independently after that. Mammals are animals that suckle their young—Linnaeus derived our entire class from that. But after we were thecodonts and before the suckling began, we developed rearing. Mammalian rearing requires a relaxation of the personality boundary between mother and child. In some cases, between father and child."

Kalenin watched her speculatively. "Birds rear."

Anya waved it away. "They developed later, after the split between mammals and reptiles. The amphibian root stock from which both classes derive do *not* rear. Therefore, both classes developed rearing separately. Bird rearing cannot utilize the same mammalian neurological mechanism."

She leaned on the table. "I saw d'Aquili's work later, and some of the TM work in the seventies. Primitive stuff, but all linked to the cingulate gyrus. When I saw that, I knew what I had discovered. But it doesn't stop there."

"Of course not," Kalenin said, encouraging her.

Anya didn't care. Fifteen years of secrets were pouring out. "Nothing comes from nothing. Two bones in the middle ear were once the jawbones of reptiles. When it comes to social interactions, human beings are the most complex animals on earth."

She counted off on her fingers. "I had found out the source of personality boundary control and, by its extension, one of the mammalian mechanisms of rearing. That was enough for other mammals. But we are human. We do not just derive everything we have and everything we are from these primitive impulses. We redefine them and put them to new use. Sasha, I hadn't just discovered the basis of rearing. I had discovered the neurology of altruism."

Kalenin didn't speak for a moment. "That's what Anapyridol does? Create altruism?"

"In part. It has anti-depressant activities. Some euphoria—how could altruism operate if it didn't feel good? But you must see the larger picture here." She forgot for a moment where she was, and she was back in Moscow staring up at Lenin's statue. "Remember the dream, Sasha. As flawed as it was, as broken as we made it, remember what we wanted to have. I can make it possible."

Anya took a deep breath. The room seemed to glow. "I have created a medical prescription for socialism."

Kalenin was silent. He leaned back in his seat and watched her. "Socialism didn't work, child. You were there. Remember that."

"It didn't work on people as they are." She leaned forward. "Anapyridol can make people as they *should* be."

"Ah," said Kalenin. "If the man will not work with the system, don't change the system. Change the man. Good Communist ideology."

"Exactly. That was what I realized back in VECTOR. By itself, irrational human nature slides inexorably towards greed and amorality."

"Amorality?"

"Capitalism is amoral." She looked at him. "Wouldn't you agree? The economics of 'price,' 'supply,' and 'demand' are mere quantifications of human action. *Humans* decide to set prices higher when supply is restricted, not equations. Restrict the supply and the need is increased. Is not increasing the price when the need is greatest a moral decision? Yet, capitalism abstracts it. It is not *humans* that raise the price; it is the invisible hand of the market. No moral decision need be considered. Is not that abstraction the very *definition* of amoral? "

"You have been thinking about this for a long time," Kalenin murmured.

She ignored him. "Putting the selfish, primitive urges of human beings in harness only glorifies them. They are no less primitive and no less selfish."

"Did you ever take Product 22?" Kalenin asked. "Or Anapyridol?"

"Do you think I have need of submission or any correction to my social compass?"

Kalenin waved the comment aside. "I take it the answer is no. I was just curious. How will you deal with Wallace?"

"Bill?" She shook her head, startled. "I don't understand."

"He's been supplying Anapyridol to the street. You must have known that. It's obvious. Who else could it have been?"

"That makes no sense. He has nothing to gain by it." She rubbed her face for a moment. "He would make far more money going through with the FDA process."

"Perhaps he wants both."

"Why? There is no rational reason—"

"You said it yourself: people are not rational. There's no earthly good reason for you to be sleeping with Wallace, but you're doing it anyway. Don't let it blind you."

Anya placed both hands palm down on the table and took a deep breath. Kalenin had always been able to do this to her. Control her with information. She wanted to ask him how he knew, but even to ask the question seemed to give him power over her. It acknowledged he had sources of information about her he would never reveal.

Kalenin pulled out a pad of paper and wrote down a number. He gave it to her. "This is my personal phone. Call it anytime. Day or night."

He leaned forward until their foreheads were almost touching. "Wallace supplying the street is not necessarily a bad thing. It will not invalidate the patents, studies, or clinical trials—some you might have to redo but there's no help for that. The FDA will want proof of your ethical purity. It all depends on how this is found out. If he is discovered by you, turned in by you, your hands are clean. His place in Lifeworks is forfeit. Who is the board going to put in charge? You. Ownership would still be his. But control would be yours."

oOo

Ethan thought his advisor might have an idea how to start. Getting a job in graduate school—if you wanted to actually sleep on occasion and perhaps go to a cheap movie once or twice a year—was something to be considered carefully. Ethan had a research assistantship rather than a teaching assistantship. This meant that the university thought his research was, in effect, his job and didn't task him with the burdensome effort of propagating his hard-earned knowledge to uninterested underclassmen. The concomitant salary, as a side comment, indicated what the university thought his research was worth.

A job outside of the RA had to be something that would pay somewhat more than a fry cook at McDonald's in Kazakhstan but considerably less than the same fry cook would be paid in Chicago *and* leave him enough time to actually do research. Ideally, it should be something related to his field. He decided to consult Henry Mathauser.

Henry was the largest man Ethan had ever seen. Joe was a big man with a big stomach. Henry Mathauser made him look small.

Mathauser was tall—well over six and a half feet. He had big shoulders, giving him a sort of cantilevered grace. His head was broad, and his hair was thinning. He was a pale man, and his lips were blubberous and blue. Henry never went outside in the sun if it was in any way avoidable. He was always impeccably tailored in a three-piece suit, a silk shirt, and an artfully knotted tie. As an affectation, he carried a cane. The suits hid the fatty wrinkles of his body, but they could not hide his mass. Henry moved slowly. When he leaned against a doorway in conversation, the doorway creaked. When he walked gently across a wooden floor, it popped and rumbled.

Henry spoke the same way he moved, in a deep, rolling, ponderous voice that always reminded Ethan of the slow movement of thick, marshy rivers.

"Is a good idea," Henry said slowly. "I have just the thing."

Henry stood up and for a moment, Ethan had the same feeling he fancied a chipmunk might have standing under a falling tree. Henry retrieved a paper from the top of the bookcase and handed it over.

"Doctor Acante is putting together a group to go down to Colombia for the eclipse at the end of February. He asked me to recommend someone. I shall recommend you."

Ethan had been hoping for something in the nuclear lab, or that Henry would suggest a raise or a new grant. Still, as Ethan went over the paperwork later in the day, he consoled himself the eclipse trip wasn't a career job and it didn't pay that badly. Ethan's area of graduate studies wasn't directly related to an eclipse. Ethan was working deep in the wrinkles of the Standard Model relating to solid-state electronics, not in the industrial intricacies of solar plasma. Though, of course, as he reminded himself, this was physics after all: physics was everything, and everything connected to everything else.

"So, what will I do, then?" Ethan had said dryly as he delivered the papers to Jim Acante.

Jim handed him an information packet. "You'll do everything we need to have done but are too pretty or decadent to do ourselves." He waved his hand in the air of his office.

Jim gave the impression that he was thin simply because he was very tall and had little extra weight. He raced bicycles on the weekend and kept furiously in shape. His hair was red, spreading from his brows and his balding head like the spindly branches of a twisted tree, and he spoke with abrasive and deformed English accent deriving growing up in London, Toronto, and Edinburgh.

"Okay," Ethan said slowly. It was like having a conversation with an English Charlton Heston.

"Hey, it's a paying gig," Jim said. "We pay for your prep time up here and the time you're working down there We pay for the flight down there and back, and all the beer and burritos you can eat. That's not too much to ask, is it?"

Ethan realized, staring at the packet, that except for his father he didn't have to tell anybody he was going. He had few friends and no girlfriend. Since it was only for two weeks, there wasn't even enough time for his presence to be missed in classes or the lab. Just a brief blink in everyone else's life.

Have you seen Ethan? I needed some help in the particle lab.

No I haven't—oh, wait. Here he is. Did you step out?

"Ethan?" Jim looked at him. "Any problems?"

Ethan shook his head. "Not at all. What do I pack?"

Jim pointed to the information packet. "It's all in there. The exchange rate. The expected climate when we get there. The expected weather on Los Llanos. How to avoid being kidnapped when we get to Bogotá—"

"Kidnapped?"

"It's a sort of an unofficial foreign aid. Wealthy Americans are taken and held for ransom. The family or the government pays the kidnappers, and usually the victim is released unharmed. Happens all the time. Nothing to worry about. Sorenson over in Biology has been kidnapped three times. Sends them Christmas cards now."

Ethan looked at him. "Define wealthy."

"Any American who can afford to go down there is by definition wealthy." Jim spread his hands. "It's not my fault that this time the best eclipse viewing is in northern Colombia. Be glad it's up there instead of other parts of the country. The Colombian government has happily decided to give us some soldiers—a Colonel Haberman. I've worked with him before. He has relatives up this way. We have to pay for his soldiers, of course. We have some equipment to protect, after all."

"I see." Ethan wasn't sure he saw anything at all.

Jim drew back. "I suppose we could do better with more money. We do what we can with what we have. If we had a bigger department, we could afford more. I think of it more as a gift to the department for work over and above the call of duty, and you should, too."

"I didn't mean anything. I'm just trying to understand it. That's all."

"Oh. Well, all right, then. Good. Orientation is on Wednesday night at the Union. That's when we'll get everybody's jobs sorted out. We have to get everything organized. After all, we only have a little bit of time there to get everything done. Eclipses don't last very long." Jim leaned forward onto his desk and started looking at manuscripts.

"How long?"

"Eh?"

"How long does the eclipse last?"

Jim looked up at Ethan, his eyes framed by his red hair. Ethan thought of a curious monkey.

"Where we're going to be, it's going to last one minute and fifty-two seconds," Jim said and turned back to his manuscripts.

"As exact as that?"

"As exact as that."

oOo

Connie sat on the bar stool, nursing his beer. He checked his watch. Jake hadn't shown up yet. Connie was worried. He had two appointments today that could change everything. The first one was with Jake. Connie didn't know what Jake wanted but it couldn't be good. The other was this afternoon with Norman. All this today, less than a week after Sam had gotten the drop on him. If it wasn't one thing, it was another.

Connie was always worried, though. He knew that much about himself. That was what washed him out of sumo. He remembered the sensei shaking his head: "You have to let all of the worry go. Leave it outside the ring. Or your opponent will merely sit back and let you defeat yourself." Which is exactly what had happened.

The trick was to make sure what you were worrying about was the real thing. Now, Sam, *he* was the real thing. Life and death. Profit and loss. That was all real. He remembered his mother talking about Jesus: No man can serve two masters. Well, Connie was just going to have to learn to do it, anyway.

Jake came in and sat heavily next to him. Wordlessly, Brendan slid a beer next to him. Jake picked it up and took a long drink. He took the cold glass and pressed it against his forehead.

Connie swore to himself. This could not be good.

"We're going to have to shut down for a while."

"What?" Connie said, surprised. He brought his voice down. "Why?"

"Because somebody," Jake glared at him, "*somebody* has been letting the girls sell drugs in the rooms. We got a tip, and I had to check it out. Me." Jake pressed the beer against his forehead again. "And now I'm working in a team, so I can't hide it."

"Look," Connie started in a desperate, low voice. "We can move it to a new place. Out into the county, maybe."

"No." Jake sounded weary. "I got no influence in the county. I've only got a little juice in town. Everything depended on sleight of hand. If nobody was looking, then it took just a little misdirection to keep the operation going. But now, people are looking."

"But—"

"The DEA is involved now. We got the word yesterday. We are supposed to investigate the appearance of a new recreational drug 'with all deliberate speed.'" Jake shook his head. "We shut down for a year or so—"

"A *year?*"

Jake continued doggedly. "Do you think I'm happy about this? Jesus, Connie! The whole thing depended on keeping the drugs and the sex separate."

Connie stared at him. "A year."

"It'll be a year if we shut completely down and let somebody else get stung for it. You'll have to cut the girls off from their suppliers or cut them loose. Junkies are too big a risk, anyhow."

Connie suddenly realized Jake didn't know he was the girls' supplier. He kept his expression carefully neutral. "Somebody else is going to move in on this."

"That would be the best thing in the world for us," Jake said grimly. "It would give me somebody to hang."

Jake stood up and drained the last of the beer. "Don't let it be you, Connie. I can bust anyone that doesn't know me. I can't afford to bust you." He left the bar.

Well, Connie thought t. *That could have gone better.*

Connie drove down to the White Castle on Gravois. He took his time and thought while he ate. He still had to deal with Norman.

Norman was sitting on the porch, waiting for him. Connie eyed the plywood covered door wordlessly. Norman motioned him to sit down.

Connie looked around. Damulin and Talbot weren't anywhere to be seen. Connie was carrying a gun and two knives, and Norman hadn't even asked him to drop them. He slowly eased down next to Norman. Not so close Norman could knife him in the back but not so far away as to be rude.

Maybe now's the time to pop him, Connie thought. Kill Norman and all this became his. Then he glanced in Norman's eyes and saw Norman looking at him. It was like a light shining through him, all the way down into his shoes, and he dropped his eyes. Norman knew exactly what he was thinking. Norman had him covered some way—maybe it was Connie's time, after all. Maybe now Norman was going to pop *him.*

"Lighten up, Connie. It's not as bad as all that." Norman smiled. "I'm going to make things easier on you. Moving the drugs and the girls is way too much for one guy. So, you'll take the girls and I'll supply the girls—and anyone else—who wants Divinidine."

Connie nodded. He kept his hands out in front of him and away from his pockets. He kept his face expressionless as the bitterness washed over him. Fiske takes away the girls and now, Norman takes away the drugs. Sam was going to kill him. For a moment, it seemed the world was conspiring against him.

Opportunity, his dead mother seemed to whisper to him. Norman didn't know what Fiske had told him.

"No," Connie said softly.

"Come on, Connie," Norman said in a hard voice.

Connie looked up into his eyes, and Cold Norman was staring back at him. Keep it together, he told himself. "I think you should take both."

"Eh?"

"Think about it, Norman. If I take the girls, I'm supplying the spot for you to distribute. You can't distribute without me."

"That's a good thing."

Connie shook his head. "No. It's disaster. There is no way we can stay out of each other's way. The man who supplies the drugs has to be the one that supplies the girls. If you do one, you've got to do the other."

Norman took his arm back and leaned against the post of the porch. "And you're okay with me taking that away from you? You and Sam schemed to get it away from the Mexican, and now you're just *giving* it to me?"

Connie shook his head. "The best way is to trade it for something else."

Norman nodded slowly. "Sam's Alton operation is still open."

"I'd rather not. I don't know Alton. What I'd really like to do is develop the Mexican's river property. Maybe a casino or a shopping mall."

Norman considered for a moment. "It's still too soon for that. We're not well enough established to pay off a clear title. Besides, the big companies have that sewed up for the moment. I don't have enough connections in Jefferson City. Not yet." He seemed thoughtful. "But it's definitely fertile ground. Let's let it go for moment. Let's say I owe you at the moment for a player to be named later."

Connie nodded. "Okay. I still need a job to get by." He made a show looking around. "Where are Damulin and Talbot?"

"Damulin's running LeRoy around. Talbot is inside, watching us."

"I figured you'd have two here."

Norman shrugged. "When you're a parent you have to make sacrifices."

Perfect, Connie thought. "Sounds like you need a third man."

Norman watched him for a long minute. "Okay. The kid thinks you're all right. You watch him. He's got this girlfriend now and he's antsy. I don't need him fooling around the operation these days. It could get messy, and he wouldn't be that much good at it."

"Oh?"

"He's a little squeamish." Norman waved his hand. "He's young yet. He'll get over it."

Silence fell between. Connie knew Norman was going over the deal in his mind, looking for cracks.

"You know," Norman said coolly. "If anything happens to LeRoy, I'll kill you like a dog."

"Sure," Connie said. "But don't worry. I'll look after him as if he were the most important thing in the world."

Chapter 1.6: February, 1998

Ethan Cori stared out the window. Though it was said that all graduate students were created equal—that is, poor, impatient, and hungry—some were luckier than others. In the room of eight cubbies, his was the only one with a window. He stared out the window at the streetlights on Big Bend. He was a long way from Alton—a lot further than the forty minutes or so of driving it actually took to get there. He was deciding what to tell his father.

As long as Ethan could remember, Joe Cori had been preaching: to the church, to his wife, to his son, to the airwaves to the world. Ethan couldn't remember ever believing him. At first, when he was a kid, Ethan had thought his dad was the greatest dad in the world—every kid whose father didn't beat him, screw him, or come home drunk every night probably felt the same. It was in their genes. But believing all that stuff about Christ and salvation was itself an act of faith: he believed in his father and therefore believed what his father believed.

Edna Cori's death caused the first crack in the edifice. It was not sudden. It took six years from a failed mammogram to the grave. Ethan was ten when it started, and it was like watching his mother's life being torn from her in strips. First the little surgery. Then the mastectomy. Then the radiation and the chemotherapy. Then the hope they'd beaten it—the best six months of his short life. Then more chemo and more radiation until Edna was a stick figure lying in a hospital bed, her shape under the covers all wrong from the surgeries. Her skin yellow waxwork. Her eyes sunken and dark. Until one night, late in the evening when Ethan was sitting next to her in the ICU, her breath just stopped. Joe had already signed the Do Not Resuscitate order and had spoken to the nurses. There was no bright flashing blue light, no loud alarm. A faint tone sounded from the instrumentation next to the bed and after a moment, a nurse came in and turned it off. Sixteen-year-old Ethan didn't respond until Joe came in and took him home. That night, Ethan decided there was no God.

From then on, when Joe spoke of a man's duty to the Lord, Ethan went up and did his homework. Little by little, he could see that Edna's death haunted Joe just as much as it haunted Ethan. It showed up in Joe's sermons as they swung violently from the reddest meat of Hell and Damnation to a gentle pleading to come to the mercy of Jesus.

Joe had been preaching across the radio and in the mail for years, but a year after Edna's death, he bought a small television station. Ethan saw it all. Clear Channel had to give up a station for regulatory purposes and sold it to Joe with the expectation they could call the note any time. But Joe, contrary to anyone's expectations, had sewn up the evangelism market by the time Ethan was getting ready to go to college. People in the area were turning off Pat Robertson and Jimmy Swaggart, clear as cable wires could make them, to watch scratchy broadcasts from the fat preacher from Illinois. The note was paid off four years early.

Hell, Ethan had thought when he drove across the Alton Bridge college-bound to Saint Louis. *More power to him.*

Now, whenever he held the phone and listened to Joe on the other end, he could barely speak with the man.

It didn't take much for Ethan to wound Joe—Ethan watched it happen. He couldn't seem to help it. Joe had even quit mentioning the ministry around him. But Ethan would find a way to bring it up and then hang Joe for it. Ethan would immediately feel bad, then angry, and the cycle, like death and resurrection, would begin anew. Joe marrying Theresa had not improved things.

Ethan could sometimes tell when his father was about to call. The air took on a pinched quality, and the phone seemed to draw all light to itself. This night, when the phone rang, Ethan was not surprised.

"Evening, Dad," he said. "It's late."

"Is it?" Joe seemed distracted.

Ethan looked at his watch. "It's after midnight."

"Well, if you're in your office, you won't be asleep, right?"

Ethan nodded and smiled in spite of himself. "That's true."

"Look, I have a question for you."

Ethan stared at the phone for a moment. This was new. "What?"

"Can you have Saint Elmo's Fire indoors?"

"Saint Elmo's Fire? Is there a storm over there?"

"No. There's no storm. At least, I don't hear anything. Outside it looks pretty clear."

"Are you seeing Saint Elmo's Fire?"

There was a pause. "No," Joe said slowly. "I'm just asking."

"I see," said Ethan, seeing nothing at all. "Well, Saint Elmo's Fire happens when the electrical potential between some object is great enough there's a discharge into the atmosphere. So, it looks like sparks or a fiery jet. It's not enough current to do any harm. I suppose it could happen indoors. Did you buy a new Van de Graaff generator or something?"

"A what?"

"A static electricity generator."

"No. Nothing like that."

Ethan waited for a moment. He could hear Joe breathing on the other end of the line but Joe didn't speak.

"Corposant," Ethan said. "That's another word for it."

"Corposant," Joe said, mouthing the word for the sound of it. "Corpo santo. Corpus sanctum. The holy body. Saint Elmo is another name for Erasmus of Formiae. Erasmus was imprisoned by Diocletian, rescued by an angel, recaptured and disemboweled. After that he was considered one of the Fourteen Holy Helpers. Erasmus was in charge of abdominal problems and domestic animals. Saint Elmo's belt was a medieval torture instrument."

"That's... interesting, Dad."

"I wonder if He used Saint Elmo's Fire in the burning bush. Speaking to Moses with jets of fire —"

"Dad, is that the only reason you called?"

Joe didn't speak for a moment. "Are you coming home for Valentine's Day, son?" he asked hopefully.

Ethan had not been home for any holiday with a religious connotation for three years. The only neutral holidays left were Valentine's Day, Columbus Day, President's Day, Labor Day, and July Fourth.

"I'm not sure," Ethan said. "I might be going to South America."

"South America?"

"Yeah. Jim Acante is leading an eclipse team down to Colombia. He wants me to go with him."

"All right."

The defeat in his father's voice was too much to bear. Come on, he wanted to shout. Damn me to Hell! Quote me some scripture. Give me something to strike at.

Then it came to him with perfect clarity: he could just quit. Stop returning calls. Stop visiting. Joe would be better off — Ethan would stop attacking him. Ethan would be better off without this rage and guilt. After all, Joe had Theresa to take care of him.

"How about the weekend after?"

"No, Dad. I'll probably still be down there."

"I see."

Ethan could hear in Joe's voice that Joe had come to the same conclusion at the same time.

"Call me when you get back. Okay?"

"Okay." Ethan hung up. That was it. Now there was nothing but the silent empty office and the harsh light of the streetlights. He was alone.

He stood and locked the office. On his way to the orientation, he started whistling. *With luck,* thought Ethan, *with all the contacts I could make, I might not have to come back at all.*

oOo

The sound of the phone being replaced woke Tess up.

"Joe?" she asked sleepily.

Joe didn't respond immediately. That was enough to wake her up. Deep in the bottom of her mind, she understood Joe's age and size, though usually those didn't concern her.

Joe's left hand was still resting on the phone as he lay propped against the headboard of the bed. He held up his right hand, moving it this way and that. A flame danced over his fingers.

Tess saw the flame and was out of the bed like a shot for the bathroom. A towel to put it out. Cold water to cool the wound.

"It's okay, Tess," Joe said quietly.

Tess stopped at the edge of the bed. She turned around.

"Just look at it," Joe said.

The flames coated his hand, tongues coming up through the gaps between his fingers and jetting from the tips.

"Joe?" Tess said cautiously as she came back across the bed. "What's going on?"

"My hand is burning," Joe said, glancing up at her with a smile. "Yet it is not consumed." He turned his hand over, and the flame spread from his palm and surrounded his fingers. Joe turned his hand again with the palm up, this time waved his fingers slowly, as if playing the piano or drumming them against a table. The fire danced from finger to finger, concentrating into a single flame. Joe spread his hand, and the fire spread with it.

"What is it?" she asked.

Joe pinched his fingers together, and the flames united into a single fire, glowing silently in the darkness. "It's a miracle," he said, then corrected himself. "No. It's not a miracle. It's the harbinger, the presentiment, the premonition of a miracle. It's the vision made to the prophet so that the true miracle will not catch him unawares." He looked up in her face. "Touch it."

"I'm a little scared."

"Don't be." He took her hand and guided it gently. When it was close enough, he cupped his hand and tilted it, and the fire cascaded from his hand into hers.

Tess yelped at the sudden warmth, but it grew no hotter than that. She poured it from one hand to another, turning her finger in it until it was a small whirlpool of flame. "How did this happen?"

"I woke up in the night." He sat closer to her so he could see the flames licking across her hands, up her arms. "It just seemed too big. Everything that's being asked of us. With the show in trouble and the money not coming in, I thought we were failing. So, I prayed. And while I was praying, the fire came from between my hands."

Tess nodded. "But you're saying this isn't a miracle? Isn't this miracle enough?"

Joe shook his head. "The light and color are all wrong. It will never show on television—nothing is real that can't be shown on television."

They fell silent. Tess poured the flame from one hand to another. "Then what will we do with this?"

Joe shook his head. "I don't know."

Tess did. "Open your mouth."

Joe stared at her for a moment, then did so.

Tess raised her cupped hands over him and gently poured the flame down his throat. Joe swallowed it down.

"Now it's inside you."

Joe whistled. "Whiskey was never so good."

Tess smiled at him.

Joe took her hands. "You're going to Colombia."

His hands were warm. "Beg pardon?"

"I called Ethan to ask him about Saint Elmo's Fire. He told me he was going to Colombia to study an eclipse. You're going down there, too."

Tess pulled her hands away. "But you're *here*."

"He works in mysterious ways. I was led to call my son—my son, the unbeliever. If ever there was a desire in my heart, it is to save him. My son told me he was going to watch an eclipse, and it came to me I will never be able to save him. You can lead a man to gospel, but you can't make him believe. But you can show him a miracle. We can show them all a miracle. Something exciting. Something we can show on television." He took her. "And it will happen in Colombia. Take a camera crew with you."

Tess watched the flames dance in his eyes. "What will the miracle be?" she asked, accepting that she would be the one to go. Trust the path, she told herself.

Joe squeezed them. "I don't know," he said humbly. "But you will. Both you and Ethan will be witnesses."

oOo

It didn't take long for Connie to have a take on how to handle LeRoy. Connie only had only to remember how it felt to be released from prison.

It wasn't a big crime—he'd held up a liquor store in Iowa City after he'd left sumo. He'd been caught in Ottumwa—which, said his lawyer, had been a good thing since he'd been caught before he'd taken the stolen car across the state line into Illinois. Federal courts were much harder on any kind of offender.

Since Connie had used no weapon in the robbery—his very size and manner had intimidated the clerk into giving him the money—and the car hadn't been worth very much, he'd been given five-to-ten in the Iowa State Prison in Fort Madison. Four years later, he'd gotten out on parole. Two days after that, he'd broken parole and moved to Saint Louis to work as muscle for the Mexican. He'd been nineteen.

Now he was thirty-two, but he remembered that heady mixture of excitement and fear that stepped outside right alongside of him, the stretched and painful grin as he breathed outside the barbed wire. The air tasted different.

LeRoy sat across the Formica table with the same grin.

LeRoy liked to watch people. Norman's goons had never had the time to just take LeRoy anywhere. Unless he'd planned and schemed far in advance— such as his date with Cindy—LeRoy stayed at home. The first week Connie took over the job, LeRoy had shyly asked to be taken where there were people. Connie had obliged. Union Station. Soulard. The Science Museum.

Then Connie had taken LeRoy to that strange and wonderful collection of objects found all over Saint Louis and brought together through Bob Cassily's unique alchemy to become the City Museum. LeRoy wouldn't enter the tiny spaces—the Tunnel of Sticks and the Caves—which made Connie just as glad, as those cramped spots were utterly beyond Connie's reach. He could no more fit into the Tunnel of Sticks than he could walk on water.

But Connie nursed a beer in the café and watched as LeRoy walked inside the giant concrete whale and found the grottoes where mosaics shone. At least, he did until LeRoy returned and dragged him to watch the carp play in the underground pond.

Afterward, the two of them went to the Steak 'n Shake for dinner. LeRoy ate absently. Instead, he watched everyone in the place as if he were ready to devour them.

Connie watched, too, but with different purpose. LeRoy's indiscriminate staring had rubbed a couple of men with dates the wrong way. Once or twice, Connie saw a young high schooler, perhaps the linebacker of a local football team, start to get up and come over. But then Connie would catch his eye, and the linebacker would think better of it.

Let him watch, thought Connie. *There's no harm. Besides, I get a kick out of watching him.*

At that point, Connie realized he was becoming personally involved.

Shit. Connie sighed, remembering Cindy. *You're getting soft.*

"Do you know what girls are thinking?" LeRoy looked at him.

Connie grinned. "You know what I used to do."

LeRoy nodded. "I know."

"Do you think I would have managed without knowing something about girls?"

"That's not what I asked." LeRoy leaned forward on the table. "I know this girl."

"Cindy. I know her."

LeRoy bit his lip and looked away. "I know you know her."

From the way he said it, Connie knew he wasn't talking about a mere verbal acquaintance. "All right. What do you mean?"

LeRoy thought for a moment. "I guess I want to know what she thinks of me. What she thinks of... well, everything. Mostly what she thinks of me. But what does she think about Steak 'n Shake? The City Museum? Baseball?"

Connie laughed. "You'd have to ask her, wouldn't you?"

"She says she wants to be friends."

Connie signaled the waitress and ordered another Coke. After she left, he said, "You know, that's the nice thing about buying a woman. You never hear words like that. By the time the transaction is conducted, the shape of the situation is fixed. And there's no way she'll ever say something as stupid as that to you."

"You're suggesting I buy her? I really like her, Connie. I can't just buy her."

Connie shrugged. "It'd be simpler if you could. But she's off the market. I knew one guy, Paco, that worshipped this girl, Libby. I mean, he really, really liked her. Paco followed Libby around for years. She wanted to be friends, too. Then one day lightning struck and they slept together, fell in love, moved in together, got married. Two years later, when I saw them again, Paco and Libby were in the middle of the nastiest, most vicious divorce I've ever seen. And I've seen plenty. On the other hand, I grew up with this kid Mike. The story was nearly the same—followed Sandra around for years. Helped her through a couple of breakups and a rough divorce—not in Paco and Libby's class but rough just the same. He's resigned by this time. He's not interested in anybody else, but he's given up hoping there will ever be anything between him and Sandra. Then lightning strikes. They get married and they've been married for ten years."

"What's all that supposed to mean?"

Connie shrugged. "I don't know. Just saying anything can happen. Time and circumstance. Lightning can strike out of a clear blue sky."

"You're not much help."

The waitress brought Connie's Coke. He thanked her. He leaned on the table so they were close. The table creaked from his weight.

"Look, kid. I know nothing from love. You want to negotiate a transaction? I know how to do that. You want to figure out how to get laid? With some girls, I can help you there. Different girls have different hot buttons. But if you really like a girl? Love her? I got nothing. Never happened to me."

"Never?"

Connie shook his head. "Not a tremor. I've met girls I liked. I lived with this nurse in Omaha about six years back. She was fun and nice in the sack. She broke up with me for some engineer at the base there. I was pissed at her some—mainly that she'd choose someone like that over me. But it didn't break me up or anything."

Silence fell between them. Connie leaned back and watched LeRoy, waiting for him to mull things over.

"Still," he said slowly. "I may not know how to get you past the friendship stage with Cindy. But I do know how to impress a girl."

LeRoy looked intrigued. "How?"

"Girls like to say how they like who a man is, rather than what he does. But girls are split. On the one hand, they like how a guy makes them feel—if he brings her roses. If he goes down on her. If he doesn't think she's fat. On the other hand, a girl has to look out for herself. They have to know what the guy can do for them. There are a lot of nice, caring guys that got dumped for some rich asshole."

"Okay," said LeRoy dubiously.

"Cindy knows you're a good guy—"

"She does?" LeRoy asked with a smile.

Connie waved it aside. "Don't be a dick. Of course, she knows you're a good guy."

"Even when I called her a bitch?"

Connie stared at him.

LeRoy looked embarrassed. "I didn't mean it. Norman always said you had to be hard when people came in—"

"I remember. She still went out with you, right?"

LeRoy nodded.

"Maybe you have a chance, after all. Impressing her might be a good thing after all." Connie made a show of thinking. "I do know of an opportunity. Sort of a start-your-own-business kind of opportunity."

"I'm listening."

"I just found out about another market for Divinidine. One Norman doesn't know about. One that doesn't even compete with him. We could exploit it."

LeRoy stared at him. "Do you know what Norman does to people who go behind his back?"

"He wouldn't do anything to *you*. You're family. The most he'd get pissed about is that he didn't find it out himself."

"That might be enough."

"Norman only gets pissed about trouble and money. In this case, there's no trouble and the money stays in the family."

"So, what did you have in mind?"

"We need a new lab. Old Bill can barely keep up with Norman's demands. You start the lab."

"A lab?"

LeRoy's face took on a guarded expression. Connie knew he was hooked. "No. *Your* lab."

"I'd have complete control?"

"Hardly. We have to keep it secret. But we can work together to keep it as much yours as possible. We just need ten thousand units of Divinidine a month."

"That's a lot of pills."

"It's not a small business. I think Cindy will be impressed."

LeRoy reached his hand across. "I'll do it."

Connie stared at the hand for a moment before taking it. They shook, and he pulled his hand back. He looked at LeRoy. My God, LeRoy believed in it, all of the "Word is Bond" and "handshake contract" crap. He deserved to get double-crossed.

Why did the idea bother him so much?

oOo

Shopping at Union Station was Portia's idea. Cindy had a completely different feeling about the place. Not only was it where she and Portia had been caught by Jake, it was also the site of the hotel where she had spent the most time over the summer. But these days Portia seemed as fragile as finely drawn wire. Besides, Portia was driving.

Portia had also toned down the god-talk, which was just fine by Cindy. Some days Cindy almost forgot about it and they were just two girls in high school.

Portia stopped at the paddle boat pond. The shed was open on one side, and the water was frozen on the far end. It was cold, and Cindy drew her coat closer around her.

Portia leaned on the railing. Cindy leaned next to her. The water had a pale blue color to it not found in nature. The bottom was barely visible through the thin water. Cindy wondered how the far end had ice. There had to be chemicals in the water.

"There ought to be fish," Portia said idly.

Cindy didn't say anything. Something about a sheltered paddle boat pond in a mall had always bothered her in some deep and obscure way. It was no more strange, she supposed, than any other tool to bring in shoppers. No stranger than the fake Eiffel tower or Venice canals in Las Vegas. But you sort of expected that kind of extravagance from a casino. Or Disneyworld, for that matter. Here, it just seemed pathetic. Cindy sniffed. The February air was sharp, even here under the shed. They'd probably drain the pond soon. Freezing couldn't be a good thing.

Portia leaned her head on the railing. "Man, I'm tired." She smiled as she said it.

Something in that smile disturbed Cindy. Portia had the look of a well fed, satisfied cat. "How come?"

"They've been working me hard." She raised her head and grinned wickedly at Cindy. "Not that I'm complaining."

"'Working you hard'?"

"The group. My... church, I suppose."

"Who's that?"

"I can't tell you. The people that gave me Divinidine. I met them through Donnie—the night of the party."

"Donnie's disappeared."

"I'm sure he is doing the right thing. After all, he's one of us."

"Who is 'us?'"

"I said I can't tell you. You know that. Unless you're saved, they are a secret. I'm only mentioning them at all because you're my friend. You need to be saved, like everybody else."

A cold ball of ice formed in the pit of Cindy's stomach. For the life of her, she couldn't figure out why she should be surprised. Deep inside, she'd hoped Jake had stopped them. Shut them down. Then Portia's fantasies would be no more than a leftover infatuation. "How does it work?"

Portia stretched her back out, holding onto the rail, looking more like a cat than ever. "I get a call from—I get a call and meet a prospective convert."

"Where?"

"Wherever. A hotel room. Obviously, they come for sex. But first we share the Divinidine. Like communion. This is my body, this is my blood. Man, church was never like this when I was a kid. After that, sex becomes, like, this sacred act. It makes sense, though." Portia leaned towards Cindy earnestly. "Joining with God should feel good, right?"

"Sure." Cindy felt heavy and sick inside. Nothing had changed. They were probably still using the same network of hotels. Cindy could probably guess which ones—Connie had taken her to a lot of hotels.

"You ought to come with me," Portia said slowly. "I mean, you probably think it's all sordid and lame. But it's not. I mean, if it were just going to a hotel to fuck, then it would be. But once you feel God move inside you—once you see with His eyes, feel Him in your skin and your mind—it's not sordid at all. It feels like something you've been looking for your whole life."

Cindy looked in Portia's eyes. It wasn't like there was some other person looking back. It was Portia. The closest friend, funniest person, brightest personality she had ever met. But now that humor, that intelligence, that wit, served something else. Served *someone* else. And everything Cindy liked, admired—even loved—about Portia was twisted around that service.

I'll save you, Cindy said to herself. If ever there was anyone that deserved saving, it's you.

oOo

Following Jim's instructive little booklet, Ethan was able to pull together everything he needed to by Tuesday. With only a few misgivings and a determined denial of the possibility of being kidnapped, he showed up at the airport. Jim was waiting for him.

"Excellent," Jim said in an abstracted voice. "Glad you're here. You've been instantly drafted to manage this camera." He handed Ethan a padded case that must have weight forty pounds. "From now until I ask it back of you—in deepest, darkest Colombia—it is your sole reason for being. If something happens to it, the best you can hope for is to get kidnapped before I find out. Your ticket is in the envelope taped to the side. Wait here and we'll all go through security together. You! Over there! Harriet! Glad you're here."

Jim walked over to a slight girl with carrot red hair. She gave Jim a look that said she'd had enough, as clearly as if she'd shouted it from the baggage terminal.

Ethan sat on the bench, holding the camera as gently as a newborn. Without thinking about it, he watched Harriet and Jim argue with one another. They were too far away to understand, but the cadence and rhythm of their words had a practiced quality. Clearly, they had known each other for a while. Idly, Ethan wondered if they were seeing one another. For that matter, if Harriet were seeing anybody at all. Her hair was short and nearly orange. It seemed to vibrate against her lime green T-shirt. The color combination had to be deliberate and Ethan found himself wondering what sort of person would make herself into such a beacon.

She caught him watching and smiled at him, nodded towards Jim, and shrugged elaborately. Ethan burst out laughing and had to turn away as Jim looked up at the noise. Ethan grinned. Maybe his life wasn't quite as isolated as he'd thought.

Somebody touched him on the shoulder. Ethan looked up, half hoping to see Harriet.

Instead, Joe looked down at him.

"Hey, son," Joe said quietly.

Startled, Ethan coughed once before speaking. "Here, Dad. Sit down."

Joe nodded and sat down. The bench creaked under his weight.

"Phil told me when your flight was."

"Yeah. Well—"

"I wish you would have told me yourself."

Ethan started to protest, but Joe waved him silent.

"We didn't part so well last time we talked, did we?" Joe chuckled.

Ethan put the camera down on the bench. "No."

Silence fell between them for a moment.

"'Hate sin and love the sinner.' I guess it's not surprising for a son to have secrets from his father. Or to have contempt for his father's work."

"Dad—"

Joe waved him silent again. "That's too strong. It came from hurt, and it shouldn't have. There's nothing in this world that can make you believe what I believe. That's between you and God."

Ethan shook his head. "I don't believe in God, Dad."

Joe nodded slowly. "I know that. I was always taught that the cost of thinking that way was, at best, eternal torment. 'The wages of sin is death.' You have to understand that's what drives me crazy when we talk." Joe turned towards Ethan. He leaned forward. "If someone you loved was stuck in a burning building and you could pull them out, you'd do it, right?"

Ethan nodded miserably. Just the conversation he never wanted to have with his father.

"That's what I'm doing. I'm trying to pull you out of a burning building."

"I know." Ethan touched his father gently on the arm. "But if somebody comes into your house and says the building is burning and there is no smoke, no fire, and everything looks normal… well, it's hard to take them seriously."

"We're talking about everlasting life, here."

Ethan shrugged. "People die, Dad. Buildings fall down."

Joe stared at him. "And the Will of God?"

"People do the best they can. In the absence of evidence, no God seems more plausible than any God."

Joe smiled at him. "'Absence of evidence is not evidence of absence.'"

Ethan smiled back. "'In a set of hypotheses, the simplest one is most likely to be closest to correct.'"

Joe nodded. "People need a miracle to believe, don't they, son?"

Ethan thought for a moment. "Maybe. But I don't think there is any such thing as a miracle—that is, something that happens outside of physics. A supernatural event. But," he said judiciously, "we don't know all the physics."

Silence fell between them again, but this time it was more of a companionable absence of conversation rather than a desperate avoidance.

"I didn't come here to argue religion," Joe said after a while. "But it is what we do, isn't it?"

Ethan laughed shortly. "Yes."

Joe stood up. Ethan stood hastily.

"I'm here to see you off. You go down there and measure the sun and the moon. That's a good thing and I'm proud of you for it." He grabbed Ethan and hugged him.

Surprised, Ethan hugged back.

Joe held him away and scrutinized his face. "You look much more like your mother than you do me. I loved her and I love you. You do understand that, right?"

Confused, Ethan nodded.

Joe released him. "Maybe we all need a miracle in our lives. Something to blow away the secrets." He shook Ethan's hand. "You have a good trip. Send me a postcard, and call me when you get back. I'll try not to preach at you."

With that, Joe turned and walked across the linoleum, and out of the concourse. Ethan stared after him, bewildered. *All right,* he thought. *Who are you and what did you do with my father?*

Jim called out to him. "Time to get going."

Jim led them all through customs. Ethan and Harriet glanced at one another a few times, but after his conversation with Joe, Ethan felt too shy just yet to talk to her. He was both relieved and saddened that they weren't sitting next to one another.

Ethan had the aisle seat on the plane. A few minutes after he had stowed the camera and sat down, a youngish woman asked him if she could reach her seat.

She thanked him graciously and sat in the window seat.

Ethan watched her a moment. Something bothered him about her. She had a fine look to her features. Her hair was short and expertly coiffed. She looked elegant somehow. Poised. Self-assured. He looked at her hand. Engaged, too. It took Ethan several minutes to realize she wasn't much older than he was.

She turned away from the window and smiled at him. "Excuse me, would you like the window seat?"

Ethan's face went red, and he stammered in embarrassment. "No. Of course not. I was just—I thought maybe I knew you."

She shook her head slightly. "I doubt it. I would remember you."

Ethan took a deep breath. "Ethan Cori." He put out his hand.

She took it. "Tess," she said. "Tess Durbin."

oOo

Bill stood in front of the closet in his office as he waited for the Anapyridol to take effect. He admired the collection of jars, each filled with ten thousand pills of Anapyridol. The right drawer of his desk held the pills he shared with the FDA. The left drawer, the pills he gave to Cindy. The rest, the vast bulk of Anapyridol, was here in this closet. Ten thousand pills per jar, ten jars per shelf, eight shelves. Between this closet and his left drawer, nearly a million pills. This was the Queen's work.

He closed the closet doors and returned to his desk. Over the last months, the landscape of the drug had revealed itself. A session began with a set of sensations as gentle as if his body were stretched over the surface of a soap bubble. These built up and then burst and faded away, leaving the first sense of euphoria tinged with a small anxiety. Then, and only then, and the most welcome moment, came the sense of something uncoiling in the back of his mind, the feeling of eyes other than his own looking outside through him. That was when he could sense the Queen.

But lately, when the body sensations faded and the adrenalin euphoria dimmed into post-drug fatigue, the feeling of the Queen's presence lingered. Sometimes, during the day, he found himself confused who was actually discussing the intricacies of contract formulation or the sales figures of generic shampoo. Was it Bill speaking or was it Her?

The confusion disappeared when he spoke with Anya, or when he touched her or slept with her. During the day, he found himself looking for work that brought the two of them in contact. Anya didn't seem to welcome these connections. Perhaps they had plateaued a little bit in their relationship. Like an old couple, each required their bubble of space.

Bill felt the familiar weight of his clothes become intolerable. He checked the time. It was late enough. He took off his shirt and started taking off his pants.

"We haven't even said hello," said Anya behind him.

He closed the closet door and turned. His pants were still around his ankles, and he stumbled and caught himself against the edge of the desk.

"I didn't expect—I thought you'd gone home," he said.

Anya smiled at him. "I don't believe you." She walked towards him. "Surely, you're taking those off for me."

Before he could stop her, she stepped around him and opened the closet.

Bill pulled up his pants and buttoned them. He drew on his shirt and waited.

"This explains a lot," she said, her voice no longer seductive.

"Anya—"

"I couldn't figure it out," she continued, staring into the closet. "I was just too close to it." She closed the door, turned and leaned against it. "Jake brought home some Anapyridol in an evidence bag."

"Evidence bag?" Bill shook his head. It seemed the world was humming around him.

"They were part of a bust," she said. "Ten years of our work. Twenty years of my career. And you're selling it on the street? Who the bloody hell do you think you are?"

Bill backed away from her. She followed him, looking as dangerous as a wolverine.

"This is everything I've ever done, you *mu'dak!* You *derr`mo!* Oh, *eto piz`dets.* This is my life's work!"

"You don't understand."

"I understand you're going to jail for this. I understand I was a fool not to figure this out in the beginning."

"Look, let me explain."

He didn't expect her to stop. There were patterns in the air now, bars and stripes of different colors. The excitement of Anya's anger had brought them out. Her voice seemed to be echoing.

But she stopped and sat down, crossed her arms. "All right. Explain."

He licked his lips. "I need a drink. Do you want a drink?"

Anya buried her face in her hands. "Sure. Why not? Why the hell not?"

He had to make her understand. "Let me lock the closet."

Anya didn't answer. Bill palmed some pills as he pulled the key out of the drawer. He locked the closet and then went to the cabinet. He'd always kept a little bar in the room as a throwback to the old days when many offices had such bars. He looked into his hand. Ten pills. He dropped all of them into the blender as he made a margarita. For a moment he thought the blender was going to fly through the roof. Then he realized it was the Anapyridol messing up his senses.

Anya looked up. "I thought you were just going to make me a whiskey and orange juice or something."

Bill tried to sound gallant. "This seems too important for a screwdriver. Though I did use orange juice."

He poured it for both of them.

Anya sipped hers quietly. She didn't seem so angry now. She drank half of it before she looked up at him. "Bill, we've got to stop this. Who are you selling to?"

Bill shrugged. "I have a contact. He buys all of the Anapyridol I can give him."

"Who would want it?"

Anyone who's tried it, he wanted to say. Instead, he spread his hands. "Apparently, it's quite attractive to some people."

Anya shook her head. "Bill," she said finally. "I actually like you. Somebody's got to blow the whistle on this, and it's got to be me. You understand that, don't you? If it's not me, the FDA will think I had something to do with it."

"I'm listening." Bill watched the clock. Seven-thirty. She's probably not eaten dinner—Anya rarely did while she was at work—so her stomach was empty. The alcohol might bring a little more into solution faster than usual. Say, twenty minutes before the Anapyridol gets into her bloodstream and she starts to feel it. It's a pretty big dose, so thirty minutes before she can see the Queen.

"But I don't want you to go to jail." She half smiled at him. "You said you had some real estate in Mexico, didn't you?"

"Ecuador," he said. "I could move to Ecuador. It's a wonderful country. You'd think it would be hot, being on the equator, but up in the highlands it's nicer than Saint Louis." He dreamily listened to the drone of his own voice. The Queen was watching now. Bill must be worthy of her. "The house is in Baños. Jungle five thousand feet down and Mount Tungurahua ten thousand feet higher. You could come with me."

Bill saw her think about that, discard it, hide her decision from her face. "I suppose I could, later. After things quieted down. I could meet you there."

He wasn't lying. It really was beautiful down there. The earth was raw and sharp. No glacier had ever flattened down the hills. Only volcanoes, wind, and water.

Bill sighed. "How would I turn myself in? I don't want to go to jail."

"I don't want you to go to jail, Bill."

She smiled sunnily at him, but he could see the smile didn't reach her eyes. Bill smiled sadly back. So small you are, he thought through the haze of colors. It seemed as if time moved slowly. He could count each tick of the second hand, wait a lifetime, count the next one.

"This is good," she said and the words echoed around the room. She drained the glass, and Bill could hear the icicles clink against one another like broken glass chimes.

He leaned back. The weight of his clothes was oppressive. He wanted to remove them but didn't. Not unless he was touching her. He wanted to touch her again. One last time? Would it be one last time?

"Bill?" The sound was as slow and thick as taffy. "Are you okay?"

Suddenly Anya was very close, looking down at him. He smiled up at her.

Ten pills, he thought. *Ten pills.* A therapeutic dose was one pill. He usually took six. Ten wasn't even close to the lethal dose. But stronger than he'd ever tried.

Anya slapped him and spoke his name. But Bill barely felt it. He didn't think he could stand, but he didn't need to. He'd be able to see his Queen easily. She was all around him.

"Bill," she cried out. "What did you do? Did you take the Anapyridol? Why?"

Bill didn't listen. He thought the room might be too small for Her. She was no longer content to just watch from the back of his mind.

Anya started hitting him with her fist. Over and over again. "You son-of-a-bitch!" she cried. "What have you done to me?"

Bill looked past her. The room began to roar.

The Queen was coming.

oOo

Jake felt like the old radio DJ slogan: "The hits just keep on coming".

In a way, the DEA starting the operation was a relief. There were always three phases to a DEA project. First was organization. The team had to be put together. Then strategy, then execution. Jake made sure he and Orphira were both on the team. Orphira was still naïve within the department. He couldn't pull the wool over her eyes, but he could still use a little sleight of hand to keep himself protected. It gave him time to shut down Connie. God, he hoped Connie would stay shut down. Jake would hate to have to shoot him.

Not that he would hesitate. When it came to keeping the lid on things, Connie was expendable. But he didn't want it to come to that. Killing people was just bad business. It brought the attention of the department down on him. If things calmed down, he might be able to start up the shop again. If that happened, he'd need somebody like Connie to front for him. A big 'if' all the way around.

The DEA agent in charge was an emotionless prick named Frank Bujold, twenty years younger than Jake. Jake had always thought Bujold knew more about Saint Louis than he let on. He wondered if Bujold knew anything about Jake's shop. Jake had reasoned that if he shut his own operation down, any busts would not point to him.

But the hits kept on coming.

The next tip came from a call referral service. This one was for the Airport Hilton room. Again, the pattern: a young call girl with a wealthy county boy. The drug was the same.

Bujold immediately incorporated the tips into the strategy. They got a court order to crack the referral service, and it turned out to be a pay telephone in Plaza Frontenac. No lead there.

They didn't press too hard on the informant, whoever it was, since the source might dry up.

By the airport bust, Jake realized something was wrong. Like the first one, the girl was polite and the boy scared. Both were cooperative. But what Jake had assumed was just normal toughness, was something different. This time he brought both of them in. Toni and Lawrence. Both were respectful—hell, Toni was more respectful than Cindy was.

Jake couldn't figure it out.

With the first two busts, they had two call girls, two clients, and handful of this drug. Jake bought a little time with Bujold by feeding him Orphira's data. He brought Orphira in and had her present it to the team. Orphira looked suddenly shy when he told her.

"You do it," she asked him. "You're the senior. They'll listen to you."

Jake shook his head. "Don't worry about it. Look, don't talk to them. I'll sit in the front row. You talk to me. Tell me what's going on." That seemed to make her feel better.

It was just a ploy to him. A bone thrown to the dogs until he could figure out what was going on. Who was the tip? Two in a row now. Both of them places he had set up years ago—who could know these places? Connie, for sure. Norman, maybe. The Mexican, absolutely. Connie and Norman wouldn't inform on themselves, and the Mexican was dead. The informant—stop. The person on the phone was reciting information. They had no idea if the tip was fronting for someone else. The tip was a young girl. An ex-call girl?

A ploy. But on the day Orphira carefully marshaled up her facts and one by one put up her ideas and conclusion, she stared at him as if no one else in the room existed. He looked back and saw, for the first time, that her dark face was round, with a faint point to her chin. Her eyes were big, and it made her face small—the word petite came into his mind. Her voice was low but strong, with a faint burr within that made Jake think about that summer down in Mississippi when he was a kid spreading asphalt in a chain gang. Jake had been caught drunk driving on a high school road trip that ended in a cell. Sixty days sweating on the gang, surrounded by that thick Mississippi drawl. The black prisoners and the white prisoners didn't mingle. The drawl from the whites sounded harsh, bitter, like men sharing a nasty joke.

The blacks had a softer, kinder sound to them. They were no less hard than the whites—everyone had to be a pit bull in that jail—but the sound of them was as smooth as deep water. Laughter and curses burst out of the voices of the whites like fetid explosions. But when he listened to the blacks from his bunk, laughter, anger, and sobs all seemed to blend together.

Jake knew even then, and had relearned since, that there was little difference between a murderous white man and a murderous black man. The world was huge and impenetrable, confusing, and complex beyond belief, and he was always going to be seeing the worst side of it as long as he was a cop. This tiny gift he brought back from Mississippi—the memory of the voices, the sound of the late night music—stayed with him and leavened his days until he came to think that any world with black people in it couldn't be all bad.

And now, as Orphira spoke, he remembered fully that sound and how he had felt in the hot stifling night, envying them, wishing he was of some other color, something different from what he was. A wordless longing after that sound, a music that seemed to come from them so naturally.

When she finished, he almost applauded.

Bujold saw none of it.

"Good work," he said, and started assigned an agent to start checking out the biotech and pharmaceutical companies in the area.

Orphira smiled at Jake when she joined him. "Did I mess myself up?"

Jake shook his head abruptly. "Not at all."

oOo

The snake uncoiled within her. It slid slowly and languorously around her until its flat angular head lay before her. Then it raised itself and stared Anya straight in the face.

"I see you." it hissed. Its baleful gaze fell upon her and burned.

"Purest dross," it said in Russian. "I could burn down you where you stood and there would be nothing left worth saving."

Anya fell to her knees. She tried to crawl away, to escape that awful scrutiny.

It said, "I'm watching you."

It came closer. She could feel the slither of its tongue across her back. In desperation she swung at it. Her fist connected with something meaty. Still, it hissed close to her. She kicked it. Beat it with her fists. Jumped up and down on it. Still, it stared at her and its gaze shone through her like the pitiless sun.

Nothing stopped it. She turned and ran and was suddenly outside. The snake was nowhere to be seen, but she could feel its gaze and scrutiny follow her.

It was freezing. Anya shivered. She couldn't really see very well. The world was made up solely of colors and textures. Nothing had substance or outline. And the world was watching her. The lights were the eyes of the snake. The earth its gaze. The air its scrutiny.

"Anya?" called a voice.

It was a void that called her. She turned to it. The void spoke to her. She welcomed it. The void was devoid of gaze. It was the only thing not watching her.

The void pulled her to one side and stabbed her arm. She cried out as cold fire crawled up her arm. She fought, but the void held her.

"No more of that. You've done enough damage for one night."

Her world and sight contracted until she was no more than a pinprick, small, hot, and raging.

She must have slept. All in a moment, she opened her eyes, fully awake. Anya was in an unidentifiable room—perhaps a bland hotel room or nameless apartment. Its only certainty was its unfamiliarity. The snake was gone, but Anya could still feel it lurking behind her eyes and under her skin.

"Ah. You are awake."

She turned and saw Kalenin cooking at a small stove built into the side of the wall. She sat up and found she was covered with a blanket.

Kalenin nodded and turned back to the stove. "I was getting the tiniest bit worried. I could have knocked out a horse with the Valium it took to make you sleep." He decanted the pot of soup into a cup and brought it to her.

"A little bit of home."

It was no more than chicken soup from the can, but Kalenin had added a little garlic and some pepper, a little dill, and for a moment Anya remembered living in a concrete block Moscow apartment with her moment. They were not pleasant memories. Anya was always cold, and the apartment was damp. But for reasons she didn't understand, her eyes filled with tears as she sipped the soup.

"Thank you," she said.

Kalenin gave her a tissue. "It's the Valium. It makes the heart tender."

Anya shook her head and dried her eyes. She sipped the soup. It was quite good.

Kalenin watched her for a few minutes. "So that was Anapyridol," he said at last.

"That was an Anapyridol overdose," she said bitterly. "Administered by a son-of-a-bitch."

"Bill Wallace?"

Anya nodded.

"Ah." Kalenin stood up and took the pot to the sink. He filled it and left it to soak. "You confronted him, I take it."

Anya nodded. "It was in the margarita. Citric acid neutralized the taste— we found that out initially in the toxicity trials. Orange juice would cover the taste in pill form." She pulled the blanket around her shoulders. "Where did you find me?

"Outside Lifeworks. I've been following you."

"You?"

Kalenin shrugged. "By proxy. I've had you followed. I was called when you started to wander down Manchester. So I picked you up. You were incoherent. I knocked you out and brought you here."

Anya stared into her cup. For a moment, she felt the snake moving inside her, a heavy, slithering parasite. She shuddered.

"After-effects?" Kalenin asked.

"Some," she admitted. "In higher doses, Anapyridol acts distinctly different."

"You didn't act very socially aligned when I found you."

"Drugs often have different effects at different doses."

Kalenin leaned forward. "You've been unconscious for a day and a half. I would expect any metabolites to be flushed out by now. At least, that's according to the specifications you submitted to the FDA."

"Exactly. It's a... psychological response."

"Really," Kalenin said dryly. "Like psychological addiction."

"Something like that." She ran through the metabolic pathway in her mind. Anapyridol in the bloodstream was broken down fairly quickly. The effect was produced by the small amount that actually bound to the receptors. No Anapyridol could be measured after twenty hours, even in the large dosage animal studies. Perhaps she was feeling the effects of a metabolic by-product. After more than twenty-four hours—

Anya started to stand. "Jake will be worried—"

Kalenin eased her back to the sofa. "It's okay. I called your husband."

"Oh, you did?" Anya looked at him skeptically. "And what did you say?"

Kalenin stared back blandly. "I said you had to go on another trip to Chicago to see Fred Hibbert regarding a licensing opportunity with Pfizer."

"He bought that?"

"Well." Kalenin looked pleased with himself. "He thought I was Mister Wallace on the phone. I can do a good imitation."

"What about Bill? He's bound to call home—"

Kalenin snorted. "That's not likely."

"Why?"

Kalenin smiled at her. "He's still in the hospital. You beat him senseless."

oOo

Connie didn't take his phone calls, so Jake had Brendan call him if he showed up at Mississippi's. Then he waited. He knew Connie could be spending a lot of time at the houseboat, but Jake didn't want to talk to him there. Too much chance of somebody getting pissed off. One or both of them could end up swimming with the catfish. No, it was better to wait and catch him on neutral territory.

After a week of checking in and around the airport hotels, another tip came in. This time at the Chase Park Plaza, where he and the Mexican had set up a spot to handle the sophisticated businessmen turned suddenly desperate tourist husbands. Bujold almost cracked a smile. Jake felt as if a rope were sliding around his neck. What the hell was going on?

Brendan sent him a message, and Jake managed to break away from Orphira to run an errand. He started to fly down Market Street until he thought better of it. If someone was setting him up, he might be followed. Even so, he stepped into Mississippi's only twenty minutes after Brendan had called him.

Connie was inside, eating a rib dinner with a kid. They were deep in conversation. Jake went around the back and got Brendan's attention. He waited with his hand on his gun until Connie came out. It had rained the day before, and then the temperature dropped. The divots in the ground were filled with ice.

Connie saw that when he came out and slowed down, his face suddenly blank.

"Close enough," Jake said, eyeing the size of Connie's arms.

"What's up, Jake? We're not partners anymore. You know that."

"Just checking on why the fuck I'm getting tips on every hole-in-the-wall we ever set up." Jake pulled out his gun but kept it pointed at the ground.

Connie held up his hands. "I don't know what you're talking about."

"Two tips. One at the Hyatt at Union Station."

"I know about that. That's why we quit."

"Another tip at the Airport Sheraton. Know anything about that?"

Connie shook his head slowly. "I'm out of the business. Norman pushed me out the same day you and I talked about quitting. I figured you were in on it. There was no way I was going to cross you and Norman. I'm not stupid."

"Norman?" Jake wanted to just shoot him. "Norman's running the girls?"

"I don't know if he is or not. He just pushed me out. You'd have to ask him."

"Do you know where the pills are coming from?"

Connie didn't speak for a moment. "I can't say anything, Jake. You know that."

Jake pointed the pistol at him. "Hell of a thing to die for."

"I tell you anything I'm a dead man, anyway. I'm out of the business, Jake. Out. My job is minding the kid in there."

"Who is it?"

"Norman's nephew, LeRoy. I got nothing to do with the girls."

Jake didn't say anything.

Connie bit his lip. Jake could tell he was trying to figure out if he could take out the gun before Jake shot him. "Jake, you said it was over. I believed you. We got us a little history here. Things might get better and we can set it up again. Don't fuck it up now."

Jake shook his head and lowered the pistol.

Connie straightened his jacket, looking cautiously relieved. "Norman doesn't tell me anything. He doesn't mention the girls. He doesn't mention any drugs. He might be fronting the stuff to them or not. I don't know."

Jake nodded. He looked away for a moment, and the gun was ripped out of his hand. Connie took him by the throat and slammed him against the dumpster. Jake tried to cry out but couldn't get it past Connie's hand.

"Hush," said Connie, and let him go.

Jake choked for a moment. When he could breathe, he leaned against the wall.

"Jake," Connie said companionably. "We weren't partners, but we had a business relationship. So I will help you."

"You know who the tip is?"

"No. What does she sound like?"

Jake shrugged. "Young girl. Knows all the spots so far. You lose any of them?"

Connie shook his head. "Not before Norman took over. Anything could have happened since then."

Connie handed him back the gun. "You need to be more careful with this."

The right thing to do right then was to slam that two-pound hunk of metal across Connie's face. No one should ever lay hands on a cop. This had been drummed into Jake's ears from his first day in the academy. From his first day as a rookie. They are out to get you. The only way to keep a wild animal under control is through fear. Intimidation. When someone touched you, they crossed the line. They had to pay.

On the other hand, Connie could probably break him in half with one hand. Intimidation had to take second place to survival. Jake looked Connie in the eyes. Connie wasn't scared of him. Connie would never be scared of him. Jake didn't know Connie well, but he knew how fear worked. You didn't make fear; you brought it out. If it wasn't there, all you would do is confirm that you were dangerous and couldn't be trusted. The risk of not trying, though, was appearing weak.

So: destroy any future relationship, or appear weak and possibly be manipulated. Choose.

All of this took place during the second or two between the time he locked eyes with Connie and when he pointedly holstered his gun. Connie was still worth working with. Jake knew Connie could see exactly the same train of thought.

"You hear anything, you let me know." Jake stuck out his hand.

"I will," said Connie and shook it.

Jake nodded. He knew that translated to: I'll let you know if I can tell you anything without harm to myself. Not quite as good as, I'll tell you anything I can because I'm more scared of you than anything else. But he would never have gotten that anyway. If he had tried, it would have been, I'll agree to anything now until I have a chance to get rid of you. Jake didn't need someone else to keep an eye on.

As he drove away, he realized things were different now. Whatever he and Connie did from now on would resonate back to this day. Great, he sighed. The hits just keep on coming,

oOo

Anya watched Bill through the doorway. He looked helpless in the hospital bed. His face was swollen. Both eyes were padded. One arm was splinted and held on the side of the bed. There was a mask over his face, but the ventilator was not on. It made her feel small to see it next to the bed. Bits of dried blood and splashes of betadine marked areas of his face and arm where she could see stitches. The room was dark and smelled musty.

There was a woman sitting in his room.

Anya eased in. "How is he?"

The woman sat up. Her face looked pale and drawn as someone who has repeatedly cried and washed her face to make sure it didn't show. She looked at the bed. "His brain is swollen. That's all I know."

"I'm Anya Fiske. I work for him."

"Kathleen Morris." They shook hands. "I've known Bill for years. He didn't have any family, so he gave me power of attorney a few years ago."

"How—" Anya stopped. "How did it happen?"

"No one knows. He was found in the Lifeworks parking lot just like this." She waved towards Bill. "He hasn't woken up. The doctor says he has some kind of brain trauma—a little coma, I suppose. They expect him to wake up when the swelling goes down."

"Ah." Anya had a little time before he woke up. She wasn't sure what she was doing here. She was still a little woozy from the Anapyridol—for a moment, Bill looked up at her with the head of a snake. She shook her head, and he was Bill again, breathing shallowly.

Kathleen took her shoulder. "Are you all right?"

"I'm okay," Anya said unsteadily. "We missed him at work. I came as soon as I could. It's a shock, isn't it?"

"It is." Kathleen nodded and turned back to the bed. "You just can't be safe anywhere these days."

"Yes." Anya backed out of the room. "Call me at Lifeworks if you hear anything."

"I will."

"I see you."

Anya jumped and turned around. It was a doctor with Bill's chart.

"Can I help you?"

"No. No, thank you." Anya would have given her shares in Lifeworks for a look at the chart, but instead she slid sideways along the wall.

Down the stairs, past the chapel, into the late fall day. She leaned against her car.

"I see you."

Anya looked around wildly, but there was no one there. She could feel it moving around inside of her.

Home, then. Home, where she snapped at Cindy, drank herself nearly senseless, and sexually assaulted Jake as soon as he came in the door. Then tried to sleep.

Life, she thought as she felt Jake start to snore next to her, *is complicated.*

Anya could feel its eyes upon her.

She sat up quickly. Jack started to wake, but she stayed still and he fell back asleep.

Anya made her way downstairs. She found her purse and pulled out Kalenin's note. After a moment's ringing, she heard a familiar voice.

"Yes," asked Kalenin. "How can I help you, Gamova?"

Kalenin didn't ask any questions. He picked her up down the street in a dark BMW and rolled up on Highway 40 without a word.

"Where are we going?"

"I have no idea, Gamova," he said pleasantly. "But I like driving west. I like driving over the big river and looking down at the water. Driving a car like this—" he patted the steering wheel. "—is reward enough, eh? But you tell me where to go."

"I don't care."

"West is good enough, then."

She stared out the window a long time. "I need help," she said finally.

"With what?"

"The Anapyridol has done something to me. It's not wearing off."

"It is fat-soluble. Perhaps you stored some and it just keeps dribbling out. Women have more such places than many men."

"This is different."

"How so? What are your symptoms?"

She told him.

Highway 40 descended into the Missouri River flood plain. Kalenin guided the BMW off the exit and onto the back roads as he listened.

"Perhaps you need an anti-Anapyridol. Can there be such a thing?"

Anya thought about it. She understood the binding site. She understood its metabolic action. She wasn't certain of the actual neurologic mechanism that was triggered by Anapyridol in the cingulate gyrus, but perhaps it was similar to endorphins. The binding site for endorphins was the same for the morphine compounds; blocking one often blocked the other. Maybe Anapyridol operated the same way.

She buried her face in her hands. It watched her. It was always watching her. "It would take years to get through just the animal studies. Bill's not going to fund it. Not after what I did to him."

"What he did to you," Kalenin said mildly. "Remember that, Gamova. He assaulted you with a drug."

"It doesn't matter. It would still take years."

"You must think outside of the box, Gamova." Kalenin turned off onto a narrow paved road. "Would we have let something this stop us when we were at VECTOR?"

"America is different."

"Not so much."

Kalenin pulled up in front of an old factory building. He stopped, and the two of them got out of the car. The ice crackled beneath her shoes. Anya could hear the river in the darkness.

"This is another venture I've been pursuing." Kalenin gestured at the building. "It looks abandoned on the outside. Inside, I've been rebuilding it— by proxy. I can put you in contact with a talented young man. Someone close to your own caliber. Someone with whom you can work."

"What about Bill?" Kalenin never promised what he couldn't deliver. The old factory had a magnetic hold on her gaze. Her own lab. "And money?"

"Do not worry about Bill," said Kalenin. "He will have enough trouble enough just healing for a while. I can persuade him not to bother you. A little settlement such as continuing to pay your salary should be enough to buy his silence. You will get your fair share. You can be assured of that. But what is money compared to this, Gamova? No more bottle washing and product development for you. Here you can do science as *we* used to do science."

She smiled at him. "All right."

I see you came from the darkness.

Not forever, she answered. *Not for long.*

oOo

Bill didn't remember waking. At some point while he was feeling miserable and full of pain, he realized he had been asleep. Part of him thought that was odd since he didn't remember falling asleep. For that matter, he didn't remember much of anything at all.

He started to open his eyes, but they seemed stuck. He shook his head, but that didn't do anything. Bill tried to rub his eyes, but his arm felt tied down.

Okay. Eyes stuck. In pain. Arm tied down. Bill had heard it was always bad idea to panic, but now seemed as good a time as any.

"Calm down. It's okay."

Hibbert's voice brought him the final step awake. Anya, he remembered. Something had happened when the Anapyridol had taken effect. He started to ask about her but stopped. He would need a story for Hibbert first.

"I can't see," Bill said. He was appalled how weak his voice sounded.

"Let's try to fix that. Keep your eyes closed for the moment."

Bill felt a moist cloth rub against his eyelids so gently it almost made him weep. *What has happened to me?*

"That should do it. Try now."

Everything was blurry. He blinked the mucous out. Hibbert was standing with a towel.

"One last bit." Hibbert dabbed Bill's eyes, and everything swam into focus. "Better?"

"Yeah." Bill looked around. He was in a hospital room. That much was obvious, as all hospital rooms look essentially identical. By that same token, he had no idea which hospital he was in. He looked down at his body. His right arm was strapped to the bed. A cast covered it from his elbow to his fingers. His neck felt stiff. He tried his left hand—it was free. He felt the contours of a neck brace. His lips and face felt swollen. Moved his hand up and felt bandages on his head.

"What happened?"

"Good question. You were found unconscious in the parking lot outside of Lifeworks. Your wrist is broken. Your face is pummeled. You have three broken ribs and a concussion. You look like somebody beat the crap out of you until you fell down, and then kept kicking you until they got tired. What happened, Bill?"

Bill tried to shrug. Shooting pains across his shoulders and back made him think better of it. "I don't remember."

"What's the last thing you do remember?"

Waiting for the Queen to come to me and Anya. Probably not the best thing to bring up. "Working. In my office. Could I have fallen down the stairs?"

"Likely not. The police checked."

"The police?"

"You were unconscious. A crime could have been committed. Wouldn't want to be uncertain about a thing like that, would we?"

Bill tried to think, but he felt drugged. Probably was, too, he thought. "How long was I out?"

"It's been four days since you were found. That Kathryn woman has been a fixture here. She's asleep down the hall. They wouldn't let her sleep in here."

Kathryn? "Kathleen."

"Exactly. Since she has power of attorney under these circumstances, she called me. Which is why I'm here managing Lifeworks instead of you. Soon enough, I expect, we'll figure out why you're here and not working your fingers to the bone so that I can effortlessly make a great deal more money. You don't think I invested in Lifeworks to *work*, did you? I'll go get her."

Hibbert turned to leave. He stopped and turned back. "Oh, by the way. Kathleen said Doctor Fiske dropped by while you were unconscious. She sends her best, I'm sure. But she asked for a leave of absence from the company. I checked and it doesn't look like she is indispensable right now, since the organization of the clinical trials is done but no data will be coming in for some time. So I told her to go ahead. Is that all right?"

Bill's mouth was dry. "Sure," he croaked.

"Good. I'll get Kathleen."

Bill barely heard the door close. Anya must have done this to him. And now she was gone. It rang in his mind like a great, tolling bell.

Anya was gone.

oOo

Jake thought about Norman over the weekend. There was no reason for Connie to lie to him—at least, no more than the obvious reasons. The downside of lying at this point was that Jake would have to go after him. As long as Connie was telling the truth, there was no reason for Jake to put him in a pine box.

Besides, Norman being in charge made a lot of sense. The only thing that kept the whole call girl operation intact was its invisibility. As soon as drugs entered the picture, that was compromised. It wasn't surprising, then, that Connie had been muscled out.

Jake considered the downside of going after Norman. Connie worked for Norman. That meant that it was possible Connie had passed on Jake's name to Norman. On the other hand, Jake hadn't seen cash nor phone call since he'd told Connie to give it up. That either meant that Norman didn't think it was worthwhile to pay Jake (a mistake) or he didn't know what payoffs were involved. Jake knew of Cold Norman—everybody knew of Cold Norman— even without the Connie connection. Unless Connie told him, Norman could not know he was involved with the girls.

There had been three tips in all. Each of them had pointed to a room Jake and the Mexican had set up for the call girl network. Going after Norman meant blowing the network apart. If he were ever going to set it up again, he'd have to start from scratch. Okay. Jake had a fair wad saved already. Part of being a good gambler was knowing when to leave the table. This might be as good a time as any.

But it would be tricky. Jake would have to expand what the tips should have said. How was he going to do that unless he got more tips? Not to mention the fact that Bujold wouldn't let the tips continue for long without investigating the source. Jake could run down the source before Bujold brought it up. If he could — the source seemed pretty smart so far to use a calling service.

Another alternative was to milk it out of anybody they'd arrested so far. Jake knew enough to how to ask the right questions and get the right answers. Here was where Donnie would have been really useful.

Except that the girls and their clients weren't exactly helpful. There were six of them. Portia, Cindy's friend, had been bailed out early and put on probation. Such was the power of money. She was pretty much off limits unless he struck out everywhere else.

That left the remaining five. From Mike Danforth, Portia's companion, to Kim Donovan, caught at the Sheraton Airport with a john named Art Wendell. They had been unfailingly polite, pleasant to talk to, and each, in the most apologetic way, had refused to give him anything to go on. The basic and most fundamental duty of a pimp was to keep his girls out of jail. The women just waited patiently. They almost looked chaste sitting there.

The men were just as bad. They were less talkative than the women but just as pleasant.

And they tried to convert him.

The women tried it with a coy look and a flirtatious smile just as they started to mention Jesus. The men were more direct and started by asking how he felt about his job. By the time he'd interviewed the first three, he was betting with himself if he'd get through all five without being handed a tract. Jake remembered kids handing out tracts on the corner when he was barely more than a kid himself. "God loves you and has a wonderful plan for your life!" that came out of one. The Four God Laws? The Four Spiritual Laws? The Law of Four? Something like that.

Maybe the women were trying to emulate Mary Magdalene or something.

Regardless, they weren't helpful. They didn't scare, and they didn't bluff. That left either faking a tip or doing some fake investigative work leading where he wanted to go.

Faking a tip was dangerous. Especially with Orphira around. But faking an investigation might work. Maybe he could even point Orphira in the right direction and she'd do the actual leg work. We can start with the two we found at the Airport Sheraton: Kim Donovan and her friend, Art Wendell.

oOo

Orphira wrote down the manager's name. "How was the room paid for?"

The manager was a small, dark man who had been born in Calcutta and retained the fluting accent. To Orphira, it sounded as if he were singing as he spoke.

"The reservation was made always by fax. Then the young man paid."

Orphira wrote that down. She had the manager print out the room reservation records for the last week. That was as far back as the reservation system data was kept locally. There were backups, but they were shipped to the home office. The faxes themselves had been tossed. She called back to the office and gave Bujold's assistant the times and the fax number.

That left the other assignment Jake had given her. Three hotels had been used: Union Station Hyatt, Chase Park Plaza, and the Airport Hyatt. First, she'd asked around the other airport hotels to see if there was a similar pattern, a particular room reserved by fax. Nothing.

Okay, then. As Jake pointed out, all of these hotels were of the same class. Whoever was behind this was going after the high-income set. There were a limited number of these hotels in Saint Louis. Orphira would have to check each one for the same pattern.

Jackpot came on the third try at Union Station. This time, the reservation was for tonight. She even had the fax. She whistled all the way back to the office.

Jake was talking to someone when she got in.

"Good news and bad news," he said when she sat down.

"Good news first."

"The reservations in question all came from the same cell phone until a couple of months ago. Now they're coming from a new cell phone."

Orphira studied Jake's face. He grinned back at her. "And the bad news?"

"Both cell phones are hacked. So, we just know they were in downtown Saint Louis when the calls were made. We don't know who made them."

Orphira mulled that over. "What happened a couple of months ago?"

Jake shrugged. "Maybe he changed long-distance carriers. You got anything?"

Orphira pushed the fax over to him. "Tonight. Room 528."

Jake looked at the fax sheet. "Let's talk to them when they come in."

They were waiting in the lobby of the Union Hyatt when a young couple walked in. The manager gave them the signal, and Orphira took a different elevator up to the fifth floor. Down the hall and a knock on the door.

A craggy young man answered the door.

"Yeah?"

Jake and Orphira flashed their badges.

"So what?" The man looked at them.

"What's your name, sir?"

"Tony Mayerville. Captain of the *Bryant*."

"The *Bryant*?"

"Barge tug. I'm here picking up load to take north."

"We'd like to talk to you about your companion."

Tony looked from Orphira to Jake. "Pull the other one. You're busting me for trying to buy a piece of ass?"

"Yeah," said Jake. "Let us in."

"Fuck you until I see a warrant."

Jake sighed. "I don't need one asshole. This isn't your home. The manager gives permission. Not you."

"Fuck you, anyway."

Orphira moved to one side so if she had to bring out her gun, Jake wouldn't be in the way.

"Let them in, honey." A woman's voice from inside.

"Shit," said Jake wearily.

Tony sighed and opened the door. "I don't know what the fuss is about. I didn't buy a Goddamn thing. I just met Linda here in the bar—"

"Linda?" Jake said as they came in. "She calls herself Linda now?"

Orphira could see past the two of them inside the hotel room. Portia was standing up next to the bed. Orphira could see how a man might mistake her for a grown woman—men are blinded by small things.

"See? No prostitution here. Just a friendly evening together."

"Right." Jake gave Tony a sour look. "So, you know she's seventeen?"

"What?" Tony blanched.

"Who made the reservation?" Jake said.

Portia said nothing.

"She did," Tony babbled. "Nothing happened. I mean, I just kissed her—"

"Quiet, Tony." Portia smiled at them both. "He's telling the truth. Nothing happened. Not that it wouldn't have. But you interrupted us."

"Yeah. Check her purse, Orphira."

Orphira opened it up and sure enough, there was the vial of pink pills. "Got 'em."

"Get lost, Tony," said Jake.

Tony didn't say a word. He grabbed his jacket and left at as close to a run as his dignity would allow.

Jake turned to Portia. "So, you made the reservation?"

Portia smiled at him. She sat down, prim and proper, on the edge of the bed. She said nothing.

"Like I figured. Grab your coat. We'll wait outside." Jake nodded to Orphira.

"She's a friend of Cindy's," Jake said in a low voice outside the room. "We got her before. We interrogated her before. I don't think she's going to change her story now. She doesn't care. We've got to find someone who gives a shit."

"You want to take her back to her parents?" Orphira set her mouth.

"Only if you're okay with it."

"Her brother disappeared."

"But she *didn't*, and she's got even more reason to run. I don't think we're going to get anything going until we can get at the guy sending the faxes."

Orphira thought for a minute. "Okay. What do you want to do?"

"The same thing. Let's hit them where they live. If we keep the pressure on, eventually we'll get something. Maybe they'll want to make a deal with us. Maybe they won't use a hacked phone. Maybe Bujold will figure out how to de-hack the phone they're using."

"Okay."

Jack opened the hotel door again. "Why don't you go in there and hurry her up?"

Orphira nodded. In the doorway, Jake stopped her.

"By the way, good work. Your dad would be proud."

Warmed clear through, Orphira entered the hotel room.

oOo

Norman's first inclination was to kill him. He stared out the kitchen window and sipped his beer as he contemplated surprising Jake Fiske in front of the Tivoli, knocking him down, pinning him to the ground, Norman's hand at his throat, shoving a 9mm in his mount, grinning once into his frightened eyes, and blowing off the back of his head.

Norman sighed. As pleasant as it was to think about, there were always problems killing cops. Norman was against it generally if there wasn't any other way. Maybe he could whack Cindy and dump her in the river. That might take the heart out of Fiske. But what would that mean to Damulin and Talbot? It was just as bad for business to kill your employees as it was to kill a cop. Much as he would have preferred to forget it, Cindy was his employee for the moment. If he offed Cindy, he'd have to find another avenue to get the pills.

Of course, with Bill in the hospital, the source might dry up completely. Then Cindy would be free range.

Norman stood up and paced around the table. Then he walked into the front room and sat, staring at his paintings. There was a solution here, but he wasn't seeing it. Something that would satisfy both his need for revenge and respect, and would get Fiske off his back.

He wondered how Connie had managed it. Three girls and three clients busted in just a month. The first thing he had done was to send Damulin to bail out the clients and get the charges dropped. But the clients had *refused!* Damulin had dropped them for the moment and tried to at least get the girls out of jail. But the girls acted the same way.

Norman had stared at the phone when Damulin told him. What the hell were they thinking?

Maybe killing Fiske was the right idea after all.

The more he thought about it, the less sense the crackdown made. Everybody knew vice was just another word for drugs. Nobody took prostitution seriously unless it was right there in the open.

Okay, Norman thought. *Let's think about it from another angle. Sometimes the solution to a problem is to redefine things so the problem goes away.*

He had a stable of girls. He had a collection of places those girls could take clients. Fiske was busting girls at those locations. Fiske was finding out where they were—how? Why?

Norman sat up. Joe was buying a lot of drugs. Fiske was busting girls— vice was drugs, remember that. Fiske wasn't busting the girls; he was busting drugs. Joe must be supplying the girls with Divinidine. The girls who had stayed in jail were Joe's girls. That's why they were acting all righteous.

But that didn't make sense unless Joe was setting up the clients, too. Norman thought about it. All of the clients were young men. Good recruitment material?

Norman shook his head. It didn't hold up. If Fiske had been after the drugs, Norman would have expected him to lean much harder on the girls to get things ready for the DEA.

Norman felt cold. Maybe the DEA was already involved. They liked running everything as if it were just normal police operations until they were ready. Then bang! You weren't worth much more than a glob of spit between a hammer and an anvil.

Shit! Connie must have figured this out. That was why he gave it up so easily.

Maybe he'd kill Connie. That would at least make him feel better.

Norman shook his head. He couldn't indulge himself. He had responsibilities. He had to do something.

Then, like the breaking of a summer morning, he saw it. Joe is giving the girls Divinidine. He's getting the clients. *But* Norman controlled the drug supply, so he controlled Joe. Norman had control of both ends. He didn't need a place. Any place would do. He could just rent a house, charge a fee for the room and the Divinidine, and rake in the money. Screw Fiske. The whole operation could just disappear.

Unless Fiske had an informer inside.

Norman shrugged. If Joe's girls and clients were willing to stay in jail, they must not be too inclined to be bought. Norman could just let Joe decide which girls went with which boy. The informer either showed up—at which point Norman would show him a new way to swim—or the Fiske's source dried up.

Norman turned it in his mind to see all the angles. It was a beautiful thing.

Of course, he still needed some satisfaction.

That came to him, too. He picked up his cell. It didn't take long to find Jake Fiske's number.

Fiske's voice mail picked up.

"Detective Fiske," said Norman sweetly. "We've never met. But you might want to know what your little girl did over the summer."

oOo

The house was dark from the outside when Cindy got home from school.

This wasn't that unusual, she told herself. After all, she was fifteen and both her parents worked. It was four thirty in the afternoon. Still plenty of light outside.

But Dad's car was in the driveway. Cindy hesitated and stood under the oak in the front yard. The air was cold. February smelled of ice. She felt hidden and safe in the oak's shadow.

She tried to reassure herself. After all, things had been going well for a while. Portia hadn't been called up for a couple of weeks—she'd been bitching about it at lunch every day. Cindy was starting to have a little hope she'd derailed the operation. School had become easier. She didn't feel eyes following her when she walked down the hall. When the teachers called her name, Cindy, there was no strange pause following it that said so clearly, *the slut*. The confidence she'd gained over the summer seemed to be paying off.

Reassured, she walked up the steps and unlocked the door. She stood in the dark doorway, listening. The house was silent.

She stepped slowly inside. "Hello? Mom? Dad?"

Cindy thought she heard something from the front room. The scrape of a chair maybe, or a soft exhalation of breath.

She stood in the hallway. What if there was a break in? What if Dad were lying in the front room, paralyzed and crippled from a blow to the head, bleeding all over the floor?

The living room was darkly shadowed from the tree outside. In the gloom, she thought she could see the figure of a sitting man, light from the single one or two rays of sunlight that had made the exhausting journey through the oak, the grimy window and the curtain.

"Dad?"

The figure moved, seemed to turn away a moment, leaned on his arms, and stood. Jake's face broke through the tiny beam, suddenly illuminated separately from the darkness, a disembodied, unshaven face looking at her.

At that moment, it was as if the barriers came down between them and an electric arc of telepathy crackled through the darkness from Jake to Cindy.

"Oh, God," Cindy moaned. Jake knew. She could see it in his face. The illusion he'd kept of his baby girl running away over the summer had been boiled away by the acid truth. She looked away up and down the hall, different words stammering through her head—"It wasn't like that." "It's a lie." "I'm sorry."—but they bled away before that floating, anguished, disembodied face. There was nothing she could do. There would always rise up between them the fact of what she had done and how he felt about it. They would build walls between them. She could see him grow older right in front of her, grow doddering and distant. He was broken. He was shattered. She could almost hear her mother shrug: *You do what you do. What is left is what is left.* The thought was intolerable.

Wordless, she went to him and eased him back into the chair. He looked up at her, mute.

"It's all right," she murmured and gently pulled against him until, like softening wax, he bent his head on her shoulder. Gradually, she could feel his neck and back ease against her.

"I'm here, Daddy," she crooned to him as if he were a child. "I'm here."

oOo

Ethan and Tess talked all the way down to Miami. She was a video producer doing a documentary about the ruins in the altiplano, the same area Ethan was going to observe the eclipse. He was pleased—it would be nice to have somebody there from America. Someone he could speak English with, at least. But Ethan couldn't help wishing that Harriet was sitting next to him instead of Tess. Tess struck him as somewhat conservative, almost matronly, with her hair done up and her respectable dress. She was wearing pearls, for God's sake. Harriet looked like someone who could shake him up. Shaking was something he could use right about now.

He had resigned himself to anonymity after they changed planes in Miami and he found himself sitting next to a man who sold pizza ovens. After an hour of being told how Bogotá was a brand new and untapped market, Ethan ordered two whiskey sours, swallowed them whole, then leaned back to wait for the alcohol to reach his brain. Just as it hit, and he started to feel his eyes cross, he looked up and saw Harriet watching him from the front of the plane. Then he fell asleep.

Harriet was nowhere to be seen when he left the plane in Bogota. Dumbly, he and the other twenty or so people followed Jim through the terminal to the bus outside. The bus stopped him for a moment as he walked gingerly past the statue of the Virgin Mary decorated with ancient Christmas bulbs. He had a headache.

Bogotá smelled.

The odor strong was but unidentifiable. He thought it was raw sewage but after a moment, he realized it actually didn't smell bad, just completely unfamiliar. Then, after twenty minutes or so on the bus, he realized he'd actually smelled it before even if he didn't recognize it. An hour after that, the odor dimmed and began to smell appetizing. It was the smell of cooking oil, cilantro, and beans, writ large across the atmosphere by thousands of hot iron stoves.

Welcome to Colombia, he thought. *When can I get something to eat?*

The bus stopped at what looked like a military depot. They all piled out and stood gaping at a line of six aging and decrepit Jeeps. Jim stood in front of them and called out each name, standing next to a soldier who calmly stared out over them as if nothing of this chaos had anything to him.

"Oh, yes," Jim said at last. "This is Colonel Haberman. He's in charge of all of the soldiers, so don't go to him with any problems. Come to me, and I'll go to him with any problems. Welcome to Colombia."

Harriet came up behind him and grabbed his arm, dragging him to the third one in the line. With rapid-fire Spanish, she sent the driver away and sat behind the wheel.

"Put your stuff in the back seat and get in. You look like the best company in the whole lot." She grinned at him.

Oh, God, he thought. *I'm in trouble. She's got a Texas accent and red hair. I'm lost.*

The six Jeeps roared out of Bogotá and up into the altiplano.

The schedule was impossible, of course. They had two days to get to the site, set up, and be ready for a solar eclipse on the twenty-sixth, and it was already the twenty-second. There was no reserve at all and there would be, Harriet assured him, some sort of cock up. It was in the cards.

Ethan nodded wordlessly and watched the road. Calling this a road was being generous. It was a wide trail that barely fit two donkeys going in opposite directions. Donkeys, Ethan noticed, were considerably smaller in Colombia than they were in Missouri. The rain didn't help the road conditions.

They didn't stop driving that night until two in the morning. At which point, Ethan discovered he was sharing a tent with Harriet. This was less important than it otherwise might have been, since she laid out her sleeping bag and fell asleep immediately. Ethan barely had time to notice before he fell asleep in the adjacent sleeping bag. It seemed as if he had just blinked and it was six the next morning, when they started driving again. He stared out the windshield morosely and noticed the trail had shrunk.

They made it to the observation area the evening of the twelfth, just as the rain stopped. By midnight, after six hours of setting up, they were ready for the next day.

"Don't worry," Harriet told him. "Jim's things are always like this. I think he enjoys the pace."

"It's all right." Ethan was covered in mud. It had rained on the way up here, and the Jeeps had no fenders.

"Go take a shower," advised Harriet.

"Shower?"

"We set them up a couple of hours ago. You didn't hear?"

"I'm surprised. I figured I would have heard running water from five miles away."

Harriet giggled. "Go on." She leaned over and kissed him. "Hurry back. You might be able to take advantage of me. After all, I'm on the rebound."

"You are?"

"Go. Shower. You stink."

Jim was standing under the hot water and letting it roar over him.

"Where's the water coming from?" asked Ethan as he started carving the mud off.

"Lake up the hill," sputtered Jim. "Propane heaters. Love working with the military."

Ethan couldn't argue.

"So, who is this Harriet woman?" he asked, trying to be subtle.

"Graduate student in archeology. Works down here on Inca digs when she can. Guides and translates when she can't. We're lucky to have her. Wasn't sure she'd come."

"Oh?"

"Terrific girl. Smarter than I am." Jim stared at him morosely. "You're sharing her tent, I believe."

"It wasn't my idea."

"I'm sure of that." Jim buried his head under the water.

"She said she was on the rebound."

Jim chuckled. "Welcome to Colombia."

Harriet was snoring lightly when he returned. He crawled into the sleeping bag beside her, disappointed and relieved at the same time.

She reached over and snuggled up next to him, and fell back asleep. She was wearing only light pajamas.

Ethan stared at the ceiling of the tent, wondering how he was going to get to sleep now.

oOo

LeRoy watched the road stretch in the headlights, a tunnel in the cold rain. The wet asphalt road ended at the gate. The parking lot on the other side was nothing more than a wide expanse of gravel, lit by a single mercury-vapor lamp. The harsh light etched everything into a hard-edged gray scale. LeRoy watched as Connie got out of the car and in the glare of the headlights fumbled with the lock. It was raining in the gloom, and he couldn't see more than the outline of the ruined factory.

Connie pushed the gate open and got back in the car. LeRoy could hear the slosh of water in the gravel as the Crown Victoria left the solidity of the road for the more ambiguous viscosity of the parking lot. The head lights picked out the front of the building.

"Walnut bowls." said Connie suddenly.

"Beg pardon?"

"That's what this place started out as. A little knick-knack factory. Chinese killed that. Then a brewery. Anheuser-Busch killed that—they don't like competition. Then, some guys from down in the boot heel bought it. Brought up chicken manure from Arkansas to turn it into fertilizer. EPA nailed that on account it's so close to the river. Even made them clean it up. Nobody's wanted it for years, and it's on my property. Now it's ours."

"All those failures don't do much to instill confidence."

Connie chuckled. "Exactly what we want. Nothing creates anonymity like continuous failure."

The factory showed its true size inside. The lights hanging high from the roof only limned the bulky shadows of the broken fermentation and reactor vats.

LeRoy tried to see it as a working factory. It was hard. "This is a lot of equipment. More than we need." LeRoy drew one hand along a table. "And it's filthy."

Connie shrugged, unconcerned. "We'll use what we need. Clean what we have to. Once in Kansas City, I ran a meth lab in the back of a kosher butcher shop. We had to keep the meth off the meat or we couldn't sell it. Kosher rules."

LeRoy stared at Connie. "Who would have known?"

Connie looked offended. "I would have. A man has to take pride in his work."

LeRoy let it go. Everybody seemed to be proud of different things. Norman had his paintings. Connie had his meth lab. For his part, LeRoy was proud of just staying alive. You have to keep your priorities straight.

The rain drummed on the roof. Over it, LeRoy heard the grumbling swish of a second car coming into the parking lot outside. Alarmed, LeRoy looked at Connie.

Connie didn't seem surprised.

"You're expecting someone?" It came to LeRoy that he could be good hostage material. LeRoy wondered what Norman would do. He couldn't imagine Norman would allow himself to be controlled, even if it cost him his nephew.

Without being obvious, LeRoy looked for escape routes. He didn't know this part of the county but the river was somewhere near here. If he could get that far. If he could keep from getting shot long enough to reach it.

"You worry too much," Connie said easily. "I'm expecting our partners."

"Partners?"

"Going to take money and labor to set this up, and we can't go to Norman for either. So, we need partners."

The car outside stopped, and LeRoy could hear the doors open and shut. Maybe he could make a deal—he knew a lot about Norman's organization. Maybe he could trade that knowledge for his life.

The door opened, and an older man came in that LeRoy didn't recognize. He was followed by Anya Fiske.

"Doctor Fiske?" LeRoy asked uncertainly.

She twitched and looked up. Her face looked haunted.

LeRoy thought rapidly. Anya was Cindy's mother, but unless she already knew what Cindy had been up to over the summer, there was no reasonable way LeRoy could confess to knowing who Cindy was.

Now Connie looked surprised. "I expected you, Kalenin. I didn't know you were bringing a friend."

"This is Doctor Anya Fiske," Kalenin said comfortably, waving towards Anya. "She was the principal developer of Anapyridol. You know it as Divinidine."

"Really," Connie said. He looked at LeRoy. "Really?"

LeRoy nodded. "She's the real thing. Without her, Lifeworks is just another baby shampoo factory."

"That's interesting." Connie shifted his weight.

LeRoy recognized the signs—he'd been around bodyguards for years now. "Why are you here, Doctor Fiske?" he said quickly. He didn't want Connie doing anything stupid.

"Doctor Fiske has her own project to pursue. There's plenty of room." Kalenin looked up into the darkness. "Plenty of room. In return, she will help you set up your own Anapyridol factory."

Connie didn't relax. "It's a setup. The feds must have figured something out early."

Kalenin smiled. "It is no setup."

"What's the project, Doctor Fiske?" LeRoy said desperately. He realized he wanted this to work. The opportunity to do something with his talent, to work with someone like Anya Fiske, was as attractive—and potentially as addictive—as crack.

Anya twitched again. She looked damaged. What had happened to her?

"I want..." she began, stopped and licked her lips. She looked around the factory as if seeing it for the first time. "I want to develop an Anapyridol antagonist."

LeRoy understood immediately. Someone she knew was addicted to it. Someone close. Cindy, maybe? He hadn't seen any signs the last time he saw her, but addicts were shrewd and Cindy was smart. It was possible LeRoy might never know.

There was nothing so cruel as losing someone you loved to stupidity. LeRoy knew it first hand, as he'd seen first his father and then his mother die from nothing more than being ignorant of sexual consequences. He felt a wave of sympathy for Anya.

LeRoy surprised himself by stepping forward and taking her hand. "You will do it," he said softly. Anya turned her face down to his. "And I will help you."

LeRoy looked around the ruined building. It glowed with potential. They could build an Anapyridol factory here. They would find an antagonist. It was all within their grasp.

Anything was possible.

oOo

Tess came by as they were running some last checks on the instruments.

"Ethan?" she called.

Harriet had been gone when he awoke, leaving behind only a faint smell of soap and a lingering sense of warmth across his belly and chest. He hadn't seen her since last night, though he kept looking for her.

"Hi, Tess," he said distractedly. "What are you doing here?"

"I told you we might be setting up near you. When I saw your group, I came over to say hello."

Ethan tried to smile at her and orient the camera at the same time. The weather had remained clear since the rain the day before, and the air was a thin, pale blue.

"Look, now's not a good time," Ethan began.

"I know. I have to get back. Hopefully, we'll see each other later. Good luck." With that she walked back down the hill to her own group.

Ethan wrestled the completed camera over to the main observation post. Jim helped him level it.

"Do you know the zealots down there?"

"Zealots?"

"The woman you were talking to. Her group is that bunch of fundamentalists here to watch the eclipse."

"Tess?" Ethan looked down the hill. "They're religious? She told me on the plane they were doing something on the ruins up here."

"There aren't any ruins up here." Jim looked disgusted at them. "She just didn't want to have to argue with you. Welcome to Colombia."

Ethan stared down the hill with a different opinion. He'd been around people arguing that particular topic his whole life. "I'm surprised she didn't try to convert me," he said, feeling shocked. Joe wouldn't have been pleased if any of *his* flock had missed an opportunity.

"Count yourself lucky."

"You have no idea."

The connection between the laptop and the high definition camera gave them trouble. The laptop refused to recognize the connection. Off. On. Reboot. Remove battery. Repeat.

Finally, the laptop recognized the camera just in time. The eclipse was due to start at 1:07 and it was 1:00 now. Jim tapped at the keyboard for a moment, and the camera began to slowly and ponderously turn towards the Sun. "Seven minute warning," Jim said. "For the next ten minutes, watch that power supply as if your life depended on it."

"I will. You've been drumming that into me for weeks."

"It's essential for all of the instruments. Not just this camera. We don't have much time."

"I know. Only have one minute and fifty-two seconds," said Ethan.

Jim looked at him.

"That's what you said, right?" Ethan checked his own instruments.

"That's right." Jim fiddled with fine adjustments on the laptop. "An hour and a half of 'well, this is okay.' Followed by a hundred and twelve seconds of transcendental ecstasy where the world makes no sense." He glanced at Ethan. "That's been my experience, anyway."

A small image of the sun popped up on the screen. Jim grinned at Ethan. "Used to be, we'd have to do all this by electronics or hand. Now, it's just a program telling the camera what to do. Stores it all on the disk."

"You have enough space?"

"I have a hundred gigs. Ought to serve." He pointed at the screen. "Here it comes."

From down the hill, Ethan could hear chanting. He couldn't make out the words, but he recognized in his bones the rhythm of a prayer.

"Bloody idiots," muttered Jim.

Ethan found it oddly comforting to hear something familiar so far from home.

He couldn't tell if the light was dimming yet, but the sun on Jim's laptop was clearly being gradually eaten away. He pulled off his dark glasses to check the instruments, put them on again to look at the sun. The Moon steadily encroached on the sun.

After a moment, it seemed the world had a flimsy look to it, as if painted on gauze. Birds shot past them, flying to roost. Now it started to look a bit dim. It grew colder.

The praying down the hill was louder now. Ethan still couldn't hear individual words, but he recognized the cadence of the Lord's Prayer.

Most of the sun on the laptop was gone.

The sun in the sky dimmed, brightened briefly, then as the laptop sun was covered, it became completely dark. Only the hazy glow of the corona remained.

Ethan pulled off his glasses and looked around. It was so sudden, so immediate, he felt disoriented. The stars leaped into view. Ethan had the dizzying sensation that they were not looking at a night sky, where the pretty lights were hung like glitter, but staring across a thin glass wall into naked space. For a moment, he thought he was going to fall. Around him he heard a couple of hushed cries.

Jim pressed a couple of keys on the laptop. "Thirty seconds."

The prayers down the hill rolled across the plains sonorously. *We burn the Yule Log for this sort of thing*, Ethan thought. *The dragon has eaten the sun. Any minute now, we will bang the gongs to drive it away and bring back the light.* Ethan put his glasses back on.

"Should start coming out of it... now."

It remained dark. Ethan pulled the glasses back off. Only the corona's glow showed the bleak outline of the moon.

Ethan fancied he could hear Tess's voice leading the prayers.

"Come on. Come on," Jim said in a strangled voice.

The sun was gone. All that could be seen was the black disk over the absence of stars that marked the triumph of the Moon. Ethan realized he wasn't breathing. *Dead*, he thought. *I have died.*

"Two minutes, ten seconds." Jim looked at his watch. He checked the laptop. "What time have you got?"

Ethan ignored him. Someone took his arm. He glanced over and saw Harriet watching the sky, smiling.

"This can't happen," Jim muttered to himself over and over, tapping keys. Ethan could hear the faint whirr as the camera followed where the sun should long appeared.

Harriet was holding his hand. Around them, the silence was broken with a rising tone of conversation as people rechecked their instruments. Somebody was swearing in a steady, hissing monotone. Ethan could hear the Lord's Prayer clearly now, its rhythm as slow and stately as church bells.

"Six minutes?" cried Jim.

Still no change in the darkness.

The Yule Log had failed. The Dragon had eaten the sun.

It would be a new world, Ethan thought. They would have to bundle against the cold. Nothing would grow, except mushrooms. He tried to remember if people could survive eating only mushrooms but drew a blank.

A brilliant diamond split the sky.

Ethan cried out and covered his eyes. He fell to his knees, blind. Harriet helped him to his feet. Ethan fumbled with the glasses and looked at the Sun. The Moon was leaving the Sun behind.

Jim was staring at the laptop screen when Ethan was able to see again. "Eight minutes. Eight bloody fucking minutes." He shook his head slowly. "It's bloody fucking impossible."

Harriet laughed, a sound like a bell in the silence brought by the sudden light. She pulled on his hand and took him back to their tent. He found that, when the need arose, he could slip out of his clothes much more quickly than he would have thought possible.

He still managed to get back to the instruments to finish his share of the work. There was now a hurry in him, an urgency, to get back to the warm blue tent. After dinner, they took their time, neither yet really knowing the other.

He briefly dreamed of a clawing, acrid smell, then nothing.

When he awoke, he was propped against a stone wall. Military men were walking to and fro about him. He was sick to his stomach and around him there was ample evidence he'd been sick in his sleep. It took a few moments to realize why he couldn't stand; his hands and feet were duct taped together.

He tried to lean against the wall to stand up but threw up again.

One of the soldiers noticed this and left at a jog. In a few minutes an American accompanied by someone in uniform walked towards him carrying some paper.

"I was wrong," Jim said as he approached Ethan. Colonel Haberman stood next to him, staring straight ahead. Ethan was beneath his notice.

Jim held out the papers excitedly towards Ethan. "It's absolutely impossible. Better than seven minutes off. But only here—nowhere else. Absolutely bloody fucking impossible."

Ethan stared sickly at him.

Jim stopped and gave him an absent smile. "Oh, yes. You're kidnapped. Welcome to Colombia."

Part 2: The God of Reptiles

"I judged I could see that there was two Providences, and a poor chap would stand considerable show with the widow's Providence, but if Miss Watson's got him there warn't no help for him any more."

—*The Adventures of Huckleberry Finn*, Mark Twain

Chapter 2.1: February, 1998

On the way to Colombia, Tess found herself behind Ethan in the check-in line at American Airlines. At the sight of his bored and unsmiling face she was struck by a sudden shyness. She watched him, and as he chose his seats, she wrote them down. If he was sitting next to her, he'd have to talk to her.

She managed to snag a seat next to him on the fight to Miami; she was willing to sacrifice working on one leg of the trip to talk to Ethan. It just meant she'd have to work harder on the leg to Bogotá.

Ethan was as pleasant a traveling companion as she could have hoped. She realized in a moment that he had no idea who she was. *Later*, she thought to herself. *Let him get to know me a little bit.* She vacillated between believing that any problems Ethan might have with her could be dealt with just by being honest and forthright and trusting in the awesome power of God, and despairing how she could possibly expect Ethan to accept her, twenty years younger than Joe and an ex-prostitute?

All through their conversation, Tess couldn't help noticing he kept eying a cute redhead a few seats away. Tess smiled to herself. Love was grand.

When they boarded for Bogotá, Tess switched with a young scientist named Jim to sit with her assistant, Portia. The plane was filled with thirty-seven converts. There were twenty-four already in Bogotá. Camping tents had to be counted when they reached the airports. Sleeping bags. Food. Everything they might need. Bogotá was the last place they could make up any lack.

The eclipse team was already set up by the time Tess and her converts reached the altiplano. In the distance, Tess saw Ethan talking with the red-headed girl he'd met on the plane. Maybe Tess would catch up with him later.

The night cooled rapidly. Tess and Portia went over the last few things in their tent.

Tess gave Portia a plastic bag. "Pass these around before people go to bed. And have Cory and Mandy check their alarms. I don't want anybody to sleep through this."

202 • Steven Popkes

Portia chuckled. "Fat chance."

"Just the same. Here are the prayers we all agreed on. I brought them with me."

Portia looked over them. "Okay. I'll pass them out."

"And no sex. Not with the cameras rolling. Grunting and rooting around when we're trying to create a miracle is counterproductive. Wait until later."

Portia nodded.

And that was it. Six thousand miles and everybody was comfortably camped out and ready. Portia left the tent and Tess leaned back against her sleeping bag. Outside she could hear the faint whine of mosquitoes and the distant grumble of a generator. She closed her eyes. Tomorrow was going to be a busy day.

oOo

Totality was to be reached by 1:00 in the afternoon—1800 UTC, she told herself. Tess had everyone take an early lunch and drop the pills at eleven. They would be peaking when it started.

Tess had them sit in concentric circles. It felt right that they should be as close together as possible. She led them in hymns and prayer until she felt the world suddenly turn as thin as a soap bubble. It was starting. She looked around and several people had that flushed, interested look she'd come to know so well.

"Pull out the prayers," Tess called out. She checked her watch. It was nearly one.

The light began to dim. Birds flew to their roosts in sudden panic. Below them, she heard in the distance farm animals suddenly complain about the unexpected impending darkness. The world took on a washed-out, gray texture, as if they had at that moment crossed from the altiplano into the afterlife.

She and Joe had thought for a long time about the prayers. They had decided on simple plainsong chants. Simple was better. Joe had thought to use the Jewish *Shema*. It was easy and direct and could be comfortably sung— singing seemed right, somehow. But it didn't quite fit what they were trying to do. Instead, they took a simple English hymn and put their own words on it. "Tis a gift to be simple," after all.

Hearing it now, with her ears and mind unstopped, feeling God himself moving inside of her, she realized it wouldn't have mattered what they chose. It was the singing, the emptying of the mind and the filling of the heart, that was sufficient.

Today, this was *her* congregation.

They murmured to each other. First one cluster of voices joined and came apart, then another, like loaves of bread clustering together as they floated on the sea.

The light was gone now. Stars surrounded the corona's glow in the sky.

Tess stood up. She swayed one way. Then another. She began to sing and the voices joined with hers. He had come to her. Together, she and her congregation had called Him forth. She felt Him move within her mind and heart, pour down over her breasts and loins, reach fingers over them all. She laughed with their joy. *You want a miracle?* He asked, and chuckled. *All right.*

Invisible lightning poured up her body from the earth. Laughing with Him, she reached up and stopped the Moon. She could hold it as long as she liked, as long as they sang, as long as her arms could remain unmoving.

She felt great and huge. Her legs splayed across continents. Her shoulders spanned the sky. The entire earth was contained within her.

Tess felt a tugging against her hands. The Moon wanted to be free. She let go and shrank. A bolt of light broke over the earth. It was too bright, and she looked away. For a moment, she could hear—and *understand!*—the happy confusion of the animals as the light returned.

Tess sank back to her knees. She blindly felt hands caressing her, and she touched them in return.

Her eyesight and consciousness seemed to return together. In the hot altiplano, she and the others were rubbing each other. Gently she disengaged someone's hand from her breast. They'd have to edit this later. Still, she had to stop this now.

"All right, everybody," she called out.

Her congregation looked up at her expectantly. This was what Joe loved, this silent and devoted attention. Tess understood him better now.

"Back to the tents. Relax and try to sleep. The cameramen have everything in hand."

She nodded to the crew and followed the rest back to their tents, taking care not to actually touch anyone. The way she was feeling right now, she'd rip the clothes off the first person that shook her hand.

In her tent, she closed her eyes and tried to sleep, but the drug seemed to have her eyelids on springs. Everything she relaxed they sprang open again. It seemed as if the world was poised on the edge of sensation: the sound of the nylon tent rubbing against the tent poles, the cool, ribbed texture of the sleeping bag against her skin, the sultry air blowing over her.

"Tess?" asked Portia as she came in the tent. "I thought I'd check—"

Tess smoothly reached up and pulled her down and rolled her over, gracefully ending up in a passionate kiss. Portia responded immediately.

oOo

Jim gave quick instructions to two bland and heavyset men in their thirties, then left them to their own devices.

They identified themselves to Ethan in halting, broken English to be Sanza and Guillermo. Ethan tentatively identified them as brothers from their resemblance to one another.

Sanza and Guillermo roughly but impersonally brought Ethan to what he decided must be his room for the moment. Guillermo left, but Sanza remained and drew out a linoleum knife. Its wicked hook blade and razor-sharp edge held Ethan's gaze. Sanza smiled as if he were trying to be friendly. He playfully jabbed at Ethan's eyes, and Ethan immediately understood: don't make any trouble.

Ethan nodded and raised his hands. Sanza expertly cut off the duct tape, stripping it off so fast Ethan barely had time to gasp. He replaced it with more comfortable handcuffs. These were joined by a chain to an eyebolt in the wall. Clearly, they had done this before.

Guillermo reappeared with plastic-wrapped sandwiches. He tossed them on a mat on the floor, along with a bottle of soda. Then he and Sanza left the room. Ethan heard them locking the door outside.

It was late morning and had grown hot. Ethan was still nauseous and unsteady. There was a mat on the floor and a chair in the corner. He put the sandwich to one side of the mat, lay down, and fell asleep.

Ethan woke up when Jim jabbed him with his finger.

"Wake up."

"I'm awake." For a moment, Ethan didn't know where he was, but the handcuffs and the chain reminded him. "Oh, yeah," he said. "Welcome to Colombia."

Jim nodded. "Eight minutes." He held up a pad of paper. "Eight minutes and 4.2873 seconds."

"The eclipse?"

Jim nodded again. "Any ideas?"

"I'm kidnapped, remember? Why should I help you?"

"Because I can have you brutally beaten at any moment," Jim said quietly. "Think. You're a smart one—everyone knew that in the department. I came up with a couple of ideas."

"Hallucinogenic gas," Ethan said. "Drugs in the coffee. Drugs injected while we were asleep—"

Jim waved him away. "Forget the drugs. Drugs don't affect cameras. Did you know those Jesus freaks were praying down the hill from us while the eclipse was going on?"

"No." Ethan shrugged. "I was busy."

"Well, you were distracted, anyway. I can understand that. Harriet has that effect on men."

Ethan stared at him. Time in the room seemed to slow down. "There's something about you and Harriet I don't know."

Jim shrugged. "How could you? She's my ex-wife."

"She set me up," Ethan spat out bitterly.

"Not really. She just distracted you. When she got up to pee, we pulled you in. But that has nothing to do with the topic at hand, does it?" Jim held out his pad of paper. "It's time dilation."

"You're nuts."

"Not at all. 493.2873 seconds. If we were on a mass—"

"Mass wouldn't have that effect. Mass would *slow down* time. The eclipse would appear to happen faster. We saw the time of the eclipse *extend*, therefore our time moved faster. It's not time *dilation*. It's time *contraction*."

Jim stared at him.

Ethan realized this had been churning in his mind since he'd awoken. "Think for a minute. You're at the edge of a black hole. Light is climbing out of the hole and light is coming in. At the edge of the hole, time has slowed down, but the speed of light is a constant. Instead of a speed shift you get a wavelength shift. From the point of view at the edge of the hole, light coming in gains energy—it blue-shifts towards a shorter wavelength. Coming out of the hole, it loses energy and red-shifts towards a longer wavelength. A time *contraction* is like being outside of the hole: time is going faster than it is near the whole. We would see light red-shift."

Ethan thought for a moment. "Except, of course, there *was* no big mass nearby. There was no nearby neutron star to slow the rest of the world down relative to us."

Jim thought for a moment. "Maybe there was a negative mass?"

"Sure. Why not? We'd get a different time relationship, but that would mean *we* were measuring on top of the negative mass of a neutron star."

"Or the rules changed."

"Which they can't." Ethan lay back on his mat. "The colonel, or somebody, drugged us and then rigged the cameras."

Jim knelt next to him. "The cameras, the spectroscope, cameras and other equipment, all show an eclipse that lasted 493 seconds. Everywhere else in the world reported 112 seconds plus or minus depending on location. It's a dilation—*contraction*—by a factor of 4.04. Could that be significant?"

Ethan pulled gradually on his chain. If he could loop it around Jim's neck, he might be able to subdue him quietly. "What? The spectroscope?"

"The factor of four."

"Four cardinal directions. There are eight phases of the Moon—two times four. The Sun and Moon represent fundamental duality—that's the number two, again. Four plus two is six, the number of the beast. Hebrew slaves were held for six years and released on the seventh. The number of Satan when he tempted Jesus. Man was created on the sixth day. 666 is the mark of the end times in Revelations." Ethan laughed. "Then, again, add one more—maybe Man? Maybe us?—is seven. The foundation of God's word. The day He rested. Adam was created on October seventh—or the first day of *Tishri*, the seventh month in the Hebrew calendar. There are seven churches in Revelations. Jesus performed seven miracles on the Sabbath." Ethan shook his head. "Pick a number and people attribute a meaning to it. None of them are worth anything." Almost there.

Jim sat up and returned to the chair out of reach. "I did some calculations. A time factor of 4.04 would require going nearly the speed of light. Or a huge local mass."

"Huge *negative* local mass." Ethan leaned back. "Was there any red-shifting in the spectroscope?"

Jim thought for a moment. "I don't think so."

"If there was that much time contraction, there would be."

"Maybe any residual sunlight was red-shifted deep into the infrared and we couldn't see it. We didn't have infrared instrumentation."

"I saw stars. So did you. Why would just the light around the Moon red-shift and nothing else?" Ethan shook his head. "Look, the factor of 4.04 doesn't mean our time moved 4.04 times faster relative to the rest of the world. It means we *perceived* time that much faster. Nerve cell impulses travel at—what?—seventy meters per second? So, 4.04 times that is about four seventy meters per second. Not even a blip compared to the speed of light." Ethan thought for a moment. "I can't do it in my head. The red-shift would be infinitesimal."

"But the instruments—"

"—would be functioning similarly faster. I mean, the quartz clocks in them would be vibrating that much faster. It's still time compression but a much lower order. It's an easier lump of physics to swallow than a local change close to the velocity of light."

"I think this goes beyond physics."

Great. He's gone round the bend. "Nothing goes beyond physics."

"Spoken like a scientist."

"Which you are—or were. Now you're a kidnapper."

Jim grinned. "Soon to be a rich kidnapper, thank you very much. After all, your father is a rich celebrity." He chuckled.

"What are you talking about?" Ethan tried to keep his face neutral.

"You think I don't know who your father is?" Jim shrugged. "This is an example of flexibility. *Adaptability.* You see, I had planned to just use myself as the victim. I'd get 'kidnapped' and ransom myself to the university. Then Haberman and I would split the ransom. He has expenses. I'd disappear like so many kidnappees do. But instead of a rotting corpse out in the jungle—food for worms and fodder for future archeologists—I'd be living well down here or even up in Mexico where a hundred thousand dollars is the wealth of kings. But *you* show up. I figured I could bring a quarter million at most. But you!" Jim rubbed his hands together. "I bet you'd bring in a good half a million or more."

"I'd rather talk about the eclipse."

"We can do that. Like I said, I'm flexible."

Ethan didn't like to speculate about physics. It smacked of religion—that was Joe's territory.

But, he thought, *desperate diseases require desperate remedies.*

"Okay," Ethan said slowly. "Then the rules changed."

Jim leaned his head to one side. "Changed how?"

"What we saw in the altiplano was impossible, right? It's impossible not because we can't explain it but because any explanation violates too many other rules. Like we couldn't have suddenly increased the mass, because changing the mass would have knock-on effects—such as turning all of the participants into jelly. Or increase of negative mass since there was no evidence of gravitational repulsion."

"Okay."

"Then we must have a situation where the rules have changed. For example, maybe the local intensity of the Higgs field decreased."

Jim shook his head. "That's the same as decreasing mass."

Ethan nodded. "True but we associate all of the qualities of mass and velocity together: increasing mass slows down time. Increasing negative mass speeds it up. Maybe there's a way to separate out the effects—change the rules so that a particular effect doesn't have the same consequences."

"One sign of intervention by the divine would be a violation of physical laws." Jim opened up his notebook. "Joshua caused the Sun to stand still. Moses brought down flaming hailstones. Jesus raised the dead. These are the sort of things you look for."

Ethan didn't take his eyes off him. Jim's voice had taken on a recitative quality. For the moment he had an audience of one: Ethan was superfluous. Ethan tried to move unobtrusively towards the edge of the bed. The chain was loose enough that he could probably reach Jim. If he could, he could drag him close enough to loop the chain around his neck.

Jim stood up and turned his back on him—but just far enough to keep out of Ethan's reach.

Ethan realized Jim was playing with him. He relaxed and leaned back on the bed. Jim turned around and smiled at him.

"You don't believe in any of this crap, do you?" Ethan said wearily. "You're just taunting me."

"On the contrary: I do, indeed. Once one leaves the realm of physical laws, all hypotheses become equal. Taunting you is just a bonus. You and I will, hopefully, figure out what happened before the ransom is paid. After that," Jim flicked his hand as if he were shooing away a fly. "We never see each other again. But for now, here's what's interesting. An eclipse occurs where the expected time isn't off by a few percent but nearly an order of magnitude—a level of error that is unmistakable. It correlates—not causation, as you reminded me, but correlation none the less—with a cult group of your father's—"

"My father doesn't run a cult. It's just a television station."

Jim shook his head. "The woman who ran it is your father's new wife. Surely you knew that?"

"Bullshit."

"Not so. Tess Cori—you did sit with her on the way down."

"Lying about her isn't going to help you." Why lie about this? What could Jim hope to gain?

"So, you didn't know. Interesting. Not important but interesting. She and her little group performed some incantations—"

"They were hymns, for Christ's sake."

Jim raised his eyebrows. "You know them?"

"One was 'How Firm a Foundation.' The other was the Doxology. They changed the words."

"They sang at the moment of the eclipse and the time was lengthened. Don't you think that's interesting?"

"Maybe *they* passed out the hallucinogens."

"Curious you would say that. They were passing around some kind of pill. You could see it clearly. Several of them held the pills up for their cameras."

Ethan didn't say anything.

"We already know a lot about how the observer interacts with the observed—superpositions and such will become the basis for quantum computing. So, what I'm thinking, after our discussion, is that some superpositions allow for changes in the rules. Were they entangled?"

"Entanglement doesn't work like that."

"We don't know what entanglement might look like from the inside. What would we observe if we were inside and participating with an entangled state?"

"Not a bunch of people singing hymns on the altiplano!"

Jim shrugged. "As I said, past a certain point all hypotheses become equal."

Ethan couldn't get past the idea that Tess might be Joe's new wife. *Might be?* Look at how blasé Jim was about it. Maybe he wasn't lying at all. Ethan had sat with her all the way to Miami. He had liked her. Not as much as he liked Harriet—before he knew she had set him up. But Tess was fun to sit next to. Intelligent. Articulate. *And* she was a pill-popping, crazy, cult woman. Ethan wondered what Joe would think of that.

Jim nodded. "I guess that's enough today."

Ethan stood up, hoping for a chance as Jim turned and started for the door.

As Ethan lunged, Jim stepped back, and Ethan fell on the floor.

Jim put his foot on his head and leaned forward slightly. Ethan felt the weight.

Jim stood watching him carefully. "Behave yourself," he said, and left.

oOo

Tess awoke, instantly filled with impatient purpose. Portia was sleeping next to her.

Tess dressed quickly and quietly, careful not to wake Portia up.

Outside, the sun was clear and the sky a cloudless blue. She had hoped to see Ethan before she left, but now there was no time. Tess had never expected any great miracle. But now that she and her congregation had been so blessed, it was imperative she return to Joe. God had given them a gift to be used, and together they would make use of it. This wasn't a private congregation any more. She and Joe had begun a movement. She could practically hear God's call.

Portia peeked out of the tent. "Tess?"

Tess smiled at her. She hoped Portia wouldn't be any trouble. "Get up girl. We've got places to be."

In an hour, they were in the buses back down the mountain. As they left the meadow, Tess noticed a ring of dead grass perfectly encircling where the congregation had been during the eclipse. God moves in mysterious ways. She pointed it out to one of the cameramen. "Make sure you get that."

Tess ignored Portia's sighs and occasional sidelong glances on the plane ride back. Let it die down. That was the best way. Nothing could come of it. She was a married woman, after all.

Instead, they made plans, discarded them, considered scripts and presentations, rewrote them, came up with possible ideas to pitch to Joe. By the time the plane turned onto Lambert Field's final approach, Tess thought they were in pretty good shape.

She made sure the congregation, especially Portia, caught cabs or limos home before she took a cab back to Alton. Tess smiled to herself. Joe didn't expect her back so quickly. She patted the bag filled with tapes and disks next to her. They would have been satisfied with a miracle small enough to be corroborated by the scientists but large enough to show up on television. This was bigger than they had imagined.

Tess paid the cabbie and quietly let herself into the house. She had hoped to surprise Joe. In his joy, maybe they would break some furniture.

Joe was sitting in the front room, his head in his hands.

Tess dropped photographic evidence of the miraculous to the floor. She knelt next to him.

"Honey?" she said gently. "What's wrong?"

Joe slowly raised his head. His eyes were blood red from weeping.

"It's Ethan." Joe took a deep breath. "He's been kidnapped."

oOo

Cindy let herself into the house. It was quiet.

"Mom?" Cindy called. No answer.

Cindy wasn't surprised. Anya had been working irregular hours. She looked like hell these days, too. Cindy hoped she wasn't sleeping very well. *Tell* me *the facts of life? I'll shove them right back at you.* Anapyridol was Mom's drug. Eventually, Jake was going to find her. It would be up to Cindy to save her.

First, she had to save Jake.

Cindy had expected anger, maybe even violence, from Jake once he knew where she had been. Instead, Jake acted as if something had blown a crater inside of him and there was little left but a hole. But, she told herself, it was going to be *okay*. She was in charge of the house now. Anya wasn't interested, and Jake wasn't capable.

Humming to herself, she pulled out a cake mix and canned frosting, set the oven to pre-heat. A cake would be good.

While it was baking, she started her homework. Limits equations and French history. She examined a picture of Marie Antoinette. It must have taken hours to get into the dress. Or maybe they had some easy technological solution. Dresses that could be opened and closed like a Chinese box. An hour to do the hair—they must have kept the same hairdo for weeks. Marie was the queen, but she had a pleased expression on her face that said courtesan more loudly than wife. Cindy read ahead and then looked her up in the index. Then she looked up 'prostitution.' There were a few references but nothing interesting.

She went upstairs and looked on the net. Apparently, Marie and Louis hadn't known what to do and therefore remained childless for years. That's what the article said, anyway. Cindy looked at Marie's picture. Well, maybe Louis didn't know what to do. Cindy's opinion of Marie was otherwise. Even so, losing your head was an awful high price to pay for ignorance.

The cake was done. She pulled it out of the oven to let it cool. *An omelet for dinner*, she thought.

Portia called while she was getting the ingredients together. Cindy answered.

"Hi," Portia said. "Did you miss me?"

"I thought you were out sick or something."

"Nope. I was in Colombia watching an eclipse."

Cindy wondered why Mrs. Rendquist hadn't called her. Had Portia run away? Did the Rendquists know what she was doing? Were they participants? Cindy had a queasy thought about mother and daughter in a sex cult. She broke the eggs and stirred them together.

"Really? How was it?" She was pretty sure Jake liked omelets. He cooked soufflés, didn't he? She cut up some small cubes of ham and diced the onion.

"Fantastic! And I met this terrific woman. Maybe I'm a lesbian."

Cindy pulled the phone from her shoulder and stared at it. Great. She put it back on the shoulder. "You've been pretty interested in boys about as long as I can remember."

"Bisexual, then," Portia said dismissively. "I thought sex on Divinidine was good before. *This* was—I don't know—*transcendental* or something."

"I hoped you would quit that stuff." Cindy's stomach felt hollow.

Portia giggled. "I'm a member of a real church now. We only do Divinidine for religious reasons."

"The sex, too?"

"That's an added bonus."

This is all my fault. Cindy felt like crying.

"So, we're supposed to bring in people we think would be suitable." Portia paused then finished in a breathy rush. "So, I thought of you. Please come. Please?"

"I don't know—"

"Please come. Please. It'll be fun." Portia was pleading.

Know your enemy, I suppose. You can't save someone if you don't know what you're fighting.

"What is it? Some kind of camp meeting?"

"Just a little introduction. Downtown at the Marriot. Tuesday afternoon, three o'clock. I'll pick you up."

Cindy sighed. "Okay."

"Terrific! I'm hanging up right now so you can't change your mind. See you Tuesday!"

"Shit." Cindy stared at the suddenly dead phone then hung it up.

She pulled the frying pan off the stove and set it aside. She could smell the heat radiating from it. She was just too sad to cook right how.

Cindy went to the front room and sat down in Jake's chair. She stared out the front window over the pile of blankets on the sofa.

She could hear the blankets breathing.

Cindy yelped and went over the back of the chair.

"Shhhh!" said the blankets.

"Mom?"

"Not so loud." Anya peeked out from under the blankets and looked around nervously.

"I didn't see your car." Cindy looked through the front window. "Oh, that's where it is. You usually park in the back—"

"Quiet." Anya peeked out at her. "He'll hear you."

"Who might hear, Mom?"

"Him." Anya shook her head and sat up. "But that's silly, isn't it?"

Cindy came around and sat back in the chair. "I have no idea."

"Of course, you wouldn't." Anya rubbed the thighs of her pants nervously. "Besides, it's ridiculous. He can either see me or not. Hiding under blankets wouldn't make any difference. I just needed to hide right then, I suppose." she laughed shortly. "An emotional expression of a philosophical idea."

Cindy stared at her. There was something fascinating about seeing someone fall completely apart. *Who are you and what have you done with my mother?* She had to struggle to keep from laughing. Cindy shook her head at herself. This wasn't funny. Maybe the problem wasn't with Anya. Maybe there was something wrong with *Cindy*.

Anya gave Cindy a brittle smile. "How are you? It seems like I haven't seen you in weeks."

"You've been working. Or something. You haven't been coming around here."

Anya nodded, picked an invisible piece of lint from her pants. "I've been busy."

"Dad's a wreck."

Anya kept her smile, but her eyes flared. "Isn't that more your doing than mine?"

Cindy shrugged. "We've gotten over it. Now it's your turn to come home."

Anya didn't seem to hear. She cocked her head as if listening. Her hands shook, and she clenched them together. After a moment, she seemed to calm down.

A moment of realization: *I'm thick.* Now that she thought of it, Anya had obviously taken the drug. Was she now joining some church like Portia? Cindy couldn't see it. Besides, whatever Anya was going through didn't seem to have any of the perks Portia was getting. Anya looked like a badly used tissue.

Reluctantly, Cindy concluded her mother might need some help. "Is there something wrong, Mom?"

Anya jerked slightly when Cindy spoke but slowly looked up, smiling. "No. I'll be all right. I just needed a nap. Perhaps you're right. Perhaps I've been working too hard. But it will be worth it." She stood up and straightened her blouse.

"All right, then," Anya said, and Cindy could have sworn it was the old Anya, sure of herself and ready to rumble.

Cindy waved goodbye to her as she left through the front door. She didn't much like the idea of having to take care of two adults. At least Anya was working—Cindy didn't get the impression that Jake was doing that so well these days.

One thing at a time, she thought. *One thing at a time. And the right thing at this time is to finish making dinner.*

oOo

Denial, anger, bargaining, depression, acceptance, thought Jake. It seemed that he'd been through steps one through three over and over again throughout the year. He wasn't ready for acceptance just quite yet, thank you very much. Depression filled the void nicely.

Without the anonymous tips, the Divinidine busts dried up. Bujold tried widening the net and checking out the hotels. Jake even had to bust some streetwalkers downtown. No data.

Jake needed to talk to Connie. He told himself it was to see if Connie knew anything about Divinidine, but it was a lie. Jake didn't want to think about what he wanted to do to Connie. It scared him when such thoughts rolled through his brain.

Jake had Brendan call him when Connie showed up. An hour after the call, Jake walked into Mississippi's. Connie was sitting with his back to the wall, waiting for him. So much for the element of surprise.

"Evening, Jake."

Jake nodded. His hands were sweaty, and the 9mm inside his jacket felt suddenly heavy.

Connie gestured to the stool next to him.

Jake sat down and ordered a beer. Brendan brought one without comment or smile. Brendan was brief and professional—Jake could tell he'd lost points. Brendan didn't belong to Jake anymore. Instead of his home turf, Mississippi's had become merely neutral territory.

It must have been written on his face. Connie's expression didn't change, but he didn't make any effort to hide his gun. If Jake wanted to start something, Connie was more than willing to oblige. Jake could read his mind as clearly as if it were a newspaper. Connie knew that Jake had figured out where Cindy had been.

Bitter, Jake nursed his beer. Intimidation had to be kept up. Fear had to be earned. He'd given up the right to both the last time he'd seen Connie.

"You have to understand, Jake," Connie murmured so that only Jake could hear. "It was ignorance and business. If I had known Cindy was your daughter, I'd have turned around that night and brought her back to your doorstep. As soon as I found out, I had her sent back."

"Norman said different."

"Norman said different," Connie repeated. "Who are you going to believe? Me, the man who worked with you? Who gave you your cut on time every month? Or Norman, the man who took it all away? Norman who messed up a good thing with some wild-ass drug. Who do you think is more trustworthy?"

Jake smiled at him. "Norman."

"Mother—" Connie controlled himself. "That's just great. That's just fucking great. So now, what do you want me to do? Put a bullet through your head? Would that bring back your daughter all pale and safe? It'd save me a world of trouble to kill you."

Brendan leaned down between him. "Not here."

Connie nodded and put his empty hands on the bar. "What the fuck do you want me to do?"

"Give me a tip on Divinidine."

Jake didn't know what he was going to say until it came out. But Connie was right: now was not the time to be trading bullets. Now was the time for consolidation, rebuilding. With his daughter. With his wife. Even with Connie. Plenty of time later to put a bullet through his lying, fucking face.

Connie didn't say anything for a moment. "What is it you want to know?"

"What is it? Where does it come from? What's going on with it now?"

"Norman's in charge. You know that."

"Norman's quit using our operations—or any hotels, as far as I can tell. All of the girls I knew have been turned out. I caught two of them working Grand. Norman's too smart to have the stuff near him and not smart enough to cook the stuff up himself. I need to know what he's doing."

Connie stared at him. "You want me to turn on Norman. Why would I do that?"

"Well, for one thing, it would help me forget how you abused my daughter. Then I'd be able to quit spending every waking moment thinking about tearing your balls off with a red-hot pair of pliers."

Connie leaned back and studied him. "That's an incentive, I guess."

Jake leaned on the bar with his elbows and continued in a low voice. "If we took Norman out there would be a power vacuum in East Saint Louis. I'd say Sam would take over, but Sam's been gone for a while. Word is he's probably floated down to New Orleans by now. You're the only person in the right position."

"What are you trying to tell me?"

Jake turned to see him. "Norman's days are numbered. You know it. I know it. He started the countdown when he got into Divinidine—nobody can start a new drug craze without the world coming down on him as soon as the secret's out. Now the secret is definitely out. DEA's in it, and they don't let go until they get their pound of meat. Let's let them have Norman."

Connie's eyes were slitted. "And you'll forget about Cindy."

Jake placed his hands on the table. "I'll never forget about it. I'll—" Jake stopped. He felt as if he were strangling. "I keep telling myself there was no way you could have known. It was just business. It doesn't help. I still want to kill you." Jake grinned thinly. "But I'll settle for your boss."

"Fair enough." Connie held out his hand.

Jake stared at it for a long moment, then brought his own up to shake it. *This is how you make a deal with the devil*, he thought. *You get him to sell out a bigger devil.*

Jake left Mississippi's and walked down the alley towards home. Halfway there, he bent over and threw up on the struggling pokeweed, broken glass, and burnt asphalt. When he was empty, he staggered to his feet. *It's not the making of the deal that's so hard. It's the keeping of the deal.*

He kept one hand against the alley fence to steady himself as he finished walking home.

He stopped at the back porch and ran the hose to wash his face. Feeling a little steadier, he stood up straight and walked through the door into the kitchen.

Cindy looked up from the stove and smiled radiantly at him. For a moment, Jake felt nauseous again. How would he ever be able to keep his bargain? How could he let Connie live?

"Hi, Daddy," she said. "You're just in time for dinner. I baked a cake."

oOo

Ethan's understanding of his surroundings was reduced by distance—a sort of inverse square law of comprehension. He remembered the wall where he had regained consciousness and the room where he was now. This room now contained his world. Small. Stuffy. Four poles with planks nailed to them for walls, similarly nailed planks for the floor, and plywood spotted with Spanish designations for the roof. The room stank from the latrine next door—in fact, the pornographic graffiti and pictures on the walls had given Ethan some ideas about the room's use before it housed him.

Jim came to see him regularly to talk about the eclipse. Ethan continued to spin wild speculations for him about what had happened. There was no continuity between the episodes. In one visit, Jim would be wildly enthusiastic about subsets of universal constants that might be changed or arranged to alter the passage of time. The next day that idea would be thrown out in favor of some kind of field effect. Field effects were discarded in order to describe the local area from the inside of a Bose-Einstein condensate. Jim decided the direction. Ethan was driven ragged trying to keep up.

Outside the event horizon of his room, Ethan knew only what semaphores came in through the door.

Sanza and Guillermo were rough with him on occasion but not untowardly so. They gave him a bucket to use and brought him sandwiches on paper plates. The beer was cold.

After about a week, Jim was waiting for him to wake up. "We need to make a movie."

Ethan rolled off the bed and stood up. "That would be easier without these." He held up his hands to show the cuffs.

"Better pictures with them on." Jim nodded to the brothers, and they came in the room and stood waiting.

"What kind of movie?"

"The movie we're going to send to your father, dummy." Jim pushed his glasses back against his face.

"I won't do it," Ethan said, surprising himself. *Bad mistake*, came a whisper in the back of his mind.

Jim shrugged. "*Muéstrale.* Make sure it doesn't show."

Sanza, on his right, sighed. He nodded to Guillermo. Both of them pulled short, wooden truncheons from their belts. Sanza clipped him gently behind the knee, and the blossoming pain brought Ethan to the ground. Guillermo poked him roughly, but not too badly, around Ethan's left kidney to get the range and then swung the heavy end deep into the flesh. Ethan shrieked and tried to curl around to that side but couldn't. Sanza booted him in the stomach, and Ethan threw up. It was careful and scientific and couldn't have lasted more than twenty seconds. Guillermo spread Ethan's legs. Sanza poked his testicles, feeling for the precious targets.

"No!" Ethan screamed.

"*Basta*," said Jim. "These guys have been in the family business their whole lives. Their father worked for Perón. You aren't even a good workout. So, want to make a movie?"

Ethan nodded weakly, his face wet with tears and snot.

Jim put his hands on his knees and stood up. "Good. *Traélo.* Bring him along after he catches his breath."

Sanza smiled apologetically and gave him a towel. Ethan took it and slowly wiped his face. He felt deeply shamed. Ethan knew—and worse, understood *they* knew—that he would have done anything, sold out anyone, to stop them. It hadn't even taken them a full sixty seconds to break him. *Not much of a person*, he thought. *Not much of a man.*

It is a strange and terrifying thing to know your limits.

oOo

Joe made it to the phone before Tess. "Hello?"

Tess saw him from behind, left fist clenched and shoulders raised in hope or fear. Then his hand opened and his shoulders slumped. Wordlessly, he handed the phone to Tess.

"Hello?" Tess watched as Joe walked heavily out of the room, a sad, proud dinosaur, having comprehended the meteor strike and only now making a symbolic gesture at escape.

"Tess?" Portia's eager voice came through the phone.

Tess closed her eyes. She didn't need this. "Now's not a good time."

Pause. "Why is that?"

Tess sighed. Teenage sexual angst seemed to just ooze through the phone. "Ethan's been kidnapped."

"Ethan?"

"Joe's son. It happened just after the eclipse. We left so quickly I didn't find out until I got back here."

"Wow." Portia paused again. "I was hoping we could talk about how to use the eclipse film. You know. Like we talked about."

I know exactly what you were hoping. Be kind, Tess. You were young once. Of course, you were working for Sam by the time you'd left school, so maybe there's not much comparison. "That will have to wait for a bit. It has some shelf life, I think."

"What are you going to do?"

"Help Joe in his time of trial. Pull together money to ransom Ethan. Lift water. Stack wood."

"What?"

"Living day to day."

"Oh." Portia spoke in a rush. "I really want to see you again."

"Oh, honey. That's not going to work, is it? I'm married to Joe. You know that."

"You were married in Colombia, too," Portia said sullenly.

"I know, but the circumstances were different. You need to find a good boy—or girl—your own age. You don't want an old crone like me. Trust in the Lord. Everything will come out all right."

Portia didn't answer.

"We can talk about it at the meeting. All right?"

"All right." Portia's voice was barely audible.

Tess said goodbye and hung up. She hoped things wouldn't escalate but had a bad feeling they would. Maybe she should have some contingency plans. She'd have to think about that. Tess firmly tabled the situation with Portia to be dealt with another time and returned in her mind to Joe and the Movement.

Portia was right, hang her. They needed to use this quickly. Not for publicity—the eclipse had legs when they wanted to use it, even though they couldn't sit on it forever. It was because of their own troops. Joe's secret congregation knew that Tess and the others had been sent down there. They had a right and an itch to know what happened. Joe should have brought everybody together as soon as Tess had returned. And if he had been in his right mind, he would have.

When you marry someone, you ought to be able to assume you know them pretty well. That's the theory, Tess thought.

Overnight, Joe had changed completely.

He had cancelled his live shows immediately and put plans for the Movement on hold. Tess tried to salvage some momentum on her own but too much depended on Joe. It was Joe who could write checks and persuade donors to open their purse strings. They needed Joe to articulate what they were going to do. It was Joe who had to convene a damned meeting.

But now it was also Joe who nearly fired his secretary—Maybelle Whitcomb—after twenty years of utterly loyal service—when she took too long to find the Colombian Ambassador's phone number. Tess could see the explosion start to happen and had shooed Maybelle out of the office, earning a black look from Maybelle and confusing the hell out of everybody else. It was Joe who was ignoring what he had to do and who hadn't touched Tess since she had returned.

I mean, I know it's his son and all, she thought. *But you have to keep your priorities.*

It was time to confront him. Life had to go on.

She found Joe in the dining room, staring west into the setting sun. The golden light flooded the room. Joe was motionless.

"Joe?" she said softly.

Joe looked up at her as if blind. He groped for her hand.

Surprised, she stepped back, then reached forward and took it. In sickness and in health, after all.

"There's no news," Joe said. "Nothing since the ransom demand. I sent them the money."

"Ransom demand?" Tess felt her spine stiffen. "You didn't say anything about a ransom demand."

"Didn't I?" Joe didn't seem to care. "I wired it as soon as they told me. Half a million dollars."

"Why didn't you tell me?" Her voice was brittle.

Joe seemed to look at her for the first time. "I should have. I just didn't think about it. I told Arnie to write them a check and send it by courier. I've been sitting by the phone ever since."

"You—" She stopped and gathered her thoughts. "What's that going to do to the Movement?"

"It'll be okay, I guess—"

"You *guess?*"

Joe shrugged. "It might set us back some."

"Joe." Things were flying apart right in front of her. The whole room seemed as if it would just blow away. "You remember how tight we are. There's not much money—we barely have enough for the Divinidine we were planning to use. Joe, we are supposed to be doing God's work!"

Joe stared at her. "God doesn't want me to lose my son, honey."

"Maybe this is a test. Maybe this is like Abraham and Isaac. Did you ever think of that? Maybe you just have to have faith."

Joe kneeled in front of her and took both her hands. "Honey—"

"I went down to Colombia and found a miracle. No—I *made* a miracle. God brought it right to my hands. We need to use it. We need the money to make use of it, not squander it. It's not our money. Do you understand what it is you're doing? Is this the devil's work right here in front of me?" Her voice rose.

Joe patted her hands. "Hush, honey. Hush for a minute. Just hush."

After a moment, she calmed down. "This is bigger than you or me, Joe. It's bigger than Ethan."

Joe patted her hands. "I've been doing this a long time, Tess. There are always setbacks. God uses human hands for his Holy Work so nothing goes smoothly."

Tess felt tears on her face.

Joe rose and found a box of tissues brought them. He pulled over a chair and sat down next to her. "Here."

She took the box and wiped her face. "I have no idea why I'm crying."

"It's a gift to be chosen to do God's will," Joe said quietly. "But we're fragile vessels."

Tess nodded.

They held hands. The sun dimmed and fell behind clouds.

"I've been thinking," Joe said in the gathering darkness. "Maybe we shouldn't try to bite off so much all at once. It takes time to change the world." He patted her hands. "Time and toil. We've done a lot. Maybe it's time to consolidate what we have."

Tess watched his face. "I don't understand."

Joe held her hands and seemed to gather his thoughts. "You were right. God has allowed this to happen. It's a sign. But the world is going to fight back against us—they always do. I've seen it all my life. 'For I did not come to bring peace but a sword.' Ethan's kidnapping is a sign. I think if we're too weak to lose a little money, then we're too weak to spread the Word throughout over the world."

Tess felt as if she were on the brink of revelation. "What do you have in mind?"

"What if we took our money and effort and built ourselves a place of safety? A place where we can consolidate what we've done and make ready to return?"

"A shining city on the hill."

"Exactly!" Joe looked away and spoke softly. "Then my son will be returned to me."

Tess smiled at him. The pure rightness of the thing was intoxicating. "I know just the place."

"Where?"

"Milan, Missouri."

oOo

When Orphira came into Bujold's office she saw two empty chairs. One for her, obviously, and one for Jake. Bujold was standing in front of the window and watching the traffic on I-270 glitter under the early spring sun. Jake was nowhere to be seen.

Bujold gestured her to be seated. "Any idea how long we'll have to wait for your teammate?"

"Detective Fiske is running down a new lead. He said for us to continue without him," Orphira said smoothly. *Oh, now you're covering for him?*

"I see," Bujold said dryly. He sat down at his desk and gestured for her to sit down. "That's a pretty good idea since his other leads have dried up. I wanted to talk to you anyway."

Orphira found herself getting tense. "What about?"

"Don't you think it's interesting that the only pay dirt we've found has come from Jake's tips? And now that the tip has shut down, we have nothing?"

"I'm not sure what you mean."

"You must have noticed this? You're not stupid, are you?

"What?"

"Are you sleeping with him? Or did you just follow Massa's lead?"

"I beg your pardon?"

Bujold stared at her without speaking for a moment. Then he relaxed and leaned back in his chair. He grinned. Orphira was not reassured.

"Sorry about that. Just checking. I had to be sure."

"Of what?" Orphira said frostily.

"Of what side you were on." Bujold tapped the desk for a moment. "I think Jake isn't playing straight with us"

Us? She saw suddenly that she was caught in a fight between two white boys.

"I see," Orphira said noncommittally.

Bujold lifted one eyebrow. "What do you think?"

Which white boy do you trust? The one with the power? Or the one that treats you well? Her instincts were always to align herself with power. Power protects, her father had always said. He'd been a cop forever. Of course, it hadn't helped her back in Silicon Valley. She'd been the best in her department, but she'd been the first one laid off. First her, then the white girls. After that, they shut down the company.

Jake *was* probably playing it both ways. Why should she protect him?

Orphira looked back at Bujold. Betrayal was one thing, she thought. But betraying him to *this* asshole was another thing entirely. "I think Detective Fiske is doing all he can."

Bujold chuckled. "Good. I like that. Protect the man you are working *with*. That's fine by me." Bujold leaned on his desk. "But if you find out something, I want you to remember the man you are working *for*." He nodded towards the door. "That'll be all."

Orphira left the office and walked downstairs to the parking lot. She sat in her car for a long time before she started it. Back to the office. Maybe it was time Jake leveled with her—yeah, that was it. Leveled with her. Or she'd toss his white ass to Bujold. Jake had been kind to her. She'd give him a chance.

She hit her forehead with her hand. Give him a chance when he was probably playing her for a fool? The best thing to do would be to get out of the car and march right back upstairs, and tell Bujold everything that had happened. Work with somebody else.

She stared up towards the office windows.

Only you didn't tell the feds on your fellow officers. She was sure Jake was counting on that. *Slimy shit.*

She remembered how he spoke to her when she'd been assigned to him. No crap. Just looked on her as a fellow officer. She'd liked that feeling. Liked the warmth that seemed to radiate from him. Liked his smile. Liked the way he'd trusted her judgment when she talked to him about his daughter. Jake hadn't been worth much in the last few weeks. Orphira didn't need a crystal ball to know something at home had gone complete sour. Something close to his heart. The daughter, maybe. Or the wife. That would make perfect sense. Jake did seem the sort of man who would love his daughter and be tortured by his wife. She wondered if there was something she could do.

Orphira leaned her head on the steering wheel.

Sweet Jesus Christ. She was falling for a white boy.

oOo

Anya sat at the table in the corner of the warehouse. Large vats of yeast were cooking. It was LeRoy's idea to genetically engineer *Saccharomyces* to produce Anapyridol as part of the fermentation process. The Anapyridol wasn't stabilized in the solution—it remained with the yeast cells.

After the beer was first racked, they filtered out the yeast, lysed and extracted the cells, then used chromatography to separate out the Anapyridol. After they eluted the drug from the columns, they just dried the Anapyridol. It wouldn't produce millions of tablets but it produced enough to fill Connie's quota of a hundred thousand.

A fine filtration on the beer removed any remaining Anapyridol infected yeast cells from the solution.

It made a nice, mild brew. LeRoy, brilliant as he had proven himself to be, was enjoying trying out the different beer recipes as much as he had enjoyed figuring out the production wrinkles. He was a genius. He was also fifteen. Thinking about him distracted Anya from the black despair inside her.

Anna had reached a block on generating the anti-Anapyridol. Worse, she continually felt Him looking around in her mind. She knew if He ever found out what she was doing, she'd be in trouble. Not that He had spoken to her. That would take more Anapyridol—something she would never do again. Give Him any more strength? *Pull the other one.*

Alcohol helped, it seemed. She couldn't tell if she just didn't feel Him or if He quit moving around. But the alcohol made it harder to concentrate, and figuring out a binder for the Anapyridol was a hard problem.

Anapyridol bound to the NMDA receptors in the cingulate gyrus. Then it was metabolized. If that were the only thing that was going on everything would have been fine. All Anya would have had to do was wait until Anapyridol was excreted out the kidneys. The data on the half-life of Anapyridol was documented as part of the toxicology trials.

By now no Anapyridol was left. Even the metabolic by-products had been broken down and peed away. But He was still there.

That meant there was a secondary effect. One they hadn't seen in either the toxicology trials or the first efficacy trials. Something she hadn't seen even back at VECTOR. This was something new. Anapyridol had effected a permanent change.

Anya went over the receptor data again and found no evidence for it. No Anapyridol or Anapyridol variant had ever bound more than transiently. No permanent bond was shown.

Anya was being forced towards thinking this was a learned response. Her brain had rewired itself in response to Anapyridol, just as blind patients learned to interpret the signals of embedded microprocessors or stroke victims relearned how to speak.

She buried her head in her hands. How would she *unlearn* something?

A shadow fell over her, and she sat up abruptly.

"Share a beer with me. Connie's gone for the night." LeRoy sat down across from her. He handed her a beer. "Tripple bock. Pretty good, I think."

"I think not." She placed the beer carefully on the table. She had no idea how many Anapyridol-bearing yeast cells were floating in the solution, and she had no plan to find out.

LeRoy sipped his small glass and watched her. "There's no free Anapyridol in the beer."

"Beg pardon."

"When I genetically engineered the yeast, I made sure the Anapyridol was sulfated. The bond doesn't break unless a strong base is used." He pointed to the beer. "Unless you have the digestive system of a caterpillar, that's safe for you to drink. You won't get a second dose."

"I don't know what you're talking about."

"I'm a genius, remember? You said so yourself. I've met Bill Wallace, and he's clearly over in the deep end talking to himself. I figure he's hearing voices and they're not coming over the intercom. But he can't be too crazy or he wouldn't be running a multimillion-dollar corporation. My Uncle Norman never trusted people who sampled the product—I'm guessing that's what Bill's doing. Am I right?"

Anya didn't say anything.

"Did you take it on your own or did he slip you something?" LeRoy sipped his beer.

"You're too smart for your own good."

"So Connie tells me. I figure he slipped it to you. I figure you're like me. I may use drugs someday but it sure as hell wouldn't be *this* drug. I like my own thoughts too much to want anybody else's."

Anya took the beer and drank some. "You have no idea."

LeRoy nodded. "Fair enough. So, you're working on a cure?"

What the hell? "Yes."

"Let me see."

She passed him her notes. He read them quickly.

"Ah," he said suddenly and leaned back. "I thought you might have made that mistake when I first saw the work."

Anya smiled thinly. "Mistake?"

"You thought it was Anapyridol doing all the work."

"We have the binding data. You've seen it."

"I didn't say Anapyridol didn't do a lot. I did see the data, after all. But look here." He pulled out a pen and sketched out a rough sketch of the molecule. "See that furanose ring with the ammonia group?" Next to it he drew a second structure. "The ammonia group is the point of attachment for glutamase when glutamate gets broken down. But see the way it sticks out in Anapyridol?"

He put his glass and her glass next to one another. "Say the glutamase attaches here. It carves off that furanose. But what's left doesn't fit and now there's nothing for the glutamase to attach to. Magic: neopyridol. It just floats off. Eventually it'll diffuse away from the site but there's nothing to metabolize it."

Anya tried to visualize the new molecule, thinner and lighter with all of the original binding sites intact. "It'll outcompete Anapyridol for the same sites."

"Right. But glutamase doesn't happen everywhere—it's only specific to the glutamate receptor sites, of which the NMDA is one—so not much is going to get produced from normal therapeutic doses. A recreational dose, however, will produce more. I'm guessing, enough to do the job."

Anya stared at the new molecule drawn on the page. The possibilities opened up to her. "There must be a second binding site."

"I wondered about that. I didn't have the data."

"I knew about it from—" She stopped before she mentioned VECTOR. LeRoy didn't seem to notice. "—before. But the Anapyridol didn't fit, so I didn't think much of it. This new molecule fits both."

"With, I'm guessing, interesting results."

In her mind, she could see the neopyridol floating in space, quickly floating over the neurons of her brain until it fit in one site and as snugly as a key into a lock. Another in the distance fit into a second lock, and both turned simultaneously. A door opened—

"This guy's going to be trickier," LeRoy said easily, looking over his drawing. "I don't think this bond is temporary. Look at that hydroxyl group. That's going to be really sticky once it fits in. We need something to bind to it and pull it out."

"Or something to tag it and tag the cell."

"Apoptosis?" LeRoy stared at her. "You want to kill your own neurons?"

"Maybe." Anya said quietly.

LeRoy whistled. "Must be some drug."

"As I said, you have no idea."

LeRoy considered her. Anya had no idea what was going through his mind.

"Let's leave that sort of thing as a last resort." He picked up her notes and examined them again. "Maybe we could add that furanose back on and convert it back to Anapyridol again. Or determine the active component of the neopyridol and block the binding site with something inert. Something the site would select preferentially."

The despair came again. Anya leaned back. Yoga. Maybe she could train it out of her mind—that wouldn't work. Yoga increased your spiritual awareness. She tried to think of anti-spiritual disciplines. Real estate? Logical Positivism?

LeRoy patted her hand. "We'll figure something out. There are still lots of possibilities."

In spite of herself, she was encouraged.

oOo

Ethan woke to see Jim seated, watching him.

Ethan sat up, coughed and spit something out. His face felt hot. "I feel sick."

"You might have malaria," Jim said speculatively. "Or not. It could be one of any number of third-world diseases. I'm surprised you haven't had the trots. But you're fortunate that way, I suppose."

"Lucky me."

"I've been considering our last conversation about the eclipse. It's not as simple as changing the rules—a delta on the speed of light or some such." Jim leaned forward, his elbows on his knees, the very picture of an earnest post-doc. "It would have to be more sophisticated. You don't change the rules. You invoke a situation where the previous rules don't really apply."

Ethan stared at him. His mind felt thick. "I have no idea what you're talking about."

"Let's say you ran a spreadsheet on a computer that's been designed to monitor aircraft engines. Presumably, the spreadsheet would work properly. If you hadn't been told, you would never know that the underlying computer running your gas mileage spreadsheet could monitor aircraft engines. Yet the capability would still be there, untapped and unguessed-at."

"You're saying the eclipse is a computer?"

"Don't be obtuse." Jim's face flashed.

Ethan stared at him. *Don't think this is Jim,* he thought. *That just fools you. This is the man that kidnapped and had his men beat you.* He shook his head and closed his eyes a moment.

"Give me a minute. I'm not at my best," he said in a low, subservient voice. For a moment, Ethan hated himself. *I should die on my feet, not live on my knees.* But the memory of Guillermo and Santos seemed to lie underneath every word or gesture and simmered his thoughts in fear.

"Fair enough," Jim said, suddenly affable.

Okay. Think. "You're saying physical rules are dependent on the situational state of the environment. If the state changes, the physical behavior changes along with it." Ethan wasn't sure how to proceed. "So, a relative slowdown of time could occur without a change in mass or velocity because the state of the environment changed?"

Jim beamed. "Exactly."

"Caused by…?"

"The prayers of that cult that was here. You met them."

Ethan shrugged. "That's a pretty powerful cult. What's so different about them, as opposed to any other religious group on the whole planet?"

Jim frowned and nodded. "I thought of that, too. But instead of trying to find reasons to say it didn't happen, let's try to explain why it did."

"Yeah." After all, it was work to dump twenty years of rational thought. "Look, there is already the observed/observer interaction at the heart of the standard model. 'Spooky action at a distance,' right? That's always generated a lot of discussion." Or you could get around the entire problem by a redefinition of isolation vs. non-isolation. Measurement wasn't special; it just broke the isolation of the experimental environment. Ethan said nothing of this.

"Right."

"So, let's say we're built into the system. The universe isn't something that happens to us. It's something we participate in."

Jim didn't speak for a moment. "Now, that's an extension of the anthropic principle a lot of people would find hard to swallow."

Everything about this is hard to swallow. Look, I'm just trying to stay alive. "So what? Science is based on the idea of repeatable phenomena. Observation, hypothesis, test—classical science. Science is a product of statistical mechanics. Single events are hard to characterize. The scientific paradigm has problems with them especially if the events themselves are suspect. If we didn't have the eclipse data, how much stock would we put in a bunch of cultists saying they stopped the moon?"

Jim stood up. "I have good news," he said.

"What?" Ethan blinked. The abrupt change startled him.

"I received word that your father has sent the money. As soon as we get it, the kidnapping will be over."

"That's great news," Ethan babbled. Going home, seeing Joe, getting back to Saint Louis—just getting out of here would be enough.

Jim watched him.

"What?" Ethan searched his face, trying to see what lay beneath.

"I'll miss you," Jim said softly. "I disappear into Mexico. Haberman is probably going south to Peru. But you, dear boy, are staying here."

"You said the kidnapping will be over."

"It will be. I kidnapped you because you were your father's son." Jim leaned towards Ethan. "But you're going to die because you slept with my wife."

oOo

"I don't know about this," Cindy said as Portia opened the car door for her and she slid into the back seat.

Cindy didn't recognize the car or the woman driving or the dark woman passenger.

"This is Tess," Portia said as Cindy buckled up. Her voice was eager and shy at the same time: Portia's I've-got-a-crush-on-this-one voice. Great.

Tess leaned back over the front seat. "Hello, Cindy," she said. "Portia's told me a lot about you. I hope you like our meeting. This is Charvak."

Charvak nodded and didn't speak.

Introductions completed, Tess turned back facing the windshield. She pulled out some papers and started going over them.

Cindy liked Tess's throaty voice. It was just like Portia to fall for a sophisticated older woman.

"Tess is giving us a ride to the meeting," Portia. "She came all the way from Alton to do it. She's great."

Great.

"Does your mom know you're going to a… meeting?" Cindy said cautiously.

"It's amazing what people will let you do if you tell them you're going to church." Portia held up a square block with a tiny keyboard. "Mom gave me one of these GPS cell phones when Donnie disappeared. As long as she knows where I am, I can do what I want."

Portia leaned forward and whispered conspiratorially. "She's scared I'll run away like you did." Portia giggled and sat back up. "But there's no need to. If I had figured out that Donnie disappearing would give me this kind of freedom, I'd have paid him to leave years ago."

"Is that what happened?"

"No." Portia bit her lip. "A letter came in the mail from him. Postmarked Venezuela. It said he was all right but he had gone on a 'spiritual quest.' He'd be back when he got back. Mom's scared he's joined a cult or something."

Cindy stared at her, not knowing what to say.

"Oh, don't look at me that way," Portia said crossly. "He's not dead or anything."

Cindy looked back outside the window. It made Cindy wonder what sort of people Portia's parents really were. Of course, visiting Portia in Town and Country seemed like visiting a cult sometimes. Maybe it ran in the family.

The meeting was taking place in the Hyatt at the airport. This made Cindy feel good—she'd never worked at the Hyatt. There was little possibility anyone there knew her.

The meeting took place in the Regency Ballroom. Other people were coming in at the same time. Portia left Cindy and followed Tess like a love-starved puppy dog, leaving Cindy on her own. That suited Cindy. She picked up a Coke and started wandering.

The room was huge—perhaps a thousand people could fit in here. One section was filled with chairs directed at a podium, but the rest was open. Most of the people were women—some of them as young as Cindy. Most were around Tess's age. There were men, too, knotted together in groups and eyeing the women speculatively. Connie was leaning against the wall, surveying everyone.

Cindy turned away from him, her face suddenly hot. *What the hell was he doing here? But then, maybe he was still their supplier.* She stood up straight, turned around, and walked over to him.

Connie watched her, no change in his expression.

"Hey, Connie," she said. Her own voice sounded shrill in her ears. "I thought you were out of this business."

Connie shrugged slightly. "Norman asked me to drop by and watch things. He doesn't like to be so public."

"You're not exactly inconspicuous."

He nodded. "I do what I'm told. I didn't think you went in for this sort of thing."

"Portia wore me down."

"A lot of them were your... professional colleagues."

"Beg pardon?"

Connie just looked at her significantly.

Oh. "I never met any of them." Cindy turned and scanned the room. "Who are they?"

"Carly and Pauline over in the corner—the redhead and the brunette. Brenda near the stage. You met Tess."

"Tess is a call girl?"

"*Was*, girl. None of them are call girls now, exactly. Some of them are still working, but now it's for the Lord." Connie grinned at her. "Evangelism that actually works." He looked away. "Say, I saw your dad's co-cop at the Westin. You ever meet her?"

"No." A shiver ran through her. Just what she needed: her dad finding out she was here.

"Pretty little sister." Connie looked around. "Any idea what *she's* up to?"

"No," she said slowly. Somehow, she thought she should. "Jake was complaining about the DEA."

"Shit." Connie looked like he wanted to spit something out. "I bet you're right. I bet the fucking DEA has stuffed itself all through this business." He shook his head. "They could even be here and I'd never know it. I was going to have to leave soon, anyway. Before the crowd gets too wasted."

"Beg pardon?"

Connie looked at her strangely. "I thought you had got into this."

"I told you. I'm here on account of Portia."

Connie leaned forward. "Recruitment to come here usually means swallowing half a dozen or so pills of Bill's pills. Followed by banging your brains out in a hotel room until you see the light of God."

Cindy stepped back. "What? *Here?*"

"I thought you knew. When you were talking about your friend, I figured she'd done the banging."

Cindy shook her head. "You've got to get me out of here."

"Maybe." Connie looked around. "You came here with Tess. She's tight with the chief preacher. I don't want to mess that up. You go and pay your respects, and if things are cool, we can go."

Cindy made her way through the crowd towards Tess. Where she found Tess, she'd no doubt find Portia. People were moving differently now. They swayed a bit. A couple of people were holding hands. Most had flushed faces. Cindy looked into their eyes and saw the pupils were dilated.

She found Tess near the podium. Portia stood next to her, waiting to be noticed. Tess ignored her and was speaking with a strong-looking, portly man. She pulled Portia away.

"I have to go," Cindy whispered.

Portia's face fell. Her face was flushed, too. Portia stroked Cindy's arm absently, but sensuously. "You promised."

"I promised to come to a meeting. I came. Now I have to go."

Tess said something, and Portia was distracted.

"Okay," Portia said suddenly and turned back to Tess.

Cindy couldn't help feeling hurt. *This is your heart*, she thought. *This is your heart on drugs.*

The big man looked up. "I've never seen you before," he said, smiling. "I'm Joe Cori. Welcome." He put out his hand. His face was only a little flushed, but he seemed in complete control.

"Thank you," Cindy said and shook his hand. "I just came to visit with Portia a little. I have to go now."

"Ah," Joe said sympathetically.

Cindy saw Joe had grasped the situation at once. *Smart man*, she thought.

"This is my wife, Tess," he said, introducing her. "I hope you can come back when you have more time."

Cindy nodded and scurried back to Connie as quickly as she could. The room seemed to be getting warmer. One couple, near Connie, had started unbuttoning each other's shirts.

"Let's go *now*," she hissed as she passed him.

"I guess. This is the best part, though. You're missing some fine action."

"Do you want to explain why we're here to my father?"

"Fair enough."

The both of them walked quickly to the parking lot. Cindy lay low in the seat until they reached I-70. Then she sat up and stared out of the car.

"You okay?" Connie looked over at her.

"I came hoping I was going to save Portia." Cindy leaned back against the leather headrest. "But at the first hint of sex, I'm out like a shot. Me, the experienced one."

Connie shrugged. "Joe's setting up for something big. Until then, Portia's not in any real danger. The clap or AIDS would burn right through that group, prayers and all. But I expect Joe is watching that pretty closely. Portia is just making experiences she can talk about to her expensive shrink someday."

Cindy glanced over at him. "Cold, Connie. Very cold."

"There's worse things that can happen to kids." He said it shortly and with an ancient air of authority.

It came to Cindy suddenly in a whole new way: Connie knew things she *didn't*. All this time Connie had driven her around—set her up with men, bought her clothes, and joked with her—he had known those things, whatever they were. Cindy had a sense there was an ocean of pain and suffering he knew intimately but of which she had zero understanding. Connie would tell her anything she wanted to know. All she had to do was ask.

Cindy remained silent all the way home.

oOo

Jake sat in his office, looking out the window. For a moment, the last six months seem to crowd in around him. He took a deep breath and things receded. It was quiet for the moment. He was alone.

He wanted a drink. He wanted to kill somebody.

The phone rang and he picked it up.

"Hey, Jake. This is Sam Forestell."

Jake looked at the phone and put it back to his ear. "I heard you were dead."

"Rumors only."

"What do you want?"

"Norman is going to dump the rest of the Divinidine tonight."

"Where?"

"I don't know where and I don't know when. You won't find him when it happens, but you might find him afterwards." Sam gave Jake the address.

Jake wrote it down. "What do you want, Sam?"

"Just doing my civic duty." Sam laughed and hung up.

Excellent son-of-a-bitch *luck*. Once Norman dumped the drugs, everything would be *over*.

The phone rang again, and he answered.

"You better have a good explanation waiting for me when I get there."

"Orphira?" Jake was bewildered. "What are you talking about?"

"I just spent a Godawful half hour with our friend and colleague, Lieutenant Bujold."

"Damn. I forgot. Jesus. Sorry."

"You better be sorry. You better have a good lead for us to follow, since that's what I told Bujold you were working on."

"Thanks."

"Thanks, *hell*. Make it happen, white boy."

Jake thought quickly. "Meet me at Riddle's."

There was a click, and the line went dead. Jake looked at his watch. Figuring she called as soon as she left, he had about forty minutes until he had to spin a story.

Jake was waiting for her in the corner booth. He found a reassurance in the size and anonymity of the place, in the hard, wooden booths and the cool texture of a Bass ale. When Orphira came in, she gave him a hard look. Something in his face must have changed her mind. Her face softened. Jake had a Corona waiting for her.

Orphira looked at it as she sat down. "I like Corona."

"I know."

She looked from him to the beer and back again. Picked it up and sipped it, watching him. "Okay. Spill."

Jake hadn't been able to think of a story. He looked up at her. Then looked down again. The only thing he had was the truth. Or at least part of the truth. "I knew what was going on in those rooms we busted."

"I figured. Were you getting something to look the other way?"

Jake nodded. "Yeah. Then we got the first tip. I talked to… the guy and got the second."

"Then he shut down."

"Not exactly. He was pushed out of the business. He's not in it anymore. It's moved. My contacts dried up."

Orphira looked into her beer for a minute. "I know about this sort of thing from my daddy. So, I know the smell of bullshit when it gets too thick. Tell it all, or I'll turn around and go back to Bujold."

Jake felt a brief flare at anger and suppressed it. "Okay. You know how this stuff works. Vice only really handles drugs. Prostitution usually doesn't get looked at unless it gets out of hand or somebody gets hurt. About seven years ago me and the Mexican—"

"You knew the Mexican?"

"We went to high school together—drinking buddies for years. We realized that a nice, high-priced ring could bring in a bundle and never get touched as long as we kept control and didn't get too greedy. We got some seed money—"

"How did you do that?"

Jake shook his head. "You don't need to know everything. We took the seed money and started out small and grew slowly. We kept our clientele off the street. Then, last spring, the Mexican got himself killed."

"How did that happen?"

Jake shrugged. "I'm not sure. I'm pretty sure he got offed by Connie Samoa—this big, black giant that moved down here from Chicago a couple of years ago. But Connie claimed the Mexican just went somewhere he shouldn't and got disappeared. Maybe. But Connie took over the ring pretty smoothly, so he must have been studying it for months. He thought I was just the cop on the beat paid to look the other way. I let him think that—I was just skimming pure profit now, anyway. Then Cindy ran off."

That's when the whole thing went south, he said to himself. *Wrong* rang inside his mind. *Not true.* That derailed your personal life but it didn't change the setup hardly at all. Maybe it even helped the bottom line.

"Ah," Orphira said. "She ended up with Connie?"

"You figured that right off, didn't you? Took me a while. People are smart when they want to be. But I didn't want to be." Jake leaned back in his chair. "Then it got really interesting. Sam Forestell was involved somehow."

"Who's Sam Forestell?"

A dead man come back to life. He couldn't say that.

Jake drained half his Bass. "Sam is one nasty piece of work. Likes carving people up with a knife. He did small murders up on the north side for years—which is pretty interesting for a white guy. Then, when Hurricane Andrew hit, he left for Florida to run hookers and help eliminate competition on some of the rebuilding contracts. Came back up here in '93 to run hookers again up on the North Side for the rebuilders after the floods. Went to Fulton for a pimp charge and came out again a couple of years ago. I didn't hear anything about it until last year, when he was doing some work with Cold Norman Parkin out of East Saint Louis."

"That's a name I've heard of."

"I'm not surprised. I don't know if Sam backed Connie originally or not. But by the end of the summer, Connie was working for Norman and Sam was running a string up in Alton. Somewhere in there, Drug X started being the Spanish fly of choice for the ring." *That was when I first saw that the whole damned thing might fall apart.* He took a deep breath and continued.

"Then Sam disappeared, just like the Mexican did. Norman pushed Connie out and started operating the ring directly. Connie's out in the cold doing bodyguard work for him. Then the ring dried up completely, as far as I know. That's where we are now."

Orphira drained her Corona. "You're a son-of-a-bitch."

"I'm better than some." Jake leaned on the table.

"So, what's your plan?"

Jake barely heard her. He pulled out his notebook and started writing down dates. Beginning of May, Cindy runs off. June, she returns. The drugs show up—they're *discovered*, at least—roll in July. September, Cindy's back at school, all's right with the world. Sam gets "killed" sometime in October. Could Cindy have been involved in Drug X? Jake shook his head. Think objectively. Then think again: could Cindy have been involved?

Jake thought about how Cindy had acted when she'd returned. Scared, mostly. More mature—comes from being a hooker, he supposed, and then kicked himself. *That's your daughter, remember?*

Not right now, he answered himself.

She came back scared. And more mature. Dependant? He closed his eyes and remembered his daughter coming home. Trembling. He'd confined her to her room for a week and she didn't say a word. He'd watched her that week. If she was using regular drugs, he would have spotted it. Had she acted like those girls they'd been pulling out of the rooms?

They were confident, mature—almost idealistic. Jake didn't think he'd ever seen Cindy idealistic. Friendly, pitying, kind—yes. But always about this puppy or that friend or this old cat. The bigger picture didn't interest her. She had no real cause. That's what was bothering him about the girls: they seemed to have some *cause* they were whoring for. Cindy didn't have that.

So, for the moment, anyway, say Cindy didn't use Drug X. Could she have been fronting it?

He thought back to her. She had been scared. Really scared. Scared down to her socks.

Had that been why she had come home?

Maybe. It didn't feel right. If she hadn't used the drug, had she seen somebody else use it? Had that been what scared her? Jake shook his head. Too distant. Whatever had scared Cindy had been personal. A threat.

Connie blamed Norman for Cindy, but that didn't wash either. Cindy came back in July. Drug X had to have been in place by August. December, the DEA had starts knocking on doors—Connie had been pushed out of the picture by then. Connie must have been in charge when Cindy started. Connie had probably not recruited Cindy—that much was true. If he knew Cindy, she'd probably recruited herself into the business. Jake felt sick, but that felt right.

Had Connie threatened her?

Jake made a fist on the table without realizing it.

Orphira looked at him, concerned. "What's wrong, Jake?"

Jake shook his head.

When had Sam come into the picture? He was out of the picture by October. Dead, so far as Jake knew. Killed by Norman. All spring and summer, Sam is backing Connie and getting his cut. Then, come June, Sam is suddenly running Alton. By September maybe?—Sam's dead and Connie's working for Norman watching his sick nephew. No, scratch that. Connie works for Norman *first*, fronting the girls, *then* Norman pushes him out to bodyguard work and runs the girls *and* the pills from then on.

Back to Norman again. Something happened around the same time Cindy came back. Did Cindy see a piece of it? Something that scared her right back home again?

Back again to Connie and Cindy.

Say Connie doesn't know who Cindy was—just some good-looking white kid he could use. Doesn't know until the day Jake meets up with him at Mississippi's and shows him her picture. Then, Connie not only knows who she is but knows he has to get rid of her.

Jake leaned back in his chair. Holy *shit*. Cindy was lucky Connie just didn't off her right then and toss her in the river.

So, what does Connie do? He goes to Sam. What does Sam do? Sam calls Norman. What does Norman do?

Norman takes over the operation and retires Sam up to Alton. Norman scares Cindy shitless—Jake knew Cold Norman—and Cindy comes home quiet as a mouse. Still, something was wrong with the idea. Why didn't Norman just make Cindy disappear? To save Connie? Connie was safe. Sam? Same answer. Cindy was no threat to Norman.

Was she a tool?

Jake stood up and rubbed his arms. Norman wouldn't have let her go unless she was of some use to him—not quite right. Norman would have let her go with the understanding that she owed him. He would come to collect.

Back to Norman again.

Shit. It was just possible Cindy knew something about Drug X.

Norman. Who, according to supposed-to-be-dead-Sam, would be out of the entire business after tonight.

Norman had drawn Cindy up deep inside this. Jake could feel it. It blew through him like superheated steam.

It all came crashing down inside of him. Jake had failed his wife, or she would be coming home. Jake had failed his little girl, or she would never have run away.

Jake's hands ached and he looked down. Slowly he unclenched his fists. He looked up at Orphira. She had a sympathetic look on her face.

She didn't know. He was about to fail her, too. The beer tasted sour to him, and his stomach hurt.

It took him a second to recapture the thread of the conversation.

A plan. Come up with a plan. "We have to lean on Connie. He knows things he's not telling. See if we can find out what Norman is doing. See if I can manage bringing all this down without taking myself down with it. Maybe Norman's been making Drug X, all along."

"That would be convenient. Take him out and everything is nice in the world." Orphira shook her head. "That's not Cold Norman's style. He'd rather front for a factory than run the factory himself. We find the factory, and the DEA will be very happy."

Jake nodded. *Show a little honesty here. String her along until you can figure out something to do.* "If DEA got distracted, I'd let Connie, Norman and Sam just fade away and get on with something worth doing."

"Like starting up your ring again?"

Jake shook his head. Color seemed to have leached out of the room. He could see the skulls below the skin of everyone around him. "I'm done with that business. What if Cindy found out?"

Orphira grinned briefly at him and stifled it. Jake was surprised. He wondered what it meant.

"I think the factory is a pharmaceutical company," Orphira said. "You saw the lab report. You can't get that level of purity in somebody's bathroom."

Jake stared at her. "Now, who's crazy? Pharma companies have better ways of making a lot more money."

"It doesn't have to be the company. Just some guy in a rogue lab. This stuff is different."

"How different?"

"I talked to those friends of mine over at SLU. This is a very specific drug. Somebody built it from scratch—probably as a research project. Then our rogue researcher steals a bunch of capsules and sells it to Norman."

"He'd have to sell a lot of it to make Norman personally interested." Jake thought for a moment. "And there aren't many local pharmas around. A couple of firms, but they're contract people and consultants. Most of the biotech in Saint Louis is devices."

Orphira nodded. "Could it be coming out of town?"

"I guess it could be," Jake said dubiously. "Kansas City? Saint Charles? East or West Coast?"

"Why don't you ask your wife?"

"Beg pardon?" Jake knew suddenly how a deer felt in the headlights of an oncoming truck.

"Your wife?" Orphira chuckled at him. "Works for a chemical company? That makes generic medicines?"

Jake didn't say anything. Talk to Anya. Yeah. Right. "I could try." He looked up. "Does that mean you're not turning me over to Bujold?" He didn't know where Norman was going to get rid of the Divinidine, but he did know where Norman would be afterwards.

"We lean on Connie. We use what we get from him to take down Norman and leave him out of it. That's enough for Bujold."

Orphira smiled at him and for the life of him, he had no idea what it meant.

oOo

Ethan remembered the day he decided he didn't believe in God. It had been a beautiful spring day. He was sixteen, and his mother had just died. He'd gone for a long walk along East Fork to get a handle on everything. The spring floods were long gone, and the torn earth was now covered with violets. The flowers were so rampant and lush, they flowed over the banks like a green and purple wave, curled down and sodden in the low and sluggish water.

He sat alone on an ancient limestone boulder, watching the water.

There was a moment like this every spring. After the thaw and before the warmth brought out the ticks and the mosquitoes. A breathless pause after the winter exhalation.

The funeral was fresh in his mind, and he had come out here for comfort. Instead, the quiet, autonomous beauty made him want to set fire to the flowers and burn them to the ground.

His hand was shaking as he drank from his water bottle. He'd packed a sandwich, but the thought of food made him nauseous.

Violets had sprung up here for millions of years. They would spring up for millions more. Ethan did not find this comforting.

"'I go now to prepare a place for you,'" he murmured. Joe had spoken at the funeral, and that had been his text. It was a pleasant image: his mother waiting for them in paradise. Was there something wrong that it struck him as a cheap and trivial idea? The invention of the weak and fearful in the face of death.

This pain, this grief, this anger felt precious, even if unbearable. Joe's promise of comforting relief seemed like a tranquilizer in disguise, no different from Thorazine or Mellaril.

If there were such a thing as God, he thought. Then His purpose and power had to be greater than human imagination. There had to be a reason to believe that belief was not naked self-service. It had to be something beyond comfort, fulfillment, or the promise of life everlasting. Something beyond human.

It came to him then the he really didn't believe in God at all. When he looked down inside himself, honestly, what he wanted to believe in was the comfort—the idea of some all-powerful, universal entity taking interest in him sitting here, watching the violets grow, didn't make a lot of sense.

His father said it took faith.

Faith meant discarding sense so you could believe strongly enough to get the comfort, like an addict accepting the necessity of the needle for the rushing warmth of the drug.

Now, better than a decade later, staring at the filthy ceiling of a hut in God knows where, Colombia, both hands handcuffed to an old iron bed and contemplating his imminent death, Ethan admitted comfort had its attraction.

You, he thought, *are going to die.*

He tried to fit it on like a new suit. "I am going to die," he said aloud.

The words disappeared into the dirt of the room. The comfort of heaven could be useful right about now. He closed his eyes.

Dear God, he prayed. *I don't want to die.* The words seemed to echo hollowly in his mind. He remembered in one of their innumerable arguments Joe saying there were no atheists in foxholes. *Just what I need*, Ethan had retorted. *Belief from the barrel of a gun.*

This isn't belief, he thought. *This is desperation.*

Someone opened the door quietly.

This is it, he thought. He tested the handcuffs again. Sure enough, they hadn't suddenly rusted through in the last forty seconds.

Harriet looked down at him. She held her fingers to her lips.

Ethan nodded.

She pulled a key out of her pocket and opened the handcuffs.

"How did you find me?" he whispered.

"Shut up. When we get out, you can ask me anything. Stand up."

He stood up shakily.

She looked him over critically. "Can you run if you have to?"

He shifted his weight experimentally. "I think so."

Harriet nodded. "Okay, then."

She led him out of the room. It was late afternoon, and the setting sun slanted through the trees. Ethan could hear commotion past some other buildings, but there was no one nearby.

Harriet walked silently. Ethan tried to imitate her. They slipped behind the privy. Ethan found out suddenly how the privy worked: a hole in the back opened down the hill. He stopped at the edge of the filth.

Harriet didn't even look back. "It's slippery. Don't stop." She kept on going.

Ethan followed. For a moment, he thought he would be sick. They passed the edge of the building, and Harriet motioned him to stop. She looked around the corner, then motioned him on.

Ethan passed the corner and saw Sanza walking towards them, carrying his dinner.

Sanza stopped. Harriet stepped forward and slipped her hand in her jacket. Sanza's eyes narrowed. *Oh, my God*, Ethan thought. *She's got a gun. She's going to kill him.*

In a moment, Ethan could foretell the future. He could see Sanza crumple and fall, the sound of the shot, the rousing the camp, Guillermo run up and see the body of his brother, look up and see Ethan, mutter in Spanish, and Ethan could understand him clearly: "You didn't know what pain was. Before."

Ethan whimpered.

Harriet glanced at Ethan and then back at Sanza, and pulled an envelope out of her jacket. She handed it to Sanza.

Sanza nodded and took the envelope with his free hand. He turned and went back towards the camp

Ethan stared at Harriet.

"What?" she said irritably.

"Nothing." Ethan tried to shake himself. He felt paralyzed.

"Come on," she said. "If he doesn't sell us out, we've got about twelve hours to go thirty miles."

She started a fast walk down the hill.

I might live, Ethan thought suddenly. With that thought, he found he could move again.

Moving felt like breaking free.

oOo

It had been two months since Connie had started the factory, and he was beginning to feel exposed. Sam's promised rewards seemed ever farther out of reach, while every day the risk of their secret factory seemed to grow. It wasn't enough to come in the dead of night to Connie's houseboat and offer partnership. There had to be some profit involved, as well.

Connie knew the day was soon coming when LeRoy would figure out the Anapyridol was not going to Norman. Connie couldn't quite see how to sell the batch to Sam without LeRoy betraying him to Norman out of loyalty — a quality Connie very much admired, when it didn't get in the way of business. Lord knows, he didn't want anything to happen to the boy. Connie had gotten outright fond of LeRoy. The boy's little puppy-dog love affair with Cindy made Connie feel almost paternal. Though from what he could tell, there was more puppy than affair going on. Somehow, knowing Cindy could have been had by any man with enough money had made LeRoy care more for her more rather than less — exactly the opposite of what Connie had expected. Made the boy interesting.

For a while, he thought that witch, Anya, was going to seduce LeRoy, The two of them worked so closely and intimately together that Connie concluded they had to be sleeping together. It was only after watching them carefully over a couple of weeks that he decided their closeness came merely from work. It didn't seem natural, but there it was, right in front of him. It made Connie uneasy. How were you supposed to predict the behavior of irrational people?

Connie contented himself with keeping the books. There was a natural comfort in adding up columns of numbers and having them all come out perfectly. His mother had always said he had the soul of an accountant. She hadn't meant it as a compliment, but you took positive reinforcement where you found it.

Do the books, he told himself. *Figure out how to turn this drug into dollars. A little casino,* he thought, dreamy-eyed, leaning back in the metal folding chair until it creaked and threatened to collapse. Nothing fancy but intimate. Where he could know the regulars. Maybe even a family thing—why not have daycare in a casino? Maybe he could bring down a few backhoes and dig a shallow channel next to the houseboat. Put in one of those little floating buildings like they used upriver in Saint Charles, only smaller. A restaurant. Maybe even a small hotel.

Connie sighed and went back to the books. It was amazing how cheap this operation was, compared to what Lifeworks had paid for their contract manufacturing. Following regulations must be expensive. Connie briefly hoped they weren't making strychnine or something. Bad drugs make bad press.

The capital outlay was done. Now all they had to do was keep the lab running until the drug was purified. Reagents and fuel for the electrical generators. That was it. Another couple of weeks, according to LeRoy, and the crop would be harvested and ready to sell.

Connie told Kalenin the production run was done and the purification started. He expected Kalenin would call Sam and Sam would then call Connie, but no call came. It made Connie uneasy. It seemed like everything was conspiring to make Connie uneasy.

He heard a rumble outside. That would be Kalenin coming with a "borrowed" tank truck of diesel fuel. Connie put down the pen and went outside. Sam was waiting for him.

Connie stood at the door. It took a moment for him to catch his breath.

Sam laughed. "Thought that might catch you unawares," he said, beaming. Sam stood up and walked towards Connie.

Connie looked frantically for the knife and didn't see it. He stepped back in through the door, reached behind it, and pulled out the shotgun.

Sam stopped. "You're not glad to see me."

"Last time you surprised me, I nearly drowned. Makes me a bit wary."

"Fair enough." Sam put his hands in the pocket of his jacket.

Connie pointed the shotgun right at his stomach.

"You don't disappoint," Sam said, grinning. "My friend, Donnie, has a pistol pointed at you."

"If I get hit by anything, I'll pull the trigger as my dying act."

"I'd expect no less. Now, how do we put down the guns without blowing each other apart?"

"How about your friend, Donnie, gets out of the truck and stands next to you, drops the pistol, and I put down my gun?"

"He's not in the truck."

"Didn't think he was. But he'd have to be a hell of a shot to cut me down before I pulled the trigger."

"Good point." Sam shrugged. "Donnie, make a noise so Connie knows where you are."

"I'm right here," came a soft voice behind and to Connie's right.

"You're quiet, I'll give you that." Connie didn't move the shotgun. "Look, Sam. I got no beef with you except how you might kill me. I just want to get paid. You want the drug. Can we be reasonable men?"

"I like that. I haven't been a reasonable man for a long time. Donnie? Put the gun away and stand where you are. Connie? If you just back up a bit, you'll see the two of us."

Connie did and pretty soon, he had the two of them in front of him. Donnie was a dark-eyed boy who looked familiar. The gun was nowhere in sight.

Sam's face crinkled, and then he started laughing. "You should have seen your face. Show him the pistol, Donnie."

Donnie slowly reached into his jacket and pulled out a length of copper pipe.

Connie didn't crack a smile. If Sam were a normal sort of criminal, this would be a trick for him to lower the shotgun. Or there would be a third man watching all of this. But Sam was anything but normal.

"Shit, Sam," he said tiredly. Hell, if Sam wanted him dead, he'd be dead. Connie lowered the shotgun. "It's not ready yet, anyway. You want a beer?"

Connie turned and walked to the refrigerator in the back near his desk. He half-expected a bullet in his back at any moment.

"Sounds good," Sam said and followed him.

He opened three Coronas and handed one to each, and took a long pull from the third. "If we're done with the jokes, I'm actually glad you're here. I just didn't expect you in person. Have a seat."

The three of them sat down on the folding chairs. Connie glanced again at Donnie and the resemblance clicked in his mind. "You're the brother of Cindy's friend, aren't you? I saw you when I took Cindy to that party."

Donnie nodded and didn't speak.

Sam patted Donnie's shoulder paternally. "Donnie doesn't talk much anymore. Donnie has other things on his mind. What mind he has left. Right, Donnie?"

Donnie glanced at Sam and turned his attention back to Connie.

Sam rubbed Donnie's shoulders gently. "Donnie is living proof that more isn't always better. He flew too close to the sun. You should take that as an object lesson."

"I will, as soon as I understand what it is you're talking about."

Sam shook his head. Without taking his eyes from Donnie, he said, "I will buy the entire batch for one million five. Cash up front. Total on delivery. Two weeks."

Connie didn't say anything. "That's more than twice what Norman's getting for his batch."

"I have wealthier clientele."

"Are you going to kill me, Sam?"

Sam chuckled. His rubbing of Donnie's shoulders seemed to have some effect. Slowly, Donnie leaned his head on Sam's shoulder. Sam's face grew suddenly tender.

"Poor Donnie's tired, isn't he?" Sam said quietly. "Consumed with holy fire. Not much left after a fire like that." Sam nodded towards Connie. "No. After I pay you, I'm going to disappear. You're going to dismantle this factory, and no one is ever going to make this stuff again. I'll have the whole batch."

This made Connie uneasy. "Are you sure you want me to destroy the factory? You might want more," he said dubiously.

"No, no," Sam said, softly. "This will be enough for my purposes. You're to erase all traces of this place."

"What about Norman's kid and the woman from town?"

Sam fell silent, considering. "Certainly, the woman can live," he said, finally. "Norman's boy can live, too."

Connie nodded, relieved.

Then Sam turned and looked long and hard at Connie. Connie felt cold clear through.

"But you will owe me," Sam said in a flat voice. "Don't ever forget that you owe me."

Connie cleared his throat. "How do you want to do this?"

Sam waved him away. "When everything is ready, Kalenin will take possession of the drugs and pay you. If he stiffs you, take care of him. You won't hear from me again." Sam stood and led Donnie, unresisting, away.

Connie followed them to the door. He watched as Sam drove off.

Then he was waving frantically after them. "What about the diesel? What about the fucking fuel?"

But they were gone.

Connie went back inside and closed the door. About an hour later, he heard the rumble again. This time, he had the shotgun in his hand when he opened the door.

Kalenin was getting down from the truck. "Give me a hand with the hose."

Connie stared at him.

Kalenin realized Connie wasn't following and turned back. He saw the shotgun and caught Connie's expression. Kalenin spread his hands. "What?"

oOo

Leroy stood in front of the mirror. He was wearing a white turtleneck and black pants. He looked like a token sixties black radical. His shoes were too shiny. His neck itched.

"You look nice." Norman clapped him on the shoulder.

LeRoy felt like an idiot. Worse, he felt like a poseur—who also happened to be an idiot.

"You think this is necessary?"

"No," Norman said calmly. "You could get nearly the same effect if you had a good roll of hundreds. But you said you didn't want to do it that way."

"She's not that kind of a girl," Leroy said. Norman rolled his eyes, and LeRoy added, "At least, not anymore."

"Whatever you say, kid." Norman handed him his jacket. "Where are you taking her?"

"Tony's."

"It's going to cost about the same."

LeRoy knew exactly what he was talking about and ignored him.

Norman sighed. "Have a good time."

"Thanks."

LeRoy didn't get nervous until he was next to Connie in the car and halfway to meeting Cindy.

Connie picked up on it without taking his eyes off the road. "It's just a restaurant, LeRoy. And she's just a girl."

Leroy nodded. This was the fifth "date" they had been on, and it only seemed to get worse.

Connie glanced at him and back to driving. "It's only hormones and sexual tension. That's all."

"Easy for you to say."

Connie barked a sharp laugh. "True enough. It's been a while since I was fifteen. It'll get easier."

"It's easy for you?"

Connie shook his head. "It's never easy."

Cindy was safely ensconced in a thick, long coat when they picked her up. LeRoy got out and opened the door for her. He caught the edge of Connie's grin as he followed Cindy into the back seat. Leroy felt his face grow warm and his ears burn.

"I dressed up like you said." Cindy smiled at him.

Now Leroy felt warm for another completely different reason. Leroy looked away at the same moment she looked down. They both giggled.

"Where are we going?" She sounded shy.

Deep inside, LeRoy couldn't believe that anything about Cindy could possibly be shy. The knowledge that Cindy had been one of Connie's girls was never far from his thoughts. But LeRoy was likewise engaged in his own criminal enterprise. Who was he to judge?

They didn't talk much on the way to the restaurant. LeRoy held the door for her again when they entered. When Cindy took off that coat, the peach glow of her dress was like the sun coming out. LeRoy felt as if he couldn't breathe.

Cindy laughed. "Just the effect I was hoping for."

Leroy closed his mouth and gave up not trying to stare at her. He wanted to memorize her every curve.

She let him take her coat and hand it to the checker. She took his arm and snuggled against him on the way to their table.

"Now, *this* is a date," she murmured.

The evening seemed full of promise.

The waiter sat them across from each other. Leroy tried to keep his eyes off Cindy's bosom, amply displayed by the low cut of the dress, and watch her mouth as she spoke, but his gaze kept wandering. He kept jerking his head up. He grew even more nervous. There were long and awkward silences.

LeRoy fumbled the order. Cindy made a couple of suggestions and LeRoy felt stupid and angry. "You've been here before."

Cindy nodded and nibbled on the breadsticks. "Over the summer."

With some man. Working for Connie. The anger evaporated and LeRoy just felt sick inside. He felt like a kid playing at being grown up. Maybe she didn't like the food. Maybe she would have wanted to go dancing. He stared at his plate. "Did you like it?"

LeRoy glanced up, and saw she was watching him.

She nibbled a breadstick. "This is a nice place. I like it fine. You're a pretty nice guy. I like you just fine, too. Don't be so nervous."

LeRoy nodded. "I like you, too. I just—"

"You keep thinking about when I worked for Connie." She said it flatly, without any particular emotion.

"I guess."

"Did you want to give me any money?"

"No. I just—"

"—want to have sex with me. Right?"

He was suddenly enraged. "Not anymore."

They stared at each other for a long minute.

"So, then, why did you bring me here?" she said quietly.

"It's a nice place. Norman thought of it."

Cindy shook her head. "I bet he did. I came here all the time. Connie suggested it to the guys. I guess Norman did, too. Maybe the two of them own a piece of the place." She looked around. "I bet half of these girls are working."

Leroy looked around the room. Cindy was probably right. There seemed to be a professional look to some of the girls here. Their faces echoed expressions he had seen on the faces of girls who had visited Norman. The thought of Cindy resembling any of Norman's girls depressed him. "So, you thought... I was going to pay you money for tonight?"

Cindy nodded. "Yeah. That's what I thought."

"And when you said this was a date, you were pissed-off?"

Cindy looked at the plate. "Not then. Not until I sat down and started looking around. Before that, well, it just felt like a date. I haven't been on a date in, like, forever."

"Can it still be a date?"

Cindy thought for a moment. She picked up the water glass and swirled it. "Maybe. I don't know. You see, when I was working for Connie, everything was scripted. I mean, you didn't know always where you were going to dinner or what you were going to do after dinner—just after dinner, anyway—but you always knew exactly where the evening was going to end up. It was like a movie you knew the ending to."

Cindy put the glass down. "But a date is different. You start the evening with some ideas of how things will turn out, but you really don't have any idea. I missed that." She chuckled. "Not that I've had that many dates."

LeRoy looked down at the table. "Norman said he pretty much cut you out of the loop. Is that true?"

Cindy nodded.

Appetizers came and stopped the conversation as they ate (as LeRoy read from the menu) Seared Sea Scallops with Black Truffles and Mussels.

With an effort of will, LeRoy eased back from the food. Some of the drugs he was on made eating too much fat too much of a good thing. LeRoy looked around and for a moment he wondered what the hell he was doing here. He forced himself to relax. The food was good. He could afford to feel expansive and companionable as he watched Cindy eat.

"I know where you live and where you go to school," he said quietly. "And I know more than I want to about your summer vacation. But that's it. What do you like to do?"

"Eat, for one," she said, wiping her mouth. "Go to movies. Go shopping. You know. The usual. Why should I talk about what I do every day? Where's the fun in that?"

"Okay. What do you like to do that you don't do every day?"

She thought for a minute. "You know what I like to do? What I really like to do?"

LeRoy shrugged and shook his head.

"Walk. For miles. Down streets and look in the windows. Along rivers. In shopping malls. Portia and I used to walk for hours. She did it to look in the stores, but I did it just to move."

"Ah." LeRoy thought for a moment. "Want to leave and go walk somewhere? We can walk on Delmar over by Riddles. It's not summer any more, but it's warm enough."

"I've never been to Riddles."

"As good a reason as any." LeRoy left enough money to cover the check and led her outside. Connie had the car waiting for them. *How does he do that?* LeRoy thought.

Saint Louis County was broken up into over ninety towns like a medieval kingdom. Delmar began at the west border of University City with Olivette, ran east out of U City out of Saint Louis County into the County of the City of Saint Louis. Riddles was in University City. Connie parked the car in the lot and waved them on as they walked west.

They stopped for a bit in the Subterranean Bookstore. Cindy showed him a picture book of the Saint Louis World's Fair. LeRoy showed her a dog-eared copy of Chuck Berry's autobiography.

"He owns Blueberry Hill down the street. At least, he used to. Norman told me." LeRoy pointed out a yellow-walled club.

They entered Riddles and were seated in the back. A big man with a blond and gray ponytail took their order. "Do you want the wine list?" he said.

Something in his eye told LeRoy that Connie had left his mark.

Cindy shook her head. "I don't like to drink."

"Me, neither," LeRoy said promptly.

"It's okay," said the waiter. "I own the place."

"Just sodas," said LeRoy.

The waiter shrugged. "Suit yourself."

"Now, this is a date," Cindy said, laughing.

"You've never been here before?"

"Never."

"How come?"

Cindy played with her fork. "My daddy… protected me, I guess. We went out to safe places. Union Station. The malls. The Arch."

"You live east of Tower Grove Park. It's not that bad." *For a white girl,* thought LeRoy.

"Safety only reaches so far. A couple of weeks ago, there was an assault four blocks away. Seems like there's a car stolen every couple of weeks. It's worse a little south of us, but it's not great where we are." Her face grew sad. "Maybe that was why."

"What's wrong?"

"Jake's pretty messed up right now," she said. "He found out about me. That hurt a lot. But Mom's been acting strange, too. He thinks she's having an affair. He didn't say, but I could tell he was thinking it." She put her elbows on the table. "It's destroying him. She says she's working a lot. But I'm pretty sure she's sleeping with Bill—at least before he ended up in the hospital. Remember Bill?"

"I remember." LeRoy wasn't sure if Anya was having an affair, but he knew how she'd been spending her nights. LeRoy had been trying to figure out what he was going to tell Cindy. On the one hand, LeRoy had built a little business. He had a factory. He had future sales. Revenue. He was a man with prospects. On the other hand, it was criminal manufacturing with dubious characters and he was working with Cindy's mother. He decided the best course was not to say anything. "Maybe she is working a lot."

"No," Cindy said shortly. "I know what she's been doing."

"You can't be sure—"

"Are you defending her?" Cindy's voice went cold. "You and your uncle are making a living off of my mother. Don't defend her to me."

Shit. He didn't say anything for a minute, trying to see a way to back track. "I don't know her."

Cindy stared at him a moment more. "No," she said, finally. "You don't."

Maybe he would never tell her what he was doing.

The silence grew long. The food came and covered the awkwardness.

After she finished her pasta, she leaned back in the booth. "Your turn. What do you like to do?" She smiled cheerfully at him.

It's not the mileage, he thought. *It's the change in moods.* He watched her, wondering what he would say.

"Biochemistry," he said, shyly.

"You're kidding."

LeRoy shook his head. "I'm really good at it. I have a knack."

"You have a knack."

He looked down. "Yes." He looked back up at her. Fiercely. "Like Michael Jordan has a knack for basketball. Like Jose Conseco has a knack for hitting home runs. Like Tiger Woods has a knack for a long drive up the green. I have a knack."

She was taken aback. "I see."

Deceit, he thought, *can lie at the heart of things.* It was deceit that killed his mother: his father had lied about his illness. It was deceit that almost killed him. His mother lied to herself when LeRoy got sick. Only when she herself began to fall ill did she admit to herself what had happened to her and her son.

I can't tell everything, LeRoy thought. *But I can tell what I can.*

"Did you get yourself tested after this summer?" he asked.

"Tested?" She looked half offended and half intrigued. "You mean for diseases and things like that?"

LeRoy nodded.

"Yeah. Jake took me someplace discrete." She laughed. "I have to go back in a couple of months. That's the deal."

"You passed?"

"Sure, I passed. Not that it's any of your business."

"I wouldn't have. I have AIDS."

Cindy didn't say anything for a moment. "You don't look it. I mean, you're thin and all, but not that thin."

"I medicate myself. I watch the literature. I read it all. I sneak into conferences when I can. I've been medicating myself since I was eleven."

Cindy looked at him as if he were crazy. "You're not a doctor or anything."

"I don't have to be. I can figure it out."

"You've figured out a cure for AIDS."

"No, of course not. There probably isn't a cure for AIDS. What I've done is treated the disease into remission. With protease inhibitors and anti-retrovirals, among others. I run tests on my own body. Take the samples and send them out and study the result. I don't have much of a lab. I know my own histocompatibility and protein complexes better than anybody. And I'm a genius."

"A genius."

"A genius," he said, excitedly. He'd never been able to talk like this. It was exhilarating. "I figured out... a molecular structure from a website."

"Website?"

"Yeah. It was up a day, and then it disappeared. I have no idea who put it up or why. But I saw right away that the compound was incomplete. It was the metabolite that was important, not the molecule itself."

"Okay, you can stop now." Cindy said quietly. "This is too much information."

LeRoy stopped. "It's true."

"If it was, you'd be better off dating my mother." She looked away. "I was wondering why you didn't try anything. I mean, we go out and do something, and you don't so much as kiss me. Just my luck to find a boy I actually like and he's got AIDS."

"You like me?"

"You didn't figure that out? Some genius."

He reached over and took her hand. She took his hand and held it with both of hers.

They didn't speak for a long time.

"So," she said. "Do the drugs keep you alive?"

"It's like running in front of a train," LeRoy said quietly. "The trick is to stay in front. I've got an edge on it. I take the cream of research and adapt it to me. So far, so far."

Cindy nodded. "So, this means we can't have sex, right?"

"You want to?"

"Sort of."

"Let's walk," he said.

They walked down the sidewalk, not crowded but not empty, either. Over bricks with brass lettering describing the giants of the blues. Past the Tivoli theatre running *The Magnificent Ambersons* double-billed with *Malcom X*. Past Blueberry Hill. Standing outside and listening. Past a vinyl record store. Standing and listening again.

She took his arm and leaned her head against his shoulder.

They crossed the street and walked back past a clothing store. Past the bookstore again. Past Riddles. Crossed the street and turned back up again, past the Tivoli, Blueberry Hill. Back and forth, talking sometimes, listening others, walking and enjoying the animal heat of their bodies in the cool air. Until Connie brought up the car and said it was time to get Cindy home.

"So," she said, sitting next to him in the back of Connie's car. "Can we kiss?"

He looked at her. "I think so. Bodily fluids—"

"Shut up." She pulled him down and kissed him gently. She held his hand all the way home.

LeRoy felt like he owned the world.

oOo

Ethan will remember that long stumbling run down the mountain for the rest of his life. On his last day, his last hour, his last thought will be of hurtling in the dark under great and towering trees, stumbling over scrub and roots, hearing the intermittent howl of unidentifiable beast or bird.

The dark closed in as they left the camp. Harriet pulled out two flashlights, red disks taped to the end to give a faint and narrow beam.

"Don't use it unless you have to," she commented. "We have twelve hours to make it thirty miles." Thirty miles to Neiva and an airport.

Harriet made him run. When he couldn't run, she made him walk. When he couldn't walk, it seemed he swayed in place, quivering downhill in the direction they had to go. The only light was the glow of Harriet's GPS as she figured out the path and the flimsy red beam of those inadequate flashlights.

Often, he fell. Each time he lay there, checking each ankle and knee, knowing anything broken would be fatal because it would keep them there in the forest. Feeling lucky for a bruise or a twist he could walk off.

Harriet wouldn't answer any questions but only guided them down an invisible trail that led to an obscure and indeterminate road. On occasion they passed between low buildings—houses or perhaps stores. Twice, a dog barked at them, but no lights came on. *No electricity*, he thought. It'd take something more than a rushed footstep to make you get out of bed on a dark night to strike a match and light a candle or a lantern. Still, they would remember and when the two of them were followed, these people, awake in the dark, would confirm to Haberman: *Sí. They came this way.*

Ethan inhaled the nut smell of cooking oil in the dark. Neiva lay in the bottom of the valley next to the Magdalena River. When the careful dawn appeared, the mountain kept them in shadow all the way to the edge of town.

Harriet looked up at the now blue sky. "Haberman's up, now." She squinted at the sky. "He's on his way."

Harriet snagged a sleepy taxi driver and gave him a bill big enough to wake him up.

The two of them relaxed for a moment in the back.

"How did you find me?" Ethan asked.

Harriet seemed reluctant when she replied. "Jim and I spent four years in Bogotá. Haberman was a—family friend, I guess. I've been to his camp several times. When I heard you and Jim were taken, I pretty much knew what had happened." Harriet looked outside the window.

"You knew Jim had faked his own kidnapping and took me along?"

Harriet nodded. "It had to be a setup. Haberman would never let Jim be kidnapped. Half the reason I was here was to make sure Jim didn't do anything stupid." She grimaced. "I thought he was still taking his medication. I still don't know how he managed to slip that one past me."

"Medication?"

"Jim is bipolar. I was surprised he managed to pull Haberman along on this scheme. You were just a bystander."

"I see."

"Hey, I wouldn't have put myself in harm's way for just any bystander. He'd have to be cute."

Jim smiled thinly. "Jim was planning to kill me. For sleeping with you."

Harriet looked away. "Yeah. Well, there's that. He was off his medication, remember? I didn't want him to do anything stupid."

"You wanted to save him."

Harriet turned back and watched him bleakly. "A woman's relationship with her lunatic ex-husband is complicated."

The taxi reached the airport as the rays of the sun came over the ridgeline. Harriet dragged Ethan through the fence. Some small aircraft were tied down nearby. She pounded on the door of the nearest hanger.

A sleepy-looking man opened the door. Harriet spoke to him in rapid-fire Spanish. The man answered and shrugged. Harriet reached into her jacked and pulled out a wad of money. The man glanced at it, then at the two of them, then stepped back and let them in.

Inside was a similar small and dirty looking plane. Harriet took him aside while the man started opening the hanger.

"Here's five hundred dollars," she said, counting it out from the wad. "And here's ten thousand or so." With that, she gave him the remainder. "Paolo will fly you to Bogotá. He will land at the airport, tie down the plane, and walk you to the taxi stand. Once you're in the taxi, give the money to him. Take the cab to the American Embassy. There are people waiting for you there."

"Where did you get all this money?"

"Where do you think?" She said in irritation. "Your dad. I'm the bagman on this operation. How do you think I got you out?"

"You were in on it all along."

Harriet looked a little embarrassed. "No. I found Jim after and persuaded him I'd pick up the money."

"How did you do that?"

"Don't be stupid."

Paolo started pulling the plane out of the hanger.

Ethan watched it. The plane seemed to be no more substantial than a kite. "How are all three of us going to fit in that?"

"I'm going back."

"What?"

Heater glared at him. "Jim is going to get himself killed unless I go back up there and persuade Haberman otherwise. You're a sweet kid and I like you. Now, it's time for you to get out of here. I've got to go mind some baggage."

Paolo waved him over towards the plane. Harriet grabbed him by the hand and dragged him over to the passenger side.

"Get in."

"I'm not leaving without you."

"If you stay here, I'm as good as dead. You want to save me? Get on the plane and get out of here."

"Come with me."

"The plane won't take both of us over the mountains." Harriet grabbed him by the neck and planted a hard kiss on his lips. "You're a good man, Ethan. I'm glad I got you out of there. Don't fuck it up."

She pushed him and he sat in the plane. Then she buckled him up and said something to Paolo in Spanish. Paolo chuckled and nodded.

"Good luck," she said and closed the door.

Paolo called out, and Harriet stepped back as Paolo started the engine.

The plane roared into life, and they taxied away from the hanger. Ethan looked over at Paolo and then back to where Harriet was standing.

She was gone.

oOo

The autumn sun had set and the twilight had entered the house. Joe and Tess sat on the sofa, holding hands.

"When do you think they'll call?" she asked. She patted Joe's hand. Picked it up and kissed it. Joe did not respond.

"The consul said the money had been picked up. They were just waiting." Joe sounded lost.

Tess put her cheek against his hand. *This is God's will,* she wanted to say. *Whatever happens, it is as He wants, and what he wants can be a trial or a blessing.* But she stayed silent. She knew the words would be no comfort to him. That would come later. She tucked them away so she could bring them out when she needed them.

The twilight deepened into pure dark. Gently, she eased his heavy head down to her shoulder. His breathing changed, and she felt her shoulder dampen as he wept. For a moment, the barriers dissolved, and it was as clear between them as ever Divinidine could have made it.

He's dead, Joe was saying to himself, over and over. *Dear Lord, he's dead.*

In the dark there was no such thing as time. She kept holding him and stroking his back, his head.

The phone rang, and every muscle in Joe's body clenched as if around a bullet. She heard his bones crack as he sat up, silent as a stone. Every connection between them broke in an instant. Joe took the phone.

"Hello," he said.

Tess held his hand. She strained to hear the conversation.

"Thank you," Joe said quietly, and replaced the phone in the cradle. He held Tess for a long minute before he spoke. "He's alive."

Tess laughed and kissed him. Joe didn't respond.

"What is it, honey?" She looked at him full in the face. His features were obscured in the darkness, but his eyes glowed.

"This is a gift," he said, hoarsely, holding her. "God has given me a gift. He's given us a sign. I can sell the station—the cable company would buy it in a shot. We have to find a suitable plot of land. Should we plan to farm? What kind of building should we have? Should we rent a bus to get there? Car pool? How many will choose to come with us? So many things to be done."

His hands gripped empty air. "We start moving our church to Milan tonight."

"No," she said, kissing him. She unbuttoned his shirt. "Tomorrow."

oOo

Things happened to Ethan as in a dream.

The sounds and vibration of the small plane were distant and insubstantial. Sometimes, the pilot tried to talk to him. Ethan might have replied. He didn't remember. How could you remember things in a dream?

Everything was removed. Distant.

The plane landed. The pilot walked him to a taxi and rode with him to the embassy. Ethan gave him the money. Once inside the embassy, Ethan identified himself and was rushed into a quiet gray office. Ethan sat down in a comfortable chair and stared across an empty desk. The room felt warm and close. Soft, in the same way the chair felt soft. Comfortable.

After a few minutes, a young man came in. "My name is Anthony DeCosta. We have some procedures to get through."

DeCosta led Ethan through some questions to determine his identity. Ethan identified Haberman as the kidnapper.

"Did you see Doctor Acante while you were held prisoner?"

"Excuse me?" Ethan couldn't parse the sentence for a moment.

"Doctor James Acante. Leader of the expedition."

"Jim. No. I didn't see Jim."

DeCosta nodded and wrote that down. A doctor came in and took him to a small room to be examined. Then Ethan was returned to the office. A meal was brought to him in the office.

There were more forms to be filled out. His picture was taken. Ethan didn't to want to think about anything. He was content to be moved to one place, prodded, moved to another. Speak when spoken to. Otherwise, he remained silent.

"All right, then," DeCosta said. "We're done with this portion. You've proved who you are. Your father was informed as soon as that was confirmed. You've given your statement. You have no medical issues of a physical nature. Would you like to call your father?"

Ethan shook his head. "I just want to go home."

DeCosta hesitated. "Are you sure? Most people would like to speak to their relatives."

"I don't want to talk to anyone." Ethan looked at DeCosta. "I don't even want to talk to you."

DeCosta shrugged. "You're booked on a flight out of Bogotá at eight this evening. You'll be in Miami by midnight, Saint Louis early tomorrow morning. It's the same flight, so you won't even have to change planes. I understand your father will meet you there. In a day or two, you'll be contacted by somebody from the State Department for any further information."

Ethan nodded.

"Any questions?"

"No."

"All right then. There's a room upstairs you can rest in. I'll have some dinner brought up."

"Thank you."

DeCosta stood up and came next to him. He leaned against the table. "We have a counselor here on staff if you'd like to talk to her."

"No, thank you." He looked up at DeCosta. He felt blank inside. Scrubbed clean of anything meaningful.

"When you get to Saint Louis, you should see someone." DeCosta put his arm on Ethan's shoulder. Ethan recoiled, and DeCosta let it drop. "You should," he continued. "It will help."

Ethan lay down on the slim bed. It felt as comfortable as a cocoon. The window was open and he heard faint honkings and clankings from the street. Voices. Shouts now and then. The screech of tires.

It bothered him vaguely that he hadn't mentioned Jim. Why would he ever protect Jim? For Harriet?

Promptly at four, two men knocked on the door and came in the room. For a brief moment, he panicked, thinking Sanza and Guillermo had come for him. But it wasn't them.

He was taken to the airport in a limousine. Outside, he watched the whitewashed walls of the streets, the people walking along the walls of residences. The tops of the walls glittered with broken glass. The people on the street watched back expressionlessly.

In the airport, standing in line to board the plane, somebody bumped him. He found himself holding a thick manila envelope. He looked up and saw no one near him. The package has his name on it. He wondered if someone at the embassy had given it to him and he'd forgotten or not noticed.

The plane took off, and he found himself watching the road that ran along the edge of the runway, trying to see if Harriet was there. There was no one watching.

He sat back and waited. For something. He was an empty bubble of emotionless anticipation. This sustained him to Miami, through the sweaty wait while people left the plane and reboarded. He held onto the envelope, not thinking about it. Holding onto it because it was something there in his hands to hold on to.

The plane continued on to Saint Louis. It landed in a dismal rain. There was some discussion between the people around him if they would even be allowed to land at Lambert. The rain was turning to ice on contact. Ethan heard the conversations around him, but they didn't touch him.

Joe was waiting for him at the gate—a special dispensation from the Department of State. Ethan watched as Joe wept to have him back.

There's something wrong with me, he thought as Joe hugged him. Ethan hugged back automatically but without any real feeling.

Tess was standing behind Joe. When he saw her, for a moment he thought he had never left Colombia. Maybe this was all a delusion. He was still lying asleep or beaten unconscious back in Haberman's compound.

Then Joe introduced her. Tess. Theresa. His new wife. Ethan was confused—he already knew who Tess was. Then he remembered Joe didn't know that. Joe explained Tess had been in Colombia on a religious retreat. *Of course,* Ethan thought. Eclipses had always inspired the crackpots, the mentally ill and the religious. Ethan half smiled. Was that bitterness? Maybe he wasn't as bad off as he thought.

When he was sitting in the back seat, watching the familiar traffic on I-70, looking at the big American hands and big American faces in nearby cars—so different from the small, intense faces he'd seen in Colombia—he seemed to find his breath for the first time. He coughed, suddenly, ragged and rough. He looked around the car. This was real. He was home. Jim had lived here for years. People knew who he was. Consequently, someone must know Harriet. There could be sense to this, after all.

Ethan looked down and saw the envelope. He tore it open and pulled out loose papers, a tablet of yellow ruled paper, and a spiral notebook. There was a scrawled note taped to the notebook. It read:

"Hope you can find some use for this. Jim didn't make it."

It was signed, "Harriet".

oOo

Norman stared across the Lifeworks desk at Bill. Bill's face still looked puffy. His eyes were sunken into shadow, and his hands shook as he sipped a glass of water.

Bill looked as if he'd been in an accident. Norman knew he'd been mugged, but that was months ago. Jesus. Didn't the man know how to heal?

"You said you wanted to see me?" Bill said in a monotone.

Norman started to speak, but the door behind them opened. Norman spun and stood up. He didn't reach for his gun, but his hand was ready to move.

A tall, aristocratic white woman opened the door and leaned in. "Bill? It's time for your pills."

Bill nodded. The woman came and brought him a tiny cup.

"This is Kathleen Morris," Bill mumbled. "She's helping out. Kathleen, this is Norman Parkin."

"Just a bit until Bill gets on his feet." She patted his shoulder. Kathleen looked at Norman narrowly. "Is this business or pleasure?"

Norman knew the look. Women protected the homestead. Norman liked the idea of this wealthy white woman viewing him as a threat.

"Pleasure," Norman said easily. "I was just checking in on old Bill. I run a club on the other side of the river, and he hadn't shown up for a while. Thought I'd make sure he was all right."

Kathleen glanced at Bill quickly and then turned her gaze back to Norman. Norman smiled friendlily at her. It was all he could do to keep from busting out laughing. He could see the wheels turning in her brain. She knew what kind of clubs were on the Illinois side. Now she was wondering what sort of clubs Bill was visiting.

Kathleen smiled back. Bill would pay hell tonight.

Bill didn't seem to notice.

"Well, I have to get back," she said. "Don't tire him out, Norman."

Norman nodded. "She's a nice piece of work, Bill," Norman said conversationally after she'd left.

Bill shrugged.

"Hell. What kind of drugs they got you on?"

"Thorazine." Bill paused a moment. "It helps."

"It helps with what?"

Bill suddenly focused on Norman with bitter intensity. He seemed to be looking out of only his left eye. "None of your business. What do you want?"

"This is your lucky day, my man," Norman said. "I'm going to take you out of the drug-dealing business. I want to buy all your stock."

"Good. Take it all."

"I figured I'd get a quantity discount."

"Fuck that." Bill fixed him with a stare out of that same eye.

Norman wondered if only one eye worked.

"I don't need your fucking money." Bill waved him away. "It's just a fucking hassle anyway. Taxes. Explanations. I want to shut down the whole thing." He lurched to his feet and limped over to the cabinet on the side of the room. He opened it up and pointed to the tubs of pills.

"Take all of it. Take it and get the fuck out of here."

Norman just stared at the tubs for a minute. "I'm going to need a cart. And a way to get out of here without being seen by your lady friend."

"Outside the door and in the hallway." Bill pointed to the other door in the room. "Goes through the labs. Follow the exit signs. Now go and leave me the fuck alone."

Norman brought in the cart and put one tub after another on it. There had to be thousands of pills.

Norman didn't feel comfortable until he had them stowed safely in the trunk. Then he kicked the cart out of the way, got in, and drove off. He called Joe on his cell phone.

"I've got what you need," he chortled into the phone. "Have you got the cash to pay for it? Right now. No waiting." Joe said yes and they agreed to meet on a back road they both knew in the farmland north of the city.

Norman sang along with the radio the whole way there.

Joe was waiting for him, standing in the dusty road, leaning against his car. Norman pulled up behind him.

Norman led Joe back to the trunk and opened it. "Here you go. This is all there is. You want more, you're going to have to figure it out for yourself."

Joe stared at the tubs. "I thought you said—" He stopped for a moment. "This is a lot more than I expected."

Norman beamed. "Don't I take good care of my clients?"

"I only have what I told you on the phone."

It was times like this that Norman loved what he did. "Well," he said, drawing it out. "You can buy the same amount we talked about. Or..." Norman pause for dramatic effect. "You can take the rest on credit."

Joe looked as if his teeth hurt. Norman had to keep himself from laughing out loud.

"For the same price?"

Norman nodded.

Joe stared into the trunk. "Could be a while before we'd be able to pay you back."

Norman spread his arms expansively. "Take as long as you like. I'm getting out of this business, anyway." Norman leaned on the car. "Look, you take the merchandise. We won't talk about terms right row. Later—say next year some time—we get together and square accounts. If you don't have the money, we'll figure something out."

Joe watched him for a while. He looked in the trunk. He looked back at Norman.

It's like fishing, Norman thought. *Set the hook and play the line. If I didn't do this, I'd have to sell cars for a living.*

"Okay," Joe said slowly. "I'll take the lot." He handed Norman a thick envelope. "Here's what we agreed on. I'll have the rest by summer."

Norman took the money. "Be seeing you then."

Together they transferred the jars into the trunk of Joe's car. Norman shook Joe's hand—which surprised them both—then got in his car and drove away. He watched Joe in his rear view mirror. The big man was staring into his trunk and scratching his head. Norman laughed out loud.

The sun had set and the twilight come and gone by the time Norman pulled off the highway into East Saint Louis. A weight had been lifted from his shoulders.

It's strange you don't recognize a cage when you're in it; only when you let yourself out. This whole Divinidine and whore enterprise had been a disaster waiting to happen. Joe's asking for a final buyout had been a stroke of luck. The additional jars Bill had supplied had just been extra gravy.

He had to consider it as an experiment: an interesting failure. It was a sign he should stick to his core business for a while. Milk the clubs. Maybe he could apply some of the things he'd learned. Clearly, there was a high-end market for pretty girls. Connie had shown him that. He could use the girls in the clubs as advertising.

That was the way to do it. Quit thinking of the girls as whores. Think of them as products. Norman could have a whole product line from streetwalker to club hooker to call girl. Connie and Sam's problem was thinking too small. Norman didn't have that problem. He'd just been distracted by the possibility of a new drug market. Sure, maybe something like that could happen. But first, let Joe explore it for him. Joe owed Norman now. Norman could collect any time he needed to—or not, as he chose. Norman's mistake had been to try to force the market instead of taking advantage of a market that already existed.

A learning experience. Norman pulled into his driveway next to Damulin's car. Connie and LeRoy were out. He was pleased that Damulin had waited for him. Norman had given Damulin the night off so he could execute this operation by himself. Now that Sam was dead, only Connie and Cindy knew about Bill, and even they didn't know about Joe. Norman wanted to keep it that way. He would have to reward Damulin's loyalty. You had to take care of your workers.

Norman let himself in. He put his keys on the table and went down the hall towards the viewing room. Maybe he could give Damulin one of the girls from the club. Or maybe a weekend in Chicago. Or maybe a girl and a weekend. No. Norman shook his head. That would be too much. You wanted to take care of your workers, not spoil them.

Norman opened the door of the viewing room. He saw Damulin sitting in the chair, staring at the Vermeer. Then he saw the blood splash on the wall behind Damulin and the empty spot on the wall where the Vermeer used to be. Then he saw an arm and pistol swinging into his face.

The blow crushed his nose and broke his cheek. The blood spurted into his eyes. That and the pain blinded him. He tried to step back and pull out his own pistol. Something smashed his kneecap. Norman shrieked and fell. He grabbed his pistol, but it was knocked out of his hand. Norman tried to roll away, but he was kicked savagely in the kidney. He curled around the pain.

Nothing happened for a moment. Norman wiped his eyes and looked up.

A man stared down at him. "Evening, Norman. I'm Jake Fiske."

Norman shook his head, trying to get the fog out of his mind. Buy some time. He felt something come loose in his mouth. He spit on the floor. It was a piece of tooth.

"What do you want?" Norman looked around the room. Every panting was gone. "And where the hell are my paintings?"

Jake looked around, surprised. "There were paintings in here? Sorry, Norman. This is the way it was when I got here." He gestured at the corpse. "Him, included."

Norman looked at Damulin, then back at Jake. Okay. Maybe this son-of-a-bitch can be reasoned with. Long enough to get off the fucking floor, at any rate. He licked his lips. "Jake Fiske. Cindy's Dad."

"I'm glad you remembered me. I remembered your phone call."

"I just clued you in on what happened. You should thank me. I was the one that sent her home."

"Yeah." Jake kicked Norman again. "You're a fucking humanitarian." He leaned over, the gun covering Norman easily. "Connie, I understand. He probably came to Sam to solve the problem and Sam came to you. She was lucky she didn't get sent to Hong Kong, or someplace. Right?"

"That's right." Norman was confused. "So, why the hell are you here now?"

"Yeah." Jake reached into his jacket and pulled out a second gun. He covered Norman with the second gun while he holstered the first gun. "About that. I can forgive my daughter. She's my own flesh and blood. I can even forgive Connie—he was ignorant. And I am grateful to you for not letting my daughter get fucked to death in some Chinese basement. But you screwed up my life. You got my daughter involved. You blew hell out of Connie's operation, which means I lost money. And now you put me in the shit with the DEA. There's no help for any of that. I'm left standing in a pile of shit." Jake shrugged. "So it goes. I gotta kill *somebody*, Norman. It's not like you don't deserve to die."

Norman lunged, but Jake kicked him in the face.

"Oh, yeah." Jake said.

"Sam said to tell you hi." Jake aimed the gun at Norman's left eye

Nothing had ever looked so big in his life. Norman couldn't help staring at it. "Sam's dead."

"You know? That's just what I said."

Norman didn't see a flash or hear a sound, but suddenly everything he had ever been was compressed into a tiny bubble in a sea of darkness. For a long moment, the darkness squeezed him and he could see a pattern across all of his life. He could see the meaning of it all. He just had time to think: *there was a plan to all of this, wasn't there?*

Then the bubble burst and he spread across everything.

Then he wasn't, anymore.

oOo

Le Roy was the one who found Norman.

Connie had dropped him off after a twelve-hour day working with Anya. Anapyridol production was close to done, but the anti-Anapyridol still seemed a long way off. LeRoy went into the picture room—that was where Norman usually was—and found him.

After the shock had passed enough for his mind to function, he called Connie.

LeRoy needed to sit down before he fell down. There were two chairs in the sitting room. One held Damulin's body. LeRoy couldn't sit *there*. The other was on the other side of Norman. He'd have to step over Norman to get to it. What if he slipped in the blood?

LeRoy sat on the bare floor. He wanted to leave the room. Run away from the house. But leaving Norman alone didn't seem right. Norman had done everything for him. Everything Norman had ever known how to do. Norman had rescued him from social services in Charleston. Norman had brought him here, into his own home. Norman had given him a job.

LeRoy had no illusions about his uncle. Norman was—*had been*—a vicious, ruthless psychopath who happened to deeply love his nephew.

He trusted me. When LeRoy had found Anya's work, Norman had taken LeRoy's word it was worth the effort. Norman had believed in LeRoy. LeRoy had repaid him by going behind his back.

LeRoy stared at what was left of Norman. The bullet had made only a small crater where his left eye used to be, but the whole back of his head had exploded. Norman had fallen back against the floor so LeRoy couldn't see into his skull. That was fine with LeRoy.

In books and movies LeRoy had seen, someone in his position was supposed to hold the body in his arms and swear vengeance. LeRoy wondered if he would feel that way later. Right now, he felt queasy and dull. He had this sense of fulfilled inevitability: this was always Norman's eventual destiny.

He should do something. Maybe LeRoy should close Norman's eyes. LeRoy reached out his hand, but he couldn't bring himself to touch the body.

He felt ridiculous. Tears rolled down his cheeks. His hand shook. Hadn't Norman done the best he could? Hadn't he given LeRoy everything he needed?

"It's okay, kid."

Startled, LeRoy turned and saw Connie. His hand dropped and touched the blood on the floor. LeRoy held his hand in front of his face and stared at it. He felt a scream building inside of his chest. He wasn't sure he'd ever stop.

Connie grabbed his arm and lifted him up, and half-dragged, half-carried him to the bathroom. LeRoy sat on the toilet and shook, staring at his bloody hand while Connie ran the shower. "Get in there and scrub yourself until you feel clean. I'll get you some clothes."

LeRoy washed himself four, maybe five times before the hot water gave out. There was a shirt, socks, pants, and underwear next to the sink. His shoes were next to the door.

Connie was sitting in the chair. Clearly, he had stepped over Norman's body.

"What do I do now?"LeRoy felt helpless.

"Do you know what happened?"

"I found him like this. I don't know anything."

Connie sighed and surveyed the damage. "Now, I guess we call the police."

"The police?"

Connie nodded. "If we got rid of the bodies, they would be coming around anyway. You didn't kill him, did you?"

"No!"

"Me, neither. They're not going to care too much what happened to Cold Norman. They're our boys, anyway. It would have been worse if he'd been killed in Saint Louis."

"Do you know who did it?"

Connie shook his head. "We'll talk about that after the police."

East Saint Louis was under state control so it was the state police that came, took pictures, and wandered around and disappeared, just as Connie had predicted. They were staties, but they were from East Saint Louis. Norman was one of their own—he'd probably gone to school with some of them. There might be a small article in the *Post-Dispatch*, but there would be no investigation.

Afterwards, Connie and LeRoy sat in the kitchen. LeRoy asked again: "Do you know who did it?"

Connie looked up at him. "Why? Are you going to go shoot him?"

LeRoy shook his head. "No."

"Norman had a lot of enemies. It could have been anyone."

LeRoy watched Connie for a moment. "But you know who it was."

Connie shrugged. "Maybe. But you don't want to know."

"Try me."

Connie shrugged again. "It was Jake Fiske. Cindy's dad."

LeRoy felt like he couldn't breathe. "You're sure?"

"Yeah. Pretty much."

"He's Cindy's dad?"

"I said that."

"How am I going to date a woman whose father killed my uncle? What am I supposed to do?"

"I said you didn't want to know."

LeRoy looked around the room. Suddenly, it felt too small.

"Do you know what *you* want to do?" Connie asked quietly.

"What do you mean?"

"Norman had three clubs he ran. He had a little piece of a couple of casinos over on the Missouri side—how he managed that, I have no idea. But it's clean money. He had the Alton girl trade, but he traded that to Sam for the Sam's Saint Louis ring. Sam's gone, but Norman didn't pick it up again. It's been a free-for-all since then. You're not in a position to cover that even if you wanted to. You don't even have a driver's license. I managed the Saint Louis ring until Norman cut me out and the DEA shut it down. Norman didn't have a lot of hard assets he could pass on to you, but he did have those three clubs and the bit of the casinos. The casinos will take care of themselves—all you have to do is rake in the money. But the clubs take management. Something a minor can't do."

LeRoy stared across the table at him. Connie had been calm, laying down the information as passionless and thorough as a blackjack dealer. "What are you getting at?"

"Do you want to replace Norman?"

"Not at all."

"I didn't think so. So, the hard assets are all you have—that and this house."

"Is there a will?"

"Surprisingly enough, there is. Along with a lawyer. Norman mentioned him to me. You'll have to talk to him."

"How do you know so much about this? Are you the—" LeRoy had to think of the word. "Executor?"

Connie chuckled. "I check on people. I knew about the clubs—it's common knowledge. Though, probably most people didn't go to the courthouse to work through the actual ownership. I did that a long time ago. I'd like to build myself a casino someday, so I did some looking around and made some contacts. That's how I found out Norman's connection. Did I ever tell you my mama thought I'd be an accountant?"

"No."

"Probably should have become one. Be worth more now. Here's what I propose. You take the gravy from the casinos. Enough to live on and pay the taxes on this place—if you want to stay here, that is. I'll manage the clubs for you with the understanding you'll sell them to me when you get older. Like you said, you don't want any part of Norman's life, right? But there's no reason to turn down good money."

"What about the Anapyridol?"

Connie waved it away. "That's coming to an end. As soon as you have the finished product, we'll turn it over and shut it down."

"It's my lab. I may not want to shut it down."

Connie shrugged. "After we settle up, you can keep the lab going on your own nickel. That's up to you. I'll help out with logistics but I won't be directly involved. Okay?"

LeRoy thought about it. "How much are we talking about?"

"The casinos will pull in something around a hundred thou a year—Norman had only small percentages. Still, that's good eating money. The clubs, after I've paid everybody off and after taxes, will probably pull down a million or so. I'll take two-thirds of that, so you'll see three hundred. All legitimate money. The Anapyridol project will give you about three hundred, illegal money. So, you'll have to launder it or use it to keep up your little lab. That's up to you."

"Four hundred thousand a year?"

"Give or take. Plus what Norman's saved. But you've got to figure the feds are going to take most of that. Maybe all of it if they think it's illegal. They're going to crawl over everything of Norman's—I'd say let them have it. You don't know nothing. And you don't, really. Besides, you're a minor. The only area you really do know something about is the Anapyridol, and I happen to know all of the leads dried up on that one before they ever got to Norman. You might get grilled a little, but if you play it stupid you should be all right. Just don't try to be smart—which is probably going to be difficult for you."

"I can act stupid." He'd had practice, back in Charleston.

Connie leaned back. "Okay, then. You have the next five years covered. You won't be a truly wealthy man, but you'll be better off than any fifteen-year-old that I know. What do you say?"

LeRoy felt as if they were cutting up Norman's corpse before he was cold in the ground. Norman would have been proud. "I say we have a deal."

"Terrific. Which brings us to the next, and nastiest, item. Have you thought about funeral arrangements?"

Chapter 2.2: April, 1998

Joe's Easter.

Their Milan Easter Celebration that afternoon would be small. Just Joe and Tess. Carla and her husband, Axel, and their little boy. Phil would be out tomorrow. He didn't say if he would bring Portia or not. But Ethan had said he would be coming. Tess would pick him up. Nobody would be arriving for hours yet. Joe had plenty of time.

Joe liked to cook—if he hadn't become a minister, he might have opened a diner. Nothing fancy. Just good food.

The Easter dinner would not be fancy, either: he had a turkey. He had made deep-fried potatoes and homemade bread. He had even baked a couple of pies. Except for the workmen finishing up the camp, Joe had been here by himself for a month. There were weekend visits by Tess, but she had been making ready the move from Saint Louis. Joe had been building homes.

The compound had been an old campground with a central shower and toilet, lodge, and banquet building, a half-dozen cabins and a collection of white canvas tents on platforms. Joe walked through the compound, making sure beds were where beds should be, sinks drained, toilets flushed. While he was not ready for everybody to move in, he was ready for the few families that would be coming out to stay the weekend. In deference to Joe, they had all agreed to hold off taking the Divinidine until Tess returned Ethan to Saint Louis. Joe planned riotous reunion upon her return.

He finished checking the lights. Then he walked back towards the lodge and the farm pickup truck. In a moment he was bouncing off the gravel road onto the pavement and heading towards town. He needed a few extra eggs and some oil, and there was a grocerette he'd spied earlier in the week that promised to be open.

The sun was now breaking through the eastern clouds, giving the wet patches a golden glow and limning the newly leaved trees with fire. The cold earth breathed fog into the morning air. The winter had been mild, but now spring was in the air.

A half mile from the farm road he saw an old man hitchhiking.

It was just too pretty a morning to be paranoid.

The old man was small, dark skinned, and looked vaguely Middle Eastern. Pakistani? Indian? Israeli? Joe couldn't tell.

"Hi," the old man said as he settled down. "I'm Fred Hibbert."

"Joe Cori," he nodded. "Been waiting long?"

"Not so you'd notice."

Fred's English was perfectly Midwestern. There was no trace of any foreign accent. Joe wondered if Fred had been born here or immigrated at an early age.

"You live around here?" Joe asked. It was always good to know the locals.

"Just passing through." Fred rubbed the condensation from the window. "I like to go walking every now and then. I put out my thumb when I get tired."

"It's a little cold to do that on Easter."

"I manage."

"Where are you coming from?"

"Saint Louis, this trip. But I live in Chicago."

"Ah."

Companionable silence.

"You're that preacher fellow that used to be on TV, aren't you?"

"'Used to be'? Have they taken my show off the air finally?"

"You did sell the station, after all."

Joe looked at him sideways. "Most people don't track such things."

"I'm a venture capitalist. I'm always looking for an opportunity."

"Were you looking to buy a television station?"

"Not my field. But I'm always interested when such things change hands."

Joe shrugged. "I'm your man. Did you have something in mind?"

"Just making conversation."

"It's not every day you meet a venture capitalist hitchhiking the back highways of Missouri."

Fred chuckled. "I guess that's so. I was poor growing up. Poverty makes you see things more clearly. But when you accrete wealth, it insulates you. I like to get out every now and then."

"You could be kidnapped. People worth money get kidnapped." Joe glanced over at him. "It happened to my son down in Colombia."

"Do tell." Fred seemed to think a moment. "Then I'm happy to be up here and not down there. Up here I think I can take care of myself."

"Understood." People were crazy.

Joe supposed he would have been recognized eventually. Even if this wasn't inside his main viewing geography. Although being recognized by a Chicago venture capitalist/crazy old hitchhiker was a new one.

"Are you still a minister?" asked Fred.

"Yes," Joe said shortly. Too shortly to be polite. "We came out here to be closer to God. I like to think of it as an extended retreat. When we're ready, we'll return."

"Ah. So, you haven't created a cult, then."

Joe almost ran off the road. "Cult?"

"You know. Like Jim Jones. David Koresh—"

"I know what a *cult* is. Is that what they're saying about me?"

"I have no idea."

"Then where did you get *that* idea?"

"You sold the station. I heard about that. You were pretty successful and getting out of the business was a surprise. Then I run into you out here. I hadn't heard about any court cases involving underage altar boys. Why would someone like you give up media evangelism?"

"Not to run a cult, anyway. It's a retreat of sorts. Like I said."

"Ah," said Fred simply.

There was something compelling about the little man. Compelling and irritating. Confidant. Joe could tell Fred was used to manipulating people. Probably good at it, too, even though Fred's poking about was almost clumsy. Joe wondered if the clumsiness was intentional.

Joe glanced over at Fred. "Why would a venture capitalist go on a walking tour of Milan, Missouri?"

"Good question," Fred said affably. "I'm rich."

"Of course."

"My business is to give money away. There is always the hope of return, but nothing is guaranteed, right? So, I'm often viewed as a sugar daddy. The amount of lies, damned lies, and statistics I'm shown is staggering. I need a good built-in bullshit detector. But it gets harder to tell fact from fiction after a while, and I need to get that detector re-tuned. So, I go for a walk."

Joe nodded. "I understand."

"Do you?" Fred looked at him. "I'm surprised. I don't subscribe to your religion, obviously. But it seemed to me, the untrained outsider, that faith was just narrowing one's vision to exclude pesky things like facts. No offense."

Joe laughed. "That's so well put, none is taken. You're wrong. Faith without doubt is fraud. Human beings are slow, fallible creatures. They cannot know the mind of God. They can't know the extent and range of His plans, His compassion, His love. Blind faith—faith without thought—implies a divine understanding beyond human ability. That's arrogance. True faith is trust in that which cannot be known with the full knowledge that as imperfect beings we cannot understand Him in this life. Blind faith, which reduces God to human perspective, is nothing short of blasphemy."

Fred stared at him. "Blasphemy?"

Joe nodded. "For a human being to state he knows the true Mind of God is to claim God's omniscience for himself—to claim, in fact, to be God. Blasphemy."

Fred stared at him. "I'm sorry. I have actually watched your show. From what I can tell, you claim that all the *time*."

"Since you've watched my show, you're clearly considering salvation." Joe chuckled. "Actually, I hope I never said that. I tried to never present anything that could be interpreted as understanding His *Will*. What I talked about was His *Nature* and the nature of His *Promises* to us."

"Same thing."

"Not at all. The Bible is all about His promises and His love. We can understand *that*. It is intentionally stated over and over in ways we can comprehend and accept. 'I am the way, the truth and the light.' 'For God so loved the world that He gave His only begotten son that whosoever believeth in Him shall not perish but have everlasting life.' 'Father forgive them for they know not what they do.' If you subtract out the tribalism, the pettiness, and the wars—all injected by fallible human beings—what you have left is a continuing description not of His designs but of His character. *That's* what I preached."

Fred watched him for a long minute. "I'm impressed," he said quietly.

"Don't confuse the messenger with the message. *I'm* not the one being impressive." Joe glanced over at Fred, trying to gauge how close Fred was. Every soul was important. Fred was looking thoughtfully out the window. Joe turned his gaze back to the road. *Let him be. You've planted the seeds, now let them grow. Too much plowing will kill the crop.*

"What are you doing for Easter?" Joe said at last.

"I'm not Christian," Fred said simply. "I don't celebrate."

"No family? No friends?"

"No family. I know some people who celebrate, but they are far away from here."

"Come to dinner with us." Joe nodded towards the town appearing around a bend in the road. "I'm just picking up a few spices and such, then I'm going back to cook the ham. Come on back with me. It'll be fun."

Fred smiled at him. Joe realized he really liked the man.

"That's the nicest offer I've had in a very long time." Fred touched him gently on the shoulder. Joe felt as if he'd been saluted by a king.

"But—" Fred withdrew his hand. "I'm not free to accept at this time. I will someday."

"Anytime." Joe meant it.

Joe pulled into the grocerette. Fred got out of the other side. They shook hands on the sidewalk. Fred's hand was small but dry and very strong.

Fred waved to him and started walking north.

Joe watched him walk past the edge of town and along the road among the farms. Then he went inside the grocerette, running through his list in his mind. *Cinnamon,* he thought. *Ethan always liked cinnamon buns. Ought to make some for the boy.*

oOo

Jake's Easter.

It was still dark out when Jake came downstairs. Anya and Cindy were still asleep. He walked to the living room and turned on the lights. The room lit up, quilted with all different colors of light.

They had gotten rid of the tree, but Cindy had rehung the lights. The wall was covered in novelty bulbs. A string of lit garden seed packs led into a string of fish. The fish led into pumpkins. The pumpkins paved the way to a string of hummingbirds. She had hung Christmas ornaments on the wires. Jake's steps vibrated the floor and caused the ceramic angel to knock against a leaping trout and made a glass pickle swung dangerously. He remembered the pickle. It had been a wedding present from someone. An ancient cloth Santa looked up from a tiny brass sleigh, clearly worried this whole bright world would come crashing down on him.

Jake stopped and the glass quieted. He walked more softly.

Everything had been taken care of. Norman was dead. The X-drug reports had dried up. The girls were shut down. Cindy had straightened up. She was a strong girl. He didn't have to worry about her anymore. The worst had happened.

But Anya looked like nine miles of bad road. She was working all the time. And she looked *haunted.* Jake didn't know how to help her. Someone as innocent as Anya shouldn't have to worry about anything.

Jake planned omelets for breakfast, then a couple of hours of lazy conversation and television and it would be pig-out time for the ham.

The omelets and coffee were waiting for them by the time Cindy and Anya worked their way downstairs.

Neither of them was at their best in the morning. Anya smiled at him sleepily and held onto the mug like a life raft. Cindy just stared at her plate. Eventually, she'd figure out that what she was seeing was breakfast.

The three of them managed the meal all right, but when Jake led them into the living room, Anya looked surprised. "What is it? Christmas?"

"It's Easter, Mom," said Cindy in a surly voice.

Things went downhill after that. Silence fell, brick by brick, into the room. The television was a godsend.

Jake took refuge in the kitchen and worked over the ham until it was tender enough to cut with a spoon. The house smelled so strongly of good food, you could eat the walls with a fork.

The meal was served and eaten, but there was still no relief.

Cindy got a phone call and shot out of the house as fast as she could—Jake couldn't blame her—and he and Anya were left alone.

For a long time, Anya didn't seem to notice Cindy had gone. After several minutes, she looked up. She looked up at the walls, around the dining room. "It's good she left. What sort of place is this for a young girl on Easter Sunday?"

"Beg pardon?" Jake looked up in surprise. "This was Granddad's favorite room." Jake could remember when he was a kid back when the Fiske family was big. His dad may have had only one kid, but that hadn't stopped his uncles. Big, ruddy men with big, ruddy sons, each with wives and children. Loud. Raucous. The smell of whisky. Cigar smoke. Ham. He looked around the room. How had things become so bare?

Anya sniffed. "I always hated this room."

Jake stared at her.

She noticed Jake suddenly. She laughed and covered her mouth with her hand. "Did I say that out loud?"

"Are you drunk?"

Anya barked out a laugh and lurched to her feet. "Not yet." She reached up into the cupboard and pulled out a bottle of rum. "But I'm working on it."

She turned and looked at him, bottle in one hand, glass in the other. "I'd go down to the bar if I were you. This isn't going to be pretty."

Jake fled.

oOo

Cindy's Easter.

It shouldn't have been sad. Anya had taken a day off. For once she didn't seem so distracted and distant. Jake had been home and cooked a ham so sweet and tender it was like eating candy. It should have been fun: champagne and party games. Instead, the three of them sat around the table, watching each other, eating in silence.

Cindy watched Anya from the corner of her eye. Anya's hair had started to turn gray—no, that wasn't right. Look at the pattern. Anya had been gray for a while. She had quit coloring her hair. How long had Anya been coloring her hair? Why did she stop? Cindy could see wrinkles beside her eyes, across her forehead, at the edges of her mouth. When had Anya become *old*? If this was the wages of drug addiction and an illicit affair, maybe Cindy should join a church. Not Portia's church. Some other one.

Cindy glanced over to Jake. He didn't look that different, but he sat loosely, as if the cord tying his body together had been slackened. He didn't look at Anya. Anya didn't look at him.

Cindy felt like she was strangling. In a moment, she would stand up and shout out what Anya had been doing. Everything would be torn asunder and laid waste, but at least the slow death of this meal would be over.

The phone rang.

Before Anya and Jake could say a word, she rushed out: *"I'll get it!"* and was up, up, and away, out of that stifling room.

"Hello!" she said into the phone.

"Hey there," said Portia. "How bad is it?"

"I'm breaking bread with the undead."

Portia laughed. "It's pretty bad here, too. Donnie just walks around, mumbling. Mom has that, 'where have I failed' look. I could give her a typewritten list, but she wouldn't understand it. Dad just looks confused. 'Why can't we all just get along?' Pretty soon, he'll stalk off to the garage. Then Mom can grieve Donnie's affliction properly. Well, she can't really do that *here* with all of us around and the gardener home with his wife and kids. But she'll do her best."

Cindy grinned. "Come save me and I'll bear your children."

"I don't know. Torturing parents and brothers is pretty attractive. Besides, I don't have a car. Or a license. I'm seventeen now. I *could* have a license. I *choose* not to."

"Hey. I'm sixteen now. Don't rub it in. Don't you have some boy toy with a car?"

There was a long pause. "Maybe," said Portia slowly.

"I'm not driving with your brother."

"Well, *duh*."

He's probably one of those Sex Christians. It doesn't matter. I've got to get out of here.

"A movie or something?" Cindy said hesitantly.

Portia understood instantly and laughed. "No sex or evangelism. We'll leave that for a later time."

An hour later, Cindy was shivering as a Prius came up. The passenger side window rolled down. "Want to get drunk and party?"

"Absolutely." Cindy got into the back seat.

The driver was a balding older man—maybe Jake's age. He smiled slightly at her but clearly was paying more attention to Portia.

Of course, thought Cindy. Didn't they pay attention to me the same way last summer? After all the weirdness Portia had been through this winter, an affair with an older man seemed almost healthy.

"You need a date," Portia pronounced. "Do you have someone in mind or do you want me to set you up?"

"I have someone in mind," Cindy said hastily. "Let me use your phone."

It always surprised her that she knew LeRoy's number. His real number—not the fake cell phones he used on business but a real land line that ran over the road and under the river into East Saint Louis.

"Hello?"

"LeRoy? It's Cindy. Me and some friends are going to go messing around. Want to come out and play?"

Silence. I've interrupted something. Well, it *is* Easter.

"You want me to meet your friends?"

"I think that's required if you're going to come out and play with us. Come on. It'll be fun."

Silence again. Cindy sighed. Sometimes she forgot who LeRoy really was. *Do I really want to be seeing a person this messed up?* It startled her to be thinking that. Should she do something about that? One way or the other? They had certainly been in a holding pattern for a month. She opened her purse and check for a condom. Such a little thing, sex, after last summer. But it still seemed so huge.

"I'd like that."

"How do you want to get together? Should we pick you up over there?" She couldn't believe she just said that. As if LeRoy lived in some sort of normal place. *Please say no.*

"I don't think that's a good idea. Can you pick me up at the airport if I take the metro? Say an hour?"

She carefully placed the condom in her purse. Let things happen if they're going to happen. "It's a date. We'll pick up food. Are you hungry?"

"I am now."

oOo

LeRoy's Easter.

After Norman's death, LeRoy's life had settled into a new routine. Five days a week, he took the Metro to Richmond Heights where Anya picked him up and took him over to the Creve Coeur lab. Much of the time they worked. Sometimes he ended up holding Anya as she cried on his shoulder—something he thought was more than any fifteen-year-old kid should have to do for his girlfriend's mother. Other times they talked biochemistry. LeRoy was, in fact, a true genius. But Anya had been working in the field for more than thirty years. LeRoy had been sailing along the edges of a vast scientific ocean. Anya, in her unconscious, broken way, laid the sea before him. It was the most exciting thing he had ever seen.

Things with Cindy didn't progress. Going out with a girl whose father had killed your own father-equivalent tended to put a damper on things. He found himself wary. Cautious. Even more than his disease warranted. The electricity that had been between them seemed to slip through his fingers, and there was nothing he could do to stop it. Cindy liked him—that was obvious. But they had progressed away from lovers and towards friends. Being friends, Connie had assured him, was the kiss of death for sex.

LeRoy wasn't sure how to feel about that since he had his own issues with sex. There was a pleasantness to routine even when the routine didn't proceed where he thought he wanted it to go. He saw Cindy regularly. Connie drove him, so the schedule had to mesh with Connie's duties at the club. But, on the plus side, he had a lot more money to spend on her.

This, weirdly, had the effect of him *not* spending it on her. After all, hadn't that been what her johns had done last summer?

LeRoy found himself coming home from their dates furious with her. Furious with himself. Angry he hadn't spent more, kissed her more. Angry he had spent money or kissed her as much as he did.

On top of it there was the *isolation* of their dating. They went out to dinner or a movie. She did not invite him home to meet her parents—not that he wanted to see Anya. *That* would be an awkward moment he would prefer to avoid: *oh, yes, worthy colleague. I am dating your daughter.*

But she did not invite him out to meet her friends. He had no friends to invite her to see, save Connie and Anya. All they had on these dates was each other. It tired them both out.

Christmas came and went, and now Easter as he sat there alone in that house. At least he had ripped out that damned front room. Connie had helped him pull up the floor and the wall, and replace it with linoleum and drywall. LeRoy could point to where he'd found Norman's body, but the stains were only in his mind.

He wasn't happy. He knew that. He wasn't terribly unhappy. But he wanted to change *something*.

Cindy called. He grabbed the moment like a drowning man clutches a straw, not from any faith the straw would keep him afloat, but because the straw was the only thing there to grab.

He sat on the bench at Richmond Heights, head down, hands clasped, lost in self-loathing. *All you have to do is reach out to her*, he thought. You know what happened to Norman. She *doesn't*. It's not her fault. Instead, he was stuck with this *friendship*. Just as well. What the hell did you have to offer her, anyway?

"LeRoy?"

He looked up. Cindy was half-standing out of a car. For the first time, her resemblance to Anya struck him, and for a moment he didn't know who it was that was picking him up.

"What are you? A bump on a log? Come on."

He sat next to her in the back seat. Cindy introduced Portia and Phil. He noticed Phil's age but didn't think much of it.

This time, he thought. *This* time I won't let Jake and Norman stand between us. *This* time I'll be with only her.

He could smell her. Bath soap and good food—he wondered if Anya cooked. Cindy always smelled like good cooking. He reached over and took her hand.

Cindy looked at him in surprise. She held his hand firmly.

This time, he thought. For a moment, Norman's broken body seemed to appear. He pushed it away.

The plan was burgers and a movie. LeRoy didn't much care for burgers—the heavy fat problem. But he agreed anyway. He could get a salad or something.

Cindy really did look like her mother. Not as exotic—he could see the leavening of Jake's influence in her features. But her cheekbones and lips were Anya's.

It amazed him Anya and Cindy were so little alike as people. Of course, he thought. He had only gotten to know Anya after she had been broken by the Anapyridol. Who knew what she had been like before?

The Steak n' Shake was open for Easter and filled with teenagers like themselves, boys and girls escaping family ties. He wished the two of them were alone. He looked over to watch Phil and Portia. They nestled together intimately, poring over the menu. *She's sleeping with him,* he thought. He wondered if Portia had been one of the girls Connie had worked. He couldn't see any other reason a man like Phil could interest a girl like Portia.

He noticed her hands. They were manicured. How many fifteen-year-old girls had manicured hands? Not very many—but he didn't know how it was out in the rich county. Maybe lots of them did. Still, it seemed strange to him that a girl as pretty as Portia, who clearly took care to look good, wore such baggy clothes. From her neck and shoulders, he could tell she had a thin figure. Why not show it? People hid themselves for a reason. Was Phil her father? He showed no resemblance. Adopted father? Somehow, LeRoy didn't think so.

LeRoy looked in the menu for something that wasn't made of raw meat. He found a chef salad that he thought would go down well. Cindy was running her finger down the sandwiches, oblivious.

Okay. What other reason would Portia have to hide her figure? Was she getting fat? Not so he could see. She must be pregnant.

Now that he thought of it, there was a slight roundness under the shirt. An overfilling of her breasts.

He looked over to Cindy. She smiled at him. She must know. He realized this was one of those things he could not initiate in conversation. Until Portia had declared her pregnancy in words, manner, or dress, they had to maintain an illusion it wasn't there. Perversely, it made LeRoy want to bring it up. He stifled the urge, but it felt like it was one more thing he was suppressing.

"We could skip the movie," Portia said as she put the menu down. "Just go somewhere. Drive."

"I know a place," ventured Cindy. "But I'd have to make a call first."

Portia handed over her cell phone. Cindy took it and dialed a number from memory. "Connie?" she said.

LeRoy was so shocked he felt frozen. He never thought the world he shared with Cindy and the world he shared with Connie would ever collide again.

"He says okay." Cindy grinned with excitement. "You guys are going to love this."

"Love what?" LeRoy hated the querulous sound of his voice.

"Connie's houseboat."

"Connie?" Portia looked up. "The Great and Hulking Beast you brought to the party?" She looked at LeRoy speculatively. "You must have hidden assets."

LeRoy blushed and turned away.

Cindy patted his arm. "He does."

It felt like the sun coming out. Maybe he hadn't screwed things up completely quite yet.

The trip down to the houseboat was an adventure in itself. The road was half mud, half slush—only a scant pair of degrees kept it from being solid ice. Twice the car hit bumps that threw Cindy into his lap. LeRoy didn't complain.

The single mercury bulb callously illuminated the peeling paint, the slight list to one side, the rainbow sheen of oil on the water. This boat had seen better days. But it was a place for teenage play. LeRoy listened to Portia giggle with delight as Cindy found the key hanging over the side where Connie had hidden it. Phil glanced over to him. Both had the same thought: *As long as they think it's fun.*

It was cold outside, but inside it was toasty. Portia immediately found the refrigerator. Phil was close behind her and suggested an alcohol-free night. For a moment, Portia's face clouded and LeRoy thought there was going to be a fight. But then her expression softened and she whispered in Phil's ear and gently licked it. Clearly, if she couldn't get drunk Phil was going to have to supply alternate amusement.

LeRoy turned away from them and went to the sliding glass doors.

Cindy brought him a Coke. "No beer tonight."

"How come?" LeRoy tried to sound innocent.

Cindy shrugged. "Maybe Phil doesn't want to get caught dragging around a bunch of drunken minors. *Banging* one might be all right but *drinking* with them might be immoral." She sipped her Coke thoughtfully. She looked up at him. "You know they're going to disappear in a minute or two. We won't see them for a while."

"I figured. Why did you suggest this?"

Cindy shrugged. "I like the water. I couldn't face sitting next to them in a movie while they were going at it."

"They'd do that? In a theater?"

Cindy laughed. "You must have grown up in a cloister. They'd make out pretty hard and then we'd have to find a place to park the car. You and I would have to go for a walk."

"Not such a bad idea."

"I guess." She sipped her soda again. "Besides. Now I've got you to myself." Cindy held his arm and leaned her head against her shoulder. "I really like you, LeRoy."

Without realizing what had happened, LeRoy found himself sitting next to her on the sofa, the taste of her lips, and her tongue in his mouth. The sound of her breathing was very loud in the room. *How did this happen?*

His hand seemed to have no place to go other than her breast, first outside her shirt, then underneath. Her skin was mysteriously warm and soft.

He had a sudden vision of his mother in the hospital, thin beyond all reason, breathing through a thick tube. He pulled back. "I can't. I don't have anything."

"I brought something." Cindy reached down and brought out a wrapped condom from her purse. "Let me help."

She unclothed him, then herself. There was a moment of terrible uncertainty followed by a feeling of perfection that didn't last nearly long enough.

Then they were curled together on the sofa, the air cool against their skin.

"Happy Easter," she murmured against his neck.

"This is the best Easter ever."

She giggled. "I wasn't sure. I thought maybe we were going to—you know—split up."

"Is that why—"

"No." She touched her finger to his lips. "I'm just glad I was wrong."

LeRoy could feel Norman nearby in his mind but now, it seemed less important. He watched her eyes, brown against the paleness of her skin. "I thought I'd already lost you."

"Guess not."

She snuggled against him. LeRoy held her. The distance was still there.

"I know your mother," he said softly.

He felt her stiffen and pull away. "Beg pardon."

"Anya and I have been working on a project together for the last several months."

She sat up and pulled her sweater from the back of the sofa and covered herself. "You should have told me."

"Maybe."

"Are you working for Bill now?"

"No. Connie set something up. She hasn't worked anywhere else for a while."

"She goes to Lifeworks every day."

"No. She picks me up at the metro and we go to a lab in Creve Coeur. Every day."

"Since when?"

"Since before Thanksgiving."

"I see."

She turned away from him. He had the sense of something shattering. "Why tell me now?"

LeRoy shook his head. He wasn't clear himself. It was something he had to say. Something she had to know. Something between them that needed to be open. "I'm not sure. It seemed the right thing to do."

"The *right* thing to do would have been to tell me months ago. The *right* thing to do is tell me before we fuck."

LeRoy nodded. "Yeah."

"Get out."

He looked up in surprise. "Cindy. It's ten miles back to the road."

"I don't care. Get out."

LeRoy looked outside. The air had grown even thicker. There was a fog over the water. It looked cold. LeRoy turned back to Cindy. It was pretty cold in here, too.

"Okay." He dressed and put on his jacket. "I should have told you a while back. Still, though I told you at the wrong time I *did* tell you."

"Do you think that changes anything?"

"No." He opened the door. What did he have to lose now? "There's something more."

"There's nothing you can say—"

"Jake killed Norman. Maybe because of you, but I'm not sure. I thought you ought to know."

She looked stricken.

LeRoy closed the door. He waited outside for a moment to see if she'd call him back. The silence was deafening. *Okay, then.*

He walked across the dock and up the muddy hill. The lab wasn't too far, as he remembered—only a mile or two. He could bunk there for the night. Anya could take him to the metro tomorrow. There could be worse things, he told himself, then walking a muddy road at night nursing a broken heart.

At that moment, unsurprisingly, it began to rain.

oOo

Anya's Easter

He is always in the back of Anya's mind, when she wakes in the morning and drinks her coffee, when she dreams of the long truck ride from VECTOR to Moscow, when she remembers that flat, dry heat of Haifa when the wind blew from the east, the wet, smothering heat when it blew from the sea. When she walks, it's as if *He* walks with her, *His* hands resting on her hands when she adjusts the microscope or reads a gel. *He* watches her every move, her every thought.

That morning, she had a nice dream from when she and Jake were first married. Jake was so careful with her. Like a delicate, porcelain Russian doll, he said. Poor Jake. He had no idea.

But you do, came a whisper from *Him.*

"Shut up." Anya sat up. Jake wasn't next to her on the bed, and the house smelled of eggs cooking on a griddle. He was cooking again.

She had become so tired of eggs over the years.

There was something nagging at her, something other than *Him.* She couldn't quite remember it until after breakfast and Jake led them into the living room. Oh, yes. It was Easter.

Oh, come the Revolution, Easter would be the first thing to go.

Cindy ran at the first opportunity—who could blame her? A girl her age needed something better than an aging cop and a possessed whore.

It was like having a bad tooth or a camera stuck in your face. She just couldn't get rid of *Him.*

She rummaged in the cabinet, looking for anything. Was there some Percocet in there? Maybe a Valium. She settled for rum.

Jake looked so shocked as he left.

Suck it up.

And suck it down, she thought. Jake has *left* the building.

Half a bottle later and she wasn't even tipsy. *His* doing, no doubt.

She called LeRoy. No answer.

Upstairs, she found the Percocet. Forty pills for Cindy's wisdom teeth and she never used a one. And they say this country is overmedicated.

Forty might kill her.

She weighed the bottle in her hand. In the old days before dentistry, people had killed themselves over a toothache. Died or managed to extract the tooth with spikes or nails. She'd always wondered at stories like this. How could a toothache possibly hurt so bad?

Now she knew.

She examined the bottle and called LeRoy again. No answer.

She put the pills in her pocket. Not quite yet.

Instead, she drove—bottle and all—down to the lab. At least, there was loneliness in the empty building. Empty, that is, but for the mice and the dogs. And *Him*.

She walked down through the pens. A couple of the dogs wagged their tails at her. She wondered if they knew they were going to be sacrificed and their brains examined. Now, *that* would be man's best friend indeed.

Her desk was in the back, an old gray steel thing left over from Fort Leonard Wood during the Cold War. How appropriate.

She went over the new batch of gels and stopped at one. This looked interesting. She printed an image of the gel so she could measure it, then pulled out her calculator.

The problem with anti-Anapyridol was engineering in the kink Anapyridol naturally possessed. The receptor required a particular configuration. No kink, no connection. No connection, no effect.

The image was promising.

She wanted to run one of the molecular simulators LeRoy had built, but he had different ones to detect different things. She brought up the PyMol program, which she knew, and things looked correct. But he was just better than she was at this sort of visualization. LeRoy would take one look and figure it out in a moment.

She leaned back in the chair. Wait for LeRoy. You're not at your best. It looks promising—the gel movement was consistent with the extra charge.

Jesus, that kid was bright. It was like watching Horowitz play the piano or something. All you had to do was *breathe* an idea to him and he had it figured out, boxed up and tested, with three variations ready for you to discuss.

She heard the door to the front of the building slam open. Suddenly alert, she looked around for a stick or a club. Something. No one was supposed to be here but her, LeRoy and Connie.

"Anya?" came LeRoy's voice.

"Back here," she called and sat back down.

"What are you doing here?" He was soaking wet but didn't seem to care. LeRoy sat down and dripped.

"Working."

"On Easter Sunday?"

She just stared at him.

He shrugged and pulled off his jacket and threw it into another chair, where it dripped. His shirt and pants were only marginally drier.

"Why are you here?" she asked him.

"Working."

"Right." She looked at him. "How did you *get* here?"

"I got a ride."

"All the way out here? With who?"

LeRoy shrugged. He pointed at the paper in her hand. "What's that?"

She passed the gel print, covered with her figures, over to him.

After a moment, he rose, not taking his eyes off the print, and started towards his desk. She followed him.

After a few moments of checking her numbers, he brought up one of the programs. After a few moments, the current attempt at anti-Anapyridol was on the screen. He twisted it around, looked behind it.

There was the kink.

"That's it, Anya. We did it," he said quietly.

She sat down across from LeRoy. She wanted to weep. But *He* was watching. Instead, she straightened up.

"But not yet," he said seriously.

"What do you mean?"

"We have the dogs and mice for a reason. We need to do the toxicity studies. Besides, looking at this, we need to make two versions."

"Temporary and permanent."

"Just as we agreed. This point here?" He pointed to the turn of the kink. "The hydrogen bond will be temporary. But if we put an ammonia group on the end of that acetyl and this puppy will *never* let go."

"How much longer?"

He studied her. "Pretty bad, eh?"

"You have no idea." She rested her head on her hands.

"No, I don't. What do you think? Two months to figure out how to ammoniate it?"

She shrugged. "Maybe."

"It's just straight chemistry now. We don't have to engineer anything. We can start the trials on this version as soon as we have enough—that's a couple of weeks. If the tox study is successful, you can get fast, fast, fast, temporary relief the end of February. Do it again for the permanent kind by May."

"Five months."

"We should take longer—who knows what it's going to do to you?"

I'm not waiting that long. As soon as the permanent compound is ready, I'm taking it. How much worse could it be?

"This is good news, Anya," he said gently.

She nodded dumbly.

"Anya?"

Anya looked up.

LeRoy smiled sadly. "Happy Easter."

oOo

Ethan's Easter.

Tess wasn't a confident driver. She didn't speak until they had negotiated University City. Ethan watched the houses and stores roll past.

A circular sameness had crept into the world. A grainy feel seemed to lie under the surface.

Ethan reached into the pocket of his jacket and pulled out the rum bottle, thinly clothed in a paper bag. He sipped it slowly. Nothing seemed important. Nothing seemed worthwhile. He wondered if this had always been true. Everything was a colorless eigenvalue. A drab superposition collapsed into existence now that he perceived it.

The rum burned in his sinuses.

Tess wrinkled her nose at the smell but didn't say anything. She concentrated her attention on driving down Skinker. Skinker to Oakland. Oakland onto I-64. Merge onto 40 West. Ethan liked Highway 40. It was more or less straight but still had the kinks and dips of older roads. Not like the rigid Laws-of-Physics control typical of interstates. Tess merged onto I-70 in Wentzville.

Once she found herself driving with limited freedoms, she relaxed.

"How are you?" Tess asked, ignoring the rum.

Ethan shrugged. "All right."

"It's a little early to be drinking, isn't it?"

"It's daylight."

She seemed nonplussed by that and didn't say anything for a few moments. "Colombia must have been terrible."

Ethan felt Jim's notebook through his jacket. He rubbed his fingers across the wire spiral. He sipped the rum. Then, for no reason he could fathom, he began to tell her what happened, starting with when he met her on the plane, the trip up the mountain, the night with Harriet, the eclipse, his kidnapping and Jim's obsession with the eclipse, Harriet's liberation, and the long trek down the mountain.

When he finished, he swallowed the last of the rum and put the empty bottle in his pocket.

"He was going to kill you?"

Ethan nodded. "That's what he said. I believed him."

Tess stared out the window and didn't say anything for over an hour. She took Moberly exit and traded interstate for state highway. "You need to talk to Joe about this."

"Joe and I haven't seen eye-to-eye for a long time."

"He's your father."

"He's a preacher before he's a father."

"So what?" Tess glanced at him, then back at the road. "You're a physicist before you're a son, right?"

Ethan laughed hollowly. "For the moment."

"What does that mean?"

Ethan reached for the bottle, remembered it was empty. "The first month, everyone is apologetic. They fall over themselves, cutting you slack. Mathauser made a point of coming in and saying he was sorry—as if it was in any way his fault. People feel bad when people they know do bad things. But that only lasts the first month. After that, they want you to get on past it."

"Shouldn't you?"

"I would if I could." He stared out the window. "Jim is dead. Harriet didn't say in her letter whether Haberman killed him, but I'm pretty sure that's what happened. Jim was crazy, but he didn't deserve to die."

"He was going to kill you!"

Ethan turned and stared at her bleakly. "You'd think that would make a difference, wouldn't you? You'd think that somehow him wanting me dead would cancel out Colonel Haberman killing him. But it doesn't seem to. I keep feeling it's my fault he's dead. We should have taken him with us."

"He would have killed you both."

"I know that. This isn't a rational thing. I think he should have been caught. I think he should have been punished or treated. I don't think he should have been killed." Ethan rubbed his face with his hands. "It doesn't make sense to feel this way. That's what I keep telling myself. But I feel that way anyway."

"You need to talk to Joe," Tess said.

The last bit of rum seemed to the tipping point. His eyes didn't focus quite right, and there was a deep, wonderful hum below everything. He leaned his head against the window and had just a brief moment to marvel at how soft it was before he was asleep.

He awoke in the car. It was parked on muddy dirt outside a bunkhouse. Ethan couldn't see anybody.

The passenger side was blocked by an old oak. Ethan had to scoot across the front seat and work his way outside. The mud caked on his shoes as he walked towards the bunkhouse. He felt dirty. His eyes were sticky and they burned. His stomach felt tender, as if he had been sick, but he didn't see anything on his clothes.

Great, he thought. *Promising physics graduate student kidnapped in Bogotá dies choking in own vomit in Bumfuck, Missouri.* That is, if he was still in Missouri. If he was "promising" in any way.

Joe opened the door before Ethan had a chance to reach for the knob. Joe's face was split by an unwavering grin Ethan couldn't recall having seen for years. He hugged Ethan and lifted him off the floor.

"Ethan!" He laughed. "I'm really glad to see you."

"Okay," Ethan said softly. and warily disengaged himself from his father. His father didn't lie. That is, he always believed whatever he said. But that didn't mean much in the God Business as far as Ethan was concerned.

"I've been waiting for you to wake up."

"It was nice in the car. Very rustic."

"It's warm today. I figured you were pretty safe, and I didn't want to wake you up until your liver had a fighting chance with the rum."

"Ah." Ethan looked down. "So Tess mentioned that."

"Number one topic of conversation when she got here." Joe stepped back inside to let Ethan enter. He picked up a plastic bag and handed it to Ethan. "Take your shoes off here—we don't like to get mud in the main building. There's a towel, soap. Phil loaned you a pair of sweatpants and a shirt to wear. Shower's that way." Gently, he pushed Ethan in the right direction. "Go on. We'll wait dinner on you."

This was as nice a moment as they'd had in five years. Ethan nodded and started walking down the hall. Maybe ten years. Since Mom died, anyway.

The shower was hot though the needle spray was thin. The sweatpants were too big in the waist and too short in the legs. The shirt draped on him like a tent. What a surprise.

It was just the five of them: Joe and Tess, Phil and some probably illegal teenager named Portia, and Ethan. But the ham was good. Ethan found that Coca-Cola tasted pretty good even without the rum.

The conversation was muted but unforced. Ethan had spent much of his life fighting Joe: about God, about religion, about how properly to mourn Edna, where to go to college. This feeling of just eating together was disorienting, like leaning on a bannister that was suddenly removed.

Don't fight, he kept telling himself. *Just go with it.*

After the meal, Phil and Portia started clearing the table. Tess disappeared into the kitchen. Joe leaned over him. "Come on to the other room."

It was a den with ancient wood paneling, bowed in spots and split in others. Ethan half expected deer heads on the wall. Joe sat down in an easy chair and motioned Ethan to the sofa.

"Tell me what you told Tess," he said quietly.

"You know about all that."

"Humor me."

Ethan warily repeated what he'd told Tess. If they were going to fight, better to be the one to start it.

"Do you have Jim's notebook?"

"Why?"

"Tess said you had something in your jacket. You mentioned the notebook."

"I have it."

"Can I see it?"

"No!" Ethan shouted, startling them both.

Joe blinked. "Why not?"

Ethan shook his head. "I'm not sure."

Joe nodded. "Let me show you something." He reached into a chest of drawers next to the chairs and brought out a video cam. "This is pretty poor quality. Check this out."

It was Tess, preaching—Ethan recognized the tone—just a sort of *la la la* like snake handlers or tongues. *Oh.* Ethan listened more closely. She *was* speaking in tongues. Ethan recognized the gibberish from his childhood. Then she pointed both hands to the sky and the eclipse came. Ethan watched the seconds timer in the window. He fast-forwarded it. Sure enough, eight minutes and some change. He handed back the video cam to Joe. Yet another proof Jim wasn't lying. "I know about this."

"Did you know Tess created the miracle?"

"What miracle?"

Joe blinked again. "The stopping of the sun in the heavens. She prayed for a miracle and it happened."

"Did you stage that?" Ethan wanted to weep with relief. Of *course* it was staged. Then he realized who he was talking to. "You *staged* that?"

"Of course not. I've been a lot of things, but have you ever known me to be a fraud?"

Ethan eased back. "Did *she* stage it?"

"It wasn't staged. It was a miracle. I had a sign and I sent her down there. She brought back evidence of the Power of God. What more of a miracle do you want?"

"I don't believe in miracles."

"The evidence—"

"All I know is something happened down there. There's no evidence it was a miracle."

"She prayed for it—"

"If I pray for light and she turns on a light switch that doesn't make recessed lighting a miracle. It's just something that happened."

"What then?"

"I don't know."

Joe leaned back. He held out his hands and flames flickered in the palm.

Ethan stared.

"It's not a burning bush," Joe said quietly. "But my hand is not consumed." He turned his hand over and watched the flames dance over his knuckles.

"You're comparing yourself to God."

"The burning bush was an expression of God—a symbol of God—not God himself. We are no different. This—" He moved his hand, turning it palm up, reversing it. The flame followed it, burning from the palm, then the back of the hand, then the fingertips. "—is no different."

"You've been learning magic tricks," Ethan said uncertainly, his mouth dry. He couldn't take his eyes off the flames.

Joe reached forward suddenly and touched Ethan's hand with his finger.

Ethan yelped and jerked his hand back. But there was no feeling of burning.

"The sacrifice of lambs was also a symbol," Joe said, leaning back in his chair. "But the blood and the death were real. This is no different." Joe closed his hand and the flames flared, then vanished.

"Tricks."

"You've known me all your life. You know better."

Ethan rubbed his hand and nodded. "Why now? Why you?"

Joe pulled a pill bottle out of his pockets. "I take these."

"What are they?"

"We call it Divinidine. I don't know where they came from. Tess gave me some and things began to happen."

Ethan looked up at Joe. "What's going on? Why did you sell the station? Why did you come up here?"

Joe shrugged and looked uncomfortable. "I sent Tess down there. I was proud, Ethan. I was going to show the world. But you were kidnapped. Pride goeth before the fall. All I could think about was you. Then, when you were sent back to me, it was another miracle. I knew we weren't ready. Most people would be just like you and say it was magic tricks and not a miracle. So, I sold the station. I gave up public preaching. We're all moving out here. We're going to learn what we have to do."

"Those pills could be anything, Dad. They could be boiling your brains to jelly. Don't you care?"

"I've felt the touch of God, Ethan. I've heard His words. I've felt Him in my skin. This is for you, too, Ethan. Now I can save *your* soul."

Ethan slowly stood up. "Take me home," he said. "Have Tess take me home."

Joe stared up at him desperately.

Ethan found his clothes and Jim's notebook, and went back out to the car. He waited. After perhaps an hour, Tess reappeared, scared and irritated. She got in the car without a word and drove recklessly down the dirt track to the main road.

"Your father's a great man," she said furiously. "All he thinks about is you."

Ethan ignored her. As soon as they neared Lambert Field, he had her let him out.

"A great man," she hissed at him.

He closed the door and stumbled into the terminal. After an hour, he was able to cajole a bored cabbie to give him a ride to the university. The whole department was closed. He turned on the lights to the office he shared with the other graduate students.

Ethan made his way to the back near the window. He pulled out the notebook and put it on the middle of his desk. He pulled out a yellow tablet from the drawer and lined up three mechanical pencils. He turned on his desktop computer and waited for it boot up, then he signed on. Every motion had the feel of ritual.

"Okay, then, Jim," he said. He opened the notebook. "Let's figure out what happened."

oOo

Orphira's Easter.

Orphira had no idea what she was doing.

It was Easter Sunday. What the hell was she doing in a bar? In *Jake's* bar? Dressed *up?* For a *white* guy?

She was parked in front of Mississippi's, tapping the steering wheel rhythmically and raging at herself. Hell, if she wanted to get laid, all she had to do was show up in any bar in Saint Louis and hike her skirt up a half-inch. Even here, in *this* bar, she could do it. And she looked good, too. The mirror said so. A big girl—not one of these anorexic supermodel wannabes but a woman with a bosom. A woman with shoulders. She filled out this dress like candy in a stocking and she knew there wouldn't be a man in the bar wouldn't have to work at looking her in the eyes when he was talking to her.

It wasn't as if she had anywhere to go, after all. Her family was dead or too miserable to visit, and her friends were all on the force. Either they were with their own families or they fell into miserable category two.

It's not too late, she told herself. There were a couple of other bars both in and out of the police persuasion. She could go get drunk with her brother officers or not. Why here?

Then came the raging part again.

Finally, she grew sick of herself. She slammed the door shut and walked into the bar.

It wasn't full, but it wasn't empty, either. There were a few couples, but most of these people had known each other for years and coming here for a visit was as normal and obligatory as making an Easter Sunday visit to the in-laws. *More fun*, she thought, *too*.

They watched her quietly but didn't give her the evil eye. She made her way to the bar. One of the older men got up and motioned her to his stool. For a moment, she bristled but caught herself.

"Thanks," she said.

He nodded and moved to the other end of the counter to speak with friends. At least, she assumed they were friends. They talked to him.

She ordered a Vodka Collins from a big, quiet man who passed it to her without comment. Next to her was the biggest black man she had ever seen. He was sipping a beer.

He caught her glance and smiled at her. "What are you doing here on Easter, honey?"

"Drinking," she said shortly.

He clutched his chest as if shot. "Just making conversation, officer."

She started and looked at him. "Do I know you?"

"You're Orphira Doyle. You work with Jake Fiske, right?"

"That doesn't tell me much."

"I'm Connie Samoa," he said quietly.

Ah. So *this* was Connie Samoa. "You're a ways from home."

"Not so far. This place is worth driving to."

"How do you know Jake?"

"I've known Jake a bit. Never thought he would be working with someone as pretty as you." Connie smiled at her again. He tipped his beer towards her and sipped it. "You never answered my question."

Orphira shook her head.

Connie shrugged. "I have to go pick up a friend, but I'm not due there yet so I stopped by. It's on the way. Some, anyway." He looked at her again. "Did you think he'd come by on Easter?"

"Who?"

"Jake."

"I wasn't thinking about it."

"I see." Connie finished his beer. "Well, he might, darling. He lives in a cold place, and some day he might come out looking for a little warmth."

"What's that supposed to mean?"

Connie shrugged. He stood up and paid his tab. "I have no idea. Happy Easter."

Connie had to turn sideways to get through the door. Orphira stared after him. Then she ordered another Collins.

She was lit by three drinks and leaning against the counter on one elbow, watching the rest of the bar. The soft glow of the vodka had taken the edges off things, and there were a couple of single men that didn't look too bad. At least, they weren't wearing rings or anything. All of them white—she felt as if she were the only woman bringing any color to the place. It was an awesome responsibility.

The door opened and Jake came in.

They saw each other at once.

"I'll be damned," Jake said.

"Let me buy a drink, first," she found herself saying. Damn inebriation. Three drinks and her mouth had a life of its own.

Jake nodded and sat next to her. The bartender had a beer waiting for him by the time he'd taken off his coat.

"Thanks, Brendan," he said. He reached over and touched her glass with the bottle. "Here's looking at you, kid," he intoned.

She laughed without catching the joke.

"Like my place?" Jake sipped his beer again.

"It's nice."

"You should try the ribs. Brendan makes the damnedest ribs. Brendan? You got any left?"

Brendan shrugged. "A couple. I'll heat them up."

"Thanks." He turned back to Orphira. "He comes in here at like five in the morning with two hundred fifty pounds of meat he's been marinating for a week. Fires up these great damned ovens in the back and cooks them slow. It's better than pit barbecue from the deep south. Best I've ever tasted — that's why I created this place. He was working in this little dive over in Lafayette Square about twenty years ago. It went bust and he ended up over at Blueberry Hill. So, I had some money —" He stopped, realizing for a moment who he was talking to.

Orphira chuckled. "Go on."

"I had some money and I wanted to open a bar and restaurant. So, I made him a partner. Built this place — not so far from my house, either. Which is a good selling point. He's been here ever since."

Brendan reappeared from the back with a plate and some barbecued meat on it. "I cut the bones off. Otherwise, it'd be too messy for a dress like that."

She hesitantly put a forkful in her mouth. It was a cloud of savory smoke.

Orphira smiled at Jake. "This is very good."

"Yeah. It sells out quick. You were lucky he still had some."

"It was my dinner," Brendan said in a low voice.

Orphira said, "Your dinner? I'm sorry —"

Brendan started laughing. "Don't worry. I'm just fucking with you." He washed a few glasses. "It was leftovers I was saving for the stray dog." Then he moved down the counter to serve other customers.

Orphira stared at him. "Am I supposed to be insulted now? Or what?"

"With Brendan you will never know."

They looked at one another and burst out laughing.

"So, what brings you out on Easter?" Jake sipped his beer. "You still have an uncle on the north side, as I remember."

"Oh, yeah. Uncle James. He could either take me to the Tabernacle of Christ, where he is a pastor and try to diddle me. Or he could take me home and try to diddle me there. After I stormed out, his poor, sweet wife would clean up the mess." Orphira shook her head. "I don't think so." She pointed at Jake. "What are you doing out of the house?"

Jake looked down at his beer. "Tell the truth, Anya booted me out. Sort of."

"'Sort of'? A woman throws your ass out or she doesn't."

"You'd be surprised." Jake was silent a moment. "Truth is, it's been pretty tough the last few weeks. Something's eating Anya up and she won't talk about it. She *forgot* it was Easter."

"Come on."

"No, really. I cook them this really nice breakfast—neither of them is worth a damn before their coffee. Then we go to the front room and Anya looks surprised and says, 'Oh, yeah. It's Easter.'"

Orphira shook her head.

Jake nodded. "Yeah. So, I cover for her—I'm pretty sure Cindy saw through it. But Cindy gets a call from her friend and runs out the door like a shot. Who could blame her? Anya decides today is a good day to die drinking and starts pounding down whatever she finds in the cabinet. She says, 'You better go. This isn't going to be pretty.' I went."

"That's tough." Without thinking, Orphira patted Jake's hand and it was like an electric shock through her body. She carefully pulled her hand away.

Okay, she thought. Now we know the rules. I get too drunk and I can't be trusted with this man. She looked at him. He's a bent cop. He looks no better than okay. He has a kind voice. He belongs to somebody else. Is that all I need to get turned on?

"Do you think she's seeing someone?" Jake rolled the bottle between his hands.

"No. Of course not." She absolutely fucking is. What the hell do you *think* she's doing? Mad scientist research?

Jake shrugged. "I've been thinking about what I've been doing the last few years. What with the girls and all, I never took advantage of that. Not once. I didn't really run the girls, but I made sure the Mexican didn't mistreat them. They were paid well. A lot better than street hookers. We tried to make sure the guys we got were clean and all. We never had any incidents. None of the girls got hit. We were very careful."

Well, that's one cure for being attracted to someone. "What's the connection here?" she said in a tight voice.

Jake didn't notice. "Now that I'm out of it, I think it might have messed me up. Connie was running my little girl." He waved at the bar. "The roof repairs. A new stove. Some of the furnishings. Her money bought a bit of it all. I can't stand the idea of her finding out."

"So?"

"So, I wonder if it hasn't changed me over the years. I wonder if it messed me up in some way I don't understand. Anya is drifting away from me, and there's nothing I seem to be able to do about it. I wonder if it's my fault." He sipped his beer again. "That's what I was thinking this morning when I got up.

A new breakfast. A new start. No more doing stuff in the dark." He shook his head. "But it didn't do any good."

Orphira watched him for a long moment. Cops are in a rare position to see people at their worst. It was equally true cops see people at their most honest, both good and bad. The man beating his wife half to death is far more honest than the same man a half an hour later promising he'd never do it again and pleading with her to take him back.

On a scale of evil, Jake was working at the shallow end of the pond.

Morality is plastic, she thought. No cop ever survived enforcing every law on the books. You had to pick and choose.

Thus began the slippery slope. She had always pussyfooted around near the top, looking down and feeling superior to those down the hill.

Jake had tried to steer that slope. He hadn't taken bribes from people trying to sway him from his duty. He hadn't hooked up with organized crime. He had found a blind spot in enforcement and had taken advantage of it in the best possible way, then took the money and built a neighborhood bar. When his setup had fallen apart, he hadn't tried to keep it going. He'd just shut it down.

Was his strange little code the thing that attracted her? Was it his way of just *talking* to her, not seeming to notice the color of her skin or the fact she was a woman? Was it the way he just *assumed* she'd be good at her job instead of her having to prove it to him?

She caught his quick glance across the top of her bosom. Okay. So, he *had* noticed she was a woman.

Okay, then. Uncle James had always preached sin and redemption. Of course, he interpreted that to mean any sin he chose to commit would automatically be redeemed. But there was such a thing as forgiveness.

She carefully touched his hand again. Held it. *If you hold the fire carefully, it won't burn you.*

"I don't think you can blame yourself for this one—at least as far as I can tell." She liked the feel of his hand.

"Yeah." He held her hand tightly. "I better get back."

"Yes," she said reluctantly. "Go on."

He stood up, glanced hesitantly at her and went to the door. He waved to her and left.

Something new, this time, she thought.

"Okay, Brendan," she said when the bartender came back to her. "Set me up."

oOo

Cindy watched the rain fall on the houseboat deck. By the time she'd figured out what she had done by sending LeRoy out into the rain, he was gone. She called after him but heard no answer. Portia and Phil were locked into their own private passion and wouldn't answer her knock, so she couldn't get the car.

Cindy thought about stealing the keys from Phil's pockets, if she could find his pants. But the rain was really coming down now, and the muddy road looked too scary to drive. If she had really known how to drive.

She sat down on the sofa, listening to the faint sounds of Portia and Phil, and cried about breaking up with LeRoy. When the tears had run their course, Cindy found a Coke in the refrigerator and sat back on the sofa. The rain pounded on the deck outside, glittering in the pool of light that illuminated the deck and the boarding ramp, bounding a circle of water and land. The water around the boat roiled from it.

Okay, then.

Her father had killed a man. Killed him on her behalf. Her mother was working in some clandestine, illegal drug lab. Cindy figured she knew which drug. She wondered if LeRoy knew what he was helping to create. Probably not. Anya was nothing if not secretive. This was the "facts of life," after all.

The two thoughts seemed to roll around in her head, two colliding steel balls in a noisy metal bowl. They drowned everything else out. She'd more or less given up on her mother, but now wasn't her father just as bad?

Not that she wasn't glad Norman was dead. She had only managed to hide the sheer relief of it around LeRoy by a careful act of will. But now that she knew her own father had killed him, the whole slope of it changed in her mind. Now she had two secrets to keep. Should she even bother? Maybe she should just blurt it all out in front of them: Anya and Bill, Norman and Jake. Everything out in the open. It would have the same horrifying, exciting thrill of watching a building explode. Much could be built in the craters left behind.

Portia re-emerged after about an hour and a half. She was wearing an oversized sweatshirt and a pair of shorts. She sat down next to Cindy on the sofa, leaned her head back, and closed her eyes. Cindy put the Coke in her hand. Portia drank it down without opening her eyes.

"Don't kill him," Cindy suggested. "We still need to get home."

"He's got a lot of life left. Give him an hour and he'll be fully recovered."

"I'm surprised. How much Viagra did he take, anyway?"

"Oh, there's no Viagra involved." Portia opened her eyes and gave her a sly smile.

Cindy had a sinking feeling in her stomach. "Christ, Portia. You didn't do that stuff here, did you? It could be hours until it wears off."

"I took no pills. Drank no drugs." Portia found her purse on the floor and pulled out a hair brush. "Nothing but the wonderful effects of Steak 'n Shake and Coca-Cola."

"Really."

"Really. After a while it's like God himself is touching you without the pills."

"What? The effects *linger?*"

"I prefer to think of it like building a muscle." She grinned at Cindy. "A really *nice* muscle."

Cindy didn't answer immediately. "I broke up with LeRoy."

Portia blinked and started. She looked around. "He left?"

"I told him to get out."

"In the rain? Girl, that's harsh."

Cindy shrugged. "I looked for him later, but I couldn't find him."

"Just because you told him to go didn't mean he had to walk out in that. He could have refused to go. He could have waited in the car."

"He didn't," Cindy said. "Men are stupid that way. Pride and all."

"Yeah." Portia looked outside. "I don't care how much I love you. I wouldn't have gone out in that." She looked back at Cindy. "What did you break up about?"

"He's been working with my mother for the last few months and he didn't tell me." Cindy decided she wouldn't even tell her best friend that her father was a murderer.

"Oh," Portia said without expression. "Was he fucking her?"

"Portia!"

"Was he?"

"No."

"I see."

"You see *what* exactly."

"That's not much to break up over."

You don't know what Anya's doing, Cindy thought. What Anya is doing to *you.* "It was enough for me."

"All right," said Portia. After a little while, she said. "You want to go look for him?"

"Absolutely."

"Okay. It's going to take a little while for Phil to recover enough to drive. He's funny that way. We'll let him sleep for a bit." Portia turned to her. "I'm going to have a baby."

Cindy stared at her, stunned. "What?"

Portia chuckled. "You're the only one who knows. I haven't even told Phil." She lifted her sweatshirt. There was a small, telltale roundness to her belly. "See?"

Now that Cindy knew what to look for, she could see it clearly. "Didn't Phil notice?"

"I kept the sweatshirt on. I told him I was cold."

"What are you going to do?"

She rubbed her belly lovingly. "I'm going to keep it. Maybe I'll finish out the semester. Maybe I won't. I don't think my parents will turn me out. If they do, I'll manage. But I don't think they will."

"Is it Phil's?"

Portia nodded. "I think so. He's a good man. I hope it's his."

"But you're not sure?"

Portia gave a Cindy a heavy-lidded stare. "God knows."

Cindy shivered.

They shared the blanket until Phil woke up. Then the three of them went out looking for LeRoy. There was no sign of him. They scoured the roads up and down, finding old and abandoned farmhouses and one ancient factory with a single mercury light burning outside. They pounded on the door of the factory for several minutes—it wasn't that far from the boat and LeRoy might have found shelter there. But there was no answer. They didn't see any evidence of another living soul.

It was midnight before Portia dropped Cindy back at the house.

She went in. Anya was asleep on the front room sofa. Cindy went past her to the back of the house. Jake was running a plumber's snake down the ducts in the kitchen.

He looked up at her eagerly. For a moment, Cindy thought she was looking at a stranger.

"A rat got in. I chased him in here, but he managed to get into the ductwork." Jake's face was earnest, open. He held the reel of the snake in one hand. The coiled spring disappeared into the floor.

A dead rat.

Perfect.

oOo

It was a four-hour drive from Saint Louis to Milan, but Donnie managed it in three. He found Sam sitting on the bluff overlooking the lake late in the afternoon. It was no surprise. Most days Sam could be found on this hill, concealed among the bushes, watching the camp on the other side.

Donnie felt dimly jealous of whoever Sam was watching. But they weren't here. Donnie was. He sat next to Sam. "What's happening over there?"

Sam put down his binoculars. He looped an arm around Donnie's neck. Donnie enjoyed the electric thrill of his touch.

Across the lake, headlights appeared and moved along the shore.

"Earlier, Joe found he didn't have pepper. Or paprika. Or something necessary for his feast. He went go down to town and get some. Then he returned and cooked. Tess came and brought with her a young man—not as pretty a young man as you, by the way. Joe's son. They said grace and ate with knives and forks. Tess passed Joe the butter. Joe passed back the stuffing. I'm sure they discussed and planned who will live in what tent, where they will school the children, and how right they are to leave the city. Tess just left to return Joe's son to the city. When she returns, they will all fuck within an inch of their life and fall into a stupor. They don't have the full group over there yet. Not for another month or two. But they will eventually."

Sam pointed back over the hill with his thumb. They snuck away from his vantage point and strode back down towards the camp. The open fires spread a smoky glow in the fog.

Sam looped his arm around Donnie's neck. "We, on the other hand, will return to camp and fuck like minks *now*. We'll swallow as many pills as we can stand. We will sacrifice the mare I bought last week and bathe in her blood. We will cut chunks from her quivering body and impale them on a pike. All night long, we will draw designs in the dirt, chant, and dance, while the meat turns on the spit, hissing and bubbling. We will eat the dripping meat, still steaming from the fire, and fuck like minks *again*. Then, when the Sun rises and we're raw and aching, those of us still breathing will stand, shaking, on this hill and sing praises to He who kept us alive."

And they did.

And it was good.

Chapter 2.3: May, 1998

Spring had come early. By the end of February, the crocuses were pushing up the snow. An occasional orchard bee stumbled through the air, dazzled and wary in the warm spring sun. Now, in April, the world was turning green.

Joe walked through the compound, a yellow tablet in one hand and a pencil behind his ear, looking for mothers. They were still few—only thirty-two had been able to make the move when he put out the word. Many of them were women Tess had known when she was working for Sam. Of those, six were pregnant, two had toddlers, and four had brought school-age children with them. Phil had come with Portia and a small coterie of other men, but it was still largely a movement of women.

Joe hoped that would change. Their group needed an equal helping of both sexes. He passed Portia returning to her tent from the shower, drying her hair in the crisp air. Her rounded belly was just beginning to show.

"Hi, Joe," she said and smiled when she saw him.

Joe grinned and waved. He thought the baby was Phil's. But Portia seemed to have her sights set on someone else. Joe wasn't sure who. He worried briefly about Divinidine's effect on pregnancy but decided to trust in the Lord. Miracles were happening every day. If God could stop the Moon, he could certainly protect a developing child.

He checked his yellow tablet. Carla, Caleb, and Jesse were the last on the list. He found their tent and knocked on the support.

Jesse, Carla's husband, stuck his head out.

"What do you need, Joe?" Jesse said as he rubbed his eyes.

"Home-schooling forms for Caleb," Joe said."I'm going into town today. I need to drop them off."

Jesse nodded and went back into the tent. Joe could hear muttered conversation. Carla came out in her robe. She handed him the forms.

"Thank you."

Carla nodded and leaned towards him. Joe patted her shoulder and turned away. The only problem with Divinidine was the way it seemed to erode the borders of relationships. Joe believed strongly in the sanctity of marriage, in spite of the occasional transgression when filled with the Holy Spirit. It was best to avoid entanglements. Besides, Tess was woman enough for him.

He walked back towards the lodge and the farm pickup truck. He tossed the tablet on the passenger seat, and in a moment, he was bouncing off the gravel road onto the pavement and heading towards town. Annie's Diner waffles were waiting, along with progressive waves of early risers: farmers, followed by the machinists in the repair shop, followed by the town physician and dentist, followed by anyone whose work began at 8: 00 AM. He was too late for the farmers and the machinists, but the remainder would be getting to the restaurant right along with him.

The sun was now breaking through the eastern clouds, setting the flowers on fire and a limning the new, green grass in a golden glow.

"Life is good," he said to God. God now always seemed to be with him, listening in the back of his mind. "I'm thoroughly past the half-century mark. I have a young wife with a young woman's perspective. I lost my son and then found him again. While he was gone, I thought about him constantly—he's a smart boy. An atheist and a physicist. Smarter than I'll ever be, and Godless in a way I cannot conceive. How did the little boy I helped raise possibly take that path?" He snapped his fingers and watched the sparks. He smiled. "There have been... other recent experiences, as well. You have to think about such things, and the thoughts change you."

Milan surrounded them suddenly. Joe braked and turned into one of the parking spaces in front of Annie's. He got out of the car. Joe stretched. "Come on in. I'll spot you breakfast."

God didn't speak. Joe had never heard a voice even when he had taken the pills. Still, one could hope.

"Suit yourself," he said. He smelled Annie's waffles and let the scent draw him inside.

oOo

Cindy put down her pencil and rubbed her hands together. She looked at them. The cold was drawn tightly over her hands. It seemed like each downy hair was clenched by the skin. She pulled her sleeping bag tight over her shoulders and settled herself firmly against the bed pillows. She saw her breath briefly in the light of the setting sun as it shown through her bedroom window.

Jake had never found the rat, and it had presumably died. At least, that's what it smelled like. Jake had been unwilling to rip apart the walls and the ductwork to find out. Anya, when she was here, and Jake, when he noticed, just bore the smell as the remains worked their way through the various stages of decomposition. Cindy decided she'd rather scrape the frost off her windows and do her homework from her sleeping bag than bear one more minute of stench.

Now it was nearly May and the smell had abated. It was unseasonably cold. Cindy had found she liked the cold's clarity and kept her heating registers closed.

Her cell phone rang. She checked the number—Portia. "Hey, Portia."

There was a strained moment of silence. "No. This is her mother."

"Mrs. Rendquist. Sorry. I saw it was Portia's phone—"

"Yes." Mrs. Rendquist paused. "She left her phone here."

"Excuse me?"

"Portia has gone missing again. So has Donnie. I had thought they had gotten it out of their system. Do you know where either of them is?"

Cindy didn't know what to say. She instantly knew Portia had gone off with those people, but she had no idea where they might be. "No, Mrs. Rendquist."

"Did she say anything? Anything at all."

Portia is pregnant and seeing a middle-aged man named Phil. Other than *that.* Cindy tried to remember if Portia had mentioned where she might be. Portia had been excited about the progress of the pregnancy, but it was still a secret—though it amazed Cindy how Mrs. Rendquist hadn't noticed it. Or maybe not. Portia had taken care to wear baggy clothes and it was the middle of winter. Would Jake or Anya have noticed it?

Cindy shook her head and brought her attention back to the phone. Portia had seemed so normal lately—comparatively speaking, of course. No evangelism. No mention of drugs.

"No, Mrs. Rendquist. She didn't mention anything to me. She seemed pretty happy lately."

Mrs. Rendquist didn't say anything for a moment. "Maybe that was a sign. Usually Portia is less than forgiving in the house. But lately she's been helpful. Happy. I should have known something was coming."

Now, *that* was a healthy home life. "When did you see her last?"

Mrs. Rendquist paused. "Wednesday."

Three days. Anya had said last summer that Jake had started looking for her the next morning.

Mrs. Rendquist said defensively, "I thought she might be staying with friends, like she did before Thanksgiving."

Cindy remembered Portia had missed a few days of school in October. She'd told Cindy she'd been sick. She must have been with *those people* then and she was with *those people* now.

"If you hear anything…" Mrs. Rendquist's voice trailed off.

"I'll be sure to call."

Cindy thought a moment. She called Connie.

"Hello, Cindy," came Connie's deep voice. "You know it's probably not a good idea to call me on your cell. Phones leave traces."

"My friend Portia's gone missing."

"So?"

"So, she was part of *that group* for a bit, remember?"

"I was mostly out of the loop at that point."

"You were at the meeting."

"I looked in on things from time to time. But Norman cut me out of it. It was Norman's show. Now, Norman's dead. You and LeRoy probably know more about it than I do."

"Did you start it up again?"

Connie laughed. "I have enough to do. Child, that business is not even on my radar."

Cindy thought for a moment. "Maybe somebody else has restarted it."

Connie's voice went low and menacing. "Better not be."

"Let's check it out."

"I'm busy. I can send one of my guys."

"Great. If we find Portia, one of your goons is going to scare her to death. Come on, Connie. She knows you."

Connie was silent for a moment. "Did you know Joe Cori sold his television station?"

"Joe who?"

"Cori. The man who was preaching when Portia brought you to that meeting, remember?"

"Right."

"It was Norman was selling the pills to Joe."

"Where's Joe now?"

"I have no idea. I haven't been tracking them."

"Would LeRoy know?"

Connie's voice went carefully neutral. "Why would he?"

Cindy hesitated. "He told me he was working with Anya—"

"Stop. I can pick you up in an hour."

"I'll be waiting on the corner."

Connie didn't say anything when she got in the car. His lips were pursed in thought. He turned north. "What about LeRoy and Anya?"

"LeRoy said they were working together. I figured it was on the same drug he and Norman got from Bill." Now she felt nervous—the same way she'd felt in front of Norman.

Connie nodded. "That and other things. But those pills did not go to Joe Cori."

"Are you sure?"

Connie glanced at her. "I was the one that brought LeRoy and Anya together. This Russian guy I know—Kalenin—set it up. He fronted for Sam Forestell. Through him, I delivered the pills to Sam. Anya and LeRoy have been working on their own little project ever since. They're not working on Anapyridol anymore."

"Maybe Sam sold the pills to Joe?"

Connie chuckled. "At this point, the only way Sam would sell drugs to Joe is laced with strychnine. Norman took over the deal from Sam. But Sam kept following Joe. He had a thing for him. Norman had Sam killed."

Cindy was confused. "But you sold the pills to Sam."

"After he was killed. Yeah, I'm still trying to figure that one out. Usually when Norman kills someone they stay dead. It's not a mistake he generally makes—*made*. Besides, Joe sold the station *after* Norman was killed. Maybe there's no connection at all." Connie caught 40 West.

Cindy thought for a while. "LeRoy doesn't know anything?"

Connie shook his head. "After Norman was killed, I took over managing what Norman left LeRoy. All of it legal and above board. The rest—well, we'll see what happens. LeRoy and I talked about everything he knew, but he didn't know all that much about Norman's businesses. Norman had cut LeRoy out of that particular loop, too—which was just fine with LeRoy. He didn't want to be a part of it. Whatever Norman was doing with the pills and Joe Cori, only Norman knew."

Cindy stared at Connie. "And Bill. Maybe."

"My thoughts exactly."

They pulled off in Creve Coeur. The lights were burning in the Lifeworks building, but the door was locked. Cindy fished in her purse and found the keys she'd stolen from Anya.

"Did Anya ever miss those?"

Cindy shrugged. "She didn't ask and I didn't tell." Cindy led Connie to Bill's office.

Bill was working over a stack of papers. He glanced up and saw Cindy.

"Cindy?" He leaned back in his chair. Then he caught sight of Connie and tensed. "Can I help you?"

"I certainly need help, Bill." Cindy sat down across from Bill. Connie leaned against the wall behind Cindy and said nothing.

Bill watched Connie. "You're keeping some pretty tough company. Jake know about this?"

"Let's not worry about what my dad does or doesn't know." She smiled sweetly at him. "We need to know where all the pills went. I know Norman was involved."

Bill glanced at Connie and then back to Cindy. "They went to Norman. I don't do that sort of thing anymore." He reached down and pulled up a cane to show them. "I'm not a well man."

Cindy put on a sympathetic face. "I heard you got mugged."

Bill shrugged. "After I got hurt, Norman made me an offer to buy them all. I sold him every pill I had. I stopped the program completely. Withdrew our applications with the FDA and everything."

"Did Norman beat you up? To get you to sell out?"

Bill stared at her. "Do you think it was Norman who did this to me?"

"It was an idea."

"It wasn't Norman. But when he offered to buy out the lot, I was ready to sell. I was done with it."

Connie leaned forward against the back of the sofa. He rested his hand lightly but firmly on Cindy's shoulder. "Who did beat you up, Bill?"

Bill didn't answer for a moment. "Anya."

Cindy sat back hard against her chair. *Anya?* Why would she beat up her lover? A chain of logic broke through. Anya was capable of almost anything—she'd hinted at it before. She was sleeping with Bill. Bill was hung up on Anapyridol—she'd seen that for herself. LeRoy said he'd been working with Anya for months. Cindy had assumed that Anya had been working with LeRoy on the side while working at Lifeworks. But maybe she hadn't been here since she had beaten the fuck out of Bill.

Connie's hand rested more heavily on her shoulder. "Why would she do that, Bill?"

Bill seemed to slump in on himself. "Because I slipped Anapyridol into her drink. She was upset—she'd found out I had been selling Anapyridol to Norman. This was her life's work, she said. I had found something better, but I knew she wouldn't take it on her own." He leaned forward on his desk earnestly. "Sometimes you have to force a gift on people." He leaned back. "But as soon as she figured it out, she went for me. I haven't seen her since."

"That's when Norman approached you?"

Bill nodded. "A couple of weeks after I got out of the hospital. I was done with it. I was done with *Her.*"

"You bastard," Cindy said, her voice rising. Anya hadn't fallen apart of her own free will. He had *done* it to her.

Connie clamped down on her shoulder and held her on the sofa. "Do you know where Norman took the pills?"

Bill shook his head. "I never knew. I never knew anything."

Cindy stood up. She wanted to leap at Bill and claw his eyes out. But Connie guided her around the sofa.

"Okay, then." Connie pushed her towards the door. "That's all we wanted to know."

Bill watched them hollowly. "Is Anya all right?"

Connie closed the door on him.

Cindy didn't think she could speak without screaming. She followed Connie to the car.

Connie sat there, watching Lifeworks out of the window.

"What are you waiting for?" she asked in a low voice.

"Waiting for you to ask me."

"Ask you what?"

He turned and stared at her.

She looked at him. "Did you know?"

Connie looked back at the building. "I never did buy the mugging story. Out here in Des Peres? In the parking lot of his own building? I figured like you did: Norman beat the crap out of him to make him sell off the pills. It didn't make much sense, but Norman was losing it towards the end. LeRoy and I had already gone into business together. We needed more expertise. Kalenin said he knew just the person."

"Kalenin?"

"The Russian guy fronting for Sam, remember? Has his fingers in lots of pies. He brought Anya. She was all messed up. Twitchy. After being around her and LeRoy for a while, I got the gist. Then Norman went and got himself killed."

"Jake killed him."

Connie froze. "Who told you that?"

"LeRoy told me on Easter."

"That surprises me. I never figured he'd tell you."

"It was after I broke up with him. He did it to make me feel bad."

Connie shook his head. "LeRoy doesn't work that way. If you sent him away, he'd think he'd have to tell you. After all, he wouldn't be around anymore to help you. LeRoy believes in the power of information. Come on. I'll take you home."

"I wish I didn't know." Cindy buried her face in her hands. "I wish I didn't know any of this."

Connie rubbed her back as she wept. She liked the warm feeling of his huge hand.

"We don't know much," he said gently. "We don't know much at all."

oOo

Since Easter, Jake had gotten into the habit of leaving the house before anyone woke. Sunrise found him at his desk, staring out the window, drinking a Dunkin' Donuts coffee, a half-eaten bagel in front of him. Weekends were the worst. There was nowhere to hide. Cindy lived in her upstairs room, as remote and untouchable as if she had her own apartment. Anya worked on weekends—at least, that's what she said she was doing. If she wasn't working, she was drinking. If she wasn't drinking, she was making snide comments, sharp enough to make him *wish* she was drinking.

Everything about his life had gone gray. The over-strength marijuana he was trying to trace down in Soulard. The basement casino he'd heard of but hadn't been able to find. The new girls that came out to waltz their wares up and down Grand when the weather turned warm. Nothing seemed to alleviate the grayness.

Jake needed to find the pimp. He should just bust the girls and then wait for the pimp to bail them out, but he found himself reluctant to do that. After work, he went to Mississippi's and stayed until he couldn't lie to himself anymore about why he was there.

Cindy was in bed or at least up in her room when he got home. Most nights, Anya was simply gone. When she was there, she was drinking whatever liquor she could find, straight from the bottle, and watching the shopping channel.

Why the shopping channel? Jake had no idea, but she growled at him when he tried to change it.

He hadn't started drinking on the job yet but he could tell, as he watched the sun come up, he wasn't far from it.

He ignored the other officers that came in at 8: 30 and tried to concentrate on the pimp. Think of it as a logistics problem. How do you find a pimp without pumping the women and alerting him?

Late in the afternoon, Milo, Duck's assistant, came in and told them they all had to come to the conference room. Duck had an announcement.

Duck was sitting at the table at the front of them room when Jake found a seat. Duck waited until everyone came in. Then he nodded, and Milo projected a picture up on the wall.

"This is Portia Rendquist. Age seventeen. Whereabouts unknown. She lives in Town and Country in a high-style mansion overlooking the lake. She's been missing for three days. The chief has called out an Amber alert on her."

Portia's picture seemed to suck all the light from the room. Jake recognized her from the arrest that night. But this was a different girl. When Jake arrested her, Portia had been high on something—filled with some vision, some zeal she wasn't talking about. This Portia was half-turned away from the camera, standing with a graceful bend in her back that showed both her tiny, pert breasts and round bottom. She had a half smile, laughing at you because she knew how hungry she made you feel. For the first time, Jake understood the clients of his now-defunct call girl ring and why they paid such exorbitant prices for one night with a young girl.

"You know this girl, Fiske?" Duck said drily.

"I arrested her."

"That's right." Duck turned back to Portia. "Fiske and Doyle arrested Miss Rendquist for prostitution down at Union Station. They did not question her unduly. The Town and Country cops did not question her at all. But you and Officer Doyle did follow her, didn't you Jake?"

"Yes, sir."

"And what did you find out?"

"She stayed in TC for the next three weeks. The investigation dried up, and Doyle and I were reassigned."

"Exactly." Duck flipped the picture. Donnie stared back at him. "This young man is also missing. Both he and Miss Rendquist disappeared around Thanksgiving for five days. But the parents thought she was with friends. Now they know better."

Somebody in the back spoke up. "She's just a runaway. She'll turn up."

Duck shrugged and turned off the projector. "Maybe. Bujold had her watched when he was running the Drug X group. Well, it turns out he is *still* running the Drug X group. Agent Bujold thinks that if we find Portia, we'll find Drug X. He has *asked* us to pursue this with all deliberate speed. So, we follow leads, talk to people. You know the drill. Just like last summer."

The grumbling was thick in the air. This was no collection of babies. This was a girl who had probably ditched her parents and was either out in California or Chicago by now. Jake ignored them. He remembered the dress Orphira had worn on Easter, how it looked painted-on. How she had smelled. At that moment, the memory was a spot of color in a gray, gray landscape.

Jake worked his way through the crowd up to the front. "Duck?"

Duck stopped. "I hate that name

"Sorry. Will Officer Doyle be joining the search?"

Duck stared at him sourly. "Do you miss your protégée that much, Fiske? Officer Doyle will also be on the case, but she is Bujold's favorite for the moment. So, she'll be working directly for him. It's unlikely you'll see each other."

Jake took his assignment sheet with him when he went to his car. He read over it, a list of addresses and possible connections. He drove out of the lot, thinking about the first address over near the Cathedral. He couldn't face it. Instead, he decided to check out the girls on Grand to see if they recognized Portia. It gave him an excuse to pump them without seeming to look for their pimp.

No go. None of the girls knew of her or recognized the picture. They were street girls. There was little connection between them and Jake's call girls. Though one girl—Jake was pretty sure she was actually a boy—did say that Portia had a *look* to her.

Nothing. Maybe Connie knew something. Jake tried to call him, but the phone was disconnected. Connie must have gotten a new cell. The old one had probably started developing a record.

Jake sat in his car, his cell in his hand, watching the hookers move up and down the street. Some laughed at the early evening customers. Some waved at cars. Some moved off for a quick sleep break before the night rush. They looked for all the world as if they were dancing. He wished he had the guts to call Orphira. He would beg her on his knees if he had to. He needed something. He needed to get in on *this*. Anything had to be better. But he had nothing to offer her. Nothing at all.

oOo

Kalenin was waiting for LeRoy at the Richmond Heights stop. He waved to LeRoy and motioned him to get inside.

LeRoy opened the door. He placed the box of coffees he always bought for him and Anya on the floor. "I thought Anya was picking me up. I didn't get any coffee for you."

"It is all right. I drink tea."

LeRoy hadn't seen Kalenin much since he and Connie had taken away the final Anapyridol production run. Kalenin had stayed to help LeRoy and Connie shut down the equipment. Then Connie took over Norman's businesses and it was Kalenin who had trucked in the deliveries of dogs, mice, and additional equipment Anya had asked for. But such things didn't happen that often. Weeks had passed since the last delivery. Seeing him now seemed a bad omen.

"Come on in the car," Kalenin said expansively. "I won't bite."

LeRoy sat down and closed the door. Kalenin waited until LeRoy had fastened his seatbelt, then sped away and merged onto Highway 40.

"Where's Anya?"

"Working," Kalenin said as he threaded his way easily through the traffic. "Chicago Labs delivered the dog samples and analysis last night after she dropped you off. When I called and told her, she went down to the lab. She asked me to pick you up. She's been there all night."

It was the first time he and Kalenin had ever been alone together before. LeRoy hadn't realized how small a man Kalenin was. Kalenin had to work at peeking over the rim of the wheel.

"Just like the old folks in Florida, eh?" Kalenin glanced at him. "Go ahead and stare. I'm a little guy. Everybody was little in the village where I grew up."

"Where was that?"

"A long ways from here in a place you've never heard of."

"I never thought of you as little."

"Nobody does." He thumped himself in the chest. "I have *presence!* Especially with the ladies." He smirked at LeRoy and turned back to the road. "If you don't think of yourself as a big man, then you have nobody but yourself to blame when other people think the same way."

"Is everybody in Russia like you?"

Kalenin gave him a sly grin. "LeRoy, nobody is like me."

"Right."

LeRoy watched out the window. Spring had covered the lawns of Brentwood with green.

"You should get a car," Kalenin said. "You're old enough."

LeRoy looked at him. "Not for two more weeks. Then I'm sixteen."

"So, get a permit. I'll pick you up and you can drive to the lab. This is America. *Everyone* drives."

"Anya picks me up."

Kalenin shrugged. "Suit yourself."

Kalenin let him out and drove off in a spray of gravel. Once inside, LeRoy could tell from the shadows against the roof that Anya was in the back, glued to the PC, long before he confirmed it by reaching her. Next to her was a box filled with samples and a sheaf of reports. She was running her finger over the screen, tracing images of stained neurons.

LeRoy put down the box of coffees and picked up the sheaf of papers. One by one he looked over the analyst's reports. All of them said the same thing. No gross abnormalities. Each of the assays had "Within Normal Range" next to it. But what did he know? LeRoy thought of himself as a biochemist more than anything else—emphasis on the "chemist" rather than the "bio." But even with everything Anya had taught him, she was still the neuroscientist.

Anya leaned back in the chair. LeRoy looked past her to the image on the screen. He recognized the ID. Anya had named the dog "Fitzie." LeRoy had no idea why.

Fitzie had been a slobberingly friendly Lab right up until they'd administered the anti-Anapyridol. The Lab had been sick for a few days afterwards—all of the dogs had acted the same way. Prone to lethargy and sleeping a lot. Small fevers. As if they'd had a cold. The other dogs had recovered fully, but Fitzie had taken to watching them. Fitzie had still been unfailingly friendly whenever LeRoy brought around the food, but as soon as he'd eaten, the dog moved to the back of the pen. Watching.

It gave LeRoy the willies, but then he figured it was because he didn't like dogs. Anya told him dogs often became wary once they'd gotten a shot or been sick in a vet's office. She'd seen it in Russia. Even so, when LeRoy had administered the sacrificial phenobarbital to each of the dogs, he made sure he did Fitzie first. He didn't want any trouble.

"Everything look good?" He handed Anya her cup.

Anya pulled the top off and sipped it. "Yes. This is the last one."

"Nothing wrong with Fitzie?"

"No. No toxicology problems with the weak-binding version. It was excreted in the urine, just as we expected."

LeRoy nodded. "I finished purifying the strong-binding form last night before I left."

Anya's hand shook suddenly. She leaned forward to avoid spilling coffee on herself. "You didn't tell me that."

"It was still drying. Besides, I have to mix up the dosages and get them ready for the mice. We're going to need more dogs."

"You should have said that to Kalenin."

"I wanted to talk to you first."

Anya nodded. "Where is it?"

LeRoy led her over to another lab table. There, in the drying oven, was small pile of fine, gray, crystalline powder resembling dirty salt. LeRoy pulled out the dish and weighed it. One hundred and forty grams. He wrote down the amount in his notebook. Then he carefully poured the powder into a vial and capped it.

Anya sniffed the air. "Water soluble?"

"Should be. Saline would probably help."

"When will the testing be done?" She looked at the vial hungrily.

LeRoy started measuring out lots. "Twelve weeks. Just like the last time. If you need a fix, use the stuff we made. That probably won't kill you." He gestured with the vial. "This hasn't been tested yet."

Anya nodded. "We should celebrate."

"After we inject the mice."

It was late when they finished, but Anya insisted on buying him breakfast. It was uncomfortable. Anya only spoke well on lab matters, and she was adamant about not speaking about them right now. She stared out of the window while LeRoy ate a thick, sweet waffle for which he had no desire.

There was nothing to do at the lab. Nothing he couldn't do back at home. Anya put him on the Metro back at Richmond heights. LeRoy wondered how long she would wait before she used the strong form. He hoped it wouldn't kill her.

Well, he thought, as the train began marching him down back home. This project was going to be over soon. It was almost over now. What did he want to do then?

So, he said to himself. *What do you want to be when you grow up?*

oOo

After Anya dropped off LeRoy at the Richmond Heights station, she turned and headed straight back to the lab. She adjusted the weight dose they had used for the dogs to fit her. But how much was enough? It had taken more than a therapeutic dose to damage her. That implied a concentration effect—perhaps there were other receptors than the ones she targeted, receptors that were deeper or less sensitive, or caused a different effect on the same receptors when they were overstimulated.

The dose for her weight approximated what she had given the human volunteers. The compound had approximately the same mass and solubility as the Anapyridol it was replacing. Of course, without extensive experimentation there was no way to determine if anti-Anapyridol bound one-for-one to the same site of the Anapyridol. Or even if it was the same site at all

The Lifeworks' tox screens for Anapyridol showed full excretion in the urine. She still had no model of how the effect could remain when all the Anapyridol had left her system, but there was no doubt it did; she could feel the untiring scrutiny even now. The original dose must have caused new connections to be created, analogous to how memories are made. It was these connections that she had to target. How did she have any assurance that anti-Anapyridol would even bind to those sites?

But then, what was the downside? She could die, slip into a coma. The drug could sear her brain and she could become a vegetable. Or worse, a thinking vegetable. Anya had a horror of losing her ability to think. Or worst, the anti-Anapyridol could have no effect at all.

Doubling the dose might do it. It was still well below lethality. But she had no idea how much Bill had given her or even if the amount to counteract it should be the same, larger, or smaller. She stared at the vial.

"Good evening." Kalenin stepped out of the shadows.

Anya almost dropped the vial. "What are you doing here, Sasha?"

"I'm just trying to help."

"Crap. I didn't see your car when I got here. Where is it?"

"Nearby. I walked."

"Why?

"I have my reasons."

"Crap, again."

"As you will. I'm here to help, nonetheless." Kalenin held out his hand. Anya gave him the vial. He shook the vial and watched the powder dance. "Do you think it will work?"

"Of course, it will work," she said, her voice shaking. *Double the amount,* she thought. *That should do it. If it doesn't, I will take more. As much as it takes.*

"I will help."

Anya snorted but didn't say anything. She measured her dose into a separate vial. She was about to mix in the saline when Kalenin stopped her

"This is a terrible place to do this. I have an apartment not far from here."

"No doubt where your car is."

"Yes."

"We'll take my car."

"I'll drive."

She put the saline, the measured vial, and the syringes in a plastic bag. *Like an old woman with her month's supply of meds,* she thought.

Kalenin's apartment was in a complex across the river in Saint Charles. Much farther than a couple of miles. He must have had someone drop him off. Connie, perhaps.

She measured out the saline and drew the dissolved mixture into the syringe. Kalenin disappeared into the bedroom of the apartment and then returned with his own small bag. Out of it he brought vials of Valium, morphine, Demerol, and a similar packet of syringes.

Anya carefully capped the anti-Anapyridol syringe and put it on the table. "What are those for?"

"What do you think the side effects will be?"

"The dogs—"

"The dosage is different, and you are not a dog. Plus, you've already been damaged by the Anapyridol. Whatever this drug does to you it will *not* be the same as the dogs."

Anya watched him steadily *Why is he helping me?* "Your point?"

"You could have a seizure or suddenly experience intractable pain as the transition occurs. Better to have these drugs in your system, already working."

She looked at the vials arrayed on the table, undecided.

Kalenin stared at her levelly. "Is there any reason *not* to sleep through this?"

"No," she said, suddenly decisive. She picked through the array of drugs. Some Valium in case of a muscle seizure. The morphine to knock her unconscious. "I don't know the proper dosages."

Kalenin left the room and returned with a Merck Index.

Anya stared at it, then at him. "You've been planning this."

Kalenin nodded. "Ever since the day we started, I knew it would come to this."

Anya nodded. She looked up the dosages for morphine and Valium and measured out the syringes. "How's your touch?"

"It's been a few years since VECTOR, but I still remember how to administer injections."

She tapped the Valium and the anti-Anapyridol. "I.M. in the gluteus. The morphine gets administered afterwards." She dog-eared the relevant pages in the Index. "Here is where to refer if I get in trouble."

Anya bent over and dropped her pants. She felt the stabs, one after the other, as Kalenin administered first the Valium, followed by the anti-Anapyridol. She pulled up her pants and sat back down on the sofa.

"Better lay down," Kalenin said, tapping the syringe to remove the bubble. He reached into the drawer and pulled out a rubber tube

"Been partying much?"

"In all the time you have known me, have you ever seen me unprepared?" He sat next to her and tied off her arm expertly. He tapped the vein until he was satisfied and inserted the needle and released the tie. Gradually, he started pressing the plunger of the syringe. Anya felt the cold flow up her arm, followed by a warmth that seemed to spread throughout her. She felt sleepy.

"Sasha?"

"Mm?" Kalenin didn't take his eyes off the needle.

"If it doesn't work, kill me." Her tongue was thick. It was hard to talk.

Kalenin glanced up at her for a moment. "I promise."

She closed her eyes and felt herself falling. She wondered if she would reach bottom.

oOo

Ethan sat stiffly across from Mathauser. Mathauser turned the pages of the manuscript over and looked at them. It was a sham, he thought. Mathauser had read it over more than once. Otherwise, he wouldn't have asked Ethan to come over to his office.

"The thing is..." Mathauser's voice trailed off. "This isn't what you were supposed to be doing." Mathauser looked up at him, confused. "What does this have to do with electron chip reduction?"

"Nothing, Dr. Mathauser."

He stabbed the manuscript with his finger. "If you wanted to move over to the high-energy group, all you had to do was talk to me."

"I don't want to leave your lab. I like the work."

"Then what is *this* all about?"

Ethan closed his eyes. For a moment, the little room in Colombia showed through the darkness. Then it whisked away. "This is what Jim was working on. This comes from the eclipse data."

"Physical explanations of mass hallucinations?"

"The instruments—"

"Altered."

"No, sir. They were not. I've checked that. It was a real phenomenon. This is a possible explanation."

"But if this is what you want to do—"

"It's not." Ethan didn't know where to begin.

This is what obsessed Jim. It's the source of these dreams I have every night, where my mother comes to me and tells me this is the way to make it go away. Where she and I work on equations until morning and it's all I can do to put them down before I forget them. It's the signature and shape of whatever

Colombian spirit that haunts me and it is the only way I can think of to exorcise it.

"It's what I *have* to do." Ethan shook his head.

"It's what you *have* to do? A more lunatic notion was never uttered." Mathauser shook his head and went over his notes. "This flies in the face of the standard model. String theory does better than that and it's not provable, *either*."

Ethan shook his head. "No, sir. My work incorporates the standard model."

"As one of many."

"Yes. The standard model—most models, actually—are predicated on repeatable phenomena. Non-repeatable phenomena that violate them are discarded as false."

"Like the eclipse nonsense."

"Yes, sir."

"It *is* nonsense. You know that, don't you?"

"You have no idea how much I wish to believe that. But the evidence that something happened is very strong. What happened can't be explained easily." Ethan took a deep breath. "If you have an explanation of what happened that squares with the evidence, I'd be more than happy to throw all this away." Ethan stared at him bleakly. "Please. I mean that."

Mathauser didn't answer. "There's a lot to like in this. I like the modeling of the different sets of physical laws in terms of finite automata. Especially your treatment of the Many Worlds Hypothesis. Turns it on its head. Good phrase: 'There is one physical universe but multiple points of view, each with its own set of rules.' Good mathematical model to back it up. You believe there was a point of view change in Colombia?"

"That's my hypothesis."

Mathauser pinched his nose and looked tired. "You're a very promising student, Ethan. You have a flair for obtuse mathematics and a clear eye for problems. You have no idea how this pains me. You can't publish this. You can't even talk about it—it would destroy your career. Physics is immune to ridicule, but people are not. They will turn on you."

Ethan nodded, dry-eyed. He had come to the same conclusion.

Mathauser leaned forward over the desk. His bulk seemed to raise his back above him. "What happened in Colombia was not your fault. You didn't kill James. You had nothing to do with it."

"I didn't kill James. I know that." Ethan sighed. "But he's dead. I'm not responsible for that, but to say I had nothing to do with it—well, that's not true. James hated me and believed in me. I hate him for getting me in that mess, and I owe him for that belief."

"That's crazy."

Ethan grinned at him. "Do you think I don't know that?"

Mathauser leaned back. He watched Ethan for a long time. He shuffled through Ethan's paper. "You're too good a prospect to be wasted on this obsession. I won't accept this as a thesis proposal. I won't put my name on it for a paper. But I'll make you a deal."

Ethan waited. He had done his part, he thought, broadcasting to the universe. Radio Ethan. He said to the dreams: *if you'll leave me alone, I can live through the rest.*

Mathauser placed his palms together over his belly. "I'm telling you this in confidence. I've accepted a position at the University of Washington. The University is creating a lab for exotic sensor technology. NASA is funding it, along with a couple of rich billionaires that want to see exploration missions named after them. It's not going to be a big lab, but I hope it will be an important one. I will be leaving at the end of the term. It was my intention to take you with me if you were so inclined."

Mathauser looked down at the paper. He took a deep breath. "I propose you finish the work you're doing on electron imaging. You already have enough for a paper and a master's degree. Neither should take you more than the end of the summer. Then I'll take you on as a graduate student when I open the lab in the fall. Once you enter my lab, you can work on this part time. One tiny piece at a time. Nothing big. If bits of it prove out, I'll back you so far as I can. Little papers. Letters. Small presentations at conferences. Nothing big enough to shake things but nothing trivial, either. In return, you do the lion's share of your work for me." Mathauser stared at him out of those tiny, stone-black eyes. "What do you say?"

It was more than Ethan could have hoped for. He could smell freedom. "I'll do it."

"Excellent. Now, go and get to work. Don't show me any more of this until next year."

oOo

Orphira had never put much stock in fate or luck. They all had the same smell as the fairy godmother and Orphira was too old to believe in fairy tales. But the way Bujold lifted her up out of Central Patrol and dropped her back into the Drug X team sure felt like creating a carriage horse out of a rat. No district duties. No trying to figure out where the marijuana drop was this week. No Jake Fiske to confuse her. This was the Promised Land.

The first thing she did was to find the prostitutes and johns she and Jake had arrested last fall. They quickly fell into two groups: those who had completely disappeared, and those who still remained. She questioned the remainder about Drug X and about Portia. The majority knew nothing about Drug X and very little about Portia. But three girls reported that one, a girl named Carly, had offered them some sort of pink pill. They had refused but had seen some of the other girls accept them. Of the girls who accepted the pills, only one name, a Selma Briteis, checked out. Orphira already knew about Selma and her room north of the Cathedral. She was one of the girls who had disappeared.

She reported this to Bujold. He frowned when Orphira listed the girls who weren't there but he smiled when she concluded there was a much larger Drug X conspiracy. Orphira watched him as she reported. Conspiracy was meat and drink to him

She went back to her desk and started collating her notes. Relatives of the disappeared girls would be a good place to start. Pimps. Past associates.

The phone rang. Absently, she picked it up.

"Doyle."

"Orphira," came a hesitant response.

She recognized Jake's voice instantly and hated herself for her instant smile. "Hello, Jake." She kept her voice neutral.

"I've got a tip. From Sam Forestell."

"He disappeared months ago. I heard he was dead."

"That's what I heard, too. But he changed my mind when he called me this morning."

"You said a tip."

"I'm guessing you checked out our arrests from last fall. Some of the girls were gone, right?"

"Right."

"I've been told where they are. Portia Rendquist is there, too."

"Where, Joe?" This cat and mouse game was getting to her. "No more bullshit."

"I want to get attached to your group."

"That's Bujold's decision."

"But you could grease it. This is real, Orphira. I'm begging you. Get me out of here.

Maybe it was. Maybe she even wanted to see Jake. But she didn't like being pushed around. "You tell me what you have and I'll think about it."

"That's good enough for me. Norman was selling Drug X to Joe Cori, the televangelist. Joe got hooked on it from a girl he was seeing. He married her."

"A televangelist married a prostitute." Orphira let the skepticism drip into her voice.

"Don't take my word for it. The marriage is in the public record. But it gets better. The drug makes you find God or something—you remember how those girls were last fall? Idealistic? As if they were working for a higher power? Well, they thought they were. Joe and his new wife sold his station before Christmas and went to northwest Missouri to build a place for themselves. A cult hotel. Now it's ready and they sent out the word. Over the last couple of weeks their little sex-for-Christ flock got buttoned down and cozy in their new home. It's a bona fide cult, Orphira. That's where the girls are. That's where Portia is. That's where Drug X is."

Orphira tried to think this through. Underage sex was a morals charge. If Portia joined the group voluntarily, was it kidnapping? That would bring in the FBI.

Jake continued. "You need more? Well, there is more. Sam says they have guns. Machine guns. And kids. Joe wants to be the next David Koresh or something."

ATF, too. It was going to be a regular federal festival.

"Any kind of lever we can use?" she said quietly.

Joe chuckled. "Joe was a widower with child before wife number two. A kid named Ethan—student over at Wash U. I thought about checking him out but figured you might like to run this."

Oh, I do. This was meat. Bujold would be drooling.

"I'll talk to Bujold." She hung up. Was it just the excitement of the case that made her smile or the prospect of playing in the same sandbox as Jake?

Both, she decided.

oOo

Mathauser's largesse stunned Ethan. He took the paper and went home. Sitting in the front room of the apartment, he went over it. There were holes in the model—he knew that. There were places in the logic where he didn't want to go. In the paper he treated singular, irreproducible events as a problem of multiple physical states, conditions where the rules of physics changed and then returned to normal, modeled as finite machines. Rules such as the nature of the passage of time, the speed of light. These were the physical constants of physics. Change one and you change the nature of others. There were countless knock-on effects.

It appeared that time had speeded up at the observation site. But the speed of light is a constant. Consequently, if they were going faster in time, light from outside their frame of reference was relatively slower—but light *couldn't* go slower. So, the frequency should have reduced—the light from outside the frame of reference, the light of the stars, the planets, the corona of the sun, should have been red-shifted.

It was not.

Moreover, their frame of reference had changed without any obvious shift of circumstance. They had not suddenly been transported away at an appreciable velocity. No large negative mass had been suddenly introduced. Hence, the rules had changed. The paper had postulated some of the implications of the rules change and the nature of the change. He'd worked out a mathematical solution where rules could change without loss of thermodynamic or momentum conservation, but he'd had to do it by declaring them as separable quantities. The implication was, though, the conservation rules were just as up for grabs as time and space. Einstein had made the equivalence principle central to his theories: physical laws were the same everywhere in the universe. It was a foundation of modern physics. Ethan had taken that away.

What Mathauser didn't know was much more disturbing. Tess had called on God for a miracle, and a violation of physics had been granted.

Ethan didn't believe in God. Or, more precisely, he didn't believe in the God of his father. If there was a God, Ethan believed it would be a God of physics. A God that presided over the trilobites. A God that decreed the Cretaceous Extinction. Not some weak God that needed to lie to his believers that the world was only six thousand years old while leaving evidence everywhere that it was not. No. Any God worthy of the name would be clever enough to operate within the boundaries of his creation.

Consequently, no God had granted Tess her wish. The truth was something far more subversive. If the laws of physics were merely rules of the game and the game could be changed, Tess's miracle had suggested a human being could change it with no more equipment than the human brain. Physics was about the objective nature of reality; principles made manifest. But a miracle showed that the subjective could be made manifest, too. The metaphor made real. How could one study the physics of the subjective? Evaluate the quantum states of a goat's entrails? Calculate the eigenvalues of the image of Christ in a shroud? Go far enough with this, and everything comes tumbling down.

Christ said that belief was sufficient. Faith was sufficient.

Ethan didn't believe it. If that were the case, miracles would have been so commonplace in the world, the word would have had no meaning.

There had been an "observer/observed" interaction recognized since the very beginning of quantum physics. Mathauser had a different point of view. It was his perspective that quantum effects were visible only when they were isolated from external influences. Superposition and other quantum effects were products of that isolation. The mechanism of "measurement" was not anthropic at all. It was a product of losing that isolation. Like many scientific effects too subtle to be observed outside the laboratory, quantum behavior required scientific isolation to be observed. That didn't mean it didn't happen outside that laboratory—likely quantum behavior happened *all the time*—just that experimental observation required laboratory conditions. There was no necessary anthropic interaction. It was a fluke that it happened to be people who were executing the experiments. The phenomena were universal.

This, though, was a different animal. *This* suggested that there truly was an anthropic principle. A direct interaction between brain and object without an intervening known physical mechanism. As if metaphors had become real objects. Real behaviors.

Okay. Accept the evidence. But physics was physics. There could be nothing unique about the human brain—that way lay the exceptionalism of human beings. That way lay magic and religion.

No. Instead, consider the *universe* as a computational engine—the brain as a unit of computation within that mechanism. That concept was what led to Ethan's reformulation using finite automata. The automata functioned according to rules and expressed those rules as observable physical phenomena. However, a sufficiently sophisticated computational engine, under specific circumstances, had access to the control panel of those finite automata—think of them as the cheat codes in an incredibly detailed simulation.

So, if the brain had that ability, why wasn't it realized *every day*?

Ethan kept seeing those pills in his father's hand. The flame dancing over his fingers.

Though the necessary computation must be part of the brain's repertoire, it could not be part of its normal behavior. Otherwise, the drug would have been unable to trigger it. The drug changed the organizational behavior of the brain, enabling access to the levers of power.

But could *any* computational engine trigger this behavior? Why didn't they see it every time a PC booted up? A cell phone started?

There was *something* special about the brain.

Ethan had started with Mach's Principle: local physical laws were determined by the large-scale physical structure of the universe. Einstein had used this to explain inertia—the quality of an object to resist changing its state of motion—in describing how the state of matter in the universe affected motion in a given reference frame.

Ethan's automata universe was similar: the total computational state of the universe had an effect on the local computational state. This had the effect of suppressing local direct access to the automata. It was, he thought, analogous to quantum phenomena. Quantum states such as entanglement and superposition might be occurring all the time but could not be observed in the noise state of normal activity. It could only be demonstrated in isolation—low temperatures and, high vacuums. At that point, superposition could be maintained. Measurement—the act of determining a specific value out of the constellation of possible values—broke that isolation.

Ethan was proposing something analogous here—*analogy*, Ethan reminded himself continually. He even reread George Pólya to make sure he hadn't misled himself. The analogy of the thing was not the same *as* the thing, but it gave possible insight *into* the thing.

In this case, the noise of the normal computational environment did not allow direct access to the local constants. Only specific mechanisms of isolation could make them available to be manipulated—and make physical laws changeable at the whim of organic computational engines.

Which brought him back to the original question: if the behavior of automata were so easily changed by people, why didn't it happen all the time?

Let us return to isolation, he thought. As in quantum phenomena, the material had to be isolated from the noise of the environment. If the analogy held true, the computational mechanisms that were *capable* of altering the automata directly were prevented by the local computational noise—other humans, maybe? The collective neurological computation of the biosphere? It had nothing to do with belief. It had to do with operation of the human computational engine *outside* of the normal computational noise—the Machian influence of all other computational engines in the larger environment. Was there an equivalent of superposition in isolated automata? Entanglement? Ethan had no idea.

If he were right—and he wanted to be wrong—then it wasn't surprising it had never been successfully investigated. How would it? Einstein, Bohr and the others had Faraday's and Newton's equations backing them up. They had three hundred years of scientific experimental results. Einstein's 1906 papers were a response to experimental evidence—the Michelson-Morley experiments for relativity and Planck's interpretation of the black body radiation results as the root of quantum physics. All of which were reproducible and produced new, also reproducible, results.

None of that applied here.

Science is statistical, he thought. Reproducibility was everything. A sample set of one had no meaning. Some yahoo out in the woods intermittently curing warts with spunk-water would never be scientifically verifiable.

Except, maybe, until now.

Mathauser must have seen it. Or maybe he hadn't. It seemed so obvious to Ethan, but he'd been thinking of nothing else for months. The darkness lurking in those simple equations describing point of view. The chaos inherent in the evaluation dynamics of subjective automata. Where did it end? Ethan turned the pages without seeing them, the figures burning in his mind like wheels within wheels. Maybe he didn't want to pursue this at all. Maybe he should be a fisherman for the rest of his life. A janitor. A bus driver.

But the drugs in Joe's hands lit up in his memory by X-ray light. What if Tess had requested turning that rock into fifty pounds of Uranium 235? Or antiprotons? Or brought a piece of the Sun down to Earth? Was it possible? Were there limits? Ethan didn't know. Magic and miracles were all fine and good when they were confined to werewolves and vampires and figures metaphorically dying for your sins on the cross. But what do you do when it gets serious? Ethan buried his head in his hands.

There was a knock on the door.

Ethan looked up. He walked to the door and looked through the peephole. A white man and a black woman were waiting outside

"Ethan Cori?" asked the black woman.

"Who are you?"

Both the man and the woman pulled out badges.

"I'm Orphira Doyle and this is Jake Fiske. We're from the Saint Louis Police Department. We'd like to talk to you about your father."

Of course. There were always consequences. Joe and Tess had discovered fire but only bothered to admire the pretty flames. They didn't realize it could burn down the city.

Doyle and Fiske came into his apartment. They sat down on the sofa. Doyle glanced down at the paper on the coffee table. Fiske didn't even do that

It's right in front of you and you can't see it. Ethan almost laughed. *Poor Joe. Poor Tess.*

"What's this all about?" Ethan asked.

"Do you know where your father is?" asked Doyle, not answering him

"Why do you want to know?"

Doyle sighed. She looked at Fiske. Fiske shrugged and gestured towards Ethan. Doyle nodded.

"We have reason to believe he's founded or joined an illegal organization involving narcotics and children. Possibly weapons."

Of course, Ethan thought.

"Do you know where he is?"

Ethan had a sudden vision of dozens of policemen pounding down Joe's door. Officers with guns. Officers triggering violent holocaust. He shuddered. *But if Ethan went with them…*

"Yes, I do. Do you want me to take you to him?"

oOo

Anya's head hurt. It hurt deeply. Profoundly. As if she'd been struck by a crowbar and the tip was lodged in the depths of her skull, bloody and beating with the rhythm of her heart.

Anya tried to hold her head in her hands, but they were stuck fast. She saw light now. Photons as an impacting crowbar. Her eyes were closed fast against the light and the pain, but it didn't help. She whimpered. Her head felt swollen on one side. There was a burning smell and a deep rumble in her ears. She felt a stinging in her thigh, and she tried to swing at it, feeling nothing but rat rage at the pain. But her hands and arms were bound

Gradually, inch by bloody inch, the pain subsided to a roar and she could open her eyes. The room was dark but still shot through with light. Every square inch was clear, as if cut into steel. Shadows were sharp. She saw that the cloth of the sofa wasn't just a texture but a mass of individual fibers. She looked around the room.

Kalenin was sitting across from her. A .45 semi-automatic was resting comfortably against his leg, its glittering muzzle pointed directly at her. He held up a syringe with the other hand. "Dihydroergotamine. For the migraine."

She tensed. Had he expected a migraine? How? What could he have planned that might require a gun? Had she done something while unconscious? Maybe she could lull him—promise him something. Anything to get these bonds off.

She looked closely at him. Recognition came instantly. "You're Fred Hibbert." She stared at him intently. "And Kalenin, too."

Hibbert nodded, never taking his eyes off her. "I wondered if that would happen. It worked, then?"

Anya hadn't thought of it. Interesting. She felt no undying scrutiny—in fact, it surprised her she would have minded. What difference would it make? "It did."

"Good

"Am I dangerous?"

Hibbert smiled. "I don't know. Are you?"

Anya didn't answer. She tested the bonds and looked down. Hospital gauze. She recognized the knot. She'd learned it in a Russian hospital. She couldn't untie it.

"Neat trick, that disguise. How do you manage it?" *Stall for time. Figure out how to get loose.*

"It's an acting technique. I'm a good actor and I've had a lot of time to practice." He tilted his head to one side. "What are you going to do, Anya?"

"Escape." He must have figured that out. She wasn't giving anything away. "Barter for it if I have to. Leave town."

"And go where?"

"I haven't thought that far ahead." But she had—she must have been dull-witted to not be able to figure things out before. She'd go back to Russia. With what she knew now and the chaos there, she could write her own ticket. Buy her own dacha. Hell. She could raise her own army.

"What about Cindy and Jake?"

She stared at him levelly. "What about them?"

"I'm guessing twenty additional points," Hibbert said softly. "Twenty to fifty."

IQ points. "More," she said. "I can be of service. I'm too valuable to discard."

Hibbert shook his head and smiled again. "That's my little psychopath. Smarter and unfettered. Would that be a good description?"

Anya stared at him. "Yes."

Hibbert moved closer to the sofa. "Open your mouth."

She stared at him.

"I'm going to free you, but I don't want to get hurt. Open your mouth."

She weighed the possibilities. If he wanted to kill her, this would be a good time. It might even be enjoyable for him. His motives were suspect, but she couldn't imagine going through all this elaborate trouble just to kill her.

The possibility of freedom was worth the risk. She opened her mouth.

He placed the barrel of the gun in her mouth. "Don't move and I won't kill you."

Anya didn't move.

Hibbert pulled a switchblade out of his pocket and flicked it open. In a moment, he had cut her bonds loose.

She flinched.

"Don't move, Anya. It's not worth the risk."

Carefully, he pulled away from her to the chair, drawing the gun out at the last second.

Anya sat up quickly and rubbed her wrists waiting for circulation to return. Her mouth was sore from the gun sight. She ignored it.

"You planned this." It was a statement.

Hibbert nodded. "One of many plans. This one worked. Most didn't."

"You were in Russia at VECTOR? You're not just a good impersonation of Kalenin?"

Hibbert replied, "I was at VECTOR with you," in perfectly accented Russian. She could have closed her eyes and identified Kalenin in the dark.

"Why?"

"That is not your concern."

Anya nodded. She hadn't expected an answer. "What happens to me now?"

Hibbert jerked a thumb to the door with his free hand. The hand holding the gun never wavered away from her. "Next to the door are your purse and a backpack. Inside the backpack is a new passport, driver's license, and tourist visa for the United States. You're a Russian citizen again."

"Money?"

"Quarter of a million. Half of your share of the money you and LeRoy got from Connie for the Anapyridol."

"What about the rest? It's mine."

"I've got plans for it. You have plenty to get started in Russia."

She stared at him, memorizing his true face. She would always recognize him now. "You have plans for me, too?"

He grinned at her. "Not anymore. You're a free woman. I'm done with you."

She started to get up.

Hibbert twitched the gun. "Not so fast. And walk in a straight line to the door. Don't stumble or I'll have some cleaning up to do."

She walked to the door and picked up the pack. It felt heavy enough to hold that much cash. She looked at Hibbert, for a moment uncertain. She had *no* idea what he wanted.

Hibbert chuckled. "Your car's outside. Don't wait around, Anya. Run. Run fast. Run hard. Cover your tracks. Run like Hell itself is coming after you. It is."

Hibbert pointed to the door.

She grabbed her purse and checked her keys, then snagged the pack. Anya was running when she hit the parking lot.

She never looked back.

oOo

It was morning. Too early to be awake but Cindy couldn't sleep. She sat up in her bed, swathed in blankets, staring out the window. It was still dark. She could tell by the ticks and creaks in the house there was no one here. Anya was God knows where. Jake was God knows where. Portia was God knows where. She wasn't talking to LeRoy, and Connie wasn't interested in helping.

There, there, she told herself, grimly. Self-pity was therapeutic.

She went downstairs to brew a cup of coffee, dragging the blanket behind her. If she were going to be awake, she may as well be wired. Who knew what the morning might bring, if she could only bounce off the walls hard enough?

The clock seemed stuck on six AM. She had a Missouri State History exam today. She should be studying. It was ninety minutes until her ride came to take her to Rosati-Kain. She almost turned on the television, but that seemed so lame she just sat down and wrapped herself closer.

Outside, she heard a car drive up. She could tell by the sound it was neither Jake's nor Anya's. A moment later, Jake opened the door and rushed into the room.

"Hey, girl," he said cheerily as he ran past her and up the stairs into the master bedroom.

"Jake?" Cindy said. She went to the stairs. "Dad?" she called up.

"Can't talk right now," came back down.

Cindy dropped the blanket on the sofa and went back to the kitchen. She looked outside. In the car waiting was Orphira. Orphira? Did she and Dad—

"Yuck," she said, blotting it out of her mind. It was bad enough imagining Dad and Mom.

Jake came back down the steps two at a time. "Okay. I'm leaving town—"

"With Orphira? I thought she was in a different district."

He stopped and briefly looked guilty. *Yuck.*

"It's a stakeout. Big drug dealer. He was somebody Orphira and I were working on before so now they've reassigned us together. Here." He handed Cindy a card from a hotel. "This is where I'll be staying."

"Milan?" Maybe she *did* need more coffee.

"Missouri. Milan, Missouri. This guy's holed up in a compound near the state park up there. He has a bunch of kids there—your friend, too, I think."

"Portia?"

"That's the one. But you keep a lid on it until you see it on the news. Otherwise, this place is going to be crawling with reporters. Will be, anyway, once they figure out who we're staking out. Don't talk to them."

She stared at him. "How did you find out all of this? Who told you?"

"Nobody you know."

It could be Connie. It could be LeRoy. "*Who?*"

Jake stopped and looked at her. She saw Jake, her dad, suddenly disappear to be replaced by Jake the Cop, gears turning behind his eyes. "Why is it so important to you?"

She stared back and tried to look like his little girl. "It could be somebody I know. From last summer."

Jake's face softened. "Yeah. Who am I to say who you know or don't know? It was Sam Forestell. Do you know him?"

Cindy shook her head, relieved. "No."

"Then don't worry." He looked over his things, inventorying. "Okay, then." He came over to and bent down to kiss her on the forehead. "I love you, Cindy. I'll see you in a couple of days."

He went to the door and stopped, turned and looked back at her. "Tell your mother where I went." Without another word, he left.

"If I see her," she said to the door.

She looked at the card and called Connie.

Connie groaned. "This better be my mother or somebody dying."

"It's me. I know where Joe Cori and Portia are."

"Good for you. Now, go find them. Call me when you get there." He hung up the phone.

She called him back but there was no answer. She left him a lengthy message of the hardest language she knew. Then she stared at the phone for a long time. It had been two months since she'd talked to LeRoy. She couldn't think of anyone else who might help her.

He answered on the second ring. "Hello?"

"Hi. It's me. Cindy.

There was a long pause. "Hi," he said finally.

"I'm sorry if I woke you."

"I was awake anyway. What's going on?"

For a moment, she didn't know how to start. "It's about my friend, Portia."

"I remember Portia. With the older guy. Pregnant."

"How did you know she was pregnant?"

"It was fairly obvious."

"You didn't say anything."

"I don't say a lot of things."

She almost said *like working for my mom,* but she stopped herself. "Portia's disappeared. Joe Cori has gone off and started a cult with those pills he got from you and Norman."

"I see." LeRoy sounded thoughtful. "How did you come by this?"

"My dad told me. He's going to some sort of stakeout. I'm worried Portia is going to get hurt."

"You're not worried about your dad?"

"Dad's a cop. He's not going to let himself be hurt if he can help it. But Portia is stupid that way."

"I see. How did Jake get all this?"

"He got a tip from somebody named Sam Forestell."

"Sam's dead," said LeRoy flatly.

"But—"

"It must be somebody else."

Cindy sensed she had the sudden chance of learning something she didn't want to know. "All right. But that's where Joe, Portia, and your pills are. I need your help."

"Why?"

"To get to Milan and save Portia. Come on, LeRoy. They were *your* pills."

"To be entirely fair, your mother invented them."

Cindy swallowed hard. "Yes. And I need to save somebody because of it. Isn't that reason enough? You helped me get them. You made your own pills with her. This is *your* fault, too. We can't just destroy everything. We have to *do* something. We have to save *somebody.*"

LeRoy was silent on the phone for a long time.

"You're right," he said slowly. "I do have to save somebody."

"Maybe you can get Connie to help. Or one of your bodyguards or something."

"Good-bye, Cindy." He hung up.

"What the fuck?" She dialed his number again. No answer. Selfish son-of-a-*bitch!* He'll save somebody all right. He'll save himself.

She called a cab to take her to the bus station. While she was waiting, she ran upstairs to her room and dug into her closet. Buried under a pile of shoes and a loose floorboard was a plastic box that held what was left of her money from last summer. She counted out six hundred dollars. That should be able to get her to Milan.

When the cab turned up, she took a Missouri map with her downstairs. "How much to go to Milan, Missouri?"

The driver stared at her.

"I need to get to Milan." She unfolded the map and showed him where it was.

The man was black and gray-haired. He stared at her for a long minute. "Are you running away?"

"No. I just have to get to Milan."

"How about you just get out of my cab and go on back inside. I'm not taking some underage white girl on a road trip."

Cindy stared at him for a long minute. "How much to go to the bus station?"

"Honey—"

"I'll give you one hundred dollars to take me to the bus station."

The cabbie sat back in his seat. "Bus station, it is."

The windows were just opening when she got there.

"One way to Milan," she asked sweetly.

The woman on the other side didn't even blink. "We don't go there. You'll have to go to Columbia and figure out with OATS or somebody how to get to Milan."

"One way to Columbia, then."

"Twenty-nine even," she said sleepily. You missed the seven AM bus. Next one is at two this afternoon and gets in at four fifteen. You might be able to get something there. Ask at the station."

"Nothing sooner?"

The woman shook her head.

Cindy paid for the ticket. Maybe she could hire a car or something in Columbia. She bought breakfast in the McDonald's and sat in the booth, trying to figure out how to make sausage on a muffin last until lunch.

oOo

LeRoy hung up and stood for a moment, thinking. The phone rang again, but he could see from the caller ID that it was Cindy on her home number. He ignored it. Cindy was right. You had to save somebody. LeRoy had managed to kill Sam. Norman had seen to that. He had helped move Bill's Anapyridol and then made some himself. He was just as responsible as anyone.

But you can only save who you want to save, and he didn't much care one way or the other about Portia. Cindy would be fine on her own. He had no sympathy for Jake. Norman was dead. The only person he thought he should do something about was Anya. By now she'd no doubt taken that witch's brew they had created. He had done nothing to stop her. In the last six months, she had taught him more about research, science and biology than he had ever known. He *owed* her.

Anya wasn't at home. LeRoy reasoned that if she'd been there, Cindy would have spoken differently. He tried to call Anya on her cell. No response. He called Kalenin. It was early, but Kalenin struck him as somebody that didn't sleep much.

The old man answered. "Yes?"

"This is LeRoy."

"How are you?"

"Fine. I'm looking for Anya."

Kalenin's voice took on a sad tone. "She's beyond my reach, I'm afraid."

"Do you know where she is?"

"No idea. You take my advice, boy. You stay away from her. She's bad medicine. She left all of her lab notes for you. I have them in safe keeping."

"Thanks," said LeRoy absently and hung up. He'd go to her house and see if he could figure something out.

The first metro rolled into the station a half hour after LeRoy arrived. It was true morning now. The commuters straggled onto the train and sat down, watching the sun play over the arch, the river, and the buildings of Saint Louis.

LeRoy waited patiently, trying to understand how Anapyridol might have affected Anya in the first place. She'd given hints, of course. A feeling of something watching her, something bigger, greater than she was. LeRoy thought it might have been her past, maybe, given some schizophrenic presence. Anti-Anapyridol should have stopped that.

LeRoy had read the original work of d'Aquili and Newberg. He knew both Anapyridol and anti-Anapyridol played games with boundary detection. But from the effects of the Anapyridol on Anya, it looked to him that she had found something entirely different.

At Union Station, he caught a cab and gave him Anya's address.

He remembered Fitzie. Fitzie had gone from being a happy dog to a dog that seemed happy when required. LeRoy had thought he'd seen it that way just because he didn't like dogs. But maybe he was on to something. There had been something *calculating* about Fitzie.

He had the cab stop a block away. After all, if there was something shady going on, why just *give* it to the cops?

Down Victor Street and left on Arkansas. Then left up the back alley to the house. Anya was there, sitting in her car, fiddling with something

He walked slowly towards her. "Anya?" he called softly.

She turned and looked at him like a bug on a rock. There was something in her eyes that stopped him. Something wild. Something feral. "Anya?"

Anya turned back into the car and rummaged for a moment. Then she turned back and pointed something flat and black at him. He heard a hornet's sound and felt something light like an insect strike his chest.

Then half a million volts of electricity shot through him and he fainted

oOo

Anya drove directly to Lifeworks. She had a plan, but it required material. Lifeworks had an abundance of material. She couldn't find her keys, but the entry code on the loading dock still worked. In and out, and nobody saw her. Lifeworks had never had security cameras. She hoped that was still true. Finally, she went through Bill's desk. A couple of thousand dollars and a Taser. She held up the Taser. Why would Bill have a Taser? Anya would never know.

Leaving Lifeworks, Anya stayed close to the speed limit all the way out to Tower Grove, thinking the entire way.

Before she reached home, she picked up some food in a White Castle and sat in the parking lot, eating thoughtfully, watching people drive through, pay, and pick up food. Kalenin's ability to disguise himself intrigued her. She should have been able to see Kalenin through any physical changes. Hair and makeup, could be seen through but all Hibbert had done was move the muscles of his face and she'd never recognized him. Anya watched faces. She watched people watching each other.

Anya didn't have much time but she judged this was time well spent. She turned the mirror so she could see her face. One older woman went through. Anya tried to make her eyebrow crease, cheek tension, and set of the mouth follow hers. A man went through. Anya tried to protrude out her lip, knit her brow, and flair her nostrils as he did. After an hour, she judged she could certainly mask her own face, though she wasn't practiced enough to make herself look like anyone else. She would have to keep her attention on it. Anya wondered if Kalenin had followed any disciplines like yoga to learn how to keep a face he had created.

She left the White Castle and pulled into a drug store. There she found some make up, hair dye, scarf, sweat pants, and hooded sweatshirt. She would need that soon enough. She put this bag next to the other one in her trunk, the bag containing the items she'd stolen from Lifeworks.

Anya pulled in behind the house. Jake's car was gone. He was likely gone for the day, but there was no way to be sure. She hadn't been tracking his schedule for the last few months.

Inside, she called out. No answer. She quickly ran up the stairs and checked each room on the way back down. The house was empty.

She went back to the car and brought out a shopping bag of Lifeworks items and a five-gallon can of gasoline. She went back in the house and set the gasoline on the floor. From the shopping bag she pulled a rubber strip, three single pint packets of A positive blood, a tube, a needle, and a saline jar. She took the needle and connected it to the tube and connected that to the jar. Then she tied off her arm with the rubber strip, tapped the vein in her arm until it was big and pulsing, then eased in the needle. When the blood started flowing into the jar, she pulled the rubber tubing off and waited, squeezing a fist regularly to help it along.

After she had about a pint, she pulled out the needle, dressed the wound. She capped the jar and put it carefully on the table.

Anya stood up, and everything grayed out for a moment. Steady. Steady. Wouldn't do to faint now.

She took the packets of blood and went into the main hallways and spattered them everywhere. Then she took the packets and put them back in the shopping bag.

The gasoline was next, and she poured out the entire five gallons in the main hallway up to the edge of the kitchen, bringing a thin strip to the door. She pulled over a few bookcases and tables to make it look good.

Anya put the packets back in the shopping bag. *Don't forget them. All is lost if you leave them here.*

Then she took the jar of her own blood and made a trail to the door, and splashed the remainder around the floor, carefully leaving a space for her to walk out. Back in the shopping bag with the jar. She'd get rid of all of this much later.

All right, then. She opened the door and took out the gasoline can and the shopping bag, and put them back in the trunk, taking a box of kitchen matches from the bag before she closed the lid

Anya sat down in the front of the car and started it. She wanted to be ready to leave when the fire caught.

Anya went over it in her mind. If the fire left anything, they'd find her blood in the kitchen leading to the back door. Forensic tests should be able to figure out it was hers. The additional blood might be identifiable as blood or not. But the heat of the fire would hopefully destroy any traces that it was not *her* blood. If they were able to even detect blood type, it would match. There would be a hunt for an abductor first—that was to be understood. A strong and terrible hunt—she was a policeman's wife, after all. Amenities must be preserved.

Once she lit the match, she would not have much time to put distance between her and Jake. She'd drive away, looking like herself, then put on a disguise and dump the car. Randomness would be her friend. The ruse only had to work for a few days. Then she would be back in Russia with enough money and knowledge to make her own place.

"Anya?"

She turned. It was LeRoy. He stared at her.

Something must have alerted him—Kalenin must have been a genius to have such a poker face. She would have to learn it. She rummaged in her purse for the Taser, shot LeRoy in the chest. LeRoy went down like a stone.

Okay, she thought. *Young black kid kidnaps soccer mom researcher.* That could work. She wrestled him into the car and sat him next to her. If anybody saw, she would be abducted.

The car was still running. She thought over what she had done. Listened to the neighborhood. Nothing to change her plans. Nothing she could hear to make her change it.

Anya went to the kitchen door, lit and flung a match in the same motion. The gasoline on the floor caught with a sudden *whump*. She staggered back from the heat, got in the car, and went on down the alley. The first black clouds started billowing out of the doorway as she left the back alley. She was driving leisurely towards Route 40 when the first fire trucks passed her, going the other way.

Up to this point, Anya hadn't given her new mental state much thought. She felt fine. Perfectly normal. But seeing LeRoy reminded her that she had felt enormously different just the day before. Now, on this forty-minute drive to Wentzville, it started her thinking.

Anya, the previous Anya, had been broken up about something watching her every move. Narcissism? Had she been so obsessed with herself she had imagined some higher force watching her? She didn't remember herself that way—and all of her memories appeared to be intact. All of the motivations for working: enhanced social control? Inherent communism? They seemed like silly dreams. Why would anyone care about such things? They were of no benefit to her.

The Anapyridol had damaged her. That much was clear. But the removal of the Anapyridol had taken much more with it. So much excess baggage.

Anya glanced at herself in the mirror. There was nothing wrong with her. She *liked* the way she looked. If the proper study by man was man, then maybe the proper study by Anya was Anya. She smiled at herself in the mirror.

But this happy state of self-appreciation didn't explain anything. Anya was different now. She had done things before without feeling badly about them— whoring herself across Mother Russia to get out, for one. That was just how things had to be done. But it seemed to her, she had married Jake for a reason other than alliance and easy sex—she could have had Bill for that with much less trouble and a great deal more to show for it. Yet she had stuck with a bad cop for years. Born a child—and she remembered how much fun *that* was.

She remembered the wedding vows. Remembered smiling and crying when the nurse had settled Cindy carefully into her arms. Presumably she was crying with joy—that's what people did, didn't they? But she couldn't remember the feeling.

Boundary conditions. Anapyridol increased the decay of boundary conditions. The fundamental mechanism of rearing. She'd thought too small. This wasn't just mammalian. Dinosaurs, birds, mammals, and some reptiles reared their young in some fashion or another. She'd enhanced a fundamental mechanism and then found a way to turn it *off*.

The emotional component of such memories must involve that same section of the brain. She'd turned off by association the emotional memories located with that area. Memory of fact, of events, remained, but the memory of the feelings were gone. They could be entirely intact but inaccessible.

Surprising, she thought. If there was one thing working in neuroscience for this long had taught her, the brain rarely did things only one way. If a stroke damaged one of the speech centers, the other could often be retrained. Of course, there were unique areas of the brain or areas that were so central and essential that there was no underlying mechanism to allow another section of the brain to take over. Though the area that could be retrained was in fine shape, the damage was such that the area was itself walled away. Perhaps that was what had happened with the Anapyridol. It widened an already existing gate and the antidote closed it entirely. She wondered if, over time, some other part of her brain would be retrained into the original function. Perhaps she might feel maternal again, clasp a man to her breast for reasons other than physical gratification. She hoped not. She liked this feeling; it was too good.

Anya smiled at herself in the mirror. She was *never* going back.

She turned on the news to see if she'd been reported. LeRoy stirred. She shocked him back into unconsciousness. She realized that she was lucky the traffic was light. Nobody was going to notice her at seventy miles an hour. But if the traffic piled on and she got stuck, somebody might recognize her later.

She turned just prior to the river and up north to catch I-70 west and then to the Earth City Expressway. A few minutes later, she pulled into the monstrous lot in front of Harrah's Casino. She found a spot not so far out that the car was conspicuous but it was still a long way from the main building. There were shuttle busses to take gamblers to the main building, but they were not yet moving towards her. She went in the back and pulled out her shopping bags. Out of one she pulled a scarf and bound over her hair. Then she remembered the old woman's tired face, and tried to think the lines of her face into that.

She looked into the car. Perhaps it would be best to kill him. No one but LeRoy, Connie, and Hibbert knew what she'd been doing over the last six months. Dead, LeRoy would be one less.

Still, adding murder to her possible crimes could be a problem if she got caught. Hibbert had warned her to run, and while she didn't trust him, she had a feeling there was something to it. Anya-before had felt something watching her, and Anya-before had not been crazy.

Let him live, then. If he were caught, he was a young black man in the stolen car of a white woman believed to be abducted and dead. That was going to cause him enough grief. *Oh, and you're a scientist? The uneducated nephew of Cold Norman Parkin? We'll write that down. Now, what did you do with the body?*

Anya walked briskly away and caught the shuttle bus to the casino. Inside, she went to the bathroom and changed. She lightly tinted her hair gray and put on a little too much mascara. She wanted to look like a well-to-do old biddy intending to be taken as younger than she actually was and having no hope of succeeding. She rinsed out the blood bottle until it seemed clean enough, then broke it and carefully slipped it into the used tampon receptacle. She kept the packets rolled up tightly in her purse. They were too identifiable. She briefly considered cutting them up and flushing them down the toilet but decided not to. If there were a blockage, this was still the casino where her car would be found. It might be too much of a connection.

She packed up her old clothes into one of the shopping bags. Then, thinking her face into the lines of that old woman, she walked out of the bathroom, out of the casino, and into another shuttle bus. This one to a sister casino in Wentzville. She now had the clothes she was wearing, the money, and her new identification. Almost done.

In Wentzville, she went inside to the bathroom and stuffed the shopping bag of clothes (minus the packets) into the trash. She played the slots for an hour. She wished she could get the news, but nothing penetrated the soft hush of the casino. It was a warm early spring day outside. She felt a sudden confidence. This was going to work.

Anya picked up her bag and started walking out to the parking lot. It was lunch now, and several cars were entering and leaving. She walked to the far edge of the parking lot and kept going into the woods surrounding the casino. She hoped there were no cameras here, but there was no way to tell.

At the top of the ridge she could see the highway. She walked along the outer road, trying to look old and dowdy. No one stopped or hailed her. She called a cab from a gas station. While she waited, she freshened up in the bathroom so she didn't look like she'd been walking too long. Then had the cabbie take her to the junction of I-70 and Highway 40.

Here were several truck stops, diners, and, most importantly, a used car lot. Inside, she smiled as prettily as an old, dowdy woman without a brain in her head. She could almost see the salesman's teeth sharpen.

An hour later, two thousand dollars poorer and in an enormous Crown Victoria, little old lady Anya took off west on Interstate 70. She listened to the radio. The fire was still being talked about. Anya Fiske had been abducted. State police were on the lookout.

She kept herself low in the seat until she left the interstate in Kingdom City. Ten hours later, in the dead of night, she was passing through Kirksville. There, she pulled off the road long enough to stop behind a tiny, sleepy hospital to deposit a collection of empty alcohol-washed blood packets.

Driving north to Canada, where her Russian passport and tourist visa would get her into Ontario. Then home to Russia. She laughed, rolled down the window, and let the spring wind blow into the car.

Anya remembered something now. She remembered the feeling of elation and excitement that dark cold night when the truck finally carried her away from VECTOR.

Anya felt as if she had been behind bars ever since she had left Russia, but now the wind was blowing through the open door of the cage. She was who she once had been. She was free. She turned the radio up and listened to old Beatles tunes tear through the night as she roared north.

oOo

When Connie got out of bed, he only vaguely remembered Cindy's call. She had said—*what?* She knew where Joe and Portia were? He shook his head, sitting on the edge of the bed. Didn't matter anyway. What difference did it make if some middle-aged white guy and some underage white girl got lost or found? It made no difference to him.

Connie liked his new apartment. It was a nice little condo that he'd picked up as part of a gambling debt. Young, rich, white kids shouldn't go gambling across the river if they couldn't cover their nut. All told, though, Connie figured he had the better deal. The kid got to keep his legs, and Connie got a new place to live.

He took a shower and toweled himself off, watching the big television. He wasn't really *watching* it; he was more enjoying the view than actually seeing what was going on. Some house fire in Tower Grove. Looked like gasoline. Something, anyway.

At that point, Anya's face appeared as an inset below the picture of the fire.

For a moment, Connie was stunned and couldn't move. Then he dove for the remote and turned up the volume.

"—arrived on the scene quickly enough that no neighboring houses were in danger. Police are also on the scene. There may be foul play. This woman, Anya Fiske, cannot be located."

Bill appeared. "Anya took a leave of absence some time ago. I haven't seen her since November."

The anchorwoman returned to the screen with a picture of Anya behind her. "If anyone sees this woman, call the number on the bottom—"

Connie muted it.

Joe Cori had Norman's pills. Cindy had said he was in some kind of standoff with the police up in Milan. So, no connection there. But Anya was a cop's wife. There was going to be a *big* hunt for her. What had happened? Connie had protected her and LeRoy well enough. Anya was crazy, but she wasn't doing anything really dangerous—Connie would have known and put a stop to it. Connie protected his investments.

Burning the house down and killing Anya? Could Sam have done that? Kalenin? That made no sense. Unless Sam took her to make more pills. But that made no sense, either—Sam had more than enough. Enough for what? Connie didn't know. Maybe there wasn't enough for whatever Sam was planning.

Too many threads. Too much speculation.

Even so, with all the search for Anya, it was a pretty fair bet that what she had been doing for the last few months was going to come out one way or another. He ticked off everyone that knew: LeRoy. Anya. Cindy. Kalenin. Sam. Cindy was likely protected, being peripheral and Anya's daughter. Kalenin could take care of himself. That left Anya, LeRoy, and Sam. He didn't know where Anya was—he'd cross that bridge when he got there. LeRoy was off the radar screen for the moment. Connie hoped he didn't have to manage that. He liked LeRoy. It would be a shame.

That left Sam. Unstable. Truly homicidal. Absolutely bug-fuck crazy. Connie felt cold. He was going to have to manage Sam. But where was he?

Joe Cori was in Milan. If Joe was in Milan, it was a safe bet Sam was somewhere nearby. The little creep couldn't get enough of Joe. That was obvious, even back when he was running Alton. Norman had told Connie that Sam had practically drooled when Norman gave him the Alton business.

Connie called Cindy's cell.

"Hello?" came from the other end. She sounded tired.

"I was sleepy when you called and didn't get everything. Tell it to me again, slowly." Connie kept himself still until Cindy mentioned Sam Forestell. "Do you still want to go to Milan?" he interrupted.

"Yes," she answered cautiously.

"We can go together."

"I'm at the bus station. What made you change your mind?"

Should he tell Cindy that her mother might be dead or kidnapped? That Sam might be after her mother? That Sam might be a cannon aimed at all of them? Let it wait. The television brought up the clip of the house, flames piled high, smoke black against the sky.

"I have my reasons."

oOo

LeRoy woke with a blinding headache and a raging fever. He sat up. His shirt was wet with drool, and he couldn't place where he was. He was in a car. What the hell was he doing in a car? God, it was hot. He rolled down the window and blessedly cool air blew in. He opened the door and leaned outside, emptying himself out instantly.

A few spasming moments later, LeRoy weakly wiped his mouth with his hand and stood up, leaning against the car. There were napkins on the front seat. He reached back in and took them and wiped his mouth, rested his head against the cool metal. Every muscle in his torso, groin, neck, chest, and abdomen, was sore.

He stood up suddenly. Was almost sick again. He swayed as he steadied himself. He looked at the car. This was Anya's car. He looked around the parking lot. He was in a Harrah's Casino parking lot. Where was she?

Slowly, it dawned on him. Anya had *Tasered* him. Maybe more than once. Then she'd ditched him here. Ditched him with her *car*. God knows what she'd done.

He closed the door and staggered away. When he had put some distance between him and Anya's car, he leaned against a light pole and pulled out his cell.

Connie answered almost immediately. "Yes." He sounded tense.

"This is LeRoy. Anya Tasered me. I just woke up."

"She... Tasered you? When?"

LeRoy looked at his cell. "A couple of hours ago."

"Really. Where are you?"

"I'm in the parking lot of Harrah's Casino."

"Walk to the main building. Do not go inside. Take a cab to Lambert Field and wait in the Delta drop off area. I'll meet you there."

"Why not go inside?"

"You're underage. Even in the hotel, it's conspicuous. Hopefully, they won't notice much if you just take a cab and get out of there. Don't wait. Do it now, before they call somebody."

LeRoy hobbled what seemed like miles to the main building. Sure enough, there was a line of cabs. He took one and leaned back in the seat. *God, he was thirsty.* Once he got to Lambert, he found the bathroom and washed his face.

Then he found a vending machine and bought three Cokes. He sat near the door, drinking one soda after the other and savoring each one.

Half an hour later, Cindy came into the ticketing area, looking around. That was too much of a coincidence. Connie probably had her with him, but there was no way to be sure. LeRoy wanted to call out but held back. After all, they had broken up. He wasn't sure what to do.

Cindy saw him and came over. She grabbed him and hauled him to his feet and hugged him. "It's good to see you."

"Yeah," he said, and cautiously hugged back.

"Come on. Connie's waiting outside."

LeRoy took the back seat and Cindy got in the front. Connie pulled smoothly out of the parking lot and onto the onramp for Interstate 70. West, LeRoy noted.

"My mom Tasered you?" Cindy turned and leaned on the seat, facing him. LeRoy nodded. "She wasn't herself."

"Why not?"

LeRoy shrugged.

"Her car has been reported stolen," Connie said. "Anya's being tracked as abducted and presumed dead. Her car will be found by tonight when the casino checks the parking lot."

"I was in a stolen car?" LeRoy said in a small voice. "The stolen car of a dead white woman?"

"She's not dead!" cried Cindy.

"No," agreed Connie. "She's not." He looked at LeRoy. "Your prints are going to be all over it."

LeRoy shrugged. "I'm not on record."

"You will be, some day."

"I'll cross that bridge when I get there."

"She faked it," muttered Cindy.

"Yes," agreed Connie. "They'll find her by and by."

"I don't think so," LeRoy said slowly. Connie looked at him in the mirror. LeRoy continued. "You didn't see her. She's different."

"Different, how?"

"Smarter, maybe. Usually when you see somebody, they're measuring you. Measuring themselves against you. Figuring out how they feel about you, if anything. Anya didn't show any of that. I was just an obstruction."

"What have you done to her? What did you do to my *mother*?" Cindy demanded.

"Tell her, LeRoy," said Connie.

LeRoy looked out the window for a moment. Then he turned back to Cindy. "Bill slipped Anya some Anapyridol back in the fall. It made her crazy and for some reason I don't know, she *stayed* crazy."

"Why?" Cindy looked at him.

When she looked at him straight on like that, it just took his breath away. He looked out the window. "Like I said, I don't know. Anya's the neuroscientist. She thought the pathway Anapyridol operated on already existed. Anapyridol only widened it. Once widened, continued use made it *stay* widened."

"Does it do that with everybody? Like, maybe with Portia?"

LeRoy shrugged. "I have no idea. I have a scientific sample set of exactly one. But Anya thought it was likely—with variation between people. For some, like Anya, it might take only one dose."

"Some," Cindy continued for him, "like Bill, might need the Anapyridol continually."

"You've seen Bill?"

Cindy nodded. "A couple of days ago. He doesn't seem like he's on anything but painkillers."

"Interesting." LeRoy digested that. "Anyway, Anya and I were working on an Anapyridol site-antagonist. If Anapyridol opened a door, anti-Anapyridol would slam it shut. I'm guessing we succeeded. She took it—I told her not to. But I'm pretty sure she figured anything would be better." LeRoy looked at Cindy bleakly. "I don't think it worked out that way. Now she's *more* crazy. She Tasered me and I woke up in her car."

"Will it wear off?" Cindy's voice shook. "Will my mother be herself again?"

LeRoy shook his head. "We made two forms, a weak-binding form and a strong-binding form; one temporary, one permanent. I wanted Anya to try the weak-binding form. She held out for something permanent."

"The police think she's dead." Connie watched him in the mirror. "You're sure she's not going to get caught?"

"How can I be sure of anything? But I don't think so." LeRoy held up his hands. "Anya was always very smart. Now she's even smarter and has no scruples. Maybe she's inexperienced—"

"Don't depend on that," Cindy interrupted. "She's told me some of the things she did in Russia. Mom's only nice when she needs to be."

"There you go." LeRoy thought for a moment. He saw Connie's eyes in the mirror. "Everybody but us thinks Anya is dead?"

"And Anya, of course," said Cindy.

"Right." LeRoy stared into Connie's eyes. Connie's eyes told him nothing. "Where are we going?"

"I told you this morning. Milan, Missouri," said Cindy. "Jake told me this morning that's where Joe Cori is. And if that's where Joe is, that's where Portia is."

"Portia," LeRoy said quietly, still watching Connie's eyes. "Connie? Do you know Portia?"

"I've met her."

"And we're going to go do battle for her or something?"

"I'm just transportation," Connie said blandly.

"I see." LeRoy looked out the window. Wherever they were going, they were going there fast. "This is from Sam's tip, right?"

Cindy nodded.

"Sam's dead," LeRoy said.

"But Jake—"

"I helped Norman kill him. He's dead."

Cindy gasped.

"Actually," began Connie. "He's not."

LeRoy felt relief mixed with horror bubble up inside of him. "Beg pardon?"

"Sam was the main backer on our Anapyridol adventure. Kalenin was his gopher."

"And you didn't tell me this because—"

"Because you wouldn't have had anything to do with the idea if you knew Sam was involved."

"Got that right

"And I needed you."

"Ah." LeRoy looked back at Cindy. "So, I'm not a murderer."

"I had faith." Cindy grinned timidly at him.

"You didn't know."

"Faith doesn't require knowledge."

"So," LeRoy said idly. "The only people who know about our Anapyridol *adventure* are Kalenin, me, Cindy, Anya, and Sam. Anya's been abducted and presumed dead, and is a cop's wife. Anybody else?"

"Nope," said Connie easily. "I kept the operation small."

"Anya's gone. Kalenin not here. Are we loose ends, Connie? Are you going to tie us all together?"

Connie changed lanes and passed a car, then returned to the easy westerly pace. "Wouldn't make any sense without Sam, now would it?"

"Sam is in Milan?"

"That's what I'm figuring."

Cindy suddenly looked scared.

"Cindy's a cop's *daughter*, Connie," LeRoy said quietly.

"I'm aware of that. I'm counting on it, in fact."

"Sam's the loose end?"

"I always known you were smart. Loose cannon's more like it. Anya's work for the last few months won't come out unless somebody talks. Joe's going down, and he's going to implicate Norman. But Norman is dead. Anya is Anapyridol's developer, so she's going to be connected to it and she's presumed dead. Bill is going to get implicated, too. I think he can be persuaded to leave you two out of it—Anya stole the pills and gave them to Norman. Bill found out and Anya beat the crap out of him. If he doesn't follow the party line, he implicates himself. He loses his company and goes to jail. If Anya doesn't reappear, great. She'll get blamed for everything. There's nothing to connect the three of us to Anapyridol except Sam." Connie didn't say anything for a long minute.

"What about the last few months?"

Connie shrugged. "I'll have to plant some money somewhere. Set up some dummy accounts. I bet I can even set up Anya for Norman's murder."

LeRoy thought for a moment. "Then who abducted Anya?"

"Anybody who wanted the money. We can leave it a mystery. Drop a few clues here and there but nothing definitive. If they find out Anya faked it, so much the better. That's my plan, anyway."

LeRoy considered it. "It's too complicated. Don't try to frame Anya for Norman. They'll do that on their own. Plant a little extra money in her accounts and have some sales attached to her. Then have Bill leak the information she beat up Bill and took the pills. That's enough. The Saint Louis police will make any necessary connections. The East Saint Louis authority can just leak the nature of the gun that killed Norman. It was a small caliber that could be handled by a woman."

Connie looked at him in the mirror.

LeRoy looked back. "You're not the only one with connections in East Saint Louis."

"Damulin was killed with a different gun. Bigger caliber."

"Damulin?" Cindy looked at them.

"Norman's bodyguard. He was killed the same night as Norman." LeRoy turned back to Connie. "Damulin was killed by Anya's accomplice. Maybe he killed Anya and ran off with the money."

"They could come after you for that one."

LeRoy shook his head. "I have an alibi for Norman's murder. Besides, it took place in East Saint Louis. I could have been standing there with the gun in my hand, covered in blood, and I *still* wouldn't have been a suspect."

Cindy looked first at Connie, then at LeRoy. "I don't want to be the daughter of a murderer."

LeRoy leaned forward and hesitantly placed his hand on Cindy's. She grabbed it and held it.

"Honey," he said gently. "You already *are*."

The tears in her eyes told him she'd realized it at that moment. "It's the facts of life, right?"

LeRoy didn't understand. "Beg pardon?"

Cindy waved it away. "Something Anya said to me once."

"Jake might go a little strange if his wife gets blamed for something he did," Connie said in an even voice.

LeRoy nodded, not letting go of Cindy's hand. "He might. But he can't come forward without taking the blame for it. Cindy can comfort him."

Cindy pulled her hand away and wiped her face. "Yeah. I guess. What if they find Anya?"

"Then Jake might come forward to save her." LeRoy thought about what Kalenin had said. "I don't think we have to worry about that. Not for a while. Besides, I think as soon as the Saint Louis PD realizes how *dirty* this is, they're going to look for any possible way to drop it. This is a scenario where they don't have mud on their faces."

Connie mulled it all over. "Either of you have cell phones?"

LeRoy nodded. Cindy said yes.

"Turn them off. Right now." When they had, he looked at them, one, then another. "Can I count on the two of you?"

Translation: *Help me or I'll have to kill you, too.* LeRoy relaxed. This was like living with Norman. This was like coming home. He nodded to Cindy. She seemed to relax.

"Sam can pull all of this apart. Do you have a plan for him?" LeRoy watched Connie.

"Not yet. We'll get close to Milan tonight and get a hotel. Then we'll check out the lay of the land in the morning."

LeRoy nodded. Connie had been thinking Anya was going to get caught. He'd had a different plan. Probably something unpleasant. But now—well, LeRoy would have to see.

LeRoy leaned back in the seat and closed his eyes. He needed to rest. "You can count on me," he murmured as he fell asleep.

oOo

Joe woke up with an odd feeling. A sense of expectation. A sense of impending excitement. He rolled away from Tess. It was early. The sun had not yet risen. He put on a robe and left her sleeping, walked down the hallway to the kitchen and turned on the big coffee urn he'd filled the night before.

Something.

He looked outside. The sky was clear. There was thick dew on the grass. He'd been hoping for cold weather, but the sun promised otherwise.

The big urn took half an hour, and this morning Joe felt impatient for coffee. He rummaged in the cupboard for a grubby jar of instant and microwaved up a cup. He made the result drinkable with some Carnation in the refrigerator.

Something was coming.

He sat down in the alcove with the coffee and stared out the window. He half-believed he could make it materialize in front of him.

Phil came in a few minutes later, Portia trailing along behind. She sat next to Joe and laid her head on the table. Phil reached up into the cupboard and brought down a box of herb tea.

Using the time-honored technique of cup microwaving, first brought to us by the venerable Joe Cori, thought Joe and chuckled.

"Eh?" Phil turned away from the microwave.

"Nothing."

Joe heard Tess getting up. It never took her long to wake up once he'd left the bed. He got up and filled two cups from the urn. He handed one to Phil and went back to the table with the other.

Tess came in a moment later and sat down across from Joe. Wordlessly, he passed her the cup he'd poured. She smiled at him.

Phil came to the table and gave the herb tea to Portia and sat down himself, sipping his coffee.

It's like ballet, Joe thought. *Like dance, the way we work together here. God is with us.*

They did not speak, enveloped in a warm radiance from the coffee and each other.

There came a knock on the side door.

Joe stood up and walked over to the door. Was this it? Was *this* what was coming?

Outside were three people dressed against the cold. One was a black woman. The other two were men.

"May I help you?" Joe said politely.

The black woman looked nervous. "Are you Joseph Cori?"

"I am."

The two men lunged for him. Joe turned to them, and the power came to him as easily and comfortably as if he'd woken up next to it every day of his life. "Leave me alone," he roared.

They stopped as if struck.

He turned to the young black woman.

Her voice was shaking. "Mister Joseph Cori, I have a warrant for your arrest. You are to come peacefully. You have the right to remain silent. You have the right to an attorney —"

"Stop that," he said mildly.

She stopped instantly.

"No." Joe looked at them. "It's not you. Don't bother me anymore. Any of you."

He closed the door on them and didn't bother to watch them. Whatever was coming had little to do with them.

"Joe?" called Tess. "You better come over here."

He joined her at the window.

Across the liquid surface of the lake strode a motley band. Mostly men, dressed in rags and skins, wearing horns on their head and carrying spears, dried blood painted on their faces and hands. They held their spears over their head and chanted as they came. Joe recognized the leader and knew this was what he was waiting for.

It was Sam, coming for him.

Chapter 2.4: June, 1998

It took time for Bill to get out of the car.

Anya had broken his right ankle and knee. She'd ruptured his kidney and broken three ribs. She'd done something to his back that didn't show up on the x-rays. It had taken two surgeries to repair the knee and put three pins in his ankle. More surgery to stitch the kidney back together. And his back just never felt *right*. No matter what the doctor did or after numerous chiropractic visits. It had taken two months of physical therapy until he could drive a car safely. Damn it, he'd had to give up the *Porsche*—using the clutch stretched cords of agony up and down his spine. These days he drove a Buick as timidly and carefully as an old man. He'd been out to see his plane, had even sat in the seat and worked the controls. It hurt worse than the Porsche. He'd sat in the cockpit and wept.

Now the Porsche was sold. The plane was sold. Kathleen had taken care of it.

He parked the car in his spot. Opened the door and placed the tip of his cane carefully on the ground. Spring or not, he looked for ice. Or oil. Or anything slippery. He'd fallen once in January, and the pain had been so striking, so vicious, he'd wet himself and had lain there, helpless in stinking humiliation, until someone had found him. He was more cautious now.

Up the stairs, one at a time, though the double doors at the top, around the corner and into his office. He sat down heavily. *Safe*. For the moment.

"You're late this morning."

Fred Hibbert was sitting in the chair across from him. Bill hadn't seen him.

Fred clucked sympathetically. "She really did a number on you." He checked his watch. "I'd be more patient, but I'm on a schedule."

"Schedule?" Bill felt lost.

Fred reached into his coat pocket and pulled out a medicine vial. He tossed it to Bill. "Recognize this?"

Bill caught it, wincing, opened the vial and shook the contents on to his desk. Familiar oblong pink pills. "Anapyridol."

"Those are from the last batch you sold to Norman."

Bill stared at him. Fred *knew?*

Fred ignored him consulted his notes. "Take forty-five."

Bill swallowed. "I don't do that anymore."

Fred nodded. "Nothing like getting the crap pounded out of you by a woman half your size to make you give up your vices." He stood and poured a glass of water. Fred put the water next to the pile of pills on the desk. "Come on, Bill. Don't you miss them?"

Bill fingered the pills. He remembered that feeling of connection, the world as big inside of him as outside, like a clear wind blowing through him.

"Don't make me force you," Fred said, conversationally.

Force me? "This is my place," Bill said, suddenly frightened. "Kathleen? Kathleen?"

Fred smiled and opened the door. "Hear anything?"

The building was silent. "What have you done?"

Fred closed the door and sat back down. "Due to possible malfeasance in your position, and being chairman of the board and largest stockholder, I have exercised my duties and shut down operations while I investigate. Could be jail time, Bill. FDA fraud. Trafficking in unapproved drugs—there's even a DEA task force just itching to find out what this stuff exactly is. The DEA hasn't connected it to you yet. But they will if I tell them. And I *will* tell them." Fred nodded slightly. "Unless you do what I say."

Bill fingered the pills again. "I've never taken so many."

"I have it on good authority the risks are negligible."

He *wanted* to take them. He had missed them. He scooped them into his hand and choked them down. For a moment, he was nauseous, but then his stomach seemed to relax. "Why?"

Fred smiled thinly. "I need to make a call."

oOo

Joe stepped through the main door and walked across the parking lot to the edge of the lake. Sam stood on the gently moving water about fifty feet away.

"Hey there, Joe," Sam called. "How's tricks?" He grinned through his blood-stained face. Around him, his followers lowered their chant and knelt on the water.

"I thought you were dead, Sam," Joe said calmly. He watched Sam stand on the water. It was an open defiance of Jesus—imitating him. Intimating the trivial nature of the miracle. *Trust not the devil's works.*

"I was!" Sam laughed out loud and leaped up. His bare feet splashed an inch deep in the water when he landed, but he didn't sink. "I'm better now."

"What do you want, Sam?"

"Come on out here and I'll tell you." Sam grinned wickedly. "Or isn't your faith strong enough?"

Joe stared back at him. He looked back at his people, then at the water. *Never hesitate*, he scolded himself, and walked out on the water to meet with Sam. It was cold and felt wet, but it was more like walking on wet sand than he expected.

He walked within a few feet of Sam. "Tell me now."

Sam applauded. "Nicely done. I've always admired you, Joe. You know that, don't you?" Sam grinned again. "I want the last battle, of course. Me against you. My Gods against yours."

"There is only *one* God!" thundered Joe.

"Snaps at it like a fish at a fly," laughed Sam. "Like a wolf on a kitten." Sam reached into his pocket and pulled out a pink pill. "In an hour I plan to be fortified. You ought to do the same."

Joe stood still. "I don't want any bloodshed."

"Oh, but I *do*, Joe. Go take your pills. I'll take mine. My Gods are thunder and lightning. Blood and pain. *My* Gods nailed *your* God to a stick."

"You have no Gods!" cried Joe.

"Prove it, Fat Boy." Sam's expression went cold. "Prove it in an hour."

Sam turned, and he and his followers walked back across the lake.

Joe turned and walked back to shore. The miracle on the water no longer occupied his mind. It was an easy miracle. Commonplace.

Tess met him. "What did he want?"

"Armageddon," Joe said quietly. "I always knew this day would come. Just not so soon."

They walked back to the compound. Tess disappeared in the back and brought back a vial of Divinidine. Joe took it and shook a dozen tablets into his hand.

"So many?" Tess looked at him.

"If God can armor me from the enemy, he can watch over my heart."

Phil refilled his coffee.

Joe took the pills and sipped the coffee, waiting for their effect.

oOoe

They left the hotel in Milan before daylight. LeRoy and Connie piled into the car. Cindy stood next to the door and looked around. "How are we going to find them?"

"I don't know," he said, settling behind the wheel. "Any ideas?"

LeRoy leaned forward from the back seat. "Let me see the map." Connie gave it to him.

Cindy turned and tried to see if there was a hill or a ridge. The sky still shone with stars but there was a glow in the east. She could see a few low, black smudges that might be small ridges. "Didn't they shine lights or something on the Waco compound?"

Connie glanced at Cindy. "You cannot possibly remember that. You were what? Seven?"

"I'm a cop's kid, remember? We hear things."

"Waco?" LeRoy looked up. "What happened in Waco? Wait a minute: what is Waco? A place?"

"A town in Texas," Connie answered. "A nut case named Koresh had a cult down there. Got into a standoff with—well, pretty much everybody. Texas rangers. FBI. ATF. Something happened—the stories don't agree—and there was some shooting. The place caught fire, and forty or fifty people got killed."

"Jesus," said LeRoy.

Cindy looked at the hills. "We know they're near the state park, right?"

LeRoy held up the map. "Got it right here."

She got in the car and closed the door. "Let's go towards the park and see if there are any cars or lights."

Thirty minutes later, they neared the park but couldn't see any lights.

"Maybe they want to take him by surprise," suggested Connie. "They wouldn't have any lights on then."

Cindy nodded.

"Take the next right," LeRoy called from the back. "It should say something."

The park entrance sign shone in the headlights. There was a policeman there. He waved them on.

Connie waved back and they continued. "Well, we found them."

"I guess an open door was too much to hope for," said LeRoy. He leaned on the front seat. "What's the plan?"

Cindy thought for a moment. "I can certainly get in there. Jake's there. I'm a lonely daughter of a brother cop whose mother has been killed. Of course, I'd go look for my father."

"He might not be there," Connie pointed out. "He may have gone back to Saint Louis. That's what I would have done."

Cindy held up her cell. "He didn't call me. If he knew, he would have called me. For one reason or another, he hasn't been told."

Connie nodded. "Okay."

"LeRoy can go in with me as my boyfriend."

LeRoy made a small, startled sound. "That would be... interesting."

Cindy ignored it. Now was *not* the time. "We hitchhiked." She nodded at Connie. "You were the last ride. You drop us off. We go in."

"Somebody might recognize me," Connie said thoughtfully.

"I don't think so. They're going to use local cops to guard the stake out."

Connie nodded. "Doesn't get *me* in."

Cindy agreed. "I can't do that. Past the guards there are Saint Louis cops, along with Jake and Orphira. *They* would recognize you."

"And everything falls apart. Let me see the map."

Connie examined it. "Says here there are trails in this park. Let's find some."

They found trail markers next to a parking lot. Next to the trail markers was a sign with a box full of park maps.

Connie opened a map and traced over the marked trails with his fingers. "Okay. I can follow this red-dot trail over to the main camp ground. I don't know where the compound is, but I bet it will be near the edge of the park here." He pointed on the map. "That's the only piece of land that borders on this side of the lake that isn't park land. The trails go out of the park there and stop. After I drop you off, I'll circle around and come back here." He gave each of the park maps. "If you need to escape, I'll be here for a bit after the trouble starts. But not for long."

Cindy and LeRoy nodded.

"What are you going to do?" Cindy felt out of her depth.

"I will *manage* the situation," Connie said quietly. "That's all you need to know."

LeRoy pulled on her shoulder. "Come on. We've got to get going."

Connie turned off the dome light as they re-approached the park entrance. He stopped the car.

"Excuse me, officer," he said, smiling. "I think these two are looking for you."

LeRoy and Cindy got out of the car.

"What do you want?" asked the cop. He shone the light on them. Cindy couldn't see his face or his badge.

"I'm looking for Jake Fiske of the Saint Louis Police Department," she said slowly and clearly. "I'm his daughter, Cindy. This is my boyfriend. He's helped me get here. It's important."

The light danced first on Cindy, then on LeRoy. The light shone on the car.

"I'll get along, now," called Connie. "You take care, hear?"

"Wait a minute—"

But Connie was driving away. The officer shone a light on Connie's car, but Cindy could see the dirt was too thick over it to ID the plate. She recognized the trick: rub oil on the plate and it caught road dirt. A hundred miles and the plate was unrecognizable.

"Damn," said the policeman. He turned to Cindy and LeRoy. He radioed for instructions and a moment later, LeRoy and Cindy were led up the hill into the park.

oOo

Connie drove on past the park and circled around to reach the parking lot without passing the entrance again. It was getting light enough that he didn't need a flashlight. He pulled on sneakers and a black sweatshirt. From the glove compartment, he took a pair of binoculars, a roll of duct tape, and a Taser. Connie wasn't above taking a lesson from Anya. He left the guns safely hidden in the trunk. As far as anyone who wasn't acquainted with him knew, he was just an early morning walker.

He looked at the map. While he couldn't say for certain where the compound was, he still thought it was in the area where the park trails stopped. The Blue Spot Trail seemed to cross a ridge that overlooked where he thought the compound was. That was where Connie was headed.

The trail was well marked, and Connie didn't have any trouble finding his way to the ridge. Sure enough, when he reached there, he could see the compound. As he watched, he saw activity on the other side of the lake. Then a crowd walked across the lake towards the compound. Odd, he thought. He didn't think it had been cold enough to freeze a lake. Maybe it had been colder up here.

He trained the binoculars on the group, and damned if that didn't look like water they were walking on. *Running* on. Dressed in rags and red paint like Indians. And leading them, *bless my soul*, was Sam. A big man whom Connie figured to be Joe Cori walked out on the water, too. Sam and Joe stood talking.

Connie looked around. Not far to the lake. Maybe two hundred yards. He could make the shot with a fair sniper's rifle. Such a rifle was hidden in his car, but there could be another way. At least, Connie was hoping.

He left his vantage point and moved off into the woods until he found a hidden thicket where he could see both the action on the lake, and the vantage point he'd just left. He took a leak, sat down, and waited. Joe and Sam quit talking. Sam walked back across the lake to the other side. Joe returned to the compound.

Damn. There were little ripples on the pond. Those boys were walking on *water*. "Isn't that interesting," Connie murmured.

A few minutes later, Connie heard someone jogging up the trail. It was a policeman dressed in black SWAT-style gear, carrying a sniper's rifle. Connie grinned and remained where he was.

The sniper set up the rifle and took careful aim. "Unit three, ready." His voice was high, reedy with tension. Connie took note.

Connie eased the Taser out and took careful aim. *Let's see*, he thought. *No vest. Good.*

Connie fired and the sniper spasmed but didn't go out. Connie came up behind him and struck him on the back of his head.

Connie listened to his breathing. Good. Nothing major. He taped the sniper's hands and feet together. He pulled out his handkerchief, rolled it up, and laid it protectively over the man's eyes. Then he duct-taped over it and over the man's mouth. Connie hauled the sniper far enough away that he could hear him without being unduly bothered.

Then Connie lay down and sighted the weapon on the compound.

I'm unit three, he thought to himself. *I have to remember that.*

oOo

Ethan watched from a distance as the three policemen approached Joe's door. He knew two of them: Jake Fiske and Orphira Doyle. The third was an ATF specialist named DuBois. This particular DuBois specialized in subduing suspects quickly without giving them a chance to retaliate.

Bujold was standing next to him. "Now, you'll see something. DuBois is the best in the business."

Ethan saw the door open. He saw Jake and the other man move towards Joe and then suddenly stop. Joe looked past them to the other policemen. "Leave me alone!" he roared. Joe closed the door on them a moment later.

The three officers came over to them.

"What the hell was *that?*" yelled Bujold.

Orphira began. "Sir—"

"What happened, DuBois?"

DuBois looked at Orphira and Jake. "He told us not to."

"He *what?*"

"He told us to leave him alone." DuBois shrugged. "You heard him."

Bujold's face turned purple. He pulled out his own sidearm and started for the front door and stopped. He lifted the pistol and aimed at the house. Ethan started to cry out, but Bujold dropped his arm.

"I'll be damned," Bujold muttered.

He turned and seemed to see Ethan for the first time. "Fiske, get Cori out of here. Go put him in a van or something."

Ethan heard Bujold call over the radio. "Unit one? I want you to take a shot at the main lodge. Don't argue." Pause and muttered static. "Unit two, you're the same? Unit three, also? Son of a bitch."

Jake brought him to one of the police vans and sat him on the bumper.

"What happened?"

"Damned if I know. He said for us to leave him alone and—well, we did. I have no idea why. Do you?"

Yes, thought Ethan but didn't speak aloud. Though this entered a different kind of phenomena, something out of his experience. He could understand how time could change—that was implied in the model. But this involved subject influence of one human on another. How did that factor into physical laws? Did consciousness have a physical representation? Could it be manipulated like light and heat?

Jake watched him. "You know something, kid?"

"I know it's better if you don't mess with this. Let me go in. I'm his son. He'll listen to me."

"Not my call." Jake's radio went off.

"You got a daughter, Fiske?" Ethan heard Bujold's voice.

"Yes."

"Well, she and her boyfriend are here. You better get over here."

"Got it." Jake turned to Ethan. "Be a good kid. Stay here. We don't want you to get hurt." Jake motioned to a uniformed policeman. "Keep him here."

The other man nodded.

Ethan settled back in the van. Something would happen. Then he would walk right in there. He didn't know if he could save his father—didn't even know if his father needed or wanted to be saved. Ethan just knew he would die trying if he had to.

oOo

Cindy was down by one of the command vans, waiting with some black kid Jake didn't recognize. He was about to read her the riot act when she ran to him and put her arms around him, crying.

"What?" Reflexively, he held her back. "What the hell? What are you doing here?"

"I haven't been able to reach you. There was a fire. Mom's disappeared. Nobody would tell me *anything*. I didn't know where to go. I remembered you were here. LeRoy and I hitchhiked here—"

Jake pulled her away and held her. "Fire?"

Cindy nodded, tearful.

"Where's Anya?"

"I don't *know*," wailed Cindy and buried her face in his chest.

What the holy hell has been going on? Holding Cindy, he turned back up the hill and saw Orphira. "Orphira? Cindy says something happened at home. A fire or something. Could you check?"

Orphira nodded and disappeared over the hill.

Jake returned to holding Cindy. He saw the black kid—LeRoy. Jake held out his hand. "Jake Fiske."

"LeRoy Parkin, sir." LeRoy took Jake's hand and shook it.

LeRoy Parkin? Norman Parkin's nephew? What the hell was Cindy doing hanging around with *him*? *Not now. Not now.*

Orphira came up behind him and tapped him on the shoulder. "Come on over here, Jake," she said softly.

"Wait here, honey."

Orphira led him about twenty feet away. "Something's happened."

"A fire?"

Orphira nodded. "Late yesterday afternoon. It was set with an accelerant."

Oh, God. "Anya? Where's Anya?"

Orphira shook her head. "Nobody knows. Her car's not there. And Joe." She stopped and drew a deep breath. "There's signs of a struggle and a lot of blood."

"Why wasn't I *told?*"

Orphira shook her head. "I don't know."

"Jesus Christ," he said, stunned. Anya? Hurt? Dead? *Killed?*

"There's an all points out on the roads for her, her car, and anybody who knows anything." Orphira put her hand on his arm. "We'll find out what happened."

"Yesterday?" Jake pulled out his cell. It seemed to be working. Why hadn't Cindy's cell reached his? He shook his head. Wait a minute. Why the hell didn't the *department* call him? He looked up the hill. Bujold was looking down at him.

"Son-of-a-bitch," Jake snarled. He ran up the hill and took a swing at Bujold. Bujold stepped out of the way and took Jake to the ground.

"Officer Fiske!" Bujold shouted. "Stand down!"

Jake tried to claw at him, but Bujold had him pinned, elbow and wrist. If he moved, Bujold would snap them both.

"You knew," Jake spat.

"I only just found out," Bujold said grimly. "You know what a clusterfuck these operations are."

"Yeah. Right."

Bujold let him up. "Go call the department. Find out what's going on and then come back to me."

Jake didn't answer. He walked off to the edge of the woods and called the station. The duty officer told him what was known: yes, there was a fire. Yes, there was a lot of blood. Yes, it was Anya's blood type. No, there had not been a DNA test yet. Yes, forensics had been over the site. No, there was no report yet. No, Anya's car had not yet been found.

He hung up and wept, the tears rolling down his face. Cindy touched him, and they held one another.

"Jesus Christ," he said to himself. A curse. A prayer. *Jesus Fucking Christ.*

oOo

When Cindy dove for her father, LeRoy didn't know whether to admire her or be appalled. It was a good act—or maybe it wasn't so much of an act. Anya wasn't dead in the body, but she was gone and dead to Cindy in spirit. Maybe it wasn't an act at all.

When Jake shook his hand, LeRoy could see the flicker of recognition. *You're the man that killed my uncle,* LeRoy thought. He hoped it showed on his face.

He wondered again how he could let that stand. He *should* take revenge—Norman would want that, wouldn't he? The fact that it was nothing LeRoy wanted seemed small.

Another day.

When Jake moved off, LeRoy stood next to Cindy. She was still sniffling. He tried to put his arm around her.

"Don't touch me," she whispered.

Ah. They were still broken up.

"I'm barely holding this together as it is. I don't want forty cops suddenly take an interest in a young black kid consoling a wailing white girl."

Or maybe not. LeRoy felt a little lift of hope and scolded himself for it.

Then Jake's partner came down and talked to him. Jake seemed to fall apart, and Cindy ran to him.

LeRoy was suddenly alone in a sea of mostly white faces. He looked around. No one seemed to be noticing him. He listened. He heard the words, "Ethan" and "Joe Cori's son," mentioned more than once.

He decided to find Ethan. If anybody could get them into the compound, it would be Joe Cori's son. Cindy was counting on him. He had no idea what Connie was doing but figured he'd find out soon enough.

The cops seemed to congregate in a line near the compound, watching it. Only a few were manning the cars parked along the line of trees. LeRoy faded back to the trees and walked along them, looking for someone who was not obviously a cop or an agent.

A couple of times, he was approached. But LeRoy looked down and mumbled a vague association with Jake. That seemed to be enough to keep him away from the front lines but not pushed summarily into the back seat of a car and locked up.

There were several cruisers, still and unlit. Two EMT vans were there, too, the technicians leaning against the front and watching, smoking cigarettes. Beyond the EMT vans were four black police vans—the cops were ready to take in everybody they found. LeRoy headed to the vans. Everybody here had a function: guard, agent, cop, technician. Only near the vans might he find people who were without a defined role. That was where Ethan would be.

A white college boy and a uniformed cop sat in the open door of one of the vans. LeRoy approached them.

The cop in uniform stood up. "You! What are you doing here?"

LeRoy glanced down. This was a local guy. Even so, it wouldn't do to leave his own name. "Larry Peters. I'm a friend of one of the kids inside. Officer

Fiske sent me over to talk to Mister Cori." He walked closer to the cop and dropped his voice. "He thought we might think of something together."

"Right. Like you're supposed to be here."

"Do I look like I *live* around here? Did I *walk* here in the dead of night? What other reason would I have to be *here*? I wouldn't even *be* here unless it was for Portia." LeRoy tried to sound respectful and indignant at the same time. He looked down. "I just want her to get out okay. You don't know—"

"Okay," said the cop. "Don't give me your life story. I don't want to be here, either. Fucking cults." The cop lit a cigarette and walked away.

LeRoy sat next to Ethan.

Ethan watched him. "Do I know you?"

"No. I'm LeRoy Parkin. Norman Parkin's nephew."

Ethan shrugged. "I don't know the name."

"You know about the pills?"

Ethan nodded. "Maybe more than most."

"My Uncle Norman sold them to your father."

"Really." Ethan's eyes narrowed. "Where did they come from?"

"That's a long story. I figure you can get us in there better than anybody."

"Maybe." He waved at the police. "None of these have been able to approach the house since the first time they tried."

"What about you?"

Ethan stared back at him. "I think I can walk right in."

LeRoy nodded. "We would just have to get past these cops."

"I don't think we even have to do that. I think we just walk that way about fifty feet." He pointed towards the house just past the cars. "Once we pass the boundary, I don't think any of these guys will be able to stop us."

"How come?"

"My father told them not to."

LeRoy laughed shortly. Then he realized Ethan was serious. He looked at the line of policemen and looked back at Ethan. LeRoy didn't trust many people, but he found himself trusting Ethan. *What the hell? Did he come all this way just to wait on the sidelines?*

He looked back at the cops. There was no way he could get Ethan back to Cindy. The line was only fifty feet in front of him, but Cindy was way back with Jake.

Okay. Well, he'd think of something once they were in there.

"Ready?" asked Ethan.

"Okay."

They walked past the uniformed cop. "Hey!"

"We're just looking at the house," said LeRoy easily. "Ethan has an idea."

The cop followed them.

When they reached the line of cars, Ethan broke into a run. LeRoy followed him.

The cop yelled and lunged, then stopped short and looked confused.

Hope they don't shoot me, thought LeRoy, trying to keep up with Ethan.

oOo

Orphira didn't know what to do. Jake was weeping, holding Cindy. Cindy was holding him, eyes now closed and dry. Consoling her father.

Should she just walk off and leave them here? Maybe. It broke her heart to see him like this. To see him moaning over that slut of a wife—*stop* it. Since when were the wages of adultery death? Orphira had been teasing, flirting with a married man. Was Orphira so much more innocent? Was Anya Fiske so much more guilty?

Best to leave them. Orphira turned to walk away. Jake blindly reached out his hand and grabbed her arm.

For a moment, the three of them, Jake, Cindy, Orphira, were a grieving family.

Then Cindy looked up at her, eyes cold. *She* wasn't mourning. It had all the look of a feral cat facing down a coyote. A look of pointless defiance. Of *what*? Orphira? The death of her mother? The failure of her father?

After a moment, Jake got a hold of himself. He wiped his nose and eyes on the sleeve of his jacket. "Orphira, I have no car here. I need to get back to Saint Louis."

"I can take you." Orphira's words came out before she thought. A series of images ran through her mind: telling Bujold she was leaving, losing her spot on the Drug X team, getting hooked up with Jake, Jake leaving the force when things came out, *Orphira* leaving the force when things came out. All from one small car ride.

And, you know? It was all right. She felt a relief slide over her. This was a good thing to do. This was a gift for a friend—maybe more than a friend but so what? The cost might be great, but gifts should mean something. They should *cost* something.

Orphira had a feeling the Anya story was going to get ugly over the next few weeks. The woman had gotten mixed up in something bad, and it had likely cost her her life. Jake was going to find out things about her he would wish he had never known. Orphira would be there. She would *let* herself be there.

There was a commotion up the hill. She saw the black kid and Ethan run across the bare earth between the police line and the compound—*they* weren't held back. Bujold, Duck, half a dozen others started after them and stopped. LeRoy played with the door and opened it. The two of them disappeared inside.

"Daddy," said Cindy.

Orphira turned. Cindy kissed Jake on the cheek. She turned to Orphira. "You take good care of him," she said fiercely.

Then she was running up the hill to the police line, dancing around Duck, slipping between Bujold's hands, running even after she could no longer be followed. Ethan and LeRoy opened the door for her and she was gone.

"*Cindy!*"cried Jake and lunged after her, stopped at the edge of the police line. "Cindy," he moaned softly.

Orphira followed him. She passed him by and went to Bujold. "Sir?"

"Yeah, Doyle?" Bujold said sourly.

"Officer Fiske's wife is missing. He needs to get back to Saint Louis. I'll take him."

Bujold looked at her, then over at Fiske, calling after Cindy. He looked down at her. "He's leaving his daughter here?"

Orphira returned his gaze. "Do you think he'll be anything but a liability? Broken up about his wife? Scared for his daughter? I'll take him. *You* should order him."

Bujold nodded. "What a fucked-up mess. Yeah. Something's going to break here, and it's not going to be pretty." He yelled past her. "Fiske!"

Jake came slowly over to her.

Bujold looked at him with a sour expression on his face. "Orphira's going to take you home."

"But Cindy—"

"*I'll* make sure she gets out okay. We're not going to do anything to get anybody hurt. We'll wait here as long as it takes."

"But she's in there."

"And there are other, smaller kids than yours in there. We're not going to endanger them, either. As long as nothing happens, she'll be safe. You remember Waco? The only reason we got in trouble there is we were in a hurry. She's your daughter. *You're* in a hurry. It's only natural. But *we're* going to be patient. I want you to go back to Saint Louis and figure out what's going on with your wife. We've got things under control here."

"I'm not—"

"*Officer Fiske!*" Bujold's voice went suddenly parade ground loud. "That was not a request. You don't want to spend the rest of the day locked in the back of a squad car. *Go.*"

Jake stumbled back against Orphira. She led him down the hill to her car and helped him inside.

She drove out the park entrance and headed south into a warm new morning, her emotions mixed: sadness seeping from Jake, desolate beside her, mixing with the bubbling urge to sing she felt inside.

oOo

Bill felt dizzy. This wasn't the same. Before, it felt as if things were lifting him, bringing him along. This felt like a freight train, an impending flood.

"Do you have any idea how old I am?" Hibbert asked.

Bill shook his head. He thought he was going to be sick.

"Of course you don't." Fred waved it away. "How could you? I was born in a little village on the outskirts of Sumer six thousand years ago."

"What?"

"Can't hear too well? I bet that stuff plays hell with the senses. It's a hammer trying to swat a fly. You get the fly, but you make a mess. My point is after all this time I *know* things. I found out things." Fred checked his watch. "We have a few minutes. Let me tell you a story."

Bill's tongue felt thick. The colors of the room pulsed and twisted.

Fred leaned back and crossed his legs. "Once upon a time, three hundred million years ago, something came here. I don't know if it came lightly, spores falling like drifting snow, or if it came like thunder riding the back of a meteor or a comet. But it came. It found things here to its liking—warm water, complex ocean life, early invasions on the land, insects—what's not to like? It decided to stay. Or maybe it didn't have a choice at that point. I don't know."

Bill's head felt heavy. He rested it on the desk. He could hear Fred's voice like the drone of far-off bagpipes.

"Over time, it insinuated itself into every living thing—chemical pathways, additional genes, extra plastids, and the like. It must have taken a while. It was limited to the exchanges between cells, and that's slow."

"Why are you telling me this?"

"I want it to realize I know what it is."

"It is my Queen," Bill said softly, his eyes closed.

Fred chuckled. "I wondered if you would think of it as a woman. It doesn't apply, of course."

"My Queen," Bill whispered.

"It's all right. *She'll* know I know."

"Do you serve her?"

Fred fell silent. Bill looked up. Fred's face was cold.

"I do not serve the God of Reptiles," Fred said quietly. Then he seemed to shake himself. "I'm guessing it took fifty million years or so. I'm *sure* she was in place by two hundred fifty million years ago—that's when the dinosaurs show up."

"Dinosaurs?" Inside him, he could feel her coming.

"She liked dinosaurs. Things went on swimmingly for another hundred million years or so. But there are other things out there like her. Conflicts are inevitable, I suppose, though I can't pretend to understand what they were about. How could I?" Fred leaned forward on his knees. "I mean, three hundred million years isn't eternity—it's not even a drop in the universal bucket. But it's closer to the idea of eternity than you or even me will ever get."

Fred leaned back. "Anyway, about sixty-five million years ago this conflict came to a head." He made an exploding motion with his hands. "Bang. No more dinosaurs. Contracts were made. Bargains struck. Treaties created. So, *she* decides to try something new, this time with mammals. They've been around a while. They're not as much fun as dinosaurs, but they have their own possibilities. After a while, she gets apes with pretty big brains. Brains she can use for her own purposes."

She reared up in him, stronger than he had ever felt her. Gigantic. *She* filled him to his fingertips, and he was small inside himself. Absently, *She* comforted his fear, but he could tell *She* was preoccupied. *She* was watching Fred.

Fred smiled. "So, Bill. Is God *in?*" he said in a purr.

oOo

Joe felt God roll through him down to his fingertips. He stood up suddenly. He could *feel* Sam walking down to the water by himself. Sam was ready. Joe was ready. He walked to the shore and waved his people back. Now was the time for war.

He walked through the door down to the lake and raised his hand. *Let there be steam! Let there be fire!*

The lake erupted, a fiery explosion exactly where Sam stood. Sam was burned alive one moment, untouched the next. He reached up and pulled down a piece of sky, tore out the lightning, and cast it.

The lightning roared down on Joe. He looked up. His skin blackened and smoked, then was whole again.

Sam started running towards him. Joe ran towards Sam. Both of them roared. They met in the middle of the lake.

oOo

LeRoy broke the windowpane and reached inside, unlocked the side door. They opened the door and entered in the compound.

There was a lightning crack and the sound of an explosion outside. Ethan ran to the opposite window. "Oh, crap," he said.

Cindy and LeRoy joined him. Outside, the lake was on fire and boiling. They couldn't see for the steam, but there were giant shadows moving. Every few moments there was an animal roar or another explosion.

"What is that?" LeRoy breathed.

"Metaphorical war," Ethan said slowly. "I'm guessing one of them is my dad. I don't know who the other one is."

"It's Sam," said Cindy. "Who else could it be? Who else has the drug?"

"You know about the drug?"

LeRoy answered. "My uncle sold it to Joe. I made the pills that were sold to Sam." LeRoy gestured out there. "But I didn't know it could do this."

Ethan looked back outside. "It can't. All it can do is enable a human being to have fundamental and direct contact with the automata underlying consensus reality."

LeRoy and Cindy looked at one another.

"What?" asked LeRoy.

Ethan didn't answer. He watched outside for a moment. "That explosion there—that one? That was Joe. My dad. I've got to go after him."

"There's Portia," Cindy said suddenly, pointing across the compound. "I can save her."

LeRoy could see Portia through the window. He watched the fire outside. Anya had invented this, but he and Norman had sold it. Norman was dead. Anya was gone. He was the only one left. He was responsible. "I'm going to find the rest of the Anapyridol and destroy it."

The three of them looked at one another. Cindy grabbed LeRoy and kissed him fiercely. "Don't get killed."

LeRoy nodded. "You, neither." He shook hands with Ethan. "Good luck."

Ethan nodded. He looked outside, then at Cindy. "Ready?"

"Ready."

LeRoy opened the door. Ethan and Cindy raced outside.

LeRoy stared after them for a moment, then he turned and ran deeper into the compound.

There were thousands of pills here. He just had to find them. There was a flash and explosion. LeRoy dove to the floor and over his head the glass exploded into the room. The floor shook.

The sounds died back to a long, punctuated grumbling, like a rolling thunderstorm He carefully brushed his face and hair without opening his eyes. Opened them. No glass slivers stabbed him. He got up to his knees and looked out the window. The battle had moved out over to the other side of the lake. Several people were lying in the mud. He didn't see Cindy—then he saw her kneeling next to someone. She was okay.

LeRoy turned back inside. The doors of the cabinets had been ripped off. Inside were the plastic tubs. He opened one of them and saw hundreds of pink pills. He looked in all the cabinets and pulled out the tubs. About right? He wasn't sure. How could he be sure? He rummaged around for something to carry them and found garbage bags. He emptied the pills into the garbage bags.

Now what? He looked outside. Whatever activity there was seemed to be taking place on the other side of the lake. *Okay.*

LeRoy ran down the length of the building until he found the door. Outside now, he was at the edge of the water. There was a trail that ran along the water and he jogged along it until he was out of sight of the compound. Then he waded out a little into the water — it was *hot* — and poured the contents of the bag into the water. The pink pills turned into a sodden mass in front of his eyes. *Going to be some funny fish in here.* If there were any fish left.

Okay, then. He started to turn back and stopped. What about Sam's pills? *They* weren't here.

Shit. The lake wasn't very big. Maybe he could just run around to the other side and find them. He couldn't *leave* them.

LeRoy started to run. Yeah, they might see him and strike him with lightning or locusts or something. So what? What did he have to lose?

oOo

Bill could feel *Her* fill him. Everything he was, everything he'd ever known was *Hers* in an instant.

"*He* knows you. I don't know you," *She* said. Bill felt his lips working.

"I'm gratified."

"Hold out your hand."

For a moment, Bill felt *Her* confinement, *Her* limitation from being inside him. *She* shook *Herself* irritably, and suddenly Bill could see more clearly than he could have imagined. Every object in the room was etched in light, annotated in symbols, seen from multiple angles. Only Fred seemed without perspective.

"Better," *She* said. His body shook and *She* noticed it, reached down inside of him, and took his heart and liver, smoothed them over and stabilized them.

Fred walked to the desk and held out his hand.

She leaned forward and licked it. Inside, Bill felt the tastes and chemicals torn apart and analyzed. Fred was suddenly of a piece with everything else.

"You should have been dead long ago," *She* said. "Thousands of years dead."

"You tried when I was born in Sumer," Fred said easily as he wiped his hand. "Again in Greece when I went to speak with Socrates. Again in Europe, 1349. Did you think me so easy to kill?"

"Don't take things personally. I didn't think of you at all," *She* said. "I didn't know you existed."

"And now you do."

"Why reveal yourself to me now?"

"I'm here representing my patron," Fred said wolfishly. "To remind you of your bargain."

oOo

"Explosives!" came over Connie's radio. "Fire in the *hole!* Unit 1! Unit 2! Unit 3! Converge on target. Shoot him, Goddamnit!"

Connie could see Sam and Joe fighting. *Mama said miracles were the devil's work since you could never tell where they came from.* There was no clear shot at Sam. Connie waited. Then Sam was down, splashing in the water. Connie took careful aim and tried to pull the trigger.

Nothing. Just like before when he'd answered on the radio.

He released it.

He would have to wait for his moment.

oOo

Joe was the angel Ramiel, angel of destruction. He decapitated Sam with a sword of fire. But the stump sizzled, and Sam picked up his head and fastened it back on.

Sam lifted his hammer and threw it at Joe. It struck him in the forehead and split it in seven pieces, each of which struck the shore. But the pieces flew back together again.

Joe was the Lion of Christ, rending Sam into pieces. But Sam spit fire into his eye and beat Joe back with leathery wings.

Shapes flickered over them as quick as they thought them. Joe rained fire, drought, pestilence, frogs, and boils down on Sam. But Sam laughed and unleashed the tornado and the glacier, the volcano, and the flood.

oOo

Cindy ran one way and Ethan ran another. The smoke and steam blew in over the lake, turning everybody into vague, Pompeii-like figures. Portia was gone.

"Portia? *Portia!*" God damn it! What the hell was Cindy doing here? Portia was her friend. Not her sister or her mother—her father was going back to see if her mother was *dead,* and she was stumbling through this muck to find someone who didn't want to be saved.

"*Phil!*" she cried.

Cindy heard something and turned, slipped, and fell into the mud, got up again and staggered in the sound's direction.

Phil loomed out in the grayness. "Cindy?" he said curiously. "What are you doing here?"

"Getting Portia out of here."

"Why would I leave?" Portia seemed to rise up out of the ground to appear from behind Phil. Cindy stepped back, startled. "Why now?" Portia said gaily. "*Now,* when we triumph over Satan!"

Satan? Right. She turned to Phil. "Look around, Phil." She waved her hand. Surrounding them were people lying still on the ground. There were injured moans coming through the fog. "This isn't going to end well."

Phil looked uncertain.

Portia grabbed his arm and pulled on it. "Come on. If we go down to the water, maybe we can see better."

The smoke blew away and cleared suddenly. Portia pointed across the beach. "Look. There's Tess."

Tess stood, attentive and rapt, watching the battle.

Phil looked at Cindy. His face hardened. "We should go, honey."

"But *Tess* is over there. *Joe* is fighting for *us*. We should be there."

Phil tried to pull her away. Portia was suddenly all teeth and claws. She started screaming.

Cindy made a fist and slugged Portia in the face as hard as she could.

Portia cried out and covered her face. Phil picked her up, and the two of them ran back towards the compound. In front of them, the door was blown off its hinges.

Cindy said a sudden prayer. *Please let LeRoy be all right.*

Then through the first door, across what remained of the kitchen, through the other door into the front yard. There was a line of policemen pointing weapons at them.

Phil stopped short.

Cindy stood in front of them. "We *surrender!*"

Bujold appeared out of the crowd and waved them forward. The three of them ran. Cindy was pulled away from them. She heard Bujold's voice.

"It's the Fiske kid. Kensington! Get her over to the cars. Marks! Take these two and put them in the vans."

She stumbled as they dragged her. Then there was a flash so bright she was instantly blind, nothing but blank white forever and ever. She hit the ground and hugged it, waiting for the shock wave.

It hit a moment later.

oOo

"You know from this vessel," Fred continued. "That I've found the means to open the window between you and them."

"Yes."

"I have also found the means to close it."

"I don't believe you. That would be lethal."

"So my patron believed, until he thought it through thoroughly. But he determined a possible avenue I've pursued." Fred pulled out a bottle from his pocket. "You are inside poor Bill. So you know what Anapyridol is. This is *anti*-Anapyridol. A permanent antagonist for the same site so excited by

Anapyridol. I can detach them from you at will. There is one already, wandering around unhurt and completely free of you."

"I will verify this."

"No doubt. My patron has determined several ways of delivering this compound that you cannot prevent. *I* don't know what they are. But *he* does. And as you will recall, he is most effective."

Bill felt her thinking. Felt her considerations operating at the periphery of his understanding.

"What do you want?"

Fred tossed up the bottle and caught it again. "I want you to fulfill your part of the bargain. That's all I've been told to say."

"Tell your patron that I apologize for the delay, but it was unavoidable."

"I expect he'll have trouble believing that."

"Nevertheless, I will fulfill my part. But it will be part of my own larger plans. I ask that he trust me for the moment."

"Why should he do that?"

"Because of the anti-Anapyridol, of course." *She* laughed. "Isn't that guarantee enough?"

Fred looked frightened for a moment. Then he regained his composure. "Of course. I will relay the message."

"Is there more?" *She* looked him in the eye.

"As a matter of fact, there is."

oOo

Ethan stood in the doorway as Cindy sprinted towards the beach, calling for Portia. There were continuous flashes in the haze over the lake, but he could see no human figures. The roar became a whisper, but the flashes remained giving a dream-like feeling to the scene.

Tess was standing at the water's edge.

Ethan walked across the sand and stood next to her.

Tess glanced at him. "I didn't expect you here."

"He's my father. You're his wife." Ethan looked at her. "You're my friend."

"Am I?" She raised her eyebrow.

Ethan nodded. The clouds over the lake scintillated, tiny pinprick stars flashing. He could hear faint firecracker sounds.

Wrong color for Cherenkov radiation, he thought. Imagine a complex electrical field of differing frequencies. There would be local maximums—would they get hot enough to dissociate water vapor into hydrogen and oxygen? Maybe the hot hydrogen would react with the nitrogen in the air and make ammonia. Those points of light looked like tiny explosions. Could hydrogen do that? Ammonia? His freshman chemistry was fuzzy. Tess crossed her arms and watched the lake. She was scared. Very scared.

He touched her on the shoulder.

The clouds suddenly piled high on one another, a seething column bubbling up into the sky. There was a quick cascade of color, red to yellow, yellow to blue, blue to violet, violet to white, and an actinic flash.

He grabbed Tess and shoved her down on the ground and covered her over with his body. The shock wave hit a moment later, and a wave of water poured over them, lifted them up, and tumbled them. He would *not* let Tess go. He *would* hold on.

They rolled over and over, underwater, until they struck the side of the compound. For a moment, Ethan thought the wall was going to give. He had a vision of rolling into the disintegrating house, trapped underwater, impaled by jagged spears of wood.

But the wall held, and he felt the slippery ground under his feet. He pushed up and found himself holding Tess up in three feet of water flowing rapidly away. He breathed hard. Tess was choking but alive.

The lake was a shallow, muddy bowl. In the center of it, two glowing giants faced one another.

Is this Joe and Sam as they see each other? he wondered. Then, in his mind, he saw the missing part of the point-of-view equation. He'd been presuming all along that the POV equation existed as a description of the observer, interacting with, but separate, from the observed. But his description of it was incomplete; the POV equation was recursive. It was the component of the rule function that determined local behavior. Of *course*, humans would be able to interact directly with rules function. Point of view was *part* of the rules function. The rules function, in fact, *depended* on point of view. Point of view included self-perception, which, then, reflected the rules function. *A wheel within a wheel.*

He helped Tess to her feet. A woman was sitting up a few feet away, holding her little boy. The boy was still.

"Caleb?" the woman said. "*Caleb!*"

Ethan ran over to her. Tess was right behind him. Without thinking, he grabbed the boy from the woman and felt for a pulse—*yes!* He placed the boy on the ground carefully, tilted his head. He could hear the CPR instructor as if he were right next to him. Check the mouth—no obstruction. Two quick breaths. No obstruction. Breathe—count the breaths. *Stop.* See if the boy started on his own. *No.* Tess knelt next to him.

The woman was sobbing.

Breathe for him again—make the count. *Stop.*

The boy shuddered, choked, and threw up into Ethan's ear. Ethan jerked back. The boy choked, gasped, and started screaming. The woman brushed Ethan to one side.

Ethan grabbed her shoulder and pointed to the compound. "On the other side. There are EMTs."

The woman nodded and ran.

Tess was kneeling next to another still form. This one was breathing but unconscious.

"Jesse," she said. "Caleb's father."

"If we move him, we might hurt him." Ethan looked around. "There's not enough water for another wave. Another explosion like that will kill us all, anyway. The EMTs will find him."

They looked around. Most of Joe's people had huddled against the trees on the far end of the beach. There were people battered into the sand, but they were gathering themselves up. It looked as if everyone was alive.

"You should go," Ethan said. He looked down into the lake bed. They were bellowing at one another. Swathed in light, they could barely be seen. "This isn't going to end well." Ethan wondered if he could pull them apart. He wondered if he would survive if he tried. The glow was tinged with violet. There was a *lot* of energy being released. Were they getting a radiation dose?

Tess shook her head. "We go in after them together."

Ethan nodded.

She grabbed his hand, and he squeezed back. They began to wade through the mud towards the middle of the lake.

oOo

They stood across from one another, breathing hard. There were no angels or gods or demons. The two of them were illuminated by their own light.

Joe still felt the power of God in his hands, in his arms. He dragged himself up.

Sam looked up at him, smaller but just as strong. Just as fast.

Sam spat at the ground. "Come on, fat boy. Is that all you got?"

Joe felt it in his hands. Felt them curl into fists. *This is what I am. This is what I always was.* He raised his fists.

Sam held out his hand, and there was a click as the blade extended.

"Come on, lover," Sam said.

Joe roared and charged.

They met in the mud.

oOo

The water slammed LeRoy against a tree, pinning him against the trunk. He held on and after a moment, he could stand. He stopped and stared. The lake was *gone*.

Whatever had been going on in the center was still going on. It looked as if the two of them were just fighting now. The little one—LeRoy figured that was

Sam—kept stabbing at the big one. The big one—Joe—kept slugging the little one. Neither one seemed bothered by the assault of the other.

LeRoy looked around. *Luck!* The sand bar in the lake was now exposed. He could make his way across without entering the water.

It was more or less solid. *No quicksand, please!* he prayed. But the sand was surprisingly firm, and he made it across. Up the hill and over, crawling on his stomach.

The hill had apparently protected the tents. They were still dry. But the raggedy people were down at the muddy edge, screaming at the battle. Quick as he could, LeRoy scooted down the hill. Which tent? Which tent?

Sam was the leader. Pick the biggest one. The one with all the colors.

He picked his way to the tent in the center. Big. Colorful. Abandoned. All good qualities to have in a place like this.

Inside, there was a collection of pillows and blankets and a plastic chest. He tried to open the chest—locked. Okay. He looked around and found an axe. Three blows, and the plastic parted like a sigh. Inside he found plastic bag after plastic bag of pills.

The screams from the beach seemed closer. Okay, he thought. That's all there was as far as he could tell. He held them in his shirt and ran away from the beach.

Over the far hill, away from the lake, he found where the lake water had gone. It was an old, open cesspool, now flooded under six feet of lake water. Exactly what he needed. He ripped open bag after bag and poured them into the stinking water.

I'm done! No more hero work for him. He had to get *out* of here.

Back over the hill and down by the lake. Anguished cries from the lake. Screams of desolation and pain from the shore. He could see Joe and Sam lying in the mud, writhing.

Forget them! He ran across the sand bar—mushy now. Hard to walk. On the other side, up the closest trail he could find. Out of sight of the lake, he pulled the trail map, now soaked, out of his pocket.

There was a gunshot.

LeRoy thought he'd been shot for a moment. Everything he'd ever wanted to do flashed through his mind. He looked at his chest. Nothing. No blood.

He made himself breathe. Gunshots meant cops. He *had* to get out of here.

Carefully, he unfolded the map. This was the blue spot trail. Up, over, take the white dot, down the hill to the car. Hopefully, Connie was waiting for him.

No time!

LeRoy ran.

oOo

"I'm not asking you to close this window," Fred insisted. "But when they call, *you* do not have to answer."

"You want me to leave them alone."

"Exactly."

"Why should I? Are they not my creations? Are not *you?*"

Fred leaned forward. "Because it is time. I do not know you—I *cannot* know you. But my patron does. And he says it is time for you to let them go."

Bill felt a sudden, intolerable sadness wash through him.

"It will make no difference," *She* said. "They don't need me. I'm only a metaphor for them to use."

"Exactly," Fred murmured. "One last thing."

"What?"

Bill felt weak.

Fred stood next to him. "Take him with you. Every poor thing he has done came from me using him and I used him poorly. He should receive some reward."

His Queen looked directly at him. *Her* fearful scrutiny turned kind. He felt *Her* hold him.

She said, "All right."

For a moment, Bill felt like he couldn't breathe. Then he realized he didn't need to.

Fred was standing over Bill's body, face stern, tears on his face. Fred looked every inch his age. "Good luck, Bill," said the old man.

"Come on, Bill," *She* said, as bright and glorious as a star. *Her* face looked a little like Anya's. "Let's go. It'll be fun."

Bill waited until Fred closed his eyes. That seemed like the proper thing to do. Then, his heart light but unbeating, he left with his Queen.

oOo

Joe held his hand steady. He could hardly stand. Sam didn't look any better. He felt everything he had flow into his hand, every disappointment, every rage, until his fist was as hard and heavy as black iron. Behind him, he felt God cheering. God was guiding him. God was giving him strength.

Sam's knife was sharp and black as a sword.

His vision wavered a moment. God seemed to hesitate. Draw in on Himself. There was a noiseless flash in Joe's vision, and God was gone.

It was like being struck blind. Joe screamed and fell to his knees. He could hear Sam. *Felt* Sam as bereft and lost as he was.

Pressure welled up in his chest. Sharp pain shot through his chest and arms like fiery electricity. Then sound receded. Vision faded. He was a long distance from the lake, from the compound, from Tess. He saw Sam nearby.

Sam cried out. Reached for him. Joe reached out.

Something struck them both across the eyes, and Joe felt himself wink out, a second after Sam.

oOo

"*Shoot!*" came screaming across the radio.

Connie looked through the sight. Joe clutched his chest and went down. Sam seemed to lean to one side, left side of his body working spasmodically.

This looks promising.

He carefully aimed the cross hairs above Sam's head. Allow for windage and drop. He pulled the trigger carefully, as he'd done a dozen times in the last hour.

This time it worked, and the gun roared.

A splatter of blood erupted from Sam's skull, and he went down.

Okay, then.

Connie laid the rifle down. He jogged back into the woods where the cop was taped up. The cop kept trying to yell, but the gag wouldn't let him. The cop's face was almost purple.

Connie ripped off the duct tape gag. The cop cried out.

Connie jogged back up the trail towards his car.

Now, all he had to do was get out of here.

oOo

Tess saw Joe clutch his chest and fall. She felt as if a hole had opened in her and the cold and lonely wind blew through. She cut that off. She knelt next to Joe. He was breathing. His pulse was thin.

"Heart attack?" Ethan said, kneeling across from her.

She nodded. "We've got to get him out of here."

Ethan shook his head. "He's too big. I'll go get one of the EMT's. They have kits for this." Ethan ran, slogging his way through the mud.

Tess leaned her head against Joe's. "Oh, honey," she whispered. "Stay with me. Don't leave me alone."

"Joe?" came a querulous voice.

Tess looked up. It was Sam. Half his face was frozen in a rictus, the other was weeping. He kept trying to stand on his right leg, but it kept falling out from under him.

"Joe?" he repeated. "You okay?" Sam struggled to stand.

Then there was a splattering sound, and a chunk of something went flying from his head. Sam stopped moving, stood still. Then fell down.

Tess heard a shriek from the side of the lake and saw a young man struggling to reach them.

Tess ignored him. She knelt next to Joe and listened to his labored breathing. She huddled next to him to keep him warm.

oOo

Cindy's eyes didn't clear until after she'd been sitting in the back of the squad car for some minutes.

Someone had been assigned to watch her—Kensington? Was that what Bujold had said? Every few minutes, Kensington asked how she was. "Blind," she responded, even after her vision began to clear.

Once Cindy's vision had returned, she looked around to figure out how to escape. She had done her part. Portia was safe. Now she had to get out of here.

Or should she? If she just stayed put, eventually they would send her home. Where *was* home now? The house was burned down—or at least so damaged she couldn't stay there. She pulled out her cell. It was still off. She turned it on. No service. *Of course.*

Cindy put it back in her pocket. Just as well. No doubt there were a dozen messages from Jake. She wondered what was going to happen next. Would there be an investigation? Would her cell phone records be examined? She had calls to Connie on it. Calls to LeRoy. Calls to Portia. Surely all that implicated her in *something.*

Maybe the best thing was to just sit tight and look innocent.

She tried the door of the squad car. It was locked. Kensington was standing about twenty feet away, smoking a cigarette.

"Hey!" she called, and tapped the window with her knuckle.

Kensington came over and opened the door.

"It's getting stuffy in there." She smiled up at him.

"You're supposed to be locked in."

"You have to watch me, right?"

Kensington nodded.

"Then why don't you roll down the window and just stand there and talk to me. I'm not going anywhere? Where would I go?" She gave him her most innocent, seductive smile, one she'd perfected last summer.

Kensington grinned. "Okay."

He had every appearance of being a boring little man in a boring little job. Cindy gritted her teeth and smiled. That was best, wasn't it? Stay here?

But as Kensington talked about police procedure and his idea of why they were *really* here (narco traffic from South America) and what *he* would do if *he* was in charge (storm the place, since the hostages were all narco traffickers, anyway) Cindy wondered why she was bothering. If she was in trouble, she was *already* in trouble. She knew what was going to happen next. When the crisis resolved, everybody was going to be taken back to Saint Louis to be questioned. Jake would come down and bail her out, if he could, and she'd go home to an empty house, somewhere. Or, if he couldn't, she'd go to juvie.

Cindy found herself thinking, *what would Anya do?* What would her *mother* do? Not the broken thing she'd become but the tough woman who'd gotten herself out of Russia? Would *she* wait for the whim of the authorities? And wasn't Cindy *her* daughter?

The gunshot rang out over the policemen. For a moment, they were frozen. Cindy had a few seconds to look around.

Then, with a shout, the line of policemen surged forward. Kensington surged with the rest of them.

Cindy saw her chance and took it. Out through the window, she ran down the hill, into the woods, and up the ridge trail. Then she pulled out her map of the forest. It was soaking. She carefully pulled it apart, dancing with impatience. White dot. She was on the White Dot Trail. That led over the ridge.

There was a point on the ridge where she could see the compound and the lake. The lake was gone—nothing left but a great mud flat. A good deal of the compound was washed away. The policemen were running into the compound and across the beach. EMTs had followed them.

Out in the lake, by themselves, were a small group of four or five people. Cindy could see EMTs working their way towards them.

She looked back at the cars. She thought she could see Phil, in handcuffs, but Portia was nowhere in sight. They would separate them, of course. Women and children together in one set of vans, men in the other.

She turned away from the scene and ran over the ridge.

oOo

Ethan heard the gunshot as he reached the compound. He turned and had time to see Sam fall. Screams of *"Gun! Gun!"* came from the police line. He got out of the way of the door, and a second later the police burst through past him. Once the first wave passed, he went in the door, through the destroyed kitchen to the parking lot. The second wave was waiting for him, guns drawn.

Ethan held up his hands. "I'm Ethan Cori. My father is Joe Cori. He's had a heart attack."

Bujold appeared behind the guns. He pointed at Ethan. "Get him over here."

Ethan was pulled away from the house. "Joe's had a heart attack. It's all over."

Bujold glanced at him and then turned and point to the EMTs. "You heard him. *Go.*"

A squad of EMTs ran towards the compound.

Ethan turned to go back but Bujold stopped him. "You wait here. They'll bring Cori out soon enough."

"I want to be with him. He's my father."

"Think I don't know that? What happened in there? Who got shot?"

Ethan shrugged. "I don't know him. The guy from the other side of the lake. Joe was fighting him. All I know is the lake got blasted. Then Joe and this guy were fighting. Then they both went down. Joe had a heart attack, and the little guy got shot. Now you know as much as I do."

"I doubt that. What *happened* in there?" Bujold's eyes were wide.

He's scared, thought Ethan. *What do I say?*

"Magic," Ethan said after a moment. "Call it magic. You being held here. Me, not. All of the flashes. The lake getting blasted —"

"The *lake* got blasted?"

"All of it." Ethan waved his hand. "Call it magic. It makes as much sense as anything else."

Bujold stared at him. "I can't say that."

Ethan shrugged.

"Kensington," Bujold called over his shoulder. "Take him to a squad car and don't lose him like you did the other one."

"Other one?" whispered Ethan as Kensington escorted him away from the compound.

"Don't start with me."

Moments later, the policemen started bring people out of the compound. Ethan watched for Tess or his father. Then two EMTs wrestled a stretcher through the door and down the yard. It was Joe Cori, gray and unconscious, an oxygen mask strapped to his face.

Ethan moved towards him.

Kensington put a hand on his arm.

Ethan threw it off. "That's my father," he said. "You can watch me as I go with him to the hospital. That way you won't lose me, okay?"

Ethan reached the stretcher and walked alongside as they rolled it to the ambulance. He looked around and saw a second stretcher, this time with Sam, covered in blood. A young man walked next to him.

Tess was brought out of the compound in handcuffs, her eyes wild and looking around for Joe.

Ethan waved to her. He pointed to the stretcher. Tess tried to break free, but the policemen wrestled her to a van.

"I'll stay with him!" Ethan called.

Tess looked desperately at him and then disappeared into the van.

Ethan sat next to Joe in the ambulance. The door was closed. He saw a hand slap the window, and a moment later, the engine roared, the ambulance shook and slowly began to navigate down the road. Ethan saw the milling policemen, arrested women and children, men in handcuffs, disappear behind a bend in the road. Lots of unhappy people but no holocaust. No holocaust.

He sat next to Joe, listening to him breathe. *Live*, he thought. *Please live.*

It was almost a prayer.

oOo

Connie was waiting in his car, the motor running.

Cindy got in next to him.

LeRoy, wet and stinking, was sitting in the back seat, wrapped in a blanket.

"How did Ethan make out?" she asked LeRoy.

LeRoy shrugged. "I didn't come back that way."

The car started moving as soon as she shut the door. It turned left out of the parking lot, left away from the park, Joe Cori, and Portia, away from Anapyridol. Cindy opened the window and smelled the morning air, fresh, clean.

Passing them, one, two, three, squad cars, police vans, and ambulances. After a moment, they were gone and behind them. Cindy could hear the distant descending siren wails of chaos.

"Excuse me," said LeRoy. "Wet back here. And cold."

Cindy laughed and closed the window. She pulled out her cell and turned it on. Forty-three messages. From Jake.

She called him.

"I'm okay, Daddy," she said as soon as he answered. "Where do I meet you?"

Chapter 2.5: June, 1998

Everything changes. Everything takes time to change.

The Waco Standoff had taken nearly three months. The Milan Disaster started and was over in a day. The media never had a good chance to cover it. But now, with the fresh smoke still steaming over the ruins, they tried to make up for lost time.

KMOV was on the scene first. Someone tipped them when the battle was still unfolding, and they managed to get a helicopter there just as the first ambulances and paddy wagons were leaving. There were many, many shots of the steaming lakebed and the ruined compound. They alerted the news office back in Saint Louis. When the paddy wagons and ambulances left the compound, the KMOV copter followed to see where they ended up. On a guess, a crew was dispatched simultaneously to Columbia as the closest full-featured hospital. The dispatchers proved right when the ambulances turned off the Interstate and headed south, sirens screaming.

There being five possible hospitals, the KMOV pilot followed all the way to make sure which one. He had just time enough to confirm the university hospital before he ran out of fuel and had to autorotate down onto the football field. Thus, there were reporters waiting. Cameras flashed, whirred, and buzzed on the ambulance when first Joe and then Sam were brought out and rushed inside.

Ethan could manage to get into the hospital with Joe only by holding onto his stretcher. The camera lights and flashes were too bright to make out the corridors. The doctors whisked Joe into the OR. The nursing staff whisked Ethan to a private waiting room where reporters were forbidden. The university refused to be intimidated by the press. There, Ethan sat for eleven long hours as surgeons rebuilt his father's heart.

The van containing Tess and Phil continued on to Central. The van containing Portia and Donnie ended up in Town and Country, where the Rendquists were waiting with lawyer and bail money. Neither Portia nor

Donnie spent a night in jail, and not a moment too soon. About the same time the Rendquists were wearily entering their home, the Missouri media figured out the story had legs

The connection to Anya came out quickly. The FDA acknowledged that tests on what little remained of Drug X strongly resembled Anapyridol, a Lifeworks pharmaceutical that recently passed its toxicology studies. (Very little of Drug X was found on the Lifeworks' premises. Funny how that happened.)

An intrusive interview with Kathleen revealed that it was Anya who had beat the crap out of Bill. Kathleen was sued because in the ensuing scuffle, she beat the crap out of the reporter.

The prostitution arrests came out quickly after that but, strangely enough, though Tess, Carly, and the other girls were well-publicized, Portia's name didn't appear. Sam's "magnetic personality" was mentioned briefly and how he had "mesmerized" several young men to follow him. Donnie Rendquist wasn't mentioned.

Joe's condition was continuously monitored, but surgical healing is not affected by media interest. Joe was only allowed to speak with Ethan, his son, and Tess, his wife, out on bail. This didn't stop the Saint Louis television stations, the Kansas City television stations, the Columbia televisions stations, Jefferson City television stations, *Saint Louis Post Dispatch*, *Kansas City Star*, *Columbia Missourian*, *Columbia Tribune* and the *Riverfront Times* from hanging outside of the university hospital and ambushing Ethan and Tess every time they came outside.

That was when the story went national.

Everyone from talk show host to anchorwoman to newspaper editor had an opinion and wanted it known. It was said that the most dangerous place in America was between a reporter and a Saint Louis cop. There was more than one way to interpret that statement.

Somebody nameless in the SLPD managed to connect Norman and Joe. That meant a connection between Anya and Norman. ABC was the first to wonder out loud if Bill had been first intimidated and then beaten into buying all those extra pills. Anya was gone. Both Norman and Bill were dead. Ethan, speaking for Joe, mentioned only Norman. Sam was in no condition to talk and, according to his doctors, would be unlikely to be in any position to talk ever again. Connie was interviewed as the caretaker for the few legitimate businesses that Norman had owned. He played dumb. He was just happy to run things for Norman's only heir, underage LeRoy. LeRoy was interviewed as Norman's sister's HIV positive kid—probably one of the few (by implication only) good things Norman ever did. LeRoy didn't know anything about Norman's business.

The East Saint Louis police report of Norman's murder was released. Damulin Rouge's death was his brief and singular moment of fame. His twelve years in the Army, discharge for heroin addiction, and subsequent support of his mother was eclipsed by his shining moment as the co-victim of Cold Norman Parkin. Norman's fatal wound, consistent with a .22 at close range, was contrasted with the caliber of the weapon that had killed Damulin, possibly as large as a .45. No actual bullet of either was ever found. The two weapons suggested two killers. The state representative for the East Saint Louis authority allowed that such a small caliber could have been used by a woman. The .45, however, might well have been too big. Perhaps there had been two killers. Perhaps Anya had teamed up with an accomplice. Perhaps Damulin had been killed by Norman himself, and Norman, then betrayed, had been killed by Anya.

Natural selection favored survival of the story that most benefited circulation and soon Anya was presented as a biochemist, both brilliant and unscrupulous, who tried to make street money off Anapyridol, even as she was getting it certified by the FDA.

Jake declined interviews. Cindy stayed indoors.

No guns were found. The only "child abuse" was sex between a few girls sixteen and over with older, unidentified, men. Several of the girls had prostitution rap sheets. Only a few pills were actually found at the scene. Presumably, as the Chief of the Saint Louis Police Department said, they had been destroyed in the flood. The SLPD began to figure out that one of their own was involved. With the odd stories they had gotten from their officers, those who made such decisions began to feel the less said about what happened, the better. The story created by the media was to everyone's advantage and was not, therefore, contradicted by mere fact.

oOo

Cardiac bypass surgery is common but not trivial. Ethan sat with Joe until orderlies took Joe from the ER and whisked him away into the nether regions of surgery. An hour of prep, nine hours of surgery—Joe was an extreme case—an hour in recovery and a transfer into the Cardiac Care Unit. Then they let Ethan in to see him.

Joe was still unconscious. He looked gray under the fluorescent lights.

Ethan held his hand. He shifted one hand to the other as he read magazines, dozed, watched the other patients. He took quick, panicky bathroom breaks; he wanted to be there if Joe needed him.

Joe seemed to come close to waking three or four times in the first hours after he was brought to the CCU. Once, he opened his eyes wide and said, "Where is he?" Then he closed his eyes and fell back asleep.

Ethan didn't have time to say *I'm right here.*

Joe had been brought to the hospital by noon. He was in surgery by one and out by ten. It was nearly midnight in the morning when Ethan was let in to sit with him. By hospital rules, Ethan should have been ushered out into the waiting area or, for that matter, never allowed into the CCU after hours. Reporters were forbidden even from the waiting room. But Ethan was Joe's only child and one of the nurses had been a big fan of Joe's show before he'd sold the station. Ethan never knew his special dispensation. He just stayed there, holding Joe's hand.

About four in the morning, the still time in hospitals when patients destined to die finally kick off and only the most desperate reporters were still camped outside, waiting for a look at the briefly famous, Ethan woke with Joe's hand on his head.

"I'm not dead," Joe whispered. He sounded surprised.

Ethan had been resting his head on a pillow jammed onto the bed rails. It took a moment to register. He pulled the pillow away from the rail and dropped it on the floor.

"Yeah," Ethan said. Ethan felt the tears come, and he couldn't trust his voice.

Joe nodded and squeezed his hand. "Is Tess all right?"

Ethan nodded. He thought about telling Joe the police had her but decided against it. "She'll get here when she can."

Joe nodded and closed his eyes. His face was no longer gray but a new-baby pink.

oOo

It was three days before Joe's lawyer, Harold Bombeck of Carroll, Bombeck, and Herbert, could make bail for Tess. If she were being held for something really serious, such as sex with a minor, as was Phil, she might not have been able to get out at all. As it was, she was being held on suspicion of holding a controlled substance.

When she got out, she had no car—it had been impounded along with Phil's, Joe's, and everyone else's. A hold had been put on her charge card. *Fine.* Bombeck took Tess to her and Joe's home in Alton and dropped her off. She pried up a floorboard she'd been ashamed of, and pulled out six thousand dollars. *Money you put away in case he dumps you. In case your pimp beats you up and you have to get out of town. Money you might need to buy somebody off.* Of course, she was married now to Joe and Joe would never leave her, never beat her, and if there was somebody to be paid off, they'd do it together. But she'd been unable to keep from hoarding the money. *Guilt money,* she thought. With it, she rented a car and broke speed limits all the way to Columbia.

oOo

Ethan left them alone. He was smart enough to know when he was a fifth wheel. He just hoped Joe would survive the encounter. He whispered in her ear as he passed, "He's only been out of surgery a couple of *days.*"

Tess nodded absently. Her gaze never left Joe's face.

They'd moved Joe out of the CCU and into the cardiac ward two days after the surgery. A security guard had been set up at the edge of the ward to keep the media at bay, but you could still tell where they were. A sort of incoherent roar drifted from beyond the big double doors. There was a spike in the noise whenever they could see Ethan through the glass.

Ethan sat in the waiting room. His stomach rumbled, but he dreaded trying to go down to the cafeteria. There was no protection down there.

He sat next to a kid of perhaps twenty.

For a moment, neither said anything.

"I'm Ethan Cori," Ethan said suddenly, turning towards the kid and sticking his hand out.

"Donnie Rendquist," said the kid. They shook hands.

"My dad's up the hall." Ethan waved towards Joe's room. "Heart attack."

Donnie nodded down the hall, where a policeman stood. "My friend's in there."

"Is somebody after him?" Ethan nodded at the policeman.

Donnie shook his head. "He's been shot in the head. He's likely going to jail if he gets better." Donnie stopped and corrected himself. "*When* he gets better."

"What happened?"

Donnie seemed to consider the question. "He wanted the wrong thing."

Don't we all, thought Ethan. But he nodded as if he knew what Donnie was talking about. "What's his name?"

"Sam Forestell."

It took a moment to register. That was the name of the tipster Orphira had mentioned.

"I think my dad knows your friend," Ethan said cautiously.

Donnie stared at him. "Oh, yeah. Joe Cori. That's the guy Sam was fighting."

"He tried to *kill* my father."

Donnie nodded. He didn't seem bothered.

A rage came out of Ethan he didn't know was there. He wanted to run through the guarded door and bludgeon Sam to death.

"Hey," said Donnie. He put a hand on Ethan's shoulder. "Your dad had a heart attack, right? Is he going to be all right?"

"Yeah, no thanks to Sam."

374 • Steven Popkes

"Sam's head was blown apart. If he lives, he's going to be a vegetable, not even able to wipe up his own shit."

"Good."

Donnie's gaze was piercing. "Your dad's *alive*, man. I was there. If Sam was after your dad, your dad was after Sam, too. Sam lost his *eye*. He lost his *mind*. Sam *lost*. Big time. You leave him alone."

Ethan settled back down in his chair, still seething. But what if it had been the other way? What if it had been Joe who had been shot, instead of Sam? Ethan had a sudden vision of his father, head misshapen, mouth open and drooling. *It could have been worse.*

What would Joe do? Joe was the injured party here. In a moment, he knew exactly what Joe would do. He could hear his voice: Forgiveness isn't about just the easy stuff—the guy that cut you off, your brother stealing the sugar. Nothing is unforgivable—that's what makes it Holy. Jesus didn't just turn the other cheek for a slap. He was right there, giving them his other cheek when they drove in the nails.

Ethan would never be a believer like his father. But could he now do less? "Does he have any family?"

Donnie nodded slowly. "Yes. He's got me." Donnie sighed as if he'd come to a decision. "I'm going to take care of him."

Sam's been punished enough. He didn't push the pills down Joe's throat. It takes two to fight, and Joe had been right there with him. Ethan felt a knot loosen inside of him. If Sam could be forgiven, then maybe that could happen to anyone.

Better watch out, he thought, smiling. *Might turn into a dutiful son yet.*

"Good luck," Ethan said. He held out his hand.

Donnie took it. The two of them shook solemnly.

oOo

Cindy didn't contact LeRoy or Connie, though she wanted to—they had agreed to that. Instead, she spent days inside Orphira's apartment, hiding from the press. It took a week for KMOV to manage to worm Orphira's address out of some low-paid SLPD flunky. Then there was an encampment of trucks and photographers outside. Cindy watched as the local broadcasters, then the national stringers, each took their turn to read scripts in front of Orphira's converted apartment building. When Fred Hibbert asked Cindy to come to Lifeworks regarding Bill's Last Will and Testament, she wasn't inclined to go until he promised her and Jake a limo. She dearly wanted to talk to LeRoy.

The lawyer's name was John Carroll and his office, or rather the office of Carroll, Bombeck, and Herbert, occupied the second floor of a Soulard office building. A real estate office occupied the first floor. Jake, looking confused, followed her into the building. He always looked confused these days. Once the stories across the television made Anya out as Norman's murder, his confusion seemed to become permanent. Cindy knew *he* knew that couldn't be true. She also knew he didn't know that *she* knew the same thing. Cindy had thought about telling him, but that would have opened another box of worms to include all of those things about her he didn't know and, if he did, would fervently wish he didn't. She decided to let things lie. If he could stand it, she could.

Carroll let them into a plush leather office and left them. It was quiet in there. Quiet like a church or a funeral. Cindy had the urge to do something messy and loud.

A moment later a small dark man entered the room. He stepped towards them and held out his hand. "I'm Fred Hibbert, temporary CEO of Lifeworks. You're Cindy and Jake Fiske."

Cindy liked that Fred had mentioned her name first.

Fred made sure they were seated on the sofa and sat in a chair across from them. "There are a lot of legal issues we have to discuss," he began. "But the long and short of it is that Bill left all of his shares in Lifeworks to Cindy."

Jake looked up. "What are you talking about?"

"Mister Fiske," Fred said quietly and sympathetically. "If I may be a bit blunt, Bill and Mrs. Fiske had a... complex relationship. One he felt bad about, even after she put him in the hospital. Apparently, he felt guilty about this."

Jake stared at him. "Did you know he put Cindy in his will?"

Fred nodded. "I didn't realize why until later. But it's not unheard of. Bill had no children. He was amicable with his ex-wives but not close with them. He had a sister who succumbed to cancer four years ago. She was his last living blood relative. All he had, really, was Lifeworks. And Anya."

"I heard he was going to get married before he..." Cindy didn't know how to finish the sentence.

Fred nodded. "He had made plans to marry Kathleen Morris. Naturally, she is devastated."

"But she's not in the will."

"No," said Fred. "And she's agreed not to contest it."

Jake continued to watch Fred. "How much are we talking about here?"

Cindy squirmed in embarrassment. *Jesus, Daddy. Can you be any more blunt?*

Fred didn't seem bothered. "Lifeworks has fifteen million dollars in gross revenue. The company was worth approximately about fifty million as long as Anapyridol was being pursued. Now that it's been discontinued, our worth has dropped somewhat. But the generic part of the operation is still strong, so I think we can safely be valued at thirty-five million. That is, of course, the liquidation value of the company. If we went public, we could command more than that."

Jake shook his head. "I didn't mean that."

"You mean how that translates to you." Fred smiled.

"I'm looking out for my daughter."

"I'm sure you are. However, the will is very clear on this point. Cindy is the sole beneficiary. The chairman of the board of directors is her trustee until she is twenty-one." Fred smiled at Jake, but there was a coldness behind the smile. "I am the chairman of the board."

Jake didn't answer.

Fred leaned back. "You shouldn't worry about this, Mister Fiske. I will take good care of the two of you. But I must be clear on my legal obligations."

Jake opened his mouth.

Cindy was sure he would do something stupid. "Mister Hibbert?"

"Yes?"

He gave her his whole attention. It was overpowering. His eyes were dark and compelling. She looked away. *Wow.* If he'd been one of her customers last summer—she didn't know what she would have done.

"Cindy—" Jake started.

Cindy patted him on the knee. All she could think of was that little two-by-four condo of Orphira's. Jake sleeping on the sofa like a zombie—being visited at night by Orphira, maybe. Or just lying there, staring up at the ceiling. Orphira walking around, making cow-eyes at Jake, barely registering that Cindy was even around. Her old home, dead rat, and ancient history, was burnt rubble back in Tower Grove.

"Mister Hibbert?" she said nicely. "Could Lifeworks back me in a mortgage?"

Fred's eyes showed understanding. Cindy knew then what she would have done if she'd met him last summer. She never would have come home.

Oh, well, she thought. *Life is full of lost opportunities.*

"Of course," he murmured.

"Okay, then." Cindy rose and picked up her house. "Come on, Daddy. There's a real estate agent downstairs. Let's go buy us a house."

oOo

The Union Station pond, complete with ducks and paddleboats, was open by early summer. Cindy waited for LeRoy at the boat house as they had agreed.

"Hey," came from behind her.

She turned and LeRoy was standing, leaning against the railing in a new sweater and pants. Cindy could tell he'd bought them just to impress her and she smiled. *Boys. They're all just boys.* For a moment, she loved every one of them for it. "You look very handsome."

"Thank you." He grinned. "You are very pretty yourself."

Cindy found herself blushing. She couldn't remember the last time she'd blushed.

"Let's rent a boat," LeRoy suggested. "I've never done it."

In the middle of the pond, forty feet from anyone else, they found a sort of privacy in the middle of the crowded mall.

She felt suddenly awkward.

"I wanted to call," LeRoy said quietly.

She nodded. "Me, too." She didn't know what to say but she could feel the moment, feel *something* slipping away. "Portia had her baby."

"Really?"

"Yeah. The *cutest* little baby girl. I think Mrs. Rendquist is happy about it. Portia's dad is going to explode about it one of these days."

"He doesn't like the baby?"

"It's not the baby. Portia is very clear that Phil's the father and that she's waiting for him. Donnie—Portia's brother—took Portia and the baby over to Fulton Prison two weeks ago—I went to help with the baby. Portia wanted to show her to Phil. He was about as proud as a man could be in an orange jumpsuit through two inches of glass. I held the baby while they talked on the little phone thing."

"What's the baby's name?"

Cindy smiled and looked away. "Cynthia Theresa Bergman. Portia insisted on the 'Bergman.' I thought Mister Rendquist was going to go nuclear when she told me."

"She named the baby after you?"

Cindy nodded. "Isn't that funny?"

"You should be proud."

Cindy felt her face go pink again. "Did you hear what Bill did in his will?"

"Connie told me."

"Who told *him?*"

LeRoy laughed. "Are you kidding? Connie's been glued to that big television of his for the last four months."

"Nervous, huh?" Cindy smiled.

"Yeah."

"So, I'm a millionaire."

"Only on paper. You own a pretty cool company, though."

She leaned forward and looked up at him. "Want to help me run it?"

"Are you old enough to run it?"

"Old Man Hibbert thinks I am. He's been letting me do things there. I've learned a lot. He says when I'm ready to own the shares outright, I'll be ready to run the company." She looked back at the water. "But you could help. I need good scientists."

"I don't want to make cosmetics."

"Then what do you want to do?"

LeRoy shrugged. "Go back to school. Do some *real* science. Do something new."

"You could do that with me."

Cindy could feel him watching her.

He spoke slowly. "Do you want a... *business* arrangement?"

She punched him in the arm. "No. No to what you said and no to what you implied."

"Ow." He said, rubbing his arm. LeRoy watched her for a moment. He spoke very slowly and clearly. "I like you, Cindy. I *really* like you. I'm not interested in Lifeworks. I'm interested in *you*."

Cindy looked back at him. "Did you know Donnie was with Sam up in Milan?"

"No."

"Even though he survived, Sam's pretty much a vegetable. So, when he was stable they decided not to prosecute. Donnie found this little apartment over in U-City. He's taking care of Sam. Cleaning him up. Feeding him. Sitting with him."

"So?"

Cindy looked down at the water. "I think that's what love is. Not the sex. Not when you look pretty or handsome. Not when you go out to movies or dancing. But when all that goes away and it's just you and a hospital bed or HIV or a new-born baby or a little apartment in U-City and you *stay*. That's love." She turned back to LeRoy. "That's what I want."

LeRoy returned her look levelly. "Give me a chance."

They watched each other for a moment. Then she looked away. "Okay."

The sun rippled across the water. In the distance they could hear people talking in the shops. Different strains of music from the stores. Laughter. A shout.

"So," said LeRoy carefully. "You want to go for a drive?"

Cindy smiled at him. "Excuse me?"

LeRoy held up car keys. "Prettiest Toyota you've ever seen."

"You got a *license?*"

"I had to do something for the last four months. Come on. Let's go someplace new."

oOo

"You've got a couple of choices," Duck said, sitting across from Jake.

Not really, thought Jake.

"I'll find you a nice desk job—say, evidence officer or records or something. Out of the public eye."

"Or?"

"Or you could retire. You've put in most of your twenty-five years. Maybe it's time to quit." Duck leaned back in his chair. "It's up to you. But you're off the street. There's not a department that wants you."

"I figured."

"You're *dirty*, Jake. Nobody wants to take a chance on you. It's a miracle we've been able to keep your part in this quiet. Everybody knows there's more to it—they can smell it. The only reason they're not asking questions is because they don't want to know. Even Internal Affairs is keeping its head in the sand, provided you're safely tucked away. If you're visible, everything will eventually come out."

The horror of sitting behind the counter, making sure evidence was properly tagged, stored, and retrieved, was matched only by the depression of making sure every little piece of information was properly cataloged in the computer system.

"I'll put in for retirement," Jake said. What was he going to *do?* Get a boat and go fishing every day? Expand the restaurant? For the life of him, Jake couldn't think of a single thing he wanted to do.

"I'll get you the forms." Duck waved him out.

Back at his desk, Jake stared out the window. The parking lot no longer sported broadcasting vans. His few moments of fame consisted of being associated with the diabolical machinations of his wife. The world seemed thin and fragile. He knew Anya hadn't killed Norman. But had there been an affair between them? Had she sold the pills to Norman? Jake didn't want to believe that. But the stories that had surfaced about Anya in Russia—working at VECTOR. Christ! He hadn't known there *was* such a place.

The simple truth of things seemed to hang in front of him. He had never really known Anya. Anya had never really known him. Now that he had to retire and she had run off, there was no chance to fix any of it.

He wanted a beer. Sweet Jesus, he wanted a beer.

He called up Orphira's cell.

"Hey, Jake." He could tell from her voice that she was smiling.

"I'm retiring," he said, suddenly.

Orphira didn't say anything for a moment. "That's not too surprising, I guess."

"Yeah. So, want to go get a beer or something? I'm free, well, pretty much all decade."

Jake could feel caution in her pause.

"Probably a mistake," she said.

"Yeah."

"My shift is over in an hour. Meet you at Riddle's?"

"I'll buy the first round."

He hung up and didn't move his hand from the phone. Anya was *gone*. She'd taken some of him with her—maybe the best part. Certainly, the better part of twenty years. But Orphira was going to have a beer with him, anyway. It came to him that this young woman knew everything about him. She knew about the call girls. She knew about the restaurant. Maybe this was what a second chance felt like. He would be better. He would *do* better.

She doesn't know about Norman, he thought. And he wasn't going to be the one to tell her. Some secrets should stay secret.

He got up and left early. What were they going to do to him? *Fire* him?

Maybe he *would* get a boat. Anything was possible.

When he got into his car, he found himself whistling.

oOo

Ethan leaned back in his chair. He stared at the figures on his laptop. The last of his electron images was being built, bit by bit, in front of him. The last experimental image he'd need for his thesis.

Mathauser and Ethan were attempting to use electron beams to etch very fine circuits, too dense for visible light. The plan was to accept the errors and use error detection techniques to mask out the broken circuits, leaving only good, clean circuits. If, for example, they started with a chip that had a random ten percent known faulty circuits that could be masked but the chip had four times the density of a chip made with comparable photon technology, it was a win. Who *cared* if ten percent of the circuits were bad? Just program around them.

The problem with the technique was two-fold. First, it wasn't always as low as ten percent. Different techniques yielded different and sometimes random error values. Second, the erroneous circuits couldn't always be routed around. They were getting an unacceptably high rejection rate.

Ethan had taken a different tack in his last set of experiments, inspired by his point-of-view equations. By using a statistical technique based on the POV state of the ground prior to the electron etching, he was able to describe the pattern of the errors. This suggested a novel architecture that would be self-organizing. The technique wasn't limited to electron imaging. If you were able to use X-rays to etch circuits, that architecture, too, would be self-organizing.

Ethan's mind raced with it. For that matter, there was no reason this architecture had to be tied to circuits at all; it was a self-organizing, self-correcting topology.

"Ethan?"

Ethan looked up. The image was done. The experimental work was done. The review was done. All he had to do now was write up the results and conclusion.

Tess was standing on the other side of the table. "You were a million miles away."

Ethan smiled. "Yeah."

"How is he?"

"Sleeping. We went for a walk earlier."

"How far?"

"Just down to the corner. He got tired so I came back and got the car. I checked on him a little while ago. He looks pretty good." Ethan made sure he saved his work, then shut down the laptop. "What did the lawyer say?"

Tess shrugged and sat down in the chair opposite him. "We're probably going to get convicted of something. The judge threw out the child endangerment charges for everybody except Phil. That was good news." Tess sighed. "Poor Phil. He's looking at five years. I'll probably be acquitted on the fraud and misuse of funds charge. Harold says they'll really hold Joe responsible for that. But there's really no way I can beat the controlled substances charge—even though at the time Divinidine was not controlled. Joe has that, plus the fraud and misuse of funds—though Harold isn't sure they can make any of the fraud charges really stick on appeal. But by then we'll likely both be in jail. Harold is trying to get a plea bargain. Two years for me, three for Joe. So far, the prosecutor's not talking to him."

"What about Dad's condition?"

"Harold says they send heart patients to jail all the time. No help there." She pointed to the laptop. "How's it going?"

"Finishing up. Should be ready for defense in a month. If I can get all the right signatures. I think the department is in a sweat to get rid of me—Mathauser has already left. They know I'm going with him."

"Joe will miss you."

"He'll have you."

Tess shook her head. "It's not the same."

Ethan agreed. "Seattle's not that far away. I'll be coming home regularly." He smiled at her. "Maybe you two should move up there. Afterwards, I mean. Make a new start."

Tess smiled at him. "Maybe we will."

For the first time, Ethan realized what a wonderful smile she had. *You know*, he thought. *Dad's a lucky man.*

oOo

Connie show his face publically in the clubs until the middle of March. By then, the news had moved into the trial phase. He split his time between managing the clubs and watching recorded news shows. He watched as the investigation fanned out, finding Norman, then Anya, connecting the two of them. Sam showed up in the stories. Connie, himself, had been interviewed but only made a brief appearance on a local station. Then the news process began to fan *in*, as facts and speculation began to be compared and matched up. The players narrowed until Norman and Anya dominated the story.

The first books on the Milan Disaster were published over the summer. Milan had to compete with a celebrity coming out as a lesbian and a follow-on to a destructive hurricane. The appearance of the books delineated the end of Milan's news cycle. Pretty much everything that had been found, decided, or speculated would be in the books.

Connie tracked Milan on the internet until the books came out. Then he went to several bookstores, buying one book here and another book there, always paying cash. He brought them home and read them, one after another.

When he had finished, he sat back and marveled how lucky they had been. The story had pretty much proceeded in the way they had hoped. There were a few minor variations, Damulin's murder being attributed to Norman himself, for example.

Connie didn't mind being lucky—better to be lucky than smart, as the saying goes—but it made him nervous. The more he thought about it, the more he saw holes. The biggest one was Sam. Why *had* he tipped the cops? To make a show? To get Joe arrested? Sam was setting up for a confrontation with Joe. What did he care if he had an audience of bluecoats?

The whole news cycle had the flavor of being *managed*. But by whom? If it wasn't Sam who had tipped the cops but someone who managed to convince them it was Sam, then who was it? And why?

He stood up and opened the curtain in his bedroom. The sun was shining. Outside, it looked hot. The asphalt was puddling in the middle of the street.

Connie had a deep and abiding feeling that things had worked out the way they did by design. It was clear that whoever was managing the news was not managing it for *him*. Connie had been in the right place at the right time by lucky accident or by someone's clever design. But *somebody* owed *someone* a debt. Connie just hoped he wouldn't be the one that would someday have to pay it back.

oOo

Joe felt close to his old self as he and Tess mounted the steps to the house. It was early morning and the air was sticky, but the heat not yet overpowering. Joe had trouble with the heat, and they had gone out for his daily walk before the sun came up.

The trial had concluded a month ago with a plea bargain. Joe would get five years, parole in two. Tess would get three years, parole in one. They were due to report in on the first of August.

It seemed a shame to get strong again, just to waste that health in prison. Joe sighed. *You play the cards you're dealt*, he thought.

The house seemed empty without Ethan around. Seattle seemed far away. Joe cheered himself up by remembering Ethan would be back before August. They'd have a few days together, anyway. Ethan and Tess were the only comfort he had against the hollow he'd felt inside of him since Milan. God had left him. He and Tess had only spoken of it obliquely. Neither had wanted to break the silence. Joe couldn't remember how he had survived on faith alone, before he'd felt the certainty of the Divine right there, in his heart. It was like being struck blind or dumb or deaf.

He stumbled on the top step. Tess stiffened against him until he found his footing. They stood there on the porch step, clinging to one another. She guided him over to the porch swing and he sat down heavily.

"Any pain?" she asked.

Joe shook his head. "Still getting used to things."

"Joe," Tess said, hesitantly.

Joe looked at her. "Yes?"

She pulled a bottle out of her pocket and handed it to him.

Joe held the bottle in his hands. Opened it. Inside were pink pills. He looked at her.

"Do you still feel... *Him?*" Her voice was uncertain.

Joe shook his head. He must get used to emptiness. *No,* he said to himself. Life was *not* empty. Tess was right *there*. Ethan was not all that far away. Console yourself with the things in front of you. But in the back of his mind, he heard the verse from Matthew: *My God! My God! Why hast thou forsaken me?* How had Jesus managed it?

"We could try again." Tess spoke quietly.

Joe shook the pills out into his hand. Fifty pills. Twenty-five apiece. More than they had ever taken.

"We could die trying." Joe stared at the pills. He wondered if his heart would take it. It had given out before. Tess was young and strong. She could manage it.

Tess nodded and held his arm. "I don't want to lose you. Or *Him.*"

"I have a bypass. I've healed up pretty well. I'm on heart medication. They've cleaned me out as much as they're going to. Later might be worse. I'm game."

She reached into his hand and counted out twenty-five for each of them. "Me, too." She went inside the house and returned with a glass of grape juice. They took the pills and shared the grape juice, and then went inside. Soon it would be oppressively hot.

Tess and Joe held onto one another. The colors came. The sounds. This was stronger, more abrupt. Joe had a feeling of pounding on a door that would not open.

They held onto each other. The colors swirled into bright light and he could feel her, open, beside him. Then a splash of brightness, and he was alone.

"Tess?" he called out, but he couldn't see anything. His eyes wouldn't resolve. He tried to touch her, but he couldn't tell if it was Tess he touched. It could have been the rug, a chair. He crawled across the floor, feeling it ripple under his fingers, seeing waves of pulsing light. Something felt like a phone, and he held it in his hands.

"Let me *see!*" he cried, and the light dimmed until he could make out the handset and the keypad.

911!

He tried to talk into the phone, but it melted in his hands.

Then there were other hands, hands he couldn't see, and he was lying down. His vision began to clear, and the bright lights resolved into ambulance lighting and windows, buildings rushing past. He looked over and saw Tess, still and gray. He touched her hand, already cooling.

"No," he whispered to himself. *This could not be happening. It's the drug. It's his eyes, his hands.* "Take me. *Take me.*"

The EMT leaned over him with a stethoscope. *My heart*, thought Joe, patched and dripping, *is breaking*.

But it kept on beating as the ambulance roared on.

oOo

Helsinki suited Anya. Old and European enough to have all those little comforts missing in the States but with just a hint of commonality to remind her of what Mother Russia should have been.

She was sitting at the café window table, watching the skaters in Railway Square. Her coffee was hot and strong. Russia had proven unsuitable—the oligarchs wanted to own her. Anya had no desire to be owned ever again. Moscow was of use only to get yet another new identity.

Anya had been in Helsinki four months. It had taken a month to make contacts and determine which of the small biotech companies would be easiest to influence and be most amenable to her proposals. Then she took a month to prepare the presentations. Now, after collaborating, then negotiating, with Bioteknik, she had assured herself a position. In just a few years, the company would be hers in all but name. Money. Power. Everything important was part of the plan.

The waiter came and refilled her coffee. She smiled up at him.

He seemed to stiffen and stare at her.

"Is there something wrong?" Anya tried to keep her voice warm and caring. Things seemed to go better when she made that effort.

"I see you," the waiter said suddenly.

"I beg your pardon."

The waiter shook himself and said something in Suomic. Then in English. "Will that be all?"

Anya nodded and he gave her the check.

Odd.

She paid the check and walked outside, past the skaters, along Kaisaniemi Park to the Hotel Arthur. People seemed to be watching her. One couple stared at her directly as she walked past. They didn't act like the Finnish people she'd met since coming here. Were they tourists? Was something wrong with her clothes?

When she entered the lobby, it seemed that all conversation stopped, all eyes on her as she walked to the desk.

"Anya Bartona," she said brightly. "Is there anything for me?"

The clerk stared at her. His face convulsed. He said clearly, in English, "I see you."

Anya backed away into a couch. The woman in the couch looked up at her and said, "I see you."

Anya twisted away as if burned. She walked quickly towards the elevators. A porter stopped: "I see you."

This was what Anya had been afraid of. It had found her at last.

The elevator opened it. All four people inside stared at her, muttering. "I see you."

Anya started to scream.

Epilogue: May, Five Years Later

The media half-life of the story was extended somewhat when Tess died in July. A tasteless television movie showing aging actors who should have known better debuted Christmas the following year and briefly reignited a flurry of articles. After that, public interest died and the Milan Disaster became a footnote for academics decrying bread-and-circuses in the media, left-wing humanitarians lamenting the power of religion, and right-wing talk show hosts celebrating the incompetence of government.

oOo

The phone rang and Joe rolled out of bed. He sat for a moment, trying to make his mind wake up along with his body. He picked the phone.

"Hello?"

"Dad?"

"Ethan!" Joe woke up completely. He switched to the radio headset and got up out of bed. "How's spring in Seattle?"

"Late this year. The May drought hasn't hit yet. Still gray and raining."

Joe nodded, even though Ethan couldn't see him. "It's a beautiful spring day here. I can see the sun breaking through the clouds—"

"Liar!" laughed Ethan. "I checked the weather down there. Raining and cold for the next week."

"Never judge a day by its weather."

"I'm going to be in town in June."

Joe could feel the grin split his face. "That's *great* news. Is NASA going to be able to do without Doctor Cori for a couple of weeks?"

"They'll have to. I have a wedding to go to."

"You're..." Joe stopped, not sure what to say.

Ethan chuckled. "No. Not me. LeRoy and Cindy."

"LeRoy?"

"Norman's nephew and Anya's daughter, remember?"

"Of course, I remember." Joe shook his head. "I'll be damned."

"Not you, Dad. *Never* you."

Joe wondered if he would be invited to the wedding. *Lots of old ghosts there,* he thought. "Listen, they can have the rehearsal dinner here if they want. We can close the diner for a day. I'll cook. If they want, of course."

"I'll ask them," Ethan said gently. "They may have already made plans."

They talked for a few minutes more. Then Joe hung up. He left his little room in the back of the diner and walked through the kitchen to the tables outside. Phil and Portia were sitting at one of the tables, drinking coffee. Little Cynthia was running around the room, trying to play tag with little Tristan. Tristan, being only two, didn't quite understand what was being asked of him.

As if any of us do, Joe thought.

Fred let himself in the door. Joe watched him. A man doesn't give up wealth and power without a reason. But Fred had been working here for a year now and didn't seem to do much beyond clean up and cook.

Joe poured himself some decaf. He turned and leaned against the counter, and watched Portia and Phil talking. The two kids. Fred, reading the paper. A moment of quiet before the diner opened. Once he opened the doors, every man, woman, and child Joe could find would be fed.

Oh, Tess, he thought. *If you were only here.*

A kid knocked on the glass door. Before Joe could move, Fred rose and let him in. They sat together in the corner next to the kitchen, talking.

Joe nodded. *Guess we're open now.*

Joe went back in the kitchen and pulled the pancake batter he'd made the night before out of the refrigerator. He checked the traps and the feeds before he lit the pilot—it was an old grill. He leaned out the door of the kitchen and looked around.

Fred was talking to the kid. "I got plans for you, kid. Big plans."

Nobody was watching.

Joe reached under the griddle and snapped his fingers. The flame leaped from his thumb and lit the pilot.

He shook the flame out and turned on the main valves. He could feel the heat waft up. Joe stirred the batter.

Thinking of Tess, Ethan, and everybody else he'd ever known, Joe Cori began to make pancakes.

Acknowledgements

God's Country has a long history. I wrote it a while back, got discouraged, then revisited it.

My son Ben and my wife Wendy Zimmerman both encouraged me and it probably wouldn't have gotten out if it hadn't been for them.

The Cambridge SF Workshop, as always, inflicted the necessary pain to make it better. This includes Brett Cox, Sarah Smith, Jim Kelly and especially Alex Jablokow, who said start over.

A special shout out goes to David Alexander Smith who pushed me to tell LeRoy's (and everybody else's) stories way back when those stories were nascent, wretched attempts. It was David who said go back to the beginning.

This is the beginning, David.

Credits

God's Country
Steven Popkes

Published by Walking Rock Publications in association with
Book View Café Publishing Cooperative
ISBN: 978-1-61138-902-9
Production Team:
Cover Design: Wendy Zimmerman
Proofreader/Copyeditor: Deborah J. Ross
Formatter: Steven Popkes

About the Author

Steven Popkes lives in Massachusetts on two acres where he and his wife raise bananas, persimmons and turtles.

He works in aerospace making sure rockets continue to go where they are pointed. He insists he is not a rocket scientist.

He is a rocket engineer.

About Book View Café

Book View Café Publishing Cooperative (BVC) is an author-owned cooperative of over fifty professional writers, publishing in a variety of genres such as fantasy, romance, mystery, and science fiction.

BVC authors include New York Times and USA Today bestsellers; Nebula, Hugo, and Philip K. Dick Award winners; World Fantasy Award, Campbell Award, and RITA Award nominees; and winners and nominees of many other publishing awards.

Since its debut in 2008, BVC has gained a reputation for producing high-quality ebooks, and is now bringing that same quality to its print editions.

www.bookviewcafe.com
Book View Café Publishing Cooperative